THE RAVEN QUEEN'S HAREM

THE COMPLETE SERIES

ANGEL LAWSON

THE RAVEN QUEEN'S HAREM

THE COMPLETE SERIES

Raven's Mark
Ebony Rising
Black Magic
Obsidian Fire
Onyx Eclipse
Midnight's End

RAVEN'S MARK

1

MORGAN

"Morgan!" I hear my name called from a voice at the front desk the instant I walk in the dormitory. "You've got mail."

I freeze and stare at my best friend, who's on desk duty. There's only one reason for her to stop me like this and for the barely contained smile she's fighting. I've been harassing her for weeks, asking daily if a package had arrived. According to the wide grin on her face, it's here.

"Hand it over." I rush to the desk, drop my satchel, and grab it with both hands. My name is handwritten, as is the return address. New York University Graduate Department.

"It feels heavy," she says. "That's good right?"

A sudden queasiness rolls in my belly. "I don't know."

"Well, open it, silly."

I nod, but just stare at the package. The contents determine the next two years of my life—no, it will determine the *rest* of my life. Where I live, my career, my associations....I take a deep breath.

"Do you want me to do it?" Shannon asks. While I consider that, two other residents walk up to the counter and she hurriedly assists them with their mail.

"No, I'll do it." I gather up my courage and tear the edge. A thick stack of papers slides out. On top is a letter. I read it aloud with shaking hands.

"*Dear Ms. Hansen,*

Congratulations! You've been accepted into the New York University Graduate Program for the Arts! In addition, we're excited to announce that you are one of six winners of the prestigious Brannon Grant, awarded to an outstanding applicant in music, visual arts, theater, illustration and drawing, creative writing, and photography.

As a recipients of this grant you will receive a full scholarship and housing for the two years of the program..."

"Holy shit, Morgan! Full scholarship for creative writing? You didn't tell me you applied for one!"

"I didn't apply."

"You must have killed it on your story submission."

With my heart in my throat I scan the rest of the letter. "I'm to report next week to my new housing and meet with my advisor immediately. School starts the following week."

"You're moving to New York next week?"

"Guess this southern girl had to spread her wings someday, right?"

"I just didn't know it would be so soon." Shannon and I had been friends since freshman year at the huge state university. She's pretty much my only family. Her sad face brightens. "Two good things are going to come from this adventure."

"What's that?"

"I'll get to visit you in New York and I'm giving you a going-away party!"

"A party?" I can't pretend I'm not a little excited about it. I can invite Ryan and maybe we can finally cross that line we've been flirting with for the last month.

Shannon grabs my hand and squeezes. "I'm so proud of you, girl."

I tighten my grip. I'm going to miss her. I'll miss everything about my home state, but I'm ready to move on toward the future and the life I know is waiting for me.

~

It doesn't take me long to pack and settle my affairs. Graduation occurred three weeks before, and with no family attending it hadn't been a big deal. Otherwise, I'd been preparing myself to find a job or go to school. Thank God the school thing worked out, because I really didn't want to go the nine-to-five route yet.

I arrived freshman year with nothing more than a trunk full of clothes and a backpack full of books. I'll leave with a little more than that; photos, a laptop, and three pairs of shoes (and a pair of boots!) I also have a small circle of girlfriends—the only family I've had since my parents' accident. Leaving them hurts the most.

I was sixteen when I lost my parents. I came home one day and they were both in the house—dead. At first they thought it was suicide. Or maybe a murder-suicide. But nothing was found in their systems except an unexplained super virus. The CDC, which happened to be located three miles away, quarantined me and the house, but nothing came from it. A freak occurrence.

The day I found them was so intense—so traumatic—that parts of my brain shut off. Most of the memories of my childhood are gone, and, according to the therapists, much of what I do remember isn't real. Somehow, in an attempt to protect myself, my brain mixed up fiction and reality, which is why I started writing. The stories flowed naturally—as if they happened to me. The events were fantastical. Impossible, but so was both of my parents dying from an inexplicable sickness. My fairytales kept me sane, and now they've won me a coveted spot in the University creative writing department. And the Brannon Grant.

Shannon planned the party at her boyfriend Max's house. She invited all the girls, Maggie, Tasha, and her girlfriend Brooke.

Everyone paired off over the last year and after a couple of false starts I'd set my eyes on Ryan, the editor of the school paper.

"Tell me about your submission," he says, pushing his glasses up his nose. We're sitting on the decades-old couches Max's parents donated to their house. Ryan has a thick, reddish beard and green eyes that shine from behind the frames. He's smart, and I met him when my writing professor suggested that the literary magazine should collaborate with the newspaper on a project.

I'll be honest, me and guys have never been a great mix. I mean, I like guys—men—males. I'm attracted to them, but when things start to heat up something clicks in my brain and things go south. Quickly. It's like a bomb inserted in my chest, right under my heart. I want a relationship. I crave it, but the slightest disinterest or even worse, rejection, sends me down a tailspin of insecurity and quite frankly, rage.

It's not an attractive quality. I admit it. I've had therapy for it.

I wrinkle my nose at Ryan's question. Although I love writing, I'm not that comfortable talking about it. And Ryan always seems to have a 'tone' when asking about my work. "Eh, it's just a weird story I've had in my head for years. I finally put it on paper and turned it in."

"So a passion project," he says, taking a sip of beer. "What's it about?"

"It's called Maverick's Murder, about a girl that grows up surrounded by a group of ravens. They're her best friends and she spends all her time talking to them while shutting out the rest of the world."

"Ravens as friends," Ryan says. He's a newspaper guy. Facts and copywriting. Fiction is lost on him. "Does she talk to them?"

"Sure."

"Do they talk back?"

I twist my hands in my lap, feeling increasingly uncomfortable. "In their own way."

"Like how?" he asks.

I force a laugh and switch the subject. "It's not a big deal. So do you think you'll have time to come to New York this summer? You'll have a free place to stay."

"Maybe," he says, but there's not a lot of enthusiasm in his reply. "Shannon, tell me about this submission Morgan won her scholarship for. She won't tell me anything."

Shannon and Maggie plop down on the love seat adjacent to the one Ryan and I are on. My best friend has a glassy look in her eye and she takes a big gulp of her red, fizzy drink. "The ravens? Lord, she won't even let me read it."

"No? What's the big secret?" he asks her.

"You know, I'm sitting right here. I can speak for myself."

"But you won't." Shannon rolls her eyes, fully aware of my attitude problem. "At least when it comes to this."

"I'm trying, but you keep interrupting." I can't keep the frustration out of my voice. I don't want to tell them about it but I also hate being dismissed. They both stop then and stare at me with overdramatic patience.

"Do you really want to know?"

"Of course we do. I want to read it!" Ryan takes my hand and squeezes. "Share your success with us, Morgan. You deserve it."

"So right, it's this little girl who makes friends with the ravens in her yard. Five of them. She gives them names and talks to them. In return they keep an eye on her and bring her treats and trinkets. Her favorite is a charm she wears on a necklace."

Maggie points to the scooped neckline of my shirt. "Like that one? Is that why you wear it all the time?"

I touch the cool medallion of silver hanging from a cord on my neck. I feel heat rush to the tips of my ears. "No, I mean, I just wear it for inspiration."

"It looks cool, though. I like the silver design in the middle."

"So, yeah, in the story, the key goes to this sort of alternate universe—"

"Where ravens talk to girls," Ryan jokes.

"And only Maverick can open the door," I continue, ignoring the my hot temper and the strain building in my chest. "This is a problem, though, because the ravens are guardians of the door and their job is to keep the two worlds apart. But one day, the door is opened and a battle occurs between the two worlds. At least one raven is injured and although they shut the door, the ravens disappear, leaving Maverick alone."

"Then what?" Shannon asks, looking more interested than I would've thought.

"Then the girl who has no friends—no family—she has to wake up and live in the real world, which isn't a nice place."

Ryan nods. "So the ravens and the key and the alternate universe were her escape from the realities of her shitty life."

I shift in my seat, uncomfortable with that accurate assessment. "Sure, yeah."

"It's original," Ryan says, linking his fingers with mine. His nose is red and I suspect he's a little drunk. "I mean, it may be a little juvenile but I'm sure NYU saw something in it worth pursuing."

I withdraw my hand from his. "What are you saying?"

He blinks. "Um, about what?"

"About my story. You think it sounds juvenile? Are you implying that makes it lesser for some reason?"

He stills, as though he's wishing he could turn back the clock, but that's the problem with Ryan. He thinks he's smarter than me. He doesn't respect my work, which means he doesn't respect me, either. "No, Morgan, that is not what I'm implying."

"Then what?" I look at Shannon, who has already lost interest and is walking over to her boyfriend. I shake my head and grab my cup. I don't need this tonight. I don't need Ryan, really. I'm moving. It's clear we're not a match.

"Morgan, come on," Ryan calls. "It came out wrong. Don't be sensitive."

Brooke grabs my arm as I pass by. "Where are you going?"

"I need to make a call," I lie, "about my apartment in New York. I'll be right back."

"Now?" It's late. Brooke isn't stupid.

"I know. I just totally forgot to do it earlier." I flash a smile to her and Tasha. "Be back in a minute."

Outside, on the tiny deck behind the house, the late spring air feels nice. I'm not sure why I'm so on edge. I think it's just the move and the raw feelings I get about my story. It's been a piece of me for so long that there are times I get confused and I think parts of Maverick's story are real—not just my imagination.

It's dumb for me to think tonight would be a good time for a hookup with Ryan. I leave in two days. I lean against the railing and stare into the small grove of trees lining the back. If I'm honest with myself, that's probably why I wanted to give it one last chance. No commitment or obligation. Other than my desire to write, it's been a life-long struggle.

Plus, it could've been a good way to get rid of that pesky V-card.

A shadow moves in the trees, triggering the hair on the back of my neck. I lean over the deck railing for a better view but feel the hands of fantasy reaching for me.

...Maverick wanders through the forest. A fluffy, gray cat weaves between her feet, herding her in a specific direction. She looks up, trying to see the sunlight, but the leaves are so thick it's nearly dark as night.

"What am I looking for?" she asks. The cat paws at her legs. She picks him up and he nuzzles against her chest. Even though he's soft, he doesn't make her feel warm. No, instead a chill races down Maverick's spine. Her hand touches the charm. It's hot against her neck and she wants to remove it.

He meows again.

Flapping from overhead gets her attention and her ravens come from above, landing one by one in the trees and on the ground. The cat hisses, clawing at her arms.

"Ouch!" she yells, and she tosses him in reaction. He lands on his

feet, close to the biggest raven, back arching defensively. Another of her ravens grabs her by the hair and tugs, back in the direction she came, but not before she sees where the cat was leading her.

A small, shimmery door deep in the woods. The stone heats against her chest, blinking at an identical flash of color ahead...

"Morgan?"

I swing around and find Ryan standing on the deck. I feel the dewy grass on my feet and turn back, realizing I'm inches from the grove of trees.

"You okay?" he asks.

"Yeah, I uh," I try to get my bearings. "I heard something in the trees. An animal or something."

Even in the dark yard I can see that Ryan's expression is apologetic. "Morgan, look, I was being an ass in there."

"A little bit."

"I know you're talented. We've worked together. I've read your stuff. It's great."

I walk to the bottom of the steps and he meets me there. "You really think so?"

"Yeah, I really think so." He takes my hand. "I just don't think you know how immersed you get in that story, which is fine. I get being into your craft, but wow, Morgan, sometimes you go so deep I feel like I can't reach you."

I know what he means. I fight a glance back at the trees. How did I get out there? Sometimes, sitting at my laptop or driving in the car, I slip into the story and feel like I'm drowning. "That's why it's so important for me to write about it."

His arm slips around my waist and I feel the warmth of his body. "You're going to do great in New York."

I press my forehead to his. "Thank you."

"And yes, I'll definitely come for a visit—if the offer still stands?"

I nod but there's no time to reply. His mouth is on mine and I just feel relief to have something—someone—to hold on to.

2

MORGAN

Even though it's only the first of June, the streets of New York are sticky with humidity. I haul my suitcase out of the back of the cab and drag it over the curb. The building number, 236, glints from brass numbers affixed to the front door. Craning my neck, I look up and see that the building is really a house, has gray stone, and is three stories high, with an attic.

"Ms. Hansen?"

I drop my chin and look at the doorway. A man stares at me, brilliant blue eyes roaming from head-to-toe. I assess him back. He's a little older than me, maybe mid-twenties. He's dressed in dark jeans and a fitted black shirt. His hair matches the color of his outfit and even though it's a casual look, it makes my travel clothes of skinny jeans and a hoodie look a little grubby. "Yes, that's me."

"I'm Dylan. I've been expecting you." He moves quickly down the steps and meets me at the curb. "Here, let me assist you with that."

"Thank you. It's heavy."

He picks it up with ease, as though it weighs nothing. Surprised, I check out his expansive shoulders and the bulge of his biceps straining against the fit of his shirt. Okay, so Dylan works out.

I follow him up the steps and notice the six call buttons just outside the door. Each has a first initial followed by a last name. I spot mine by the number four. I smile and point. "That's mine?"

"Yep. When you have a visitor they'll have to be let in by you or someone else in the house."

"I've always heard New York is dangerous. Is it really that bad?"

"For a beautiful woman like you?" he says, with an earnestness that makes me blush. "You'll always need to be careful."

He opens the door and I walk in first, eyes popping at the interior. This isn't a house. It's a mansion—decked out in the finest décor. My boots slide on the marble floor and massive gilded mirrors flank each wall. A sparkling chandelier hangs overhead and an enormous staircase is in the back of the room, leading to the next floor.

I walk over to one of the mirrors.

Jesus, I look like hell.

My long, dark hair is a mess, having mostly fallen out of the bun I twisted it into hours before. Dark circles highlight how tired I am, giving my blue eyes a haunting look. A drop of brown soda left a stain just below my neckline when the airplane hit a patch of turbulence. And my favorite boots look shabby and cheap against the pristine floors.

My silver charm glints in the mirror and I make eye contact with Dylan's reflection. I touch the intricate design, feeling oddly exposed. For a brief second I consider that something about his face looks vaguely familiar. When I turn on my heel and face him directly I no longer see it, but he does give me a warm, reassuring smile.

"This is graduate housing?" I ask, once I've come to my senses.

"For scholarship winners, yes. The house was donated by the Brannon family in the 1930s, specifically to be used for extraordinary students with creative majors. It's called the Nead."

"Wow," I look around the foyer again. "That's pretty amazing. I can't believe I get to live here. Sure beats the dorm at my university."

"Despite the grandeur it is a comfortable home with plenty of space to work on your projects. I'm happy to give you a full tour now, or would you prefer to see your living quarters first?"

"I think I'd like to see my room." I point to the stain on my shirt. "I may need to freshen up a little."

Dylan guides me up the stairs, pointing out small details along the way like some notable pieces of artwork and the passage to a back staircase that leads to the kitchen. On the first floor, he explains, there is a dining room, library, and living room. Each upper level has two suites per floor. The suites include a bedroom, private bath, sitting room, and studio, each specific to the creative needs of the student.

My room is on the third floor, just beneath the attic, which, according to Dylan, has been retrofitted for two additional rooms.

"There's a rooftop garden I can show you later," Dylan says, opening the door to my room.

"Holy shit," I blurt before covering my mouth. "Sorry, but wow, this place is insane."

The room is luxurious—like something out of a high-end home decor magazine. I take in the small sitting room with a comfortable-looking couch facing a top-of-the-line television. The bedroom is to the left and I gaze at the king-sized bed with exquisite bedding. The bathroom has a shower and a tub with wide-mouthed ravens each holding a large marble in their mouth as the feet. Across the way is one more room.

"Your writing chamber." Dylan says, standing back so I can go in.

The antique desk faces a wall-length window that overlooks Central Park. A little nook, with pillows and a blanket, is built into the wall, with what I assume is one of the best views of the city.

A new computer, laptop, and printer have been set up on the desk. A small chair and table are across the hall. Bookshelves line the walls, halfway filled with classics and books on craft. I clutch the back of the chair at the desk and look around the room.

"I'm dreaming, right?"

"Excuse me?"

I blink three times—which sometimes helps lull me out of my fantasies. Dylan and the room are both still here. "This can't be real. The house, the scholarship..." I walk over and squeeze his bicep. "You."

He looks down at my hand and licks his lips. "I assure you, Morgan, it's all very real."

"So I just go to class, work on my projects, and live here?"

"Yes." His eyes are an intense ice blue and are both intriguing and unnerving at the same time. "One of the stipulations of the scholarship is that dinner must be eaten by all residents together—daily—no exceptions. The meal will be prepared and served in the dining room. If you have specific dietary needs you'll just need to leave a note on the board in the kitchen. The cook will take care of it."

"So everyone that lives here will eat together?"

"Yes. It's a way to foster companionship and creative inspiration between artists. Now that you've arrived, we'll have our first meal this evening."

"Our? You're one of the students?" I ask. I don't know why but I didn't think he was one of the residents.

He leans against the door frame and I get a better view of his long, lean body. "Yes. I am. Does that surprise you?"

I look around the room and settle my eyes on the window and the magnificent view outside. "I'm beginning to expect the unexpected."

3

DYLAN

I exit Morgan's room and the composure I've held since she arrived falls away like a sheet. I inhale, catching my first real breath in minutes. She has no idea of her power, of her effect on me and eventually, the others. I assume they're already aware of her presence in the mansion, and if they aren't, they will be soon.

I head straight to my room, needing a minute to myself. My suite is directly above Morgan's and it's like I feel her alluring presence the instant I walk in the door.

My quarters do not exactly contain a studio—more like a library or artifact room. I'm the historian of our select little group and today is noteworthy, and before the day's end I'll document it extensively.

Morgan has returned to the nest.

I'd hoped she would recognize me, and for a brief moment in the reflection of the mirror, I thought she did. I'd known her memory was severely impaired. I just wished there would be a spark of some kind.

I sit at my desk and pick up the sheath of papers Morgan submitted with her application. Her writings implied the memory of her childhood was still intact—that the power she possesses is still flowing through her veins. It's up to each of us to help reveal the memories, and it will be our duty to help her control that energy.

Leaning back, I close my eyes, reliving the past hour. Morgan is no longer the girl under our protection. She's a woman that has come into her own, just as we always knew she would. Beneath her disheveled humanity is a beautiful woman—I'd let that slip during our tour. If given the chance I'd say more. I'd comment on her passionate eyes, her sensual lips. I'd reach for the slim curve of her neck. The charm of protection rests between the swell of her breasts and it's clear she has little idea of her effect.

She's still a virgin, that was apparent first off. Crossing that barrier will be both necessary and dangerous. Mythologically speaking, Morgan's power comes from her heart and body. Taking care of her is of utmost importance; showering her with affection, providing unconditional support.

In the past this was forgotten—to great destruction. We know better. We understand her heart as well as her mind. Her innocence will make her first days here even more precarious. The others... they'll have a hard time staying away from her soft skin and alluring flesh. Although our fates are intertwined, Morgan must be the one that determines our destiny. Our future depends on her.

I stare out the window. We aren't the only ones aware of Morgan. Her innocence and power.

That's why we've brought her here.

4

MORGAN

Besides the suitcase I traveled with, I do have other belongings. I sent a few boxes ahead and they were waiting for me in the closet of my suite. Dylan showed me where he stored them, told me he would be on the third floor in his rooms, and left me to unpack.

It doesn't take long until my closet and dresser are filled with clothing. The bathroom cabinets hold all of my toiletries. The biggest hassle is the box of books and mementos.

Like many authors, I started writing as a child and I'd filled dozens of journals with my ideas—most about Maverick and her ravens. I'm carrying a stack of these books from the bedroom to the studio when I trip over the coffee table, dropping the stack with a clatter against the hardwood floors and howling in pain.

I slump to the floor, holding my busted toe, when I hear footsteps racing down my hall. I look up, expecting to see Dylan but instead find a smaller, absolutely gorgeous man coming my way.

"Are you okay? I heard you scream."

"Yeah, I'm just a bull in a china shop." I grimace at my swollen toe. "Whoever thought it was a good idea to put me in a classy place like this may be crazy."

The man helps me to the couch and I feel a sharp undercurrent of electricity between us. I stop cold. He pulls his hands away from my body and offers me one in greeting. "I'm Sam—your floor-mate." He points down the hallway. "I live right down there."

"I'm Morgan." He doesn't let go of my hand and I feel my cheeks heat as he studies me. "I heard you were coming—I just didn't know…"

"Know what?"

"How beautiful you are." He touches my cheek and it should be weird—super weird—but it's not. I only feel the shock of energy between us.

I swallow and say, "Stop. That's two men today that have called me beautiful. Is that what it's like in New York? Because I thought the men laid it on thick in the South."

His forehead wrinkles. "Who else called you beautiful?"

"Dylan--well sort of, he just said I need to be careful in the city."

Sam tightens his grip on my hand. "He's right. You do."

"You would know. Are you a model or something?" We hold eye contact for a beat and I absorb his features. They're disturbingly striking. Sharp cheekbones. Perfect lips. Green eyes that suck me in like an inviting pool. His hands are warm and I feel the strength in his touch. He's not big like Dylan but he's strong.

Amusement flashes in his eyes. "No, I'm not a model, but I work with some. I'm here on a photography scholarship. Maybe you'll pose for me sometime."

"I doubt that's a good idea. I'm not really the model type." I look at the mess on the floor. "More like a hot mess type."

"Hmm." He pushes a strand of hair over my shoulder. "We'll let the camera determine that."

I flex my toe and determine it's not broken and reach for the stack of books. Sam grabs them from me and says, "Where do these go?"

"In the studio."

And that's how I met Sam.

THERE's time before dinner and if I don't get in my daily writing I start to feel twitchy, so I grab my latest journal and settle into the cozy window seat. With a new pen and a fresh sheet of paper, I add to my ongoing story.

Maverick first noticed the birds when she was a kid.

The instant she walked outside, they would be there. Large, with sleek, glossy feathers. Round, brilliant eyes. They would appear slowly, one at first, flying down from the sky and perching on a branch. He would call to the others and they would follow—four more ravens, with wide, shadowy wings to guide them down to the treetops.

This went on for years. Maverick walked outside and her ravens greeted her. The other kids in the neighborhood thought she was strange, walking to the bus stop every day talking to 'herself'. They didn't notice ravens in the trees or hopping along the lawns nearby.

Over time, her relationship with the birds became so intense she stopped having friends entirely, preferring to sit in the backyard on a soft blanket. She socialized with the ravens. They brought her trinkets, pieces of metal and shiny beads. Marbles from lawn ornaments. Jewelry they'd plucked from somewhere with their beaks.

She fed them bread and birdseed and told them endless stories about her day. The way the teacher smiled at her essay, or the one particular girl named Callie in the 6th grade that called her names. The next day during recess she spotted the familiar shadow arc across the playground and watched, both fascinated and terrified, as a large, black bird snatched the bejeweled barrette out of the girl's flaming red hair. Callie howled, screeching in pain. She pointed upward and all the teachers and students gathered around.

Not Maverick. She watched the raven fly away with a shiny trinket in his beak.

That afternoon, the clip--along with a tuft of auburn hair still attached--waited for her on the backyard blanket.

That was the day she decided to name them...

A knock on the door pulls me from my writing and I walk to the front door of my suite. Sam waits on the other side. He's cleaned up from his casual shorts and T-shirt from earlier and is now wearing perfectly fitting jeans and a light blue shirt that makes his eyes twinkle like jewels. His hair is long, knotted at the top of his head in a man-bun I'd find ridiculous on anyone else, but not him.

"I thought I'd walk you down to dinner, if you'd like?"

I look down. I never changed. "Give me a second? You can wait in the sitting room."

"You look fine."

I shake my head. "First impressions and all of that."

My closet is sparse, so it doesn't take long to pick out an outfit. I go for a strappy sundress and sandals with heels. I brush out my hair and apply a little makeup. I don't want it to look like I'm trying too hard but I also don't want to look like a hobo next to Mr. Model out there. Not to mention the rugged good looks of Dylan. I slather on a little mascara and a hint of blush and walk out of the room.

"Damn." Sam stands as I enter the room. "Just when I thought you couldn't get hotter."

"Stop." He shrugs but pulls out his phone and takes a quick photo before I can stop him. "Hey! At least let me see it."

He shakes his head but I notice the hint of a frown as he slides the phone back in his pocket. He offers me the crook of his arm and, reluctantly, I hook mine with his.

"Do you know anything about the others in the house?" I ask as we approach the staircase and head to the second floor. "I've only met you and Dylan."

"Sure." He points to the two rooms on the second floor. "Damien lives on the top floor with Dylan. Clinton and Bunny live down here."

"Bunny?" Relieved to hear another girl may be in the building, even if she has a stupid name. "What's her focus?"

"Bunny is a dude," he gives me a strange look. "I'll let him explain the name. He's a visual artist—painting, drawing, collage."

We enter the foyer, my arm still linked with his. Sam's proximity and the delicious scent of soap and musk make my heart flutter in a way that is totally inappropriate and out of character. I tell myself it's because I'm tired and need a little extra support, but that doesn't explain the tightening in my lower belly. I follow him through the archway under the stairs and down a hall lined with wood. I stop cold in the doorway of the dining room and feel Sam's hand slip to mine.

The first thing I notice is the mural. It covers all three walls, minus the one made of glass. Hand-painted trees shoot up with lush leaves creeping toward the eighteen-foot ceilings. My eyes zoom in on a girl wandering in the woods, chin lifted, with a smile on her pink lips. I step forward and Sam releases his grip. I spin, trying to take it all in. Five ravens dot the landscape. One with a jewel in his beak, another with wings spread. One more hops on the ground while a fourth soars overhead. A fifth watches the girl from his perch in the tree.

"What is this? Who made this?" I ask, feeling my heart race like a hummingbird.

"It's been here since the house was built," Dylan says. "The Brannon family was big into Gaelic lore."

I turn and face him. He's wearing a blazer that make his shoulders look a mile wide. His black hair is cut short on the sides but a bit longer in the front. It's then that I notice the others...all men, all equal shades of gorgeous, flanking Dylan's sides.

"Morgan, I'd like you to meet our other housemates," he says. "Damien, Bun, and Clinton."

Without being told, I know who is who. Damien stands to his right, much taller than the others but lean with hard muscles visible though his shirt. He wears a shiny belt buckle and two rings on his fingers. Tiny earrings glint in his lobes and his eyes flash violet when he looks at me. And man, does he ever look at me. His gaze is consuming, like he's drinking me in. His head is shaved and two tattoos peek out from the collar of his shirt.

"You're Damien," I say, finding my voice.

"Hello, Morgan."

I look to Dylan's left. "And you're the one they call Bunny."

The nails on his right hand are thick with paint and splatters cover his shoes. He's smaller than the others, even Sam, but he has the most soulful coppery-brown eyes that match his spiky hair. Bold glasses frame his face and everything about him is adorable. His shirt sleeves are long, but one side seems unusually baggy and sits at an odd angle. I tilt my head as it dawns on me. He has a disfigured arm. He lifts up on his feet when I know his name and his mouth splits into a grin. "It's good to see you, Morgan."

Standing at the end of the table, with his hands wrapped around the back of the chair, awaits our final housemate. His jaw is clenched, gray eyes hard as steel. His dark, shoulder-length hair is loose against his massive shoulders. I thought Dylan was big—but no—Clinton must spend most of his days in the gym. Which is equal parts impressive and frightening. I feel dark energy rolling off of him and he seems to do his best not to make eye contact. When he doesn't speak, Dylan says, as though the man isn't in the room, "This is Clinton. Ignore him. He'll eventually warm up."

I stare at the men around the table, each standing behind an empty chair. The only one left is at the head and it's clear they've saved it for me.

"Now that introductions are over, is everyone ready to eat?"

Groans of happiness burst from each man, including Clinton, but they all look at me like they're waiting for my word.

"I'm starving," I say, lowering myself into the chair. "Let's eat."

5

MORGAN

Dinner is served by an older couple named Sue and Davis. I learn soon enough that they're married and together they've been responsible for cooking and cleaning for the residents of the mansion for decades.

The men speak animatedly during the meal, discussing their various projects. I can't help but finding myself caught up in their talk—as though they've known one another longer than a few hours. When there's a brief lull in the conversation I ask, "How long have you all lived here?"

A weird quiet settles on the group but Sam finally speaks up. "We've all been here for over a year."

I scan the men, all in various states of looking at me or at their empty plates. "All of you?"

Dylan nods. "Yes, your spot just became available."

"And I'm the only female?"

He nods. "It's a little untraditional, I guess. I hope you don't feel uncomfortable." Not as awkward as walking in and seeing the historic painting on the wall behind me depicting a scene my story.

"I don't mind. I never got along very well with other people, females in particular." I don't count Shannon. That relationship was an anomaly.

"What about you?" Damien asks. "Where are you from?"

"I grew up in Georgia. I lived just outside Atlanta until..."

Bunny frowns, his eyes curious. "Until what?"

"Until University. I mean, I still lived in the state, just in a college town."

Again, an awkward silence settles over the table. This always happens. I can't offer much about my childhood. I don't want to discuss my parents. I'm a clean slate until about four years ago and none of that is very interesting. I could discuss my work but it feels too private.

I determine the break in conversation may be my signal to head back upstairs. I move to stand but Dylan clears his throat and lifts his hand for me to wait.

"I just wanted to say that I think we're in for an exciting year of study, creativity, and friendship." He looks at me directly with those intense blue eyes. "The guys and I met before you got here, Morgan. The dean gave us a heads up about there being only one woman in the mansion. We all swore on our honor to respect and take care of you."

I look at the others and they all nod in agreement. I can't decide how I feel about the honor thing. They're *very* handsome men. Any one of these men seem like a good choice for finally losing my virginity. The random thought makes me blush and I make eye contact with Clinton, of all people. I take it back, any of them but Clinton. No chance.

"I appreciate your sensitivity, but it's not like I haven't been on my own for a while. I'm an adult."

"Of course you are," Sam says. "But standards needed to be set. You can count on us. All of us. We're all here to accomplish greatness and it's in our best interest to have an understanding from the start. "

I suspect it's the exhaustion from the day, but their words trigger a wave of emotion. I fight back the sting of tears. "Thank you for being so sweet."

I stand and they all rise in unison, each man completely different but in this very moment resolved to support me. It's been a long time since I've felt such unconditional approval. No one back home, not Ryan or even Shannon, ever understood my work or even my crazy brain. In just one day, I already feel closer to these men than I thought was possible.

6

SAM

After hours of trying to sleep, I finally give up. I stare at the vaulted ceilings and curse. Sleep is elusive. Dark dreams walk on the other side and I know why.

Morgan.

The instant she walked in the house it was like something shifted. I felt her footsteps. Her heartbeat. Her mere presence shot straight to my groin. She's down the hall, I remind myself, all I have to do is go down there. One thing will lead to the other and this *thing*, this oppressive energy, will release. Fuck, it doesn't even have to be me (I would certainly prefer it to be me) but she could screw any of the men in the house and we'd all feel a bit of relief.

I toss the sheets to the side and get out of bed, ignoring the tight constriction between my legs. "Not now, dude," I tell him. "It's not happening."

We all know the rules. Morgan chooses her mates. She must find the right man to release her powerful energy into. It's just unfortunate that her pheromones drive us wild in the meantime.

I flip the switch on the wall and a series of lights clicks on, buzzing overhead. I walk into my studio—the darkroom is to the left.

If there's one way to kill my libido, it's coming in here. Photos hang from the wall in various sizes and compositions. The skyline, fountains in the park, portraits of men and women around the city. I look at a scene and set up my shot, but what I see through the viewfinder is chilling.

I look at a photo I took down in Times Square two weeks ago. It had been a lovely spring day, with tourists enjoying the weather and blue sky overhead. That's what they saw. Me?

The final result hangs with the others. Dark clouds press down behind the buildings. The flashing lights of the billboards are off, replaced with cracked gray screens. The streets are abandoned, other than litter piled against the empty buildings. A dead child lies in the street.

The walls are plastered with similar images. Each one I take turns into this. I can't control it, but each photo I process has the same result.

I know in my heart that unlike most photos, the images do not represent what has already happened. No, it's not a sign of what's here.

It's a sign of what's coming.

7

MORGAN

I wake after a night of dreamless sleep to the smell of bacon and eggs wafting through the air. My stomach churns and I realize I'm starving. From the angle of the sun out my window, I get the feeling I slept a little later than normal and I tug a hoodie on over my tank top and head to the kitchen. I'm tying my hair in a knot when I enter the kitchen and find Bunny eating at the table alone. His feet bounce on the floor, bobbing up and down with a fast beat.

He looks up from reading a magazine. He does a fast double take when he realizes it's me, and there's no mistaking that he's checking me out. I tug at the strings on my jacket.

"Morning," he says in a hoarse voice.

"Did you oversleep, too?" I ask. I'm ecstatic to find the coffee still hot and a covered plate of food on the stove. I groan when I see the fluffy biscuit next to the eggs and bacon.

I walk over to the shiny, stainless steel kitchen table and raise my eyebrows. Bunny nods for me to sit.

"I'm a night owl." He takes a sip of his coffee. I try not to focus on his missing arm but as in all situations, the more you try not to look at it the more you do. The close proximity does give me the chance to see that his arm is still attached, it's just not fully functional, and his hand is mangled and mostly useless.

"Is that when you work?" I ask, digging into my eggs. They're delicious. "I've tried writing at night but early morning seems to be the best fit for my creativity."

He smiles and his soulful eyes light up. "Then we're opposites. For some reason I can't get moving until after midnight. It's like the rest of the world needs to be asleep for me to focus."

I shovel in a mouthful of eggs and a strip of bacon. After washing it down with a swig of coffee I say, "So tell me about your paintings."

"They're uh...well, would you like to see them? That may be easier than explaining them."

"I'd love to."

We clean up our dishes, leaving them in the sink as instructed by a note on the counter. I suspect Sue doesn't want people touching things in her kitchen. Together, Bunny and I walk up the massive staircase and I finally gather the courage to ask, "So how did you get the name Bunny?"

"I don't know, I've just always had it."

"Your parents named you Bunny?"

He laughs. "No, but my parents are from Ireland. My real name is hard to pronounce. Bunny is just easier."

I glance at him from the side. "It's the bouncing thing, isn't it? You're constantly moving."

A slight grin appears. "Could have something to do with it."

We climb the stairs past my floor up to the attic. The area is divided into two sections but the rooms are different. Bigger—with massive, vaulted ceilings and arched windows that overlook the city. The cavernous rooms have a haunting glow of daylight and instead of the area being split into suites, it's just a massive studio. An unmade bed is tucked in one corner and mural-sized canvases lean against the walls.

I stop mid-stride when I see them.

"You made these?" The canvases give me a physical reaction, like

I'm surrounded by something holy. I walk up to the nearest one—it also happens to be the biggest. The rectangular piece is as tall as the ceiling. A million stars splash against the blue-black backdrop and a woman floats in the middle.

Her eyes are enormous. Her pupils are dark with irises a deep shade of sapphire. Her mouth is heart-shaped and red, and a tiny raven is perched atop her long black hair. The woman's neck is graceful and thin, stretching from the bottom of the canvas. In her hand is a jewel that sparkles like purple fire against the backdrop.

I blink and look at the others and they're all similar—each a variation of the girl with the raven and the intense, haunted eyes. In some, she holds a stone. In others, a locket hangs from her neck, nestled between her alluring swell of breasts. She wears a variety of dresses, most delicate and fine. In a few she's nude. More than once I wonder if it's actually a photograph I'm looking at and not a painting at all, but the drops of oil and acrylic on the floor tell me otherwise. Upon closer inspection I realize they're not simply paintings but intricate collages built from paper, objects, and paint.

I glance back at Bunny, who is standing several feet behind me. His hand is shoved in his pocket and it makes me wonder.

"How?" I blurt, before I can censor myself. "This requires such skilled work. Doesn't your disfigured hand hinder you?"

He shrugs. "It's a bit of a challenge at times but I'm able to create even with my injured arm."

"It was an injury? An accident?"

He doesn't reply and it's a fair response. Who am I to ask something so personal? He walks past me to a small work table covered in brushes and paints. Knives, scissors, and spades stick out of well-used containers. I watch as he selects one thin paintbrush with a tiny tip. He dips into a small jar and walks back over.

"Can I?" he asks, holding the paintbrush to my cheek. His eyes are on fire, burning closer to copper than brown.

"Sure." I bite down on my lip as he moves closer, aware of a heat rolling off of him. He brushes the hair off my cheek, eyes focused and intent. I sense his heartbeat thumping with slow, easy beats. He leans close, hovering the brush just over my skin, until first touch when the tip surprises me with the cool paint. I laugh, because it tickles, but brace myself as he goes to work. The strokes of the bristles are soft and soothing; I'm lulled quickly into ease. Bunny's body is close enough that the hem of his flannel brushes against my arm. I get a whiff of his delicious scent. I have to stop myself from pressing my nose into his shirt. I study his face, his lips and mouth, and in the peace of the moment I want nothing more than to press my lips against his, just to see if they feel as soft as they look.

I'm so into this thought, into the moment, that I feel myself leaning forward just as he steps back and says, "There. Perfect."

I reach to touch the paint, cool and wet on my cheek, but stop myself, knowing it will smear. He returns from his work table with a small circular mirror and asks, "Want to see it?"

"Yes!" I'm giddy like a little girl.

He holds it up for me and I hunch, trying to catch the right angle, and then I see it. It's a delicate twist of vines, similar to the one engraved on my locket.

"I liked the design," he says quietly, as though he's revealed a piece of his soul.

"Thank you, Bunny," I say and continue my walk around the room, absorbing every one of his pieces.

8

MORGAN

I spend the afternoon working on my book. The story is bothering me—a nagging feeling that I'm missing something important. I sit back in the window seat and review what I've written so far.

Maverick has spent her childhood with the ravens and they've become like a second family—maybe her real family. She feels a sense of peace when they're around, but lately other forces have come into play. The girl is older now, in high school, and even I have to admit it's time for the protagonist to branch out a little. Meet new friends. Maybe a boy.

But what boy would want to be with a girl that speaks to animals? Also? Boys suck.

I stare out the huge window, pressing my forehead against the glass. Down in the park, birds burst in and out of the treetops. Up here it's quiet. No birds at all. Not even pigeons roosting in the eaves.

I look down, as much as is possible. From this angle it's clear the house has a nice-sized back yard, and in it, a figure catches my eye. I see the top of a head—hairless—and I think it must be Damien. He wanders in and out of a small structure and curiosity gets the best of me.

I didn't shower after Bunny painted my face. I didn't want to lose the magic of the moment and a quick glance in the mirror proves the painting is still on my cheek. Quickly, I slip on my shoes and run down the stairs. Sam's door is shut and when I pass by the second floor I pause briefly when I hear low, soulful music drifting down the hall.

I know that Damien and Clinton share this level and the former is outside. That means Clinton is behind the haunting melody, and as much as I want to follow the music, I know better than to barge in on Clinton. His reaction to me the night before was less than warm. In fact, he made it clear he has a problem with me being here. Dylan basically confirmed it.

I leave the music behind and head to the kitchen, seeking a door to the back yard. I swing open the heavy door and find Sue standing over a table of freshly washed vegetables. The small woman with graying hair and a stiff-looking uniform holds a knife with a wide blade and has a pile of red peppers nearby. A bowl full of different colored eggs sits on the counter.

"Do you need something, dear?" she asks.

"Are those fresh?"

"There's a coop on the roof."

"Really?" I smile. "We had chickens when I was a kid. My father built a coop in the backyard. Oh man, they nearly drove him mad."

"But they provided plenty of eggs?"

"Well, not really. There were a few incidents." The memory floods back and I grasp for it before it fades. "The first was when we had this one crazy chicken that just vanished in the back. Like one minute we were chasing it. The next poof, he was gone."

"And the second?"

"Something got in the coop. My father had to clean it up. That was the end of the chickens." I watch her work for a minute. "So, I'm just looking for the way out back. Thought I'd check out the yard."

"Just through that door there," she replies, pointing with the knife. "Are you going out to see Master Damien?"

"Sort of?" I answer honestly. I'm a little embarrassed that she knew right away what I was up to. Sue has a knowing glint in her eye. I suspect it's difficult to get anything past her.

"Well, take him a plate, will you? He gets so busy out there he forgets to eat."

"Sure, of course."

She walks over to the refrigerator and extracts a plate covered with foil. I take it from her. "There's enough for two in there."

"Oh, I don't plan on..." I glance down. "I just wanted some fresh air."

Sue shrugs and waves her knife. "Well get along, then. Dinner is at seven sharp. We're having salmon."

"Sounds delicious," I say, backing away and reaching for the door knob. "I'll make sure Damien gets this."

"Thank you, dear."

The warm afternoon heat blasts against my skin the second I step outside and I unzip the front of my hoodie. I cross a small porch and follow a path of slate pavers around to the main part of the yard. A wide, bigger porch sits across the back of the house and nestled in the corner is a cement structure with a metal roof. The building is plain and wide ventilation shafts poke through the ceiling. A strange chemical smell wafts through the air.

The door is open and I'm given a moment to watch Damien before he notices me. He's standing at a long, metal work table with a thick, leather apron hanging around his neck and tied at the waist. Leather work gloves cover his hands and he uses a small torch on his project. His muscular arms are bare, the hint of his white tank visible under the leather. His black work pants fit perfectly, snug across the butt. A pair of workmen's goggles are pushed to his forehead and he concentrates on a small object under a circular magnifying glass.

Extreme heat rolls out of the room even with the large fans mounted to the walls. I shift uncomfortably, wanting to take off my hoodie, but unable to with the plate in my hands. Damien is incredibly focused, but something happens and he drops the torch with a clatter on the table.

"Fuck," he mutters, tossing his gloves across the room. He wrings his hand.

"Damien!" I step through the doorway uninvited and ask, "Are you okay?"

He looks up, wincing from the pain. "Morgan? What are you doing down here?"

I hold up the plate. "Sue wanted me to bring you this." I set it down on the table and approach him. "Can I see it?"

"I just cut it. Nothing big. It happens."

I reach for his hand and see the slice in his length of his finger. "Do you have a first aid kit?"

He stares at my hand for a moment before looking back up at me. He swallows. "Over there, in that cabinet. Blue box."

I move quickly, grabbing the box among all the other supplies in the cabinet. I rummage though and find bandages and ointment. Leading Damien to a stool near the work table, I get out the medicine and slather it on the bandage. We clean the wound and wrap it up.

"Better?" I ask. I'm standing between his spread legs, his feet perched on a rung at the base of the stool.

"Much," he says in a quiet voice. We stare at one another for a moment and I sink into his beautiful eyes. They're the most unique shade of violet. He strokes a finger over my cheek, the one that Bunny painted and his lips twist into a wistful smile.

"What?"

"You look good marked like that."

I reach to touch the dried paint. It should be flaking off by now but it's not. Damien's eyes and hand move to the charm resting on my chest. I removed my hoodie before cleaning his finger. The studio is almost unbearably warm and I'm well aware of the sweat drenching my thin tank.

"This charm," he says, fingering my necklace. A shiver rolls up my spine. "Where did you get it?"

Normally I lie. I say that I found it in a boutique or an antique shop. The truth always clings to my tongue but not today. Not now. "I don't know," I say, placing my hand over his. "It's like I've always had it."

"You don't remember who gave it to you?"

"No, just that it's important to me." I realize we're still touching and my heart starts to race. It's an odd moment, I feel like he may kiss me, and bizarrely I really want him to. An intense yearning fills my lower belly and I lick my lips. Something about this place or these guys make me horny as hell. I mean, they're hot. That makes sense but at the same time I've never reacted to a person—much less *people*—like this.

Damien's eyes follow my every movement. "The food," I mumble. "It's getting cold."

He frowns, eyes on my mouth. "The what?"

"The food Sue sent." I take a step back and he drops the charm, as though he's coming to his senses.

"Ah, right. Yes." He scratches the back of his neck. I move to get the plate—to put something—anything—between us.

"So your studio is outside and not in the house?"

He takes the plate and leans against the doorway. "Yeah, the fumes from soldering are toxic. It's safer for me to work out here."

"And your specialty is metalworking?"

"Jewelry and designs. Welding. I make whatever inspires me. Come on, I'll show you." He turns and drops the foil on the work table. Fishing around a drawer, he appears with two forks. He offers one to me.

"I'm not hungry."

"Sue clearly gave me enough to share." He raises an encouraging eyebrow and the pierced hoop glints in the studio lights. Damien is covered in decorations. Tattoos, piercings, rings, and bracelets. Silver, mostly, but it shines in the light. Now that he's bandaged and we've created some distance, I study him a bit closer.

Two wolves are tattooed in dark gray and black on each shoulder, intricately designed. He lifts the fork to his mouth and a silver ring on his finger catches my attention. I ask, "Did you make all the jewelry you're wearing?"

"Most of it." He eats a roll by shoving the whole thing in his mouth at once. After he swallows he says, "Like you, I have some sentimental pieces."

"Which one?"

"Which do you think?"

My eyes roam his body. His buff arms and chiseled chest. I only have an idea of what his abs look like and the thought twists me into knots. I skim over the studs lined up his ear. Beneath the tank I see the outline of metal and know his nipples must be pierced as well. I focus on the amulet hanging from his neck on a leather cord. Although it's beautiful, I don't think it's special. Not like my charm.

My attention returns to the ring and I catch his hand in mine as he takes another bite of his lunch. He chews as I run my finger over the carved silver. I realize almost immediately it's a long blade twisted around his finger.

"This one."

He watches me closely. "Why?"

I shake my head but feel the hum of energy coming off the ring. "I'm not sure but I know it's the one."

"Metals and jewels carry many properties. Protection and power. Health and wealth. I use different ones to accomplish a variety of things, endurance or even strengthening resolve."

I touch the ring again and feel the hum. "What about this one?"

"It's gold fused with palladium. It signifies guardianship."

I'm not sure what that means but simply say, "I could tell it's special."

We stare at one another and he brushes a piece of hair off my cheek. "You're the one that's special, Morgan. Never forget."

9

DYLAN

Once dinner is complete, the table is clear, and Morgan's room has gone quiet, the others, one by one, gather in the first floor library. Clinton arrives last and locks the door behind him. It's the first time we've all met since she arrived at the Nead.

We take our places; Bun and Sam on the plush couch, Damien sits on a leather armchair facing the expansive back windows. Clinton never sits, instead hovering by the entrance. Me? I stand.

The five of us have known one another for eons. We're not quite brothers, but close enough; soldiers, warriors, even a criminal or two. Assigned as guards between the worlds. For Morgan.

"She seems to be settling in," I say to the group. "Unpacked. Working. Freely walking around the house."

"She came to see me in my studio," Damien comments. "Although she has a lot of questions and I believe a hint of intuition, she's blind to her purpose here."

There's been a fire in his eyes all evening. I expect us to all have one soon—Morgan is like an infection passing to one another. I glance at Bunny and note, even beneath the gentle exterior, he seems a little more spirited.

"Did you get the same sense?" I ask him. "I'm aware she spent time in your studio. She took the mark well?"

"She's curious. I suspect she feels the energy between us." Bunny looks at each of us. "She has no idea that the charm she wears is a protective symbol. The rune I marked on her cheek should reinforce it."

Morgan's energy is volatile. There are a few ways to suppress it. Runes and charms seem to help. Relying on us will be even better. But she's not there yet.

I walk to the bar and pour myself a drink. The amber fluid tastes like fire against my throat but immediately warms. I need something to satiate the urges. I know the others do too, and I pour four more glasses and pass them around.

Handing the last to Clinton, I ask, "How are you holding up?"

He swallows the drink whole. "It's hard to be around her and not..."

"I know, brother. We all feel the same." But even as I say it I know it isn't true. Clinton has a deeper sense than the rest of us. He always has. He's the one that knew the time had arrived for us to rejoin with Morgan. That watching her from afar was no longer possible. The demons are banging on the gates and without the bond forged by the six of us together, they'll get through.

I look at Damien. "You'll create her ring?"

Damien nods. "She seemed receptive to the one I'm wearing. The metals are infused with magic that will allow her memories to flow a bit faster, while not overwhelming her."

It's the best we can do. The clock is ticking but Morgan's powers are great. Unleashed all at once, she could destroy exactly what we're trying to protect. Ultimately, she must initiate the bond. It can't be the other way around.

I look at the other guards; we've been chosen for our strength and abilities. We're here to forge a bond with Morgan, a girl with more power than she could ever imagine she possesses.

"What happens if she doesn't figure it out?" Sam asks, but he knows the answer. The gates will open and death will spill into the streets, consuming any and all living things.

"We won't let that happen. Each of us will do exactly what it takes and what is in our personal skills to build the bond with Morgan." I give each man a knowing look that they all return, including Clinton, who nods before glancing away. "We can't allow the apocalypse to begin."

10

MORGAN

It's dark when I wake and the only sound in the house is a haunting melody drifting up from the first floor.

I feel an ache in my stomach and decide to go to the kitchen. Since I've arrived at the mansion I've felt unsatisfied with a constant, unquenchable hunger. A thin strip of light lingers under Sam's door, and I almost stop to see if he wants something, but the music downstairs takes on a deep vibration that I feel in my bones. I'm lured down the steps.

Clinton's door is shut but I approach it anyway. I pause before the mahogany panel and with a closed fist, rap on the wood. For a moment I worry he can't hear me. I'm also terrified that he will. My heart pounds in my chest of what lies behind that door. I know Clinton won't hurt me, the men swore their allegiance, but something about the smoldering, sexy man sets me on edge.

I'm about to turn away for the kitchen when the music abruptly halts and footsteps echo off the floor. The door opens and he stands before me, hulking in the small space.

We stare at one another. His eyes are gray and tense. His hair is tied at the neck, although short strands hang by his sharp cheekbones and my fingers curl into a fist to keep myself from pushing them back. I try to keep my eyes from his chest—it's bare and so very, very perfect. From the brown, round nipples to the fine trail of hair that travels from his abs to the low-slung pajama bottoms hanging from his hips. A drawstring swings from the waist.

"I heard your music," I finally say, well aware it's come out in a whisper. "I was sleeping and then, the music and..."

He glances up the stairwell but the entire house is quiet. If Sam or Bunny are working, they're too immersed to notice what's happening down here.

He pushes the door wider—an invitation—and even though I still feel a sense of danger I step through and enter Clinton's suite. There's no mistaking the heat of his eyes on my back as I walk down the hall and I'm hyper aware of my clothing—or lack thereof. Tiny shorts and a thin, gray T-shirt. The air is cool in the room and I attempt to cover my aroused nipples by crossing my arms.

His suite is nearly identical—just below my own. The walls are dark wood paneling and heavy, red fabric drapes over the windows. His instrument, a cello, rests on a stand in the middle of the living space. I can't help but walk over to the fine piece.

"You play beautifully."

He speaks for the first time. "Thank you."

I'm taken aback by the softness in his voice. It's a sharp contrast to the hard muscles and hostility on his face. The tension ratchets up a notch and the ache, now moving across my body, up to my chest and down between my legs, grows more intense. "Will you play something for me?"

The look on Clinton's face is one of resignation, but he moves to the chair and sits. His legs spread and the juxtaposition of the massive, half-naked, burly man playing an exquisite classical instrument is nearly too much to handle.

He reaches for his bow and grips the neck with one hand. His biceps tense and his abs tighten. I sit on the leather couch across from him. The first notes are low and long, vibrating in my chest.

I'm overwhelmed by the music and lean back, closing my eyes. The melody washes over me and soon I'm drifting...

Maverick crosses her backyard into the woods. Her house is visible from the path and the fluffy gray cat leads her into the darker corners of the forest. The charm around her neck hums in warning as they travel. It's not the first time they've made this journey, Maverick and the cat. They've tried several times but the ravens kept pulling her back.

"They're going to be angry," she tells him. He glances at her with his aloof yellow eyes. "They don't like me to leave the yard."

It's true that the ravens get testy if Maverick travels without them. They're a constant in her life. She's grown now—more woman than child—almost sixteen. She doesn't need the ravens as much anymore. She has a few friends at school. A boy named Jason asked her to the dance. She feels the judgment from her birds when she leaves in a vehicle or the night she kissed Jason by the front door.

Even with those small rebellions, she knows better than to go off with the cat. Weird things happen in the forest. There's a darkness lurking. It's where the one raven lost use of his wing fighting with this very cat. It's where the chickens from the coop went missing.

It's where the strange light flickers when she gets too close.

She knows not to come here but the cat always leads her and truthfully, Maverick feels a compulsion to follow.

Leaves crackle under her feet. Homecoming is next weekend. Even as the charm vibrates against her chest, Maverick is thinking of the dance and the dress she and her mother bought at the tiny boutique downtown. She climbs over a large log, the cat waiting for her patiently at the edge of a bend. The girl catches up and around the corner she sees the bright purple light, beckoning her forward.

"Is that it?" Maverick touches her necklace. The light a few steps away looks wavy, like a mirage.

"Mew," the cat replies, twisting through her legs. She no longer needs his encouragement. The light calls to her and she moves forward on her own. When she looks down it's no longer the forest floor but a stone path. The trees have vanished and the sky is a royal blue over-

head. The girl looks forward and the light is now a solid door, arched at the top with a purple stone in the middle. A golden door knob beckons her to twist. Her mission is clear. Open the door.

Maverick feels the gentle touch of fingertips at the base of her neck and turns, finding a handsome blonde man removing the charm.

"Who are you?" she asks, feeling an explosive warmth in her chest. He's powerful—that is clear, and her body thrums from his touch.

"I'm here to escort you to past the boundary line. Are you ready?"

He tosses the charm to the ground and a second wave of power surges through her limbs—an exhilarating sense of freedom. A familiar cry screeches in the distance but the man guides her elbow and he whispers in my ear, "Open the door, Maverick."

Shadows fly overhead as she rests her hand on the knob—

I snap out of my dream--or was it a vision--and sit up straight. Clinton stops playing and rests the cello on the stand.

"What?" he asks, eyes wide.

My skin is on fire and my heart races. I take one look at the man before me, at his bare chest and strong jaw and cross the room. Without asking—without a single beat of a pause—I walk the short distance and climb into Clinton's lap, pulling him close.

"Morgan?"

His breath is warm, sweet from alcohol earlier in the night. I feel the power from my dream rolling through my veins and I know, without a shadow of a doubt, that if I don't release it, I will be consumed whole.

Clinton's hands move to my back and I squirm against him, seeking relief. He groans at the pressure and his grip tightens. I feel his excitement, large and hard, straining against the thin cotton of his pants, and the cold glint in his eyes from earlier is gone, replaced by a hunger that matches my own.

"Do you feel it?" I ask in a voice that sounds like a whine. "The energy?"

"Yes," he replies gruffly.

"Take it away." I writhe against him. "Can you?"

He nods and takes one last look at me before kissing me hard. I exhale at the feeling of his mouth against mine and crush my body against the solid weight of his chest. His shoulders and arms are rock hard and the cords of his muscles tense with the slightest move. His mouth tastes like sugar and I lick his lips, while curling my fingers into the fringe of his hair. Clinton shudders beneath me like a man on the edge and the hard exterior turns into something different—something wild.

With each heated kiss the surge of energy diffuses, shifting from explosive to heady want. Our bodies collide and I feel the sharp tips of my nipples rubbing against the granite planes of his chest. I want to feel his skin against mine. I want to lick the sweat off his body. His fingertips lift the hem of my shirt and graze my belly. I'm overwhelmed, lightheaded and consumed. He kisses along my neck, his other hand cupping my breast. I want him to go further, and I encourage him by sinking my nails into his chest, but his hands don't move and I finally pause, breathing shallow.

"I don't—" I start, feeling the lie on my lips. I *do* want. So badly, but this man, Clinton, I don't know him, even if he feels perfect and familiar beneath me.

He presses his forehead to mine. "Feel better?"

Strangely, I do. Under the lust I have a renewed sense of balance. The power surges have subsided and I nod. I reluctantly extract myself from Clinton's arms. "I'm not sure what came over me."

He tilts my chin up. "I'm here for you. Whenever you need it."

There's a deep meaning to his words and before I take him up on his offer I decide to leave. An hour ago I was afraid of this man. Now I've felt nearly every inch of his body. Something about this house has lit a fire in me—creatively and physically--and as I walk back up the stairs to my room I wonder how I'll survive.

11

CLINTON

Letting Morgan walk out of my room was the hardest fucking thing I've ever done.

Harder than my cock right now, which trust me, is like vibranium, the special metal Captain America's shield is made out of. It's like Thor's hammer. Or the Hulk's fist.

Why the hell am I comparing my manhood to childhood superheroes?

I lean my head against the front door of my suite and breathe, trying to gain a little composure. Dylan called it at our little family meeting tonight. Morgan is killing me. I feel her every mood, her every desire. It's my special talent, in this form or any other. I sense it all: Danger, desire, fear, excitement. It's how I know if there are predators around. It's how I know if it's safe to hunt. It's my role in the group. It's about survival.

And right now the girl has brought all of those emotions into the house, giving the boys an extra dose of hormones and me a raging, never-ending hard-on.

I turn and slide down the door, my heartbeat slowing. I could have had her tonight. Picked that virginity like a cherry from a vine, but despite the want, it shouldn't be me. I won't be gentle. Not like Sam or Bunny. Those two will take care of her. Make sure it's done right. No, the urges she brings out in me come from deep inside.

She needs a mate.

Not just a fuck.

I see my reflection in the cabinet down the hall and I push my hand through my hair. Like I told her, she can use me whenever she wants, but beyond that? I've got a job to do and it's about her wants, not mine.

12

MORGAN

Over the following days, I find a balance that I know deep down comes from my encounter with Clinton. I wake early and write, using my time to get down a flood of words. Not only did Clinton quench my lustful desires, the gates opened in my mind and I can't get them down fast enough.

Admittedly, some of my dedication is due to the fact I'm hiding from Clinton. I can't express verbally or on paper what came over me that night. I've never felt such all-consuming want. I mean, sure, there were guys I'd been interested in. Even a few hard-core celebrity crushes in college, but I threw myself at the man, and the following evening at dinner, even though my urges had quelled, I kept my eyes on my plate and excused myself quickly.

I'd probably still be in my room if I didn't have an appointment to keep. I'm on my way to my first meeting with my graduate professor when raindrops begin to fall. I run down the city block with my bag clutched to my chest, barely making it inside before sheets of rain hit the streets.

"Wow, that was close," I say to the woman at the desk while

shaking the water out of my hair. "I'm here to see Professor Christensen."

Her eyes flick to the computer monitor. "Morgan Hansen?"

"Yes, ma'am."

"You can go on in. He's expecting you."

I walk down the short hallway and find his name on a small plaque by the door. I knock twice and a voice invites me in. The older Professor stands behind his desk in greeting. "Ms. Hansen, I'm happy to meet you."

"You can call me Morgan."

"Please have a seat, Morgan." I stare at the man, with his graying hair and thick beard. "Is something wrong?"

"No, sorry. You just look familiar."

He smiles. "I get that a lot. I'm told I favor Brad Pitt."

His expression is dead serious but I figure out soon enough that he's joking—although, to be fair, there's a touch of Brad in his baby blue eyes.

"I wanted to start off by thanking you for setting up the scholarship and housing."

He stiffens slightly before gesturing to the seat across from his desk. I take it and by the time he's in his own chair the easy charm has returned. "The Brannon scholarship is unaffiliated with this office. They do their own research and selection. You aren't having any problems there, are you?"

"Oh, no. My housemates have been very welcoming. And my quarters are the perfect space for writing. I've accomplished so much since I arrived."

"Good." He leans back in his chair and it creaks under his weight. "That's an eclectic group of men. I wouldn't want you to feel uncomfortable in any way."

"Aren't all artists eclectic?" His tone feels a little off, like he's issuing a warning. But I'm not here to talk about my housemates. I shift the subject. "Since this is our first meeting, can you tell me a little bit about what I should expect in the program?"

That brings a smile to his face. "As you know, this is a special graduate degree. You've been chosen to continue working on a specific project that we've seen extraordinary promise in—your novel. The first sections you sent in with your application were phenomenal."

Pride swells in my chest. "Thank you."

"Maverick's search for her true meaning is heartbreaking. And her relationship with the ravens? Impossible—yet we know from science and mythology that ravens are a magnificent species. Smart, cunning, clever. You've captured all of those elements in your book while bringing us the true humanity in Maverick's emotional journey."

His words hit me in the chest. I've never had someone understand my writing—my true intent—without me having to over-explain it in the process. Christensen nailed it on the first chapters. "That means so much to me."

He lifts his eyebrows. "Now, don't think my compliments mean there's not a lot of work to be done. The University and my office want to do everything we can to make your novel a success. Resources, research assistants, oh and I have arranged a partnership for you."

"What kind of partnership?"

"With another author. You'll bounce ideas off one another, read each other's work. It can be very beneficial." He hands me a card with a name, number, and email on it.

"Anita Cross. Is she in this program?"

"No, she didn't qualify but she's still an outstanding author. I suspect you'll learn so much from one another."

I slip the card into my bag. "I'll get in touch with her soon."

"Excellent." He glances at his watch. "If there's nothing else, I'll let you go. I'm sure you have words to get down."

"Every day!" I laugh. But it's true, even sitting here right now I'm itching to get back to work. Maverick has been running through my head all day. It's like she wants to tell me something and I can't quite figure it out.

~

THAT EVENING, after another quiet dinner, I pass Clinton exiting the dining room. I expect him to ignore me but he stops and grabs my arm. In a quiet voice he asks, "Can we talk?"

My heartbeat kicks up a notch and I nod.

I follow him into a quiet corner just off the kitchen. "I apologize if I crossed a line the other night."

"You?" I laugh. "I'm the one that basically jumped you. If anyone should apologize, it would be me."

"There's no need to apologize, Morgan." He brushes his hair over his ear. "Expressing yourself sexually is nothing to be ashamed of. It's a healthy reaction to stress."

I'm not ashamed but I do feel the flush of heat come to my cheeks. "Do I seem stressed?"

He looks me over, eyes sweeping over every inch of my body. "Not as much as you did when you walked in my room."

With that he walks off, leaving me flustered in the corner. I compose myself and walk through the library, picking out a book to read. I then exit through the back French doors leading to the porch. I've spent the whole day working or meeting with Professor Christensen, a break is warranted.

The porch is wide and made of stone. Twinkling fairy lights hang from the ceiling and comfortable furniture crowd around a circular pit with a roaring fire lit in the middle. I take a seat and pull out my book, content to read as the sun drops behind the nearby buildings, casting the whole yard in a fiery glow.

It's peaceful back here. I'd almost think I was back in suburbia, and my only interruption is Davis coming out and asking if I'd like a drink.

"Some of the wine we had for dinner," I suggest. Everyone at the table had at least one glass.

"Right away."

The creak of the door alerts me to his return but when I look up I spot Sam holding two glasses. "Can I join you? Seems like a nice night."

"Of course," I reply, scooting over on the cushiony couch. I've got my bare feet perched on the fire pit, enjoying the heat on my soles. "Shouldn't you be out photographing that sunset?"

"There's more than enough natural beauty right here." He grabs his phone and takes a quick snap. Before I can react he takes a series of just me.

"You know I don't like it," I tell him as he slips the phone into his pocket and sits next to me.

He shrugs. "I don't tell you what to write, you don't tell me what to photograph."

That's the kind of logic I don't approve of, I think, knowing he's right. We drink our wine and watch the red trails of the sunset fade into evening. Sam and I sit close together on the couch and I don't protest when he links his fingers with mine.

"You've been quiet at dinner." He rests his glass on the arm of the chair.

I glance over and catch the ridiculously sharp angle of his jaw in the firelight. His eyes twinkle and I want nothing more than to tug at the tie holding up his hair and watch it spill over his shoulders.

"I've just been immersed in my book, I guess. It's hard to come back to reality sometimes."

"I know the feeling. I spent eight hours in the darkroom yesterday."

Incredulous, I move so I can see him better.

"What?" he asks.

"It's just really nice to hear someone say that. None of my friends at school ever got my intensity or drive. They made me feel like a freak for the amount of time I spent working on my novel."

Sam uses a finger to push a strand of hair off my cheek. His hand lingers on my neck. "Your friends must not have the creative passion you possess."

Between the heat of the fire and Sam's proximity, I break into a sweat. It's only been days since my encounter with Clinton but the familiar ache returns to my loins, this time stronger than ever. If Clinton was here I'd take him up on his offer for another round. But he's not. Sam is and my feelings for him are just as strong.

He frowns and asks, "What's wrong?"

"Can I tell you something you won't divulge to the others?"

"Of course."

I'm glad with the firelight he can't see me blush. "I kissed Clinton the other night." I wait for the reaction and start to pull my hand away but he only tightens his grip. He also doesn't look remotely surprised. "Did you know? Oh my God, did he tell you?"

"Who?"

"Clinton!" I whisper-yell.

He laughs. "No, he didn't tell me anything but...well," he makes a face, "secrets are difficult to keep in this house."

I'm not exactly sure what that means but I add, "It was a one-time thing. Completely out of character. At least my character, that is."

Sam gives me a long look. He's not intimidating like Dylan or Clinton but he carries himself with confidence. Why wouldn't he? He's fucking gorgeous. When he looks at me though, with those emerald green eyes, I feel like he can see into my soul.

"Did you feel better after being with him?"

"We didn't have sex."

"That's not what I meant."

I look down at my hands and remember what Clinton said about not feeling shame. "I felt better actually. Like, when I went down to his room I had all this pent-up energy—just bubbling up inside. Once we kissed and, you know, we let that out on one another I felt more balanced." Sam's fingers tighten around mine. "I'm not really experienced in things like this. I hope I haven't ruined the dynamics in the house or something."

He shifts toward me and clasps a hand behind my neck. "God no, Morgan. Dylan told you that first night. We're here for you in any way you need."

His tongue darts out, licking his lips and for the second time I feel like I could fall into a man. When I don't respond with anything other than a rapid heartbeat and shortened breath, he tugs me into his arms until I've got my back pressed against his chest. His feet bookend mine, soles burning against the hot fire, and my dress has shifted up, exposing my upper thighs. I feel the length of his hardness against my lower back and I fight the urge to press into it.

Why? Because this is crazy. I *feel* crazy.

Slowly, Sam begins to trail his fingers up and down my arms, leaving a blaze of goosebumps in their wake. His breath is hot against my neck and he whispers in my ear. "Let it go, baby. All that doubt and anxiety. You're carrying the weight of the past on your back and it's a boulder that will take you down."

His words don't make sense but his fingers do, and they move across my thighs and under the curve of my breasts. I will my hips to stay on the cushion but I crave his touch, right at my center, and just when I think I can't bear the teasing any longer, the tips of his fingers dip between my legs, grazing over my most sensitive spots.

"Have you ever had an orgasm, Morgan?"

"Yes," I breathe, trying to find my voice. And trying even harder not to think of that bumbling night with a potential boyfriend. That relationship, like all the others, didn't end well. "Just once, really."

"I can tell. You're wound tighter than a clock. We've got to release a little of this, okay?"

"Ohhkay." I shudder when he moves further, pushing past the lace of my panties. His lips kiss up and down my neck, sucking and licking every inch. My toes curl on the fire's edge and I clench my hand around his knee. He strokes the hot nub between my thighs, the one desperate spot begging for all the attention. His fingers move with precision, like he doesn't want to waste a beat. His free hand moves to my breast, tugging at the strap until he can reach the hard peak of my nipple. I moan at the dual sensation. No, I've never felt anything like this.

I grow slick from his touch and I lean my head on his chest. I feel his heartbeat, rapidly thumping against my back. His movements grow quicker, my hips thrust in time, I almost—almost—beg him to do more, go further, but the coil in my lower belly tightens and tightens until I'm wound so far there's nothing to do but gouge my nails into Sam's legs and cry as I shatter into a million pieces.

"Sam," I breathe, trying to regain control of my senses. But all the stress and tightness in my body is gone. I'm limp as a ragdoll against his body. All I want to do is curl up and soak in the moment, but I force myself to sit up and straighten my top, then the hem of my dress. My panties are drenched and I don't even want to know what my hair looks like. He confirms this by smiling at me and smoothing out my hair.

"God, you're beautiful," he says, leaning forward to kiss me. His lips are warm and inviting. "I always knew you would be, but it's like looking into the sun. Blinding." He kisses me again and again and again, until the moon rises high and we both sleep.

13

SAM

"I fucked up."

Dylan looks up from the book at his desk. It's a massive tome, six hundred years old, with brittle pages and faded ink. I spot a familiar design at the top of the page. The sword that Damien forged into a ring—the same one he's creating for Morgan.

"What did you do?"

"She's just so..." I can't believe I did it. I'd been so careful. We all have, but seeing her like that. Red cheeked and post-orgasmic. I just let it slip. "I made a comment about how I'd always known she would be beautiful."

Dylan's jaw ticks. "Did she react?"

I can't help the smirk. "Honestly, I think she was too fucking pleased to notice."

"Yeah, we all caught on to that. The whole house shuddered when she finally came."

I expect congratulations on being the one to push her over the edge but no, I fucked up. That's why I'm here.

"As obnoxious as it is, you're probably right," he says, leaning back in his leather chair. "She was probably too distracted and even then, we may have to continue to nudge her toward the truth anyway. I think we're running out of time and her memory is slow to recover."

"I know. My photos aren't getting any better." In fact, they're scary as fuck. The darkness is looming and if we don't get the bond forged, we're all screwed.

"Did you get a feeling?" he asks with a straight face. To be chosen bears a lot of responsibility. Morgan's mate will no longer just be her guardian. He'll be her partner and take the brunt of her powerful energy. "Like you were the one?"

"I felt something—she's special. The desire to please her is overwhelming." There's no mistaking the pain on Dylan's face. We all feel the need to pleasure Morgan. "But she didn't push it further. I gave what I could but as you know, the choice is up to her."

Dylan nods and looks back at the book in front of him. He's studied the lore on Morgan and the gate for many years. He carried the knowledge in him even when he took the form of a raven. But this is the first time I've seen lines of worry by his eyes.

"We have time," I assure him. "Her memories are coming back. She's writing a lot and the two energy releases have helped. I think she's aware that she may need to rely on us more. Once that happens, she'll be more receptive to understanding the truth and her role in everything."

"And you think she'll make the right choice?"

We both know this is where the whole problem lies. Morgan must know the truth about her past; what has happened and the destruction she caused.

"I don't know," I reply. "But soon we'll find out and we need to be prepared one way or the other.

14

MORGAN

Under the guidance of the handsome blond man, Maverick twists the door knob. The ravens screech overhead, angered by her actions, but the surge of power between her and the door feels right.

Something finally feels right.

The lock gives, springing inside, and she feels the click of release. Maverick tilts her head to look at the ravens flying overhead. She can barely hear them now and their bodies look like nothing more than shadows. The man's hand comes down on her shoulder. "It's time, Maverick. Open the door."

With a firm grip on the knob, she does just that, pushing it forward until she can see to the other side. A veil of gray shrouds the distance, but the cold is unmistakable. Black tendrils of smoke weave around her ankles and the air smells of wet ash.

She steps forward, leaving the sunlight behind, and jumps when the land crunches beneath her feet. The girl bends and touches what appears to be stone covered in soot, but it only takes a moment to know it's bone.

A wave of nausea rolls in Maverick's stomach.

She looks to the man and says, "What happened?"

"You've opened the gates of Hell, sweetheart." The beautiful man's face shifts, eyes turning black and skin melting away. *"Welcome back."*

Maverick screams...

The sound echoes in my ears and bounces across the room. I wake covered in a thick layer of sweat.

"No, no, no, no," I cry, jumping out of bed. I brush my ankles to get rid of the smoke.

There's no smoke. No ash. I blink, taking in the fact I'm in my room at Nead mansion. I'm not even sure when I came back up here. After midnight for sure.

Confusion and fear cling to my throat and I race to the window. I brace myself for destruction, for the kind of annihilation in my dream (*memory?*) but the city below functions like normal. Taxis and buses zip down the road. Green, thriving trees fill the park. People walk in that brisk, city way of theirs.

I lean against the window sill and rub my face and eyes.

Jesus, what a nightmare.

Across the room on the bed I spot my journal, open with a pen in the crease. Pushing back the blankets, I grab the book and flip through the last pages, ignoring the lingering feeling in my gut.

She looks to the man and says, "What happened?"

"You've opened the gates of Hell, sweetheart." The beautiful man's face shifts, eyes turning black and skin melting away...

I'd written it—not just dreamed it. I run a hand down my face. It had been so real.

A knock on the door draws me from going back down the rabbit hole. When I open it, Davis stands on the other side. "You have a visitor."

"Now?" I look down at my pajamas. "Who?"

"Ms. Anita Cross." His eyes linger on my neck. "Should I ask her to leave?"

I reach for the spot, remembering Sam's mouth being there the night before. "No, give me five minutes. Ask her to wait, please."

I pass the journal and snap it shut, as if that will keep the darkness away. In the bathroom I lean into the mirror and look at the dark bruise on my neck. Dammit, I think, reaching for my makeup. He fucking marked me.

∼

AT THE BOTTOM of the stairs Davis stops me and says, "I escorted Ms. Cross to the library."

"Thank you, Davis."

"I also have a package for you." He holds out a small purple box. "Damien asked me to deliver it to you."

I look at the square box. It's not heavy and I tuck it into my jacket pocket and thank Davis again.

On the way to the library I hear voices in the kitchen. Damien and Sam from the sound of it. My stomach flips just hearing Sam's laughter. What he did to me last night. Wow.

Anita walks around the library, eyes skimming over the books. She's around my age but with light hair instead of dark. She's tall with curvy hips and a pronounced bust. A flare of possessiveness ignites and I shut the door behind me. I don't want the boys to see her.

They're mine.

Anita turns when the door clicks shut and I shake off the desire to toss her from the house. "You must be Anita," I say with a plastered grin. *What the hell has come over me?* "Sorry to keep you waiting. I was up late and finally crashed."

"No worries," she replies. Her own grin seems genuine. "I was just looking around this amazing library."

"The Nead Mansion is the gift that keeps on giving. I'm very lucky to have won the scholarship."

"Professor Christensen showed me your submission. Luck had nothing to do with you winning. You're an amazing author."

We're a study in contrasts—me and Anita. Besides the hair color, she's wearing a sleek, gray, pencil skirt that accentuates her curves. Her white, form-fitting blouse reveals an ample view of her cleavage. And her hair is perfectly straight in a way I didn't even know was possible.

I stand across from her in ripped jeans and a hoodie with nothing but a bra underneath. The jacket is zipped to my chin in an attempt to hide the bite marks from my housemate.

"Well, he told me some amazing things about you, too," I say, which is a bit of a stretch. "I can't wait to get started and review your work."

"Oh, that's why I stopped by today. To drop you a copy of my manuscript. I figured I'd give you a head start on reading it, then at our first 'official', she uses air quotes, "meeting, we'll both be on the same page."

She opens up her satchel and pulls out a thick, bound sheath of paper. A flash drive is affixed to the cover. "Paper and digital. Whichever you prefer."

I take the heavy materials from her. "Awesome."

The box from Damien holds my attention—as well as keeping Anita away from the others in the house. I pause at the door, listening for voices, but quickly escort her to the front door, where Davis waits, ready to usher my guest out.

"Next week?" she asks. I nod. We've agreed to meet at least once a week. I clutch the manuscript she gave me. That means I'll have to find time to read this whole thing before I see her again. "You'll send me your updates?"

"As soon as possible. I promise."

After she leaves I turn and find Bunny standing one floor up, watching our exchange. The weird flicker of jealousy returns and there's something in the look we share, like he knows what I've been doing with the others. Sam did say there are no secrets in this house.

My hand brushes against the box Davis delivered to me from Damien and I look down. When I search for Bunny again, he's gone; whatever moment we shared has passed.

"I'll be outside," I say to Davis as though he's keeping track. He probably is for all I know but he replies with a, "Yes, ma'am," and I walk back through the library and out the back doors. I pass the couch and unlit fire pit from the night before and touch the spot on my neck.

What am I doing? These men and their good looks and unconditional support have me rattled. The commitment to their craft and unmistakable sexual energy is difficult to ignore. I will myself to stop, but it's like a craving I can't control. I keep walking toward Damien's workshop, carrying the box in my hand, feeling a distinct tug between my navel and the man I know is inside.

"Hey," he says as I cross the threshold of his sweltering studio. It's not a question. He doesn't seem remotely surprised to find me in his doorway.

"You left this for me?" I hold up the box and he puts his tools down on the table. He's not wearing his apron, but a ripped and faded pair of cargo pants and a black shirt with the sleeves torn off.

"Yes, I made it for you. Do you like it?"

"I haven't looked at it yet."

He frowns and walks over, taking the box from my hand. It opens with a slight creak and inside is the most beautiful silver and gold ring I've ever seen.

"You made this?"

It's a stupid question. It's obvious and I've seen his work. But to be given something so exquisite...it renders me speechless. Damien fills the silence by removing the ring from the box and taking my hand. He slips the ring on my finger—my ring finger—and it's a perfect fit—almost as if it molds to my finger. A spark of electricity jolts through my body as the metal warms to my skin and I feel charged.

I feel aroused.

The worry and jealousy with Anita earlier vanish and I look up into his eyes. "Thank you."

"Never take it off, Morgan."

"I won't."

His hand reaches for my neck and he thumbs the spot where Sam left his mark. I should be embarrassed but I'm not. I feel something different, a deep need. Not the kind I experienced with Sam.

"Sam..." I start but he cuts me off.

"I know all about you and Sam. The house quaked when you orgasmed last night, Morgan. Your power and your energy are barely contained."

It's a fucking weird thing to say but I know that he speaks the truth. I felt a tremor when I came on the back porch. I saw the knowing in Bunny's eyes earlier in the hallway. We're all linked and I have no doubt I'm the conduit.

I reach my fingers into the waistband of Damien's pants and tug him close. His eyes search mine and I tilt my head upward. He responds by placing both hands on my face and kissing me hard.

Emboldened, I move my hand to the front of his pants and feel the hard lengthening of his erection beneath the fabric. His kisses turn frantic and his hands leave my face to graze down my shoulders and arms.

"Tell me what you want," he says, dipping his hands around my backside. I want him. All of him, but I also feel the urge to control. To take. I thumb the button on his pants.

Damien backs into the work table, tools and instruments scattering in the process. I tug his pants down, revealing the enormity of his size. This isn't my first time doing this. I'm a virgin, not a prude, but the sheer size flusters me until I look up and Damien rubs his thumb over my lip.

"You've got this, babe," he tells me, and it's the most awkwardly wonderful thing to say. It's like he knows. Like all the others, they know my heart and desires. My *needs*.

I do *have* this.

With a strong push against his chest, Damien falls back, leaning his elbows against the counter and I take him in my hand, stroking the velvet tip. He groans in approval.

I lick my lips and kiss him before dropping to my knees. His hand moves to my hair and with a tentative lick I feel a different type of power course through my veins.

I am invincible.

I am complete.

These men are mine.

15

MORGAN

I leave Damien weak-kneed in the studio. I never knew how doing *that* could be so...empowering. To have a man like Damien, strong and confident, call my name out in worship...I just didn't know. But now I do. And there's more, too.

I feel it clearly now. I cross the yard and look up to the attic dormers. Someone, there's little doubt who, is watching from way above. Keeping guard. It's time for me to speak to him.

I pass back through the library and then the down the hall. Sue is busy in the kitchen preparing for dinner and rich, delicious scents travel down the hallway. True hunger rumbles in my belly, not the false kind I've felt for the last week. I touch my lips, still puffy from being with Damien, and feel satiated for the moment.

I take the long walk upstairs, eventually stopping in front of Dylan's rooms. I've never been invited in before, but something tells me he's been waiting for me to arrive on my own. This is only confirmed as the door opens when my hand hovers mid-knock and Dylan awaits, dark and brooding on the other side.

His blue eyes hold mine, and I can't quite read what he's thinking, but I step into the giant studio without further greeting. I have questions and I know without a doubt he has the answers.

The first is on the tip of my tongue but one look around the room throws me into silent awe. The walls are covered floor to ceiling with books, their binds old and cracked. An ancient map hangs from the ceiling with tiny black pinpoints. There's a cluster near my university in Georgia and another surrounding our building here in New York.

I spot a red pin at Professor Christensen's office. Another at my ex-sort-of-boyfriend's apartment down south, and several others dotted around familiar locations.

A photograph on a massive mahogany desk catches my attention from across the room. I leave the map and my growing questions and approach the work space.

"What is this?" I finally ask, pointing to the picture. It's a little girl, around three, with a halo of dark curly hair. She stands on chubby legs in a green, grassy yard pointing to the sky. I have a vague recollection of wearing the glossy red sandals strapped to the girl's feet. "Where did you get it?"

He stands in the doorway, tall and broad. His shoulders block out half the light. Dark, leather cuffs are clasped around his wrists. "Your parent's house."

That stops me cold. "What do you know about my parents?"

"Morgan, I know everything about you. I was there the day that photo was taken. I was there the day your parents died. I've been with you since the beginning."

I swallow, because the instant Damien put the ring on my finger memories have trickled in my mind like they'd never left. "You're one of my ravens."

It isn't a question.

"Yes. I am."

I reel. It wasn't just a story. They were real. Not just Dylan, but the others as well. "All of you?"

"All of us." His eyebrows cinch together. "But you know that, don't you?"

"I don't know anything," I say honestly. "But I do feel something." I hold my hand to my chest. "Something's happening to me. The dreams. My writing. My encounters with the others."

He steps forward and I'm dwarfed in his shadow. He touches my chin. "It's a reawakening. It's been predicted, and as much as I have been waiting for this day, it means the darkness is also rising."

My hands tremble from his nearness. The other men in this house? I've craved their touch. Dylan? I want to pour myself into him and let him harness the energy of the past, present, and future.

"This is crazy, Dylan. Am I crazy?"

"No, little bird, you're not crazy. You're the strongest of us all. The steel that binds us all together. Things were different when you were younger. We could freely communicate with you, albeit in a different form. But then the darkness took notice and things changed. Your family shattered. Your memory was taken. Our forms altered. Much to our dismay, we had to leave you."

Anger replaces my confusion. "You abandoned me."

"I'm sorry," he says. "There was no other way. The darkness was too close. Leaving was the only option."

Emotion overwhelms me and I gather my wits. "What is the darkness?"

He guides me over to the far side of his massive work table. Spread across the top are photos of me and my childhood home, further proof that what he's telling me is either the truth or he's the worst kind of stalker. The photos have a grainy, out of this time quality about them. As difficult as it is to understand how and why Dylan has these photos, it's the next stack that sends terror up my spine.

The photos are completely modern and could have been snapped at any moment. The images are recognizable, Times Square. The Statue of Liberty. The Brooklyn Bridge. They're impossibly realistic other than the faded gray tone and the absolute destruction they depict. The streets are abandoned—desolate with gray, stormy skies overhead. Bleached skulls pile next to rusted vehicles. Choking vines twist up concrete buildings. Death hovers just off camera but it's clear pure evil is behind such annihilation.

I spot the marking in the corner and rub over it with my thumb. "Sam took these?"

He nods. "Sam doesn't see the world we do. He sees into the future and his camera speaks the truth."

"This is why he didn't want me in his studio?" He took photos of me. Quickly, I flip through the ones on the desk until I find the one from my first night at the mansion. The image is stark, my face bold and haunting in the decaying room. Ivy rolls up the walls and a giant hole in the building reveals the night sky. The most disturbing thing? I'm not dead. No. I'm alive and full of life. My eyes shine the darkest black and a twisted smile lingers on my lips.

I drop the picture and rub my eyes. What the fuck is that? I'm happy about the bad things coming? It shouldn't be a surprise, not after everything else. The apocalypse is coming and I'm fooling around with a different guy every other night. Oh and they're guys who, once upon a time, were ravens. My ravens.

I wander across the room. Finding a red velvet chair, I sit. "My writing. It's just memories isn't it?"

"Yes, with some embellishment."

"And this scholarship? It's not real. It's just a way to keep me close."

"The scholarship isn't real but your acceptance into the graduate program is. We had no idea where you were until that submission came through. An associate notified us of your application. We were able to bring you back home."

Home. This wasn't my home. Once upon a time I lived in a nice suburban house, in a normal neighborhood with my parents. My eyes flick to Dylan's. "My parents. The virus that no one could identify. The tests and doctors…what was that?"

He walks over and kneels. With my hand in his he says what I've always feared. "The darkness killed your parents, Morgan. Just like it will kill everyone else if given the chance."

"How?" I ask, recalling the strange illness. But the memory is strong. I've written about it more than once. Dreamed a dozen times. I touch the charm hanging below my throat. The one Maverick discards and feels a rush of power. "The gate. I opened it."

He nods.

"I killed them." I look at Sam's photos, dread creeping over every inch of my body. "Why would I kill them?"

He links his fingers with mine. "That's why we're here, Morgan. To keep the unthinkable from happening again. To help you control your urges—your needs."

There's no mistaking what kinds of urges he's speaking of. My heightened desires and unquenchable thirst for these men since I arrived is undeniable. "And if I don't control those urges?"

"Then you're likely to open the gate again."

"Why, Dylan? That makes no sense? Why would I want to do this to my family? To the world?"

His eyes take on a sheen of sadness when he replies, "Because you're the Morrigan."

"The Morrigan?" The name sounds familiar, something I've read in the past.

"The queen of the ravens. Harbinger of death and war. It's in your nature and every reawakening starts the cycle again. It is our duty, the five of us, to stop you."

16

MORGAN

Even though I'm still reeling from my talk with Dylan, I go to my quarters and change for our mandatory dinner. Despite the fact I showered and cleaned up, I still have the taste and feel of Damien on my mouth. With every floor I pass, I note the lingering effects of the men in the mansion. There's the phantom heat of Bunny's painted mark on my cheek. My stomach twists at the memory of Sam's teeth on my throat and the pleasure of his hands between my legs. The image of Clinton's eyes are scorched in my mind just like the heat of his lip as I poured my everything into him.

I carry these sensations with me as I walk past the second level and down to the main foyer. It's with a new understanding that I enter the dining room and take my seat at the head of the table. The men wait for me with attentive, expectant expressions. I take them in one by one.

Dylan, the only one that hasn't touched my skin, is still part of my soul. I speak to him first. "I was eight years old the first time you came to me. Nothing more than a shadow in the trees. You followed me to the bus stop and were there each day when I returned. It was you that arrived before the others—a sentinel—making sure I was safe."

I shift my gaze to Sam. "You were always the kindest and never afraid to get close. I remember sitting on the blanket in the yard. Watching you fly tree to tree. You'd call out and I'd try to copy your voice. We'd talk for hours—just chattering away. You became my best friend when no one else wanted to be around."

Damien leans forward and I touch the ring he forged for me. "The first gift you brought to me was a shiny silver marble. Next, a trinket made of gold. I had a whole stash in my room but I was only able to keep one. The only one that truly mattered." I touch the charm on my chest. "I didn't remember until today where it came from. Or why I had it. But I remember now that you brought it to me one sunny afternoon. The cord was already strung through the loop and you all watched from your branches as I hung it on my neck. You were protecting me—even then. I didn't realize I had a job. I didn't know I would fail so badly."

I look apologetically at Bunny with the last sentence. He reaches across the table with his good hand and I shake my head. "It's my fault you lost use of your arm and hand. I never should have followed the cat down the path. He came to me day after day, leading me to the gate, and every time I followed."

"You didn't understand," he says.

"No. That's the thing. I did. I felt the energy and the power and I wanted more. I knew I was meant for something beyond this world. I just didn't realize it would lead to such destruction. I didn't know you would get hurt."

"I survived, Morgan. I'm still here—with you."

I squeeze his hand but look down the opposite side of the table, to the man at Dylan's side. Clinton is the strongest of the guardians. "The most protective. The most reserved. You were always the last to arrive because you were keeping watch over all of us."

"I'm the one that failed that day."

"You can't bear the weight of my actions alone, Clinton."

"We were commanded," he says, leaning forward. His eyes shine like steel. "You were a child. We knew what was on the other side and the ramifications of the gate opening."

"I was a child with the power of a goddess."

The room goes silent now that our history is spread on the table.

Across the room Dylan leans back in his seat, arm resting by his side. He doesn't look concerned. No, he looks emboldened, like my returned memory is the answer to all his prayers.

"What do we do now?" I ask the historian. But he gave me a summary in his quarters. I need the men, my ravens, to absorb the darkness; if not, the Morrigan will return full force, open the gate, and the apocalypse will begin. I understand this now. I understand my heightened desires.

"We do nothing," he replies, gesturing to the other men. "But you must make a choice."

I frown. "What kind of choice?"

"Between us."

I stare across the table. None of the men looked remotely surprised, unlike me where it's just one blindside after the other. "I don't understand."

"To fight the darkness, Morgan, you must find a partner of equal strength. Someone who can take the brunt of the energy burning beneath your skin." Dylan's blue eyes shine. "Ravens mate for life and you are the Queen. You'll need to choose from one of us—one of the guards."

His words are like a punch to the gut. Mating for life? But it still rings true in the center of my chest. My eyes skim past each one. The strong, the smart, the beautiful, the creative, and the caring, and I realize with stark clarity that I'm not upset about the directive.

I'm upset that I can't have them all.

17

MORGAN

An ancient book detailing the tales of the Morrigan sits on my bed when I arrive in my room that night. A note rests on top.
Embrace your history. -Dylan
I read the heavy book, absorbing the words and illustrations. The Queen of the Ravens was the Celtic goddess of war. A terrifying, wrathful woman who reveled in evil. She was known as the Triad. Woman with three parts.

The woman named Morgan.
The Raven Shifter.
The Goddess of War.

In each telling of the Morrigan's story she falls for a man, a warrior hero, Cu Cuchulainn. Cuchulainn rejects the Morrigan over and over, igniting such rage that she kills him and uses her pain to fuel an epic and all-encompassing war.

Beneath a drawing of the dark-haired queen, the book explains that the Morrigan's vengeance was so overwhelming she was trapped in an alternate universe where she could wallow in war and strife for eternity. Her only allies, a murder of five ravens, had been assigned by the gods to rein her in. Over time the ravens became devoted guardians to the Queen, falling in love with her one by one. To find peace she must find her one true mate from the guardians.

I push the book to the side and lean back against my pillows. The last twenty-four hours have been surreal and for a moment I seriously consider if I've awoken in a mental ward. Maybe the Nead is nothing more than a sanitarium. I google the word 'Nead'.

"You're fucking shitting me," I say to myself, tossing the phone across the room. Nead is the Gaelic word for nest.

But that's just it, I think, wandering across my suite and into my writing chamber. I look at the journals lining the bookshelf—a lifetime of stories about this very thing. I don't *feel* crazy. I feel like everything in my life has a new sense of clarity. My childhood. The obsession with ravens. The weird dreams about the forest and the cat. The mysterious death of my parents and the loss of memory.

And the men. Oh boy, the men. If all of this is true, one of them is my true love. My mate.

I touch the ring on my finger and exit my rooms. It's time to round up my guardians.

18

MORGAN

The men come into the library one at a time.
    Dylan first, as my sentinel.
    Bunny next, covered in paint and flashing me a sweet smile.
    Damien appears from the backyard, smelling of metal and sweat, a shiny object between his fingers.
    Sam enters from the hallway, giving me an easy-going hug on the way to his seat.
    And Clinton arrives last, arms crossed over his chest, wary and watchful.
    "Thank you for coming," I say. "It's been a long day. Or two, actually. I've had time to do a little reading and soul searching. As hard as this whole thing is to believe, I know in my heart the stories you have told me—and the ones I have been writing on my own for so long—are true. I think I knew it all along."
    "It's my understanding that one of you is my mate." My heart hammers in my chest. "After the last few weeks I know I'm not in the position to make that choice—not right away. I need more time."
    "Time is of the essence, Morgan." Dylan says. "The gate weakens every day."

By gate I think he really means me. I weaken the longer I go without a mate and someone to take the darkness from me. But Morgan, the woman, is part of the triad of the Queen, and she needs tended as well. That part of the Morrigan needs to be sure. It's not something I can jump into.

"If we're going to do this it has to be on my terms," I tell them. "It's a decision I need to be absolutely sure of. If what you're saying is true, there's no room for error. I must find the perfect mate and right now I have no freaking idea which one of you that is."

"How do you plan on deciding?" Sam asks and the others all lean closer, listening intently for my answer.

"You have thirty days to prove yourself to me. I want a single month, thirty days, to ensure that I'm picking the right one." I exhale, trying to rid myself of the nervous tension in my stomach. "At the end of that time period I'll make a decision."

Dylan, as always, is the first to stand. He bows and says, "As you wish, Goddess."

The others follow, bowing in my direction, and for once I notice a bit of rivalry as they look at one other.

Things are about to get very, very interesting.

EBONY RISING

PROLOGUE

The apocalypse has been here before, carried on the wings of a goddess. Her anger spilled blood with a blade. Her tears brought plague down on the earth. Her fear hovers in the shadows, waiting for the next heartbreaking rejection. The next betrayal.

She knows it will come.

It always does.

Because the goddess leads with her fist but kills with her heart.

No one can alter destiny.

Not even the chosen.

1

MORGAN

Sweat clings to my skin, pooling in my lower back. My hands are slippery, encased in the heavy, padded gloves.

"Two minutes," Clinton commands, starting his stopwatch. "Now."

With arms that feel like lead, I pummel the sandbag, hardly making it sway. I'm not weak; I'm just exhausted. I wake at dawn for three hours of nonstop writing to fulfill the obligation of my acceptance into the University arts program. But once that's complete I move on to the rest of my required lessons.

Two hours of physical training every other day. Two in ancient history. The same divided between art, chemistry, and divination. Evenings, after our mandatory dinner, I mostly spend alone. I've noticed the guys tend to slip off—sometimes leaving the building. No one has extended an invitation for me to join them.

"Faster!" Clinton shouts.

I glance at him in the mirror. Just seeing him ignites a spark of energy that fuels my movements. Clinton is not just good-looking—he's hot. He's a huge man with muscles on top of muscles. His abs are more nine-pack than six, and I'm pretty sure his jaw is sharp enough to cut glass. I swipe at the bag, getting in a hard jab, eyes focused on the dark hair that grazes his shoulders. With each punch I pretend I'm trying to get my hands in his hair, which is one step closer to getting his mouth against mine.

The Goddess' power flares deep within.

His eyes watch my every move. He assesses my form, speed, and skill. Tomorrow we'll work with blades. The next day, hand-to-hand combat. His job is to help me become strong enough to fight the Darkness. Because it's not about if it will come, it's about *when* it will come. And I need to be ready to fight it off, unlike last time.

"Focus, Morgan," he says. But the energy wanes and my muscles scream. My biceps feel like Jell-O, barely able to make contact. Clinton steps behind me, easing his arms next to mine. He takes over, guiding each punch, landing them with more power than I've ever mustered.

The stopwatch beeps and he cradles my arms in his.

"Time," he whispers huskily in my ear. Goosebumps ripple across my hot skin. Even though I'm burning up, a shiver rolls down my spine and I push my body against his.

"How was that?" I ask, knowing the physical part of the training is over. Well, maybe not *all* of the physical. We're just not going to need the punching bag any longer.

"You've improved." He holds up the watch and the number blinks.

02:15

"Wait," I snatch it from him. "I did an extra fifteen seconds?"

"Yes, you did. You're stronger than you think."

I spin, pressing my palms against his chest. It's impossible to think of my own strength when faced with his. I run my hands down the soft cotton of his shirt, feeing the hard muscle beneath.

Clinton is so tall that when we stand like this, face to face, he rests his hands just under my ass and lifts me up until I wrap my legs around his waist. He does that now, amplifying the tingling shiver in my spine. The only thing I can think of is his mouth and--from the way he looks at me, like a hungry wolf--he's thinking the same. I get a tickle of anticipation and lick my lips.

"I think I deserve a reward for a workout like that."

"Do you now?" he replies gruffly. But I feel his hardness against my lower body.

"Hmmhmm."

A wicked grin appears on his mouth. "I'm not one to deny my queen."

Queen. It's weird. So, so weird.

He tightens his grip and tosses me onto the thick, padded, training mat. I yelp as I fly through the air, but it's out of excitement, not fear. Leaning back on my elbows, watching the hulking man stalk toward me, I inhale.

Okay, there's maybe a little fear.

The kind where I'm terrified I'll break my own rules. Cross the barriers I've firmly established between me and my potential mates.

Clinton crawls over me and I wrap my hands around his massive biceps, reveling in his size. He's the strongest of my guardians—the ancient shape-shifters that followed my spirit through the millennia. When his lips finally meet mine I feel a surge of mystical power—our connection—and I move my hand to the back of his neck, tugging on his hair. His hand travels down my body, grazing my bare stomach, and ghosting over the heat of my core. I steal his breath, absorb his strength, and whine when we part.

The stopwatch, lying a few feet away, beeps.

"My time is up, sweetheart," he says, grimacing as though he's in pain. One look between his legs and I understand his struggle.

I grab him by the shirt and tug him back down. His eyebrow lifts. "Just one more minute. Bunny won't mind."

He laughs, shaking his head, because we both know that even if Bunny cared he wouldn't say a word. He's the sweetest of the group. Despite this, Clinton kisses me long and slow, dragging it out until I feel it in the soles of my feet. When we separate I lean back on the mat and rake his hair over his ear. "I guess there's a reason for the time limit," I say. "Another five minutes and the choice would have been made for me."

Clinton helps me off the ground, plucking me with ease, like a flower from the grass. "Unfortunately it doesn't work like that, Morgan."

"I know, I know."

No, I don't get the luxury of letting the boys fight it out over me and letting the best man win. No. It has to be the right one. *The* one. And I have to make the decision.

I'm on a quest for my mate and the clock is ticking.

2

MORGAN

I wash the sweat and exhaustion off in the shower. The small tryst with Clinton recharged my weary muscles, and like each physical encounter with my guardians, I come away more balanced.

With a towel around my body I walk out of the bathroom and into the spacious bedroom. It's all part of the suite given to me when I came here a month ago. I thought I'd won a prestigious writing scholarship. In truth, although I did win a coveted spot in the writing program at New York University, the housing grant was something different.

This house--or rather, this mansion--was called The Nead. Gaelic for *The Nest*. I'd come to live here with five skilled artisans. They each had an interest in their craft as well as a deep bond with me—something I didn't know until I arrived and the secrets of the past were spilled.

I walk past the bed, where two open books lie. Homework from Dylan. He's insistent that I read up on every reference to the Morrigan that exists. Why? I stare down at the illustration of a beautiful, dark-haired woman. Her eyes are dark with power, her lips full and red. There's a crow perched on her shoulder and dead bodies at her feet. The Morrigan is a terrifying force that if betrayed will rain ruin down on the living.

I am the most recent incarnation of the Morrigan.

My guardians are doing everything they can to ensure I keep my power in check and find the chosen one out of the five. My mate will be the anchor to my soul. The tie that binds me to earth and keeps the Darkness lurking just outside our realm at bay. But, until I choose, my power has to be kept in check and the best way to do that is to let the guardians absorb my dark energy. The best way to do that? One sexy encounter at a time.

I've spent the last few weeks processing the strange situation. Some, like my friends back home, surely would think I've accepted it too easily. Who am I to just blindly accept that I'm an ancient goddess holding the fate of society in my hands? Maybe I should have laughed it off when Dylan told me the truth. Maybe I should have run like hell, considering that these men want me as nothing more than a sexual plaything.

But I knew instantly in my heart that the stories I'd been writing were true. That Maverick, the little girl in my book, isn't a character I imagined. She's a reinterpretation of myself.

Of my ravens.

When Dylan revealed my destiny he explained everything I'd been feeling since I was a child. The joy the birds brought me, the vision-like imagery for my book, the moments of anger and uncontrollable emotion. And the fact I knew, deep down, I was saving myself for someone special.

My phone chimes, letting me know I'm already late for my session with Bunny.

I grab my shoes and head out the door for another date with destiny.

"Sorry," I say, entering Bunny's attic studio. "I'm late. Totally my fault."

He looks up from his low worktable, once wood but now just a thick pile of paint and goop. A cup with a stirring stick is in his good hand and his sweet smile nearly cracks my heart.

"It's fine."

I cross the room and stand next to him. The substance he's mixing is gold and shimmery. I rest my hand on his shoulder and feel the instant heat between us. "It's not. It's important for me to keep my time with everyone equal."

He nuzzles his face in my neck and I feel the ticklish prick of his spiky copper hair. "You took a shower after training and smell delicious. It was worth the wait."

I wrap my arms around him. "You're too good to me."

With a light kiss to my neck he holds up the container and says, "Come on, I want to try something new today. Can you grab those brushes?"

Bunny lost the use of his left hand and arm when he was in the shape of a raven. I was there when it happened and it's my biggest regret and most lingering guilt. I'd led an agent of the Darkness, in the form of a cat, deep into the forest. Bunny tried to stop us. The result was a terrible disfigurement, including limited use of his arm and hand. As a raven he could no longer fly, but as a human he miraculously still creates the most amazing pieces of art.

I pick up the slender cup holding a variety of brushes of all lengths and sizes. Bunny is already across the room where a table has been set up. A thick cloth covers the top.

"What's this?"

"Today I'm going to paint you." His eyes flash coppery-brown behind the dark frames of his glasses.

"Bun, you paint me every day." I glance around the room at the dozens of massive canvases lining the walls, floor to ceiling. They each have the same theme. Me.

He smiles and moves closer. He smells like chalk and oil paint. A scent I've grown to love—almost crave.

"No, you don't understand." He rests his container on the table and runs his hand down my arm. "I'm going to paint *you*. Your body will be my canvas."

This ignites a small fire in my belly. I've never been naked in front of Bunny before, even though he has a variety of paintings depicting me nude. Interestingly, they're all incredibly accurate. The tiniest moles and birthmarks specifically detailed. I'm afraid to ask how he knows.

"We don't have to if it makes you uncomfortable." His eyes flash with worry.

"No," I assure him. "I want to. I really do."

The next moment is charged as Bunny turns to give me some privacy. I stop him and say, "You can watch," because the barriers between us need to be broken and this is just one of them.

Bunny freezes in his spot, Adam's apple bobbing as I reach for the button on my shorts. I shimmy them over my hips and push them aside with my foot. Reaching for the hem of my shirt, I quickly pull it over my head. Bunny's right hand clenches into a fist at the sight of me in nothing but my pink lace bra and panties.

"Jesus," he mutters, eyes roaming over every inch of my body. He starts at my red painted toes and travels up my legs. He licks his lips, eyes skimming over my belly button. I reach for the clasp at the back of my bra when he blinks. "Wait."

I frown. "What?"

"Can I do it?"

I nod, wanting nothing more than to feel his touch as he undresses me. The spark of energy flares between us. Like the others, Bunny is an extraordinarily handsome and unique man. He's much smaller than Clinton and Dylan. They're ridiculously large, tall and broad-shouldered. Bunny is thin but solid. A wisp of air but he carries the same intensity and power as the others. I wouldn't want to see him angry.

In my adolescent memories Bunny holds a special place. Not just because of the injury but from before when he would hop around the ground, following me everywhere. That's how he got the name Bunny. I gave it to him.

His artist's fingers are long and agile. His movements are precise. He doesn't need brawn, he has skill, and even one-handed he removes my bra with a quick flick of the wrist.

The strip of fabric drops to the floor. I feel his breath on my belly when he hooks his fingers into the sides of my panties. They fall in the pile and in less than two minutes I'm bare in front of him. I wrap an arm around my waist nervously.

"Can you take off your necklace?" he gestures to his arm.

"I thought I was supposed to wear it and the ring all the time." Damien forged the ring from precious metals to provide protection.

"Just for a bit—it will be fine."

I remove the necklace. Then the ring comes off, placing them in a small dish on his worktable.

With a dry paintbrush he presses the tip in the hollow of my throat and drags it down between my breasts, stopping only when it tickles the sensitive spot below my navel.

My nipples harden from the sensation and Bunny's pupils constrict in reaction.

"I think you should get on the table," he says quietly. I nod, keeping my eyes away from the bulge in his pants. As gracefully as I can, I hoist myself up on the surface, and following Bunny's instructions I lay flat on my back. I'm thankful there are no mirrors or reflective surfaces, but at the same time, ever since I committed myself to this endeavor—searching for a mate—I've lost a fair amount of modesty. Mostly it comes from the constant hunger. The intense desire that courses through my body all the time. I know it's the Darkness calling and the only salve is to dull the ache with the guardians.

No, there's no time for embarrassment.

I stare at the ceiling as Bunny preps his supplies wondering what he thinks about me like this. He's so quiet and shy. With the others, they let me take the lead, although I get the feeling I'm pushing their self-control to the edge. Choosing a mate must be my decision and they're all willing to let me take charge, although they are active and engaged participants. But Bunny? I've never felt his hand or fingers on me like I have with the others. I haven't tasted his skin other than a few lingering kisses. Because of this, I think of him all the time. Curiosity may get the best of me.

He suddenly appears, blocking the high ceiling. He smiles and says, "This may feel a little cold at first but as it reacts to your body it will warm up."

"Is it paint?"

"Sort of," he pushes his glasses up his nose. "I mixed a base acrylic paint with a compound that Damien created." Damien works with precious metals and jewels. "I thought maybe we could bring about a heightened experience."

I tilt my head. "How so?"

"I'm hoping we can ground you to earth and strengthen the gate between you and the Darkness. Maybe open a conduit to your decision-making process, so you know," he swallows, "you can make a choice between us sooner."

"It's worth a shot." I lay my palms flat on the table. "Let's do this."

Bunny starts in the center of my belly, above my navel and below my breasts. The first touch jolts through me like a shard of ice and I jump on the table. "Holy shit."

"I told you."

But like he also said, the cold dissipates and turns into a blanket of warmth. I relax back on the table and with a focused look, he begins working diligently.

The tip of the brush sears like a piece of ice traveling across my skin, but I anticipate the slow, burning heat. It's a strange mixture of pain and pleasure that only grows when he extends the paint away from my belly and toward the other, more sensitive areas.

He works with three different brushes—two held between his teeth. Since I can't see anything but his face I watch his expression as he reacts to my every movement. His pupils constrict at the same time as my nipples. His mouth twitches when the bristles tickle across my hips. A line of concentration slashes between his brows. We both bite down on our lip when he decorates my left breast and then my right with the most excruciating patience.

The desire is not just from his touch, but from the properties in the paint. I feel the magic seeping into my flesh and my stomach tenses at the rush of raw energy.

Bunny moves down my body with long strokes against the dip of my sides and the arch of my hips. His brush travels downward, swirling across my legs. He spreads my thighs and I clutch the table. I know I've left a wet spot down there.

"Why are your cheeks red?" he asks, pulling the extra brushes from his teeth. He's fully attuned to my reactions. "Are you uncomfortable? Just tell me."

"No," I reply, staring at the ceiling. He's standing above my hips and thighs. "It just feels really good and even though I'm trying to keep my mind out of the gutter, my body has a mind of its own."

"Don't be embarrassed," he says. "You're exquisite. The most glorious canvas I've ever had the pleasure of working on. Do you want to see?"

My first thought is no. I don't even like to look at myself in the wide mirror outside my shower. But Bunny is an incredible artist. I feel an intense urge to see it myself. "Can I?"

"Of course."

He walks away and I instantly miss the heat of his body near mine. The magic, I think, must not only react to my skin but his proximity as well. It makes me wonder what would happen if he were even closer.

Bunny returns with an oval mirror and holds it over my body. My eyes widen when I see what he's done. Nearly every inch of my skin is covered in, what I now understand to be from my research and studying, runes. I lift my hand to a symbol above my breastbone.

"You can touch it. They dry quickly."

I'm careful at first, worried anyway. But the paint is dry, feeling more like it's part of my skin than just applied on top. The designs shimmer when I touch them, as if activating their magic. The warmth hasn't left my body. It's only grown stronger and as Bunny watches me looking at myself, the spark burns.

"I feel the magic," I tell him. "Do you feel it?"

"I do," he whispers, lowering the mirror. "I need to complete the runes before the mixture spoils."

He starts to move back between my thighs but I grab his shirt and drag him back.

"Morgan?"

"No," I tell him, pulling his mouth to mine. "No more painting. No more magic. I need you to fuck me. Now."

3

BUNNY

M organ's lips sear against my own, channeling the magic and lust into a force I'm not sure I can withstand. I'm not like my brothers. The ways of women are not innate. I'm not sure how to give her pleasure. Would she even want it from someone like me?

Her body hums, the whole house probably hears it—feels it. A deep soulful vibration that rattles around my heart before landing in my groin. She sits on the table in front of me, body covered in golden glyphs. Each one a spell of protection—created to keep the Darkness away. But I feel the power beneath the surface, under her heaving breasts and sparking in the pit of her belly. It's in her fingertips, her breath, it's coiled tight in between her legs.

The Morrigan, even the small bit residing in this woman's soul, is strong. Her thirst unquenchable. She needs to be needed. She *wants* to be wanted. To turn her away is like firing a shot in a battle that can't be won.

My job—our job—as guardians is to contain that fire before it spreads, and until she finds a mate there's only one way to do it.

She comes at me again, round, full breasts smashing against my chest. Her lips are blistering hot and her eyes have turned a shade darker. I thread my fingers through her hair and groan when she bites my bottom lip.

"Please," she begs, but I know it's the magic talking. Even when she moves her hand to the front of my pants, I know she's not ready to declare her intent. "You're here to protect and serve me, Bun. The Morrigan wants to be fed."

It's the first time she's referred to herself by her given name—the woman we swore to protect when gods still roamed the earth. I step back and take in the ravishing, naked woman before me.

"Spread your legs," I command, my mission clear. She needs me and I crave to serve her. Morgan leans back and presses her palms against the table top, widening her thighs. Her tits jut forward and I curse my disfigured arm for not being able to touch them both at the same time. Instead I use my finger to circle around each of her nipples, raising them into a hard peak. I guide a path lower, between her breasts, over the runes fading into her skin and down to the soft hair between her legs.

Her hips tilt forward in invitation and, stepping closer, I nudge them even wider. Her eyes watch with anticipation, licking her pink lips as I swipe my tongue across mine.

Bending between her legs, I inhale her scent and brace myself for pleasuring Morgan in a way the others haven't yet.

4

MORGAN

The coil tightens, twisting and twisting until my breath comes in tiny pants.

My fingers curl against the table's edge, holding on for dear life. Bunny's breath tickles my clit, until it throbs, begging for more, more, more.

Between my legs he works his tongue the way he uses his paint brushes; with skill, precision and unbelievable patience. The slow lathing turns rapid and I cry out his name.

"Almost," I promise, loving the way his hand grips my thigh, and I tug the hair near his ears.

"Take your time."

It's clear he's not in a hurry. He never is, but my body needs release. Our eyes connect seconds before the orgasm rips through my body and for a second I think I may fall into the deep coppery pools. But the coil snaps, sending me tumbling down the edge, nerves raw and explosive. I groan and box his ears with my thighs.

"Fuck," I mutter, leaning back on the table. Every inch of my body is slick with sweat. The area between my legs aches. I rest for a moment, staring at the ceiling, trying to catch my breath. When the fog in my brain clears I sit and look for the man that just showed me the stars. Bunny stands before me, eyes worshipful.

"Did that help?" he asks, the tip of his ears red.

"Bunny," I say, dragging him back over by the shirt. "That was incredible." I touch his chin. "Thank you."

His eyes flick over my shoulder where I know a large clock hangs on the wall. "You don't want to be late."

We both know I have a history lesson with Dylan next. We also both know I don't want to be late. Dylan's not a big fan of tardiness.

Before I move I tug Bunny down for a kiss. I taste myself on his lips and his mouth still carries the fever of want. I feel awful getting pleasure without offering any in return, but the men assure me this is their duty. My needs come first. I'll make it up to him later.

When I stand, wobbling slightly on my feet, I discover the golden runes have disappeared. "Where did they go?"

"Your body absorbed them. You'll carry the magical protection for some time."

"Do you really think it will help me select a mate?" I ask. Bunny picks up my discarded clothes. His eyes never leave my body as I redress.

He touches my temple and trails his finger down the side of my face, along my neck and stops at my breast. "Your mind, body, and heart need to merge to the same place. The spells should assist. It will always be your decision, Morgan, but with your emotions and desires so heightened, a little assistance can't hurt."

We stand across from one another and I feel a change from the woman that walked in the room. Not only in myself but in the relationship I have with Bunny. His mouth has touched my most sensitive and private of places but I have a feeling his paintbrush tapped into something even more elusive.

My soul.

5

MORGAN

A small break is worked into my schedule between my appointments with the men in the house. Originally I thought it was just good time management. Like a break between classes at school. I've learned over the last week that these small respites are mostly used to shower. I spend half the day covered in either sweat from training or the lingering scent of sex. The men, astonishingly, don't seem to mind, but I think it's awkward. The whole sharing one another concept seems strange, even if they don't think so.

After my encounter (that's what I call them, because "after my epic orgasm" sounds weird) with Bunny I rush downstairs for my second shower of the day. My phone chimes the instant I cross over the threshold of my room.

Shannon, the screen says. A photo of my best friend from college smiles back at me.

Shit.

I won't even deny it. The first month I was in New York I barely thought of my friend. I missed emails and texts. I ignored phone calls, but two days ago Dylan reminded me of the importance of keeping up with family and friends.

"I don't have any family," I snapped back, feeling slightly defensive. "I killed them, remember?"

He rolled his eyes. "You didn't kill them, Morgan."

No, but when I was a teenager I let the Darkness past the gate. My parents were the victims of the toxicity that followed. Luckily the ravens—my guardians—were nearby and shut the entry point. It was too late for my parents but at least no one else suffered.

"When your friends call, engage with them. It's normal. It's healthy."

"What do I tell her?" I asked, specifically thinking of Shannon. "That I'm too busy fucking around with five guys to return her call?"

His jaw clenched. "We're not fucking around."

I couldn't help but laugh. Dylan was right. He and I were definitely not fucking around. He'd barely touched me. The others? Sure, there was no actual fucking, at least not yet, but a lot of everything else. "Fine. I'll answer the next time she calls."

The phone vibrates in my hand. Now is that time.

I swipe the screen. "Shannon?"

"Holy crap, Morgan. You finally answered!"

"I know, I know. I'm sorry." I walk down the hallway to the bathroom. My eyes widen when I take in my appearance. My hair is wild. The makeup under my eyes is smeared and my neck is blotchy from Bunny's lips.

I can't even imagine what my inner thighs look like.

"I'm the worst kind of friend," I say, feeling a wash of guilt that isn't just about Shannon. Juggling five guys is *not* normal for me, even considering the supernatural implications.

"I've just missed you," she says. "I miss college. Adulting sucks."

"How is your job?" I ask. Shannon has a degree in dance and music theory. So naturally she's teaching dance camp to three-year-olds.

"Exhausting. Why did my parents let me get such a worthless degree?"

I laugh because even my creative writing degree is a crapshoot. I just lucked out and got into a graduate program. There's no assurance I'll ever make a dime from my writing. "I'm sure it will all work out. So tell me how things are going back home."

Shannon launches into details about our small group of friends, most of whom I haven't thought of since I left. Living in New York, writing all the time and then discovering I'm some kind of goddess who has the power to take down humanity has kept me distracted.

"I saw Ryan the other day," she says.

"Ryan?" I ask, hardly paying attention. Seriously, I'm the worst kind of friend. I'd dropped my pants and inspected my legs. The runes are still gone but a large, pinkish hickey is forming on the soft flesh of my upper thigh.

"You know, the hipster-hottie from the school paper you were sort of dating before you left?"

"Duh," I say. "The train was ratting by. I just didn't hear you. How's he doing?"

"Not much—he got that internship at the Atlanta Journal." She pauses. "I think he misses you, too."

I almost laugh. "Shannon. He does not miss me."

"No, seriously, Morgan. I saw him the other night. He asked about you."

"We didn't even part on the best of terms, you know." I think of Ryan and his little hipster glasses and thick beard. I crushed on him hard even though he was a bit of a douche about my writing. Too whimsical and juvenile. The image of that boy back in college compared to the men living in his house? Talk about juvenile. I bite my tongue and say, "Ryan's great, but I don't think I'm interested in a long distance relationship."

There's a moment of silence.

"Shannon?"

"Oh my God. You met someone!"

"What? No."

"You did!" she shouts. I hope she's inside. "I can hear it in your voice. Tell me all about him."

Tell her? I fight back a real laugh this time.

Tell her about him?

Or rather *them*.

How do I even begin to explain what's happening in this house? In the world, even? How do I suggest that I've got a smidge of goddess in my soul and she's not a good one? Hell no, she's the Queen of the Ravens, the Goddess of War and wrathful as hell. With the energy and power coursing through me right now I'd chew up a guy like Ryan and spit him out.

I take a deep breath and say, "There's no guy. I'm just busy. Living the city life, you know? Studying and working my ass off. Figuring out how to live with a bunch of housemates. It's just crazy and there is no time for a relationship right now."

"Housemates?" Shannon was my roommate for four years. I'm not surprised she's curious.

"Yeah, five guys."

"You're living with five guys."

"Are they hot?"

I drop in the chair in my sitting room and lean back against the pillow. Dylan told me I needed to keep in touch with my friends. So that's exactly what I do.

~

"You're late," he says when I finally get to his room. The door is ajar, clearly left open for me to enter when I arrive. Dylan sits in a buttery soft leather chair near his attic fireplace. The ceilings are huge and vaulted—it must be freezing in the winter. A thick book rests in his lap.

"Sorry." I struggle to catch my breath from running up the steps. "I got a phone call. From my friend Shannon, you know, the one you told me to stop ignoring."

He raises a perfectly arched eyebrow. Everything about Dylan is perfect. He's tall. Muscular, but not bulky. Short, jet-black hair. Brilliant cobalt eyes. Other than Clinton, Dylan is the only guardian I find intimidating. He's smart, quick, and I lose myself when I'm near him.

"You've missed your lesson," he says, ignoring my excuse. "We'll be a day behind." As I step closer I notice him take a sharp inhalation and his eyes narrow.

The call kept me from taking a shower and I have little doubt he smells the sex on me. I brace myself for...something. Jealousy? No, the guardians aren't jealous. They've encouraged my sexual experimentation. They know better than anyone that I must have an outlet. Desire? I roll my eyes. If Dylan truly desires me I wouldn't know. Since the true intention of me being in the house was revealed, to fight back the Darkness, he's kept his distance. Maybe I'm bracing myself for nothing other than his judgment. His eyes are laced with opinion. Even so, he places the book on the table next to his and keeps whatever is running through his mind to himself.

"Maybe I can come back tomorrow for a make-up session." I offer. "It's Tuesday and other than my writing time in the morning, I just have a meeting with Professor Christensen and Anita."

He seems to consider this. "You received your runes today?"

"Yes." I push up my sleeve but there's nothing to see. "Fully spelled."

"And you had an intensive training session with Clinton this morning?"

I nod, thinking of Clinton's mouth against mine. "Quite vigorous."

He sighs and rubs his forehead. "I did hope to go over the Raven Wars with you this afternoon."

"The Raven Wars?"

"The two-hundred-year battle that started with the Morrigan's betrayal by Cu. There are lessons to be learned in the history."

Despite my exhaustion, my interest is piqued. "Good, then let's meet tomorrow. I'm eager to get to work." I meet his steely eyes. "Unless you have other plans?"

I wait to see if he tells me where he and the others go on occasion. It's not like they're not allowed. They can leave. Predictably though, Dylan doesn't even blink. "One o'clock sharp."

I smile. "Perfect."

I turn to leave but hear Dylan call my name. "Make sure you take a shower before dinner," he says, swallowing thickly. "You smell like sex and I'm not sure the others can take it."

I nod and quickly leave the room. As stoic as Dylan tries to be, the tight feeling in my belly tells me that the others aren't the only ones that can't handle the smell of sex on me for long.

6

DYLAN

I release a groan and drop my head into my hands when Morgan walks out of the room. After a moment, I stand and grab a pre-dinner drink. There's no doubt I need something to settle my nerves. Being in the house with the Queen as she releases her energy on the others is testing my resolve. What once was a thick rope tying me to the Morrigan is now a thin thread pulled taut by want and desire.

I gulp the warm, amber liquid in one swallow and place the book I'd been reading on my study table. Even though I sounded pissed when I spoke to Morgan, I wasn't. I'm not. Unlike the others, I've kept my connection with her strictly professional. Even Bunny broke down today, pleasuring her so thoroughly her orgasm ricocheted through the house like a boomerang.

My turn is coming. It's part of my duty and allegiance to being her guardian. She must test each one of us to see if we're not only compatible but actually her mate. The fate of society depends on it. The Darkness knows no bounds and the energy she contains is unparalleled.

The clock chimes behind me, alerting me to the fact it's time to prepare for dinner, where once again I'll be faced with Morgan and her alluring temptations.

I plan to hold her off as long as I can. Not because I don't want her. I do.

That's the problem. I want her too much.

7

MORGAN

She blinks, and from her position and the hard surface under her back she knows she's back on the table. She feels the whisper of a paintbrush on her toes. She glances at the ceiling and it's not the vaulted beams of the attic but the square mahogany tiles of the dining room. With a look upward, she spots Bunny and smiles.

"What are we doing here?" she asks. "Did the runes not work?"

Her voice comes out muffled, like she's underwater. Bunny stands above her head, speaking but she can't hear what he's saying. A raven caws in the distance and he smiles, but it doesn't reach his coppery eyes. She opens her mouth but a figure catches her eye and she looks to the side.

It's Sam with his handsome, charming smile. A knotted bun of hair sits atop his head, making his cheekbones even more dramatic.

He holds a thin paintbrush dipped in gold and paints her left breast with delicate precision.

Before she can react, she feels the pinprick of both her nipples pebbling in pleasure and looks to her right.

Damien uses his own brush to coat her flesh. The crystal chandelier makes the smooth dome of his head gleam. His violet eyes focus *intently on his work. His hands are quick and worshipful. A tremor coasts down her body.*

Near her belly she feels the cool smear of paint followed by a sharp hunger in her loins. Morgan lifts her head to get a better view of Clinton placing kisses with gold-coated lips past her belly button. She smiles when she sees him, pleased. Another set of hands, strong and capable, push her legs apart. She searches in the hazy light, expecting to find Bunny but instead it's Dylan between her thighs. A surge of warmth destabilizes her.

The lights flicker and in the dark she realizes the paintbrushes have become hands, mouths, and the velvet tips of hidden skin. Morgan blinks again and she's on all fours. She can't see her guardians but she feels them. Lord, she wants them. From the mouth suckling on her breast to the whisper of kisses on her neck. There's the delicious feel of a tongue lathing against her most sensitive part, sending shockwaves up her body. There's the heavy feel of a man behind her, his cock sliding between her cheeks.

A dim light fills the room and Morgan is astonished to find it coming from herself—from the runes glinting with life.

She turns her head to see which guardian is behind her, beg him to do it, take her virginity. She's ready for the next step. With any of them. All of them...

A loud horn blares and I lurch forward, jostling against the seat.

"Sorry," I say to the woman next to me, shifting back over to my seat.

"Are you okay?" she eyes my face. It's heated. My armpits are drenched under my thin summer sweater. My panties are drenched and I'm thankful my skirt is black.

"I just don't like small places. It makes me feel claustrophobic." I stand and pull the cord. I need to get off the bus. Get some fresh air. What kind of dream was that—on the bus of all places?

The bus doors open with a *whoosh*. I stumble off, taking a gulp of the warm but fresh air. My feet touch the pavement and I'm grounded, the confusion of my dream—or was it just a fantasy? —dissipating.

The university office is only a few blocks away and my heart rate settles as I get closer. A shadow passes overhead and the ruffle of feathers draws my attention upward. A sleek, blue-black raven roosts above the office building. It ducks his head and blinks at me with one eye.

I feel a sense of familiarity and also a spark of anger. Are they following me? I know they're technically my guardians, but I've never been told they would do this. I also didn't know they could still shift.

Leaving the raven and the muggy air, I duck inside the building and head to Professor Christensen's office.

The secretary waves me in. I have a standing weekly appointment to discuss my novel, *Maverick's Murder*. I started writing this novel in my head many years ago, and then in college submitted a section to my creative writing teacher. She suggested I use it to apply to graduate school.

In my head, *Maverick's Murder* was nothing but a story—a story I was deeply invested in. I thought about it. Dreamed about it. Frankly, I obsessed over it. Now I understand why. *Maverick's Murder* isn't about a girl and her birds. It's about *me*, the Raven Queen and my murder of crows. My raven guardians.

The first passages in the book are memories. Slightly altered retellings of how, as a child, I had five guardian ravens that followed me around. They'd been assigned to me by the gods to monitor the Morrigan's Darkness that resided inside. Agents of evil, in my book a cat and a prince, lured me into the woods behind my house to open a gate that flows between this world and another. On the other side is something I can only describe in the book as death; a vengeance wanting to consume the lives and souls on Earth.

It's not pretend. It's real, and if the Darkness lures me back again and that portal opens, the apocalypse will begin.

Professor Christensen's door is open and I'm surprised to hear another voice in the room. The professor is incredibly punctual—

always waiting for my arrival and dismissing me when it's over. I stop just before entering, recognizing the voice. It's Anita Cross. My critique partner.

I tap on the door and peek inside. They both smile when they see me.

"Morgan, come in."

I greet them both and add to Anita, "I didn't know you were going to be here."

"My fault," Professor Christensen says, leaning back in his seat. He's distinguished as always, with his gray hair and expensive suit. "I had the crazy idea to get you both in here together. I wanted to hear how things are going."

I'd read the first five chapters of Anita's book. Her writing is spectacular—to the point it makes me feel a little inadequate. Interestingly, her book is a dystopian theme, focusing on an America in the distant future. Plague has taken the country and the survivors create a new breed of royalty.

I take the seat next to Anita. She's poised and perfect-looking, of course. Not a hot mess of sex fantasies and sweat. "I've truly enjoyed reading Anita's work. She's an amazing author."

"She says the same about you," he replies. "Which is why I decided to give you both a little assignment. You're almost too flattering of the other's work. Like you're afraid to help the other push a bit deeper. I'd like you to come up with three questions for the other author's main characters, trade, and then answer truthfully. Dig into the meat of these creations, their true motives and desires."

"That's a great idea," Anita says, scribbling the instructions on a note pad in her lap. I reach into my bag and rummage around for my own, dropping my pen three times in the process.

Today is not my day.

"I'd like you to get on this immediately," Professor Christensen says. "Text one another the questions in the next twenty-four hours. Meet up again on Thursday to exchange ideas." His blue eyes move between us. "Sound good?"

I'm mentally going over my schedule. Besides writing, I have my lessons back at The Nead. I'll just have to rearrange some things. "Yes, that sounds great."

"Morgan, maybe we can meet at your place. You have that fantastic library."

I don't like the idea of another woman in my home. I'm not exactly jealous—more protective than anything else. I'm also concerned about the increasing amount of magic being performed. Before I can come up with a good excuse Professor Christensen nods his head and says, "That's a fantastic idea. There's so much history to that house. I hope you make the most of your stay there."

I have little choice but to relent. "We can meet at my place. I'll text you the time, okay?"

"Perfect," Anita says as she stands to leave. I struggle for an extra moment to get my notebook back in my too-full bag. "Morgan, can you stay for just a moment?"

"Yeah. Sure."

He stands and moves to close the door. When he returns to his desk he says, "How are things with your housemates?"

I brush a curl of hair out of my eyes. "Good. They're great, actually."

A thin line creases on his forehead. "They're not too distracting? I'd hate for something to derail you from your work."

"Distracting?" I fight the heat in my chest. Hell yes, they were distracting. But also sweet, encouraging, and teaching me how to survive. "That hasn't been a problem at all. Some days I barely see them."

Unless I'm dreaming of them. Touching them. Testing their mettle as I seek my mate.

"Good, good. I just wanted to keep up. It's an unusual situation."

I frown. "Have you ever met any of them before, Professor Christensen? Are there specific reasons for your concerns?"

He clears his throat. "No, I haven't, but a few have reputations in the community. Underground exhibits and performances. I admit it's nothing more than rumor but it's my job to advise you."

Now I'm annoyed but try to keep the tone out of my voice. "Are you finding my submissions lacking? Is there a problem with my work?"

"No."

"Well, then I need you to trust that I'm an adult and can manage my personal life."

"It's just that you have no parents to rely on—"

"My parents?" A cold, angry feeling sparks in my chest. "Professor, I made it through my senior year of high school and four years of college without their guidance. I think I can manage."

I grab my bag off the floor and exit the office, even though I hear him calling my name. Out on the street, I gather my composure. Christensen may be an overbearing ass but he did do me a favor by revealing the rumors about the boys. I knew they were going somewhere at night.

Now I plan on finding out more.

8

MORGAN

Davis, the butler at The Nead, waits for me in the foyer when I arrive at home. He hands me a tray of lunch. I thank him and he adds, "Don't forget your appointment with Master Dylan at one o'clock."

"Sharp," I say, rolling my eyes and shoving a piece of cheese into my mouth. "Got it."

Although there's nothing specific to confirm this, I'm getting the feeling Dylan is trying to push me away. It's stupid. He's the one that broke the news about me being the Morrigan and about the need for me to find a mate. He understands the importance—as much as anyone else. Except when I'm with him it's all history and business and death and war. As I approach my door, I know that even though we haven't crossed any intimate barriers with one another, it's going to happen. It has to. Soon.

Maybe today.

Quickly, I shower, rinsing off the sweat and grime from my bus ride. My mind wanders to the assignment given to me by Professor Christensen. Anita's book has three main characters—each seemingly lucky to have survived the deadly virus that wiped out a huge portion of humanity. They take on roles of leadership as communities rebuild. One female and two males. They fight over her affection and the glory of producing the first heir to their new world.

I lather and wash my hair, feeling the suds drip down my body. It brings to mind my dream on the bus. The feeling of all the men touching me at once. *Five men.*

What have I gotten myself into?

I rinse out the shampoo and turn off the water. I only take a few seconds to dry off and slip into the closest thing: a black and white print sundress. The straps are made of thick, glossy ribbon that tie in a criss-cross in the middle of my back. The dress doesn't require a bra but I do find a pair of black lace panties in the top drawer. Once things heated up between me and the guardians I made a trip to the nearest lingerie boutique. It seemed necessary.

The clock by my bed says 12:57 and I do not want to incur Dylan's wrath again. With damp hair and zero makeup, I grab my homework and leather-bound notebook before racing up the stairs to Dylan's quarters.

I run into Bunny at the top of the stairs. Fully aware that I'm pushing the time I grab him by the arm and ask, "Do those runes have any side effects?"

He frowns. "Like what?"

"Dreams? Fevers?"

"It's possible," he replies. His clothes are covered in paint and there are two blue smudges on his cheek under his glasses. "Did something happen?"

"Not bad." No, that dream wasn't bad. It was...just a lot. "Honestly, I was probably just tired. Things have been a little hectic."

A line of concern slashes across his forehead. "If you need to slow down, say something to Dylan. He'll understand."

I glance at my watch. 12:59. "Shit, I gotta go." I lean over and give him a quick kiss on the lips, feeling a bit of my anxiety burst. God, these men are better than Xanax. "Bye!"

Running down the hall, I notice Dylan has left the door ajar once again. I step over the threshold right at one p.m.

"I made it," I say, walking into the main study. Dylan leans over a table, his eyes focused on a book. "Hello?"

He glances at the empty chair across the table from him. "Sit. Get out your assignment."

I follow instructions, pushing back the heavy wooden chair and flipping through my book. The room is silent—there's not the constant strain of music like in Clinton's room or the gym. Nor the hum of machinery from Damien's workshop out back. Sam is eternally talking. To himself. To me. To the images in his photographs. And Bunny is so engrossed in his paintings sometimes you forget he's there entirely.

Dylan's presence is unmistakable. He's the sentry, of course, the first of my guard. He's always been there to make sure I'm safe and there are no predators or dangers around. Even in the silence it's impossible to ignore him. His size. His face. The assured confidence that rolls off his body.

"Did you complete your reading?" he asks, finally looking at me. His eyes take in my still-wet hair and plain face. Unlike the others that brighten when they see me, Dylan's expression is indifferent.

"Yes." I push the book forward to reveal the page. The books in Dylan's library go much deeper than any account of the Morrigan's history via an internet search, or even the university's well-stocked library. "According to the lore, the Morrigan was not always so angry. She had a happy childhood but she did have the heart of a warrior. Which is why she was smitten with the Cu Cuchulainn. She thought they could run the battlefield together."

Dylan watches me as I speak.

"Cu didn't believe a woman could match his strength, but he did find the Morrigan's body worthy of a tryst. They made love by the river bank—one that soon would flow with blood from the battle—and when they united, she thought they would be partners forever."

"Then he rejected her," Dylan says.

I point to a passage in the book. "He took her virginity—then her heart. He mocked her desire to fight side-by-side. He left her, stole from her, abandoned her, and that's when something fragile and dangerous in her broke." I look into Dylan's brilliant blue eyes. "She summoned her rage. And the ravens followed. She sent the birds to be a harbinger of death so Cu would understand his fate was sealed. Then she turned on his army and slaughtered them on the battlefield. The blood from the slain men soaked in her feet, building a force of rage that scorched the world and blocked out the sun. The land turned barren. The sky an ashy gray. The gods shut down the entry points between worlds, locking that one away from this one."

Dylan leans back in his seat, crossing his arms over his chest. "Throughout history the barriers have been weakened and broken, allowing the essence of the Morrigan to cross over. The black plague was one time. The Spanish flu was another. The sickness sometimes infected individuals directly. Attila the Hun. Franco. Genghis Kahn. Queen Mary. And of course, Hitler and Mussolini."

"Wait, the sickness infected them and turned them into mass murderers?"

"Yes. Sometimes it took decades to stop either the actual illness from wiping out humanity or the people that carried the virus." He sighs. "The difference now is that that same sickness is inside of you, Morgan, and the gods anticipated it. They gave you the five of us as your guardians. Only we have the strength to tolerate the pain and aggression that builds up inside."

"But only one of you is my true mate."

"Yes." His jaw tics. "Eventually, the ones not chosen will leave for new assignments."

Leave? I don't like the idea of that at all.

I push back my chair and walk across the room to the expansive wall of windows that looks out over the city. The sky is a bright blue. The park below a vivid green. I feel Dylan behind me, a charged current passing between us.

"The whole thing is very surreal," I finally say.

"I imagine it's hard to comprehend. The gods blessed you with snippets of the Morrigan's memory and the ability to write them in your book. Just as they have done the same with the guardians and their skills. It's so important that you're strong enough, because the time will come when you'll be tested. It has happened to each one of those leaders I mentioned. Do you realize that most of them came from lower positions in society? Regular soldiers. Peasants. Failed students. Pathetic leaders of rebellions. Yet they all lit a spark in their followers. That spark is the Darkness."

"And one day it will come for me?"

"Again. It already has once. That day behind your family's home. The day your parents died. We shut it down, but other opportunities will arise. Soon."

I know the warning is true. I feel it in the way my skin itches. The way my stomach twists with constant desire. Still staring out the window I ask, "Why won't you touch me?"

"Excuse me?"

"You haven't touched me, Dylan. Not like the others. If it's so important for me to pick a mate—test *your* strength—and control the Darkness, then why haven't you stepped up to the plate?"

He pales, making his eyes seem brighter and jet-black hair darker. "I've been focused on your studies. Have the others not fulfilled your needs?"

"Some of them," I reply. "But you know exactly how I'm doing. We're all tuned in to one another. You feel what I feel. Something is holding you back and I'd like to know what it is."

For the first time in weeks I see the flicker of real desire in Dylan's eyes. In an attempt to be patient I bite my lip and wrap my arms around my waist. The neckline of my dress plunges just enough to get an eyeful of cleavage. His eyes skim my flesh. I won't throw myself at him. We'll have to come to an understanding and right now I can't figure out what's going on in his head.

To my surprise, he reaches for me and thumbs my bottom lip. In a sudden, unexpected rush he says, "You're the most alluring woman I've ever laid eyes on, Morgan."

"Then why don't you want me?"

In the next moment the tall, muscular man looks inexplicably vulnerable. "I want you more than you can imagine. You're like the fire of a thousand suns and I'm a tiny moth with no hope but to burn my wings. You're like a gallon of wine for a man dying of thirst. You're the stars that guide a sailor home."

His words sound like poetry, but other than the hand that moves from my mouth to my neck, he still hasn't moved an inch.

I inhale and say, "Let me guide your way. Let me quench your thirst. I'm here for you just like you're here for me."

"I can't." He shakes his head. "Not yet."

This time I do make the first move. I step forward and grab him by the front of his shirt, wrinkling the fine, blue linen. I tug him downward, pulling him into a reluctant kiss. His lips are hot as fire, his breath sweet like honey. He caves just an inch and his strong hands cinch around my waist.

Dylan's hips brush against my belly and I feel the hardness beneath the fabric of his pants. There's no mistaking his want. So something else is holding him back. I pull myself away from his mouth and ask again, "Why are you afraid?"

He presses his forehead against mine and his jaw tenses. Just when I think it's a lost cause he says, "You entice me, Morgan. Like no other in any other time or place. You ignite a hunger in me that I worry I cannot control." His lips move to my neck and he kisses a fiery trail from one side to the other. "I don't want to just make love to you. I want to consume you. I want to plunge deep inside and leave a mark. I want to fuck you senseless. I want to claim you."

"Is that so different from the others?"

"No," he replies gruffly. "It is the same, but I'm different. I don't have the control they do."

"I don't believe you," I can barely hear my voice over the hammering of my heart.

He lifts my chin and says very slowly, with incredible intent, "I will break you, Morgan. You are not ready for my passion. I will tear you apart."

Those words. That declaration. Jesus. I step back, unsteady on my feet.

His expression is instantly remorseful. "I'm sorry. The truth is too much."

I look up in his eyes.

"You don't get to tell me what I can handle, guardian."

"What?" His eyes are wide with confusion.

I place a hand on each hip and gesture to Dylan's favorite reading chair. "Take a seat and get ready to do your fucking job."

My sentry. The leader of my guard does exactly as he's told, lowering himself into the chair with a noble grace.

I move before him and prepare to show him exactly how strong I am.

9

DYLAN

The edge in Morgan's voice—the commanding tone—snaps me to attention.

I sit. I wait. I watch.

She stands before me, hair curly and wild, in the tiniest slip of a dress. A black bow holds it all together in the back and I nearly yanked it off the minute she stepped in the room.

I'd been honest with her. Every word I said was the absolute truth. I'm terrified of my reaction to her. There's no chance I'd take it easy on her. No fucking way I'd be gentle. And although I can push back it would be disrespectful to flat out tell her no. When it comes to the displacement of the Darkness, I have no greater obligation. She's my Queen and I'm here to serve her.

Morgan approaches me, her dark eyes lit with determination. Resting her palms on the arms of my chair she leans over, giving me an exquisite view of her ample breasts, and whispers next to my lips, "You may be afraid of yourself, Dylan, but I'm not. I think you're tense and need a little release."

My cock is already hard. It's been hard for weeks now, listening to Morgan work her way through the men in the house. Every kiss, every touch. Christ, the orgasms. I don't know about the other guardians but when she unravels, I lose time. My body freezes as she channels all her energy into that one final explosion.

I look into her eyes. "I'm at your mercy, Morgan."

She smiles and hovers her mouth over mine. My lips ache, wanting to touch hers, and just when I think I'm going to lose control she kisses me, soft and seductive.

Then she hikes up her skirt and climbs on my lap.

My reaction is a hiss and I grit my teeth. Her eyes widen for a brief moment but narrow once she realizes the reason for my reaction. She presses down with the core of her body, fitting my twitching cock against the miniscule slip of silk fabric separating our flesh.

"You're strong, Dylan. More than the others. You're the glue holding this whole thing together. I get that." Her lips sear against my throat and her fingers unbutton my shirt. Her fingers are cool against my hot skin and the scrape of her nails down my chest and over my nipples lights a fire in my groin. She licks my mouth. "But you deserve to let go. Enjoy yourself." She swallows. "Enjoy me."

She pushes me back into the leather cushion and slides down my body. I regret the heat from her core leaving my cock but her hands move to the buttons on my pants. She unfastens them with graceful ease. I lift my hips and watch her tug them down, removing them entirely. My fully erect cock springs from between my legs, aching with unparalleled desire as she inches her hands up my thighs.

I can tell she doesn't plan on making this quick and easy. No, the determination in her eyes implies she's committed to a deeper connection than just getting me off. As her lips explore the muscles below my hips, I reach for the ribbon behind her back and yank. The bow slips, loosening the straps of her dress. She stands and it falls to the ground in a pool of fabric by her feet. The silver charm at her neck glints against her skin.

My cock pulses at the sight of her. My heart hammers against my chest. She's beautiful. Her breasts are perfect and her hips swell with a sensuous curve. Her ass is round and fleshy. My hands fist, fighting to stay off of her and let her maintain control. I eye the perfect brown of her nipples, the hard peaks that confirm her excitement. I smell the musky scent of want between her legs—even through her black lace panties.

"Lean back," she tells me.

I jut my chin and comply, sliding down so my cock waves between us like a surrendering flag. My position brings a smile to Morgan's puffy, pink lips. Seeing me in a state of relaxed submission with my belly exposed and vulnerable assets in the air give her all the power. Just because she's on her knees does not mean she's servicing me. No. It's clear the roles are reversed. She owns me right now.

And I'm two seconds from begging her for more.

She saves me from doing it, cupping my balls with her cool, delicate hand. My body seizes. Her grin grows and I watch through hooded eyes as her hand moves up the rod-hard shaft and her tongue wets her lips.

She leans forward, her breasts pressed against my knees. Her thumb swirls against the tip of my cock, spreading the slippery cum down the sides. Unable to withstand it any longer, I reach for her. Her hair, her cheeks.

Together we guide her mouth down the hard warmth and I exhale, shuddering out the tension and desire I've carried for weeks and weeks.

Up and down her head bobs, and I weave one hand into her curly locks and another cups the heavy weight of her breast. She's done this before, with Damien, gifting him with the pleasure of her mouth.

My excitement grows and my hips rise to meet her mouth and she braces herself accordingly. Leaning back so I can see her whole body. Her pert nipples. The dip of her lower belly.

"Fuck," I growl at the tightening in my balls. I want it to last forever. I want to bury my face in her hair, sleep with my hands wrapped around her body.

To my surprise she pulls her mouth away but continues to use her hands, slip-sliding up and down my cock. "Give me your light. The goodness," she cries and I realize what she wants me to do.

With a guttural moan I come, chanting her name with each thrust. Cum flows from my cock, coating her body in thick, hot spurts. My head spins. My balls ache. My breath comes raggedly. For a brief moment I'm back in the sky, soaring amongst the clouds, while my girl waits for me below.

I blink and fall back against the cushion, spent of every ounce. I watch through the haze of ecstasy as Morgan uses her free hand and rubs her fingers in the slick goo.

"What the hell?" I say, narrowing my eyes as the runes reveal themselves, glimmering and glinting on her breasts and stomach.

She looks down and back up. Her eyes shine bright. "Withholding on me doesn't make me stronger, Dylan. Each one of you has to do your part. I respect your concerns over my body but you can't shy away from your duty."

There's no fight in me anymore. She's proven her point. I'm not the one in control here. I tug her off her knees and into my lap. We're both sticky and her body shines like the sun. I bring her mouth to mine and kiss her passionately, sharing the source of energy that courses between us all.

She pulls back and says, "I was wrong about one thing."

I push a curl of hair off her cheek. "What's that?"

"You didn't need a little release." Her hand rests on my shoulder. "You needed a big one."

10

MORGAN

Late afternoon sun warms the window seat. I've got my notebook in my lap and I'm struggling with the assignment given to me by Professor Christensen. It seemed easy at the time; three questions for the main characters of each other's books. Anita's book has a character, a young man named Cass. He's the son of an original survivor—a very powerful man—whose family has created a dominant class in their post-apocalyptic world. Cass does not see eye to eye with his tyrannical father and he's heir to the throne. On his father's deathbed he's told that their power comes from a magic source. Cass must decide if he's going to use the power the same as his father did or toss it aside altogether and become one with the people.

With my pen, I scribble down a few questions:
Does Cass have the strength to survive with ordinary citizens?
Will the people even accept him as one of them?
Who will take over if he steps down from the throne?

My stomach rumbles and I check the time. Dinner is in ten minutes. With every encounter, the table becomes a little more intimate. The earlier activities with Dylan provides another link in the chain. I've tested them all and I'm not closer to finding a mate than I was when I started. Each of my guardians is worthy. They're talented and smart. Strong and capable. They put my needs and safety first.

There was no condition that I had to lose my virginity to my mate. I'd clarified that in an awkward and abrupt conversation with Dylan two weeks ago. But it still seemed like the right thing to do, so I held off. How would I even decide which man was to be my first real lover? They're all equally compelling and proving themselves quite skilled sexually.

Although I'd still done nothing more than a little dry humping and making out with Clinton, I've experienced enough with them all that it seems even more likely I'll have to make a wild guess as to who will be the first.

I walk to the bathroom and drag a comb through my curly hair. My lips still look a little enlarged and my cheeks carry a red tint from the encounter with Dylan. I'd never known a man so stubborn. He certainly brought out my rebellious side and I loved seeing him crack under pressure and just let go. I smile at my reflection. That had been delicious. *He* had been delicious.

I hear a knock at the door and rest my hairbrush on the counter. I slip on my shoes and find Sam waiting outside the door. He looks amazing, as always, even dressed in his causal knee-length shorts and button-down shirt. Tonight the shorts are a dark navy blue and the shirt a preppy-plaid. His warm, brown skin makes his green eyes shine. His hair is tied in a knot at the back of his head.

"Ready for dinner?"

"I am, thanks for waiting for me."

He exhales and I see a glimmer of exhaustion. "I've been in the studio all day. I needed to see someone else. Lucky for me, the most beautiful woman in the house lives down the hall."

I snort. "I'm the *only* woman in the house."

He frowns. "What about Sue? She'd take offense to that."

"You're being ridiculous."

That earns me a grin and he links his arm with mine. Sam

escorting me to our mandatory dinner has become a tradition—one I like. Slowly I've come to appreciate each of the men for their individuality, and Sam, at the end of the day, is probably my very best friend in the house.

A friend with benefits, but a friend all the same.

"How was your meeting with your professor today?" he asks as we arrive in the foyer.

"Good. I was just working on an assignment. He's determined to have me and my critique partner work more together. She's coming here on Thursday."

"Here?"

"Yes, we'll meet in the library." But his question makes me pause and I hold on to his elbow. "Can I ask you something?"

"Sure."

"Do you guys have any friends? People you work with? I know you all slip off occasionally at night. Where are you going?"

"That's a lot of questions, Morgan."

"I'm just curious. I've never seen any of you speak to someone outside of the house before. Are you not allowed?"

"We're not hermits," he says, but his eyes are guarded and Professor Christensen's comment about rumors of their activities lingers in my mind. "I shop for supplies—meet models in the park and shoot photography all over the city. I know the others do, too. We're just dedicated to protecting you and everyone else. There's not a lot of time left for socialization. We have one another—and you." He gives me a wistful grin. "Although I could definitely go for a night out at the pub, you know?"

"Maybe we could go sometime?"

He links his fingers with mine. "Maybe."

We enter the dining room. Clinton waits at the door and I give his hand a squeeze as we pass. The others wait, with drinks in hand, near their seats. I greet Bunny across the table and run my hand over Damien's shoulder. Dylan watches my every move, waiting for me to take my spot at the head of the table. I've quickly learned that my guardians are sticklers for old-fashioned manners and never sit before I do. Sam pulls out the chair for me and I take my seat. The others follow.

Sue and Davis arrive with dinner, a steaming pan of lasagna, salad, and buttered bread. Generous glasses of red wine sit before each of us and I'm not shy about taking a drink. It's been a long, complicated day.

The vibration coursing through the room tells me that everyone is aware of what happened between me and Dylan. Talking sex isn't polite dinner conversation, so I dig around for a little guardian history.

"I have a question," I say, allowing my pasta a moment to cool. "How did you become guardians anyway?"

Looks are exchanged down the table. No one answers right away so I fix my attention on Dylan. There's no doubt he knows the answer. He takes a long gulp of his wine and says, "Mythology says we were created from the blood, bone, and ash left on the battlefield from your people."

"The ones the Morrigan slaughtered?" That idea leaves an uneasy feeling in my bones. She killed them and then the gods bound them into an eternity of servitude?

"She was betrayed," Clinton says, the muscle in his jaw tensing. "Cu Cuchulainn let the Darkness loose. Our ancestors were the victims. The gods created us to make sure it never happened again."

I rest my fork on my plate, my appetite gone. "How long have you actually been alive?"

"Alive?" Bunny asks, his expression full of wonder. "It seems like since the beginning of time. First as blood. Then bone. Later, tears and ash. I lay on the ground, buried among the charred remains of death. A god scooped me up and placed me in his pocket. For a millennia, I settled in the warmth until he remembered I was there. He held me in his palm and blew his breath on me, like a strong wind, and I scattered amongst the clouds. Rain dropped me to the ocean until I was pushed and pulled into the waves of hurricane. The god declared me ready, snatched me from the air and molded me in his hands. I returned in the form of a raven, my mission set in my mind: Protect the world from the Darkness and the Darkness from herself."

The entire table has taken a quiet, somber feel. I look at each guardian. "Did the same happen to each of you?"

"More or less," Sam replies. "It was an honor to be chosen and created by the hand of a god."

A lump forms in the back of my throat. "You don't blame me—her—for this at all?"

A choking sound comes from Damien and it takes a moment before I realize he's laughing. "I don't think you understand what a gift it is to serve in this capacity." His violet eyes flash passionately. "We're blessed. Guarding you—providing an outlet for your energy and power. There is nothing more fulfilling."

"We were a speck," Clinton adds. "The gods made us a force."

"Serving me and my--" I swallow, "--needs, cannot be that great." I mean, I haven't picked a mate. I won't let them have sex with me—yet. The whole house is a ball of tension.

Dylan leans forward, elbows on the table. "You do not understand the extent of our abilities, Morgan. We're more than what you've seen."

"Then show me! You're each amazing with your talent and art, but there's something deeper inside. I can feel it." I take a deep breath. "I feel it in your touch. In your bodies. You're so strong."

Expressions of pride settle on the faces of my guardians. Oh boy, they liked that. Dylan is the one to reply for the others. "It's a double-edged sword. We *are* strong. We are beyond capable. And we do hone our skills each and every day. But if we have to show you what we can do, then we've failed."

"Why?"

"It means the Darkness has slipped by us and the gates of hell have opened." He gives me a hard look. "Don't ask for something you can't take back."

I nod in understanding. For all their tough bravado, these men are playing with fire—me—and if they're not careful they will set off a bomb they can't contain. I pick up my fork in an effort to change the subject and move on with dinner.

What I don't tell them is that during Bunny's story, listening to the pain and the wonder of the gods' decisions, the rune over my left breast burns like the fire of a thousand suns.

And I like it.

11

DAMIEN

With the package in hand, I cross the entry foyer, hoping to catch Dylan in his rooms. Davis, always seeming to know my intent, stops me from the pantry off the kitchen.

"Master Dylan is down in the training room."

"Is he?" He hadn't mentioned an extra session, but I suspect I know the reason. "Thank you, Davis, you saved me from going up three flights of stairs."

I cut down the side hallway and take the back stairway to the basement training room. Midway down I hear the loud, thumping bass Dylan cranks up during workouts. I push open the door and see he and Clinton are in the middle of one of their crazy circuits. The moves are intense and I can't help but stop in the doorway and watch.

Although we're all superb physical beings, Dylan and Clinton are the biggest of the guardians. Dylan is tall and lean, his muscles tight cords that run along his back and arms. Clinton is just massive. A huge beast of a man. When you see them like this—or really any of us in the training room—it's not far-fetched to believe we were created by the gods.

With Clinton timing, Dylan begins the last round of nine

circuits. Nine pull-ups, nine push-ups, nine dead-lifts, then platform jumps, planks, and four other back-breaking exercises. Dylan groans in pain as he pushes through the final round, screaming as he drags a hundred-pound weight from one side of the room to the other.

"Time," Clinton says.

Dylan screams in pain, relief, and accomplishment before picking up the weight and throwing it across the room. It lands two feet away from me with a crash on the rubber mat.

"Hey," I call out. "Don't take that stress out on me."

They both look up and Dylan gives me a sheepish grin. He's breathing heavy and sweat soaks through his gray t-shirt.

"You want in?" Clinton asks, racking the weights.

I shake my head. "I worked out earlier and I'm about to head out for a while." I hold up the package. "I finished."

Clinton drops the last weight in the rack with a heavy thud and Dylan stares at the felt-wrapped object in my hands. I unwrap it, excited to show them.

"Damn, she's gorgeous," Clinton says.

"Can I?" Dylan asks, holding out his hand.

"Yeah, of course."

The sword is solid but lightweight. The hilt is carved with protective runes and I embedded magic-infused gems into the guard. Dylan takes the sword by the grip and holds it upright. "Beautiful."

He performs a few moves, the blade cutting through the air and glinting in the harsh training room lights. Satisfied, he flips it over and offers the handle to Clinton, who tentatively takes the powerful weapon.

"You'll start training her tomorrow?" Dylan asks him.

"First thing." He raises an eyebrow, skeptically. "You're sure this is a good idea?"

"It's part of the prophecy. We have to teach her properly. God forbid the gate falls and she's unable to fight."

"What if she uses it against us?" I ask. It's the question we all have. I know I feel the creeping Darkness every time I'm near her. The longer it takes her to find a mate, the more apparent it is.

"I have faith Morgan is strong enough to withstand the evil and will fight for the good," Dylan replies. He looks between us. "Do you not?"

"I think she needs to pick a mate and channel her energy as intended. Her indecision is concerning," I say.

Clinton's eyes narrow. "Are you jealous? Because—"

I hold up my hand. "No, I'm not jealous. It's hard to be jealous when every time she or anyone else in this house gets off and you feel it too. It's the best of both worlds and I'm sworn and dedicated to my service. But instead of the Darkness diminishing as she explores her choices, I just feel it getting stronger." I look at Dylan. "Do you not?"

"I concede that Morgan herself is getting stronger. I'm not sure about the Darkness." He walks over to grab his towel and wipes the sweat off his face. "She'll have to choose at the end of the thirty day span. She has twelve days left. After today, I'm confident that she not only understands her role, she's embracing it."

"Was that before or after she sucked you off?" Clinton asks. I search his eyes for a hint of the jealousy Dylan accused me of but it's not there. It's a genuine question.

Dylan holds him with a hard stare and simply replies, "During."

12

MORGAN

The city lies before me, like a kingdom. The lights spread for miles, dotting the landscape with tiny stars. The heat of the day has dissipated and the green grass under my feet is soft and warm.

After dinner, Sam asked if I wanted to see the rooftop garden. Although Dylan mentioned it when I'd first arrived at The Nead, I'd forgotten it existed. We passed by Bunny's studio (where he'd disappeared to right after the meal was over), and into a narrow alcove with what looked like a small, built-in seat. I'd never paid much attention to it. Sam hopped up on the platform and opened a small door on the low ceiling. It wasn't a seat but a step.

Sam offered me his hand and helped me up. My muscles were sore from my morning workout and the climb up the narrow, wooden staircase seemed to go for miles. He waited for me at the top and snapped my photograph as I walked into the garden for the first time.

Long stretches of grass. Small fruit trees. Flowering bushes and plants line flat-stoned pathways. Sam stretches his arms like he'd been dying to do it all day.

"Come on," he says, taking me to a small bench facing the west. "We're just in time for the sunset."

I split my time between watching the orangey-pink ball of fire disappear and Sam work his camera. It's a nice one with a complicated lens and attached flash. He takes pictures of me, the sunset, and the city below. I know the photos aren't normal. None of his pictures turn out the way things look now—but tainted by the influence of the Darkness. Sam's cameras capture the image of what the world will be —not how it currently is.

"Can I see how it works?" I ask once the sun has disappeared and the sky is streaked with purple. Stars dot the sky behind us to the east.

He walks behind me and circles his arms around my body so the camera is before us, capturing an amazing view of the city below. I feel the heat of his breath on my neck and the thump of his heart against my back. In my ear he says, "It looks normal through the viewfinder." I squint and see the buildings in the distance. Nothing weird. He snaps a few photos and then clicks a button, making the images appear on the small screen.

"Holy crap," I say, pulling the camera closer. Sam leans his chin on my shoulder. On the screen the beautiful, lit-up city is gone. There's nothing but the shell of jagged, bombed-out buildings and a hazy, ominous mist hovering over the decaying city. "This happens every time?"

"Yes."

"So, even though we're doing all this to stop me—the Morrigan—from opening the gate, this is still going to happen?"

"Yes," he says but then frowns. "Well, maybe. Right now? Yes. Can we change it? We think so."

"How?" But I know the answer. I feel it in my bones. The hunger and the want. I must take my mate and release the negative energy inside into the one I've chosen. They hope the Morrigan will be appeased with a bond. I lean against the edge of the building and face Sam.

He cups a hand behind my neck. "I know it's hard and I know it's a lot to take in. You came up here to be a student and now you're dealing with all of this."

"I'm not even close," I confess. "I have no idea who I want to pick." I gaze into his sincere, sympathetic eyes. "When I'm with you, I want you. When I'm with Clinton or Damien or Bunny or Dylan...I want them. You each give me the feeling of safety and security. You all bring out my deepest desires. I trust you all. With my body—with my life. I don't know how I'm supposed to choose."

"You have a few more weeks."

I slip my arms around his waist and pull him closer. "Two months ago," I tell him, "I sort of liked this one guy at school. He was cute-ish, with a hipster beard and glasses kind of like Bunny's. But he wasn't that into me and he was sort of a pretentious dick."

Sam raises an eyebrow.

"I thought Ryan was the best I could get, you know? I never had great luck with guys. I had no idea the five of you would not only be here but had been waiting for me all along."

"Maybe that's why you never clicked with anyone." He presses his lips to mine. "You knew, deep down, we were here."

"Is it weird?" I ask him. "Knowing I'm with the others? That we do...stuff together?" Even in the shadowy garden I know Sam can tell I'm blushing. I'm getting better about it—talking about sex—but even so, it's still awkward at times.

He stares at me for a minute and then asks, "Did you ever hear how we transformed from ravens to men?"

"No."

He takes my hand and leads me to a wrought-iron bench with a spectacular view. Roses bloom nearby and I smell their heady fragrance.

"When you opened the gate the last time and the Darkness got through, things became chaotic. We'd been sent to watch and observe you in the form of a raven. The instant the Darkness crossed over it was like suddenly we were too large for our skin. I was in the air searching for you when I fell from the sky, landing hard on the ground. My bones broke and stretched. My feathers dropped from my body. My skin peeled away. I, and the others, were left in the forest in new bodies," he uses his hands to gesture, "these bodies, with the understanding we needed to get the gate closed and find you."

"But you didn't find me."

"No, but we closed the gate." Sam looks out over the city. "It was a hard battle. And we fought it on both sides, until we managed to close it up once more. You were gone by then—disappeared into thin air—but we knew this was a good thing. You needed hiding and we were no longer able to follow you like we had once before."

"So then what?"

"We were brought up here, to The Nead. We worked and studied, refining our skills until we found you again." He takes my hand. "To answer your question about how we feel about this; we've known this day was coming for a long time. We've prepared for it. We've trained for it. We will do anything for you, Morgan. Anything. Jealousy isn't an option."

His words are sweet. Heartbreaking really, but something else bothers me and I finally just ask. "I know I'm supposed to choose my true mate. But what about you all? Is it just an obligation? A duty? Or does love not matter in all of this?"

He laughs and shakes his head. Lifting my hand to his mouth, he kisses my palm. "You own our hearts, dear Queen. Our minds and our souls. The guardians not chosen will break into a thousand pieces when you finally pick the one, but it's a risk we are willing to take. It's a risk we *must* take."

"This is just so freaking weird."

The sky is fully dark now and the city casts a glow over the garden. I take a deep breath, absorbing the flowers and trees. Absorbing Sam. Even though our time together has been chaste—nothing more than a few kisses--I feel a sense of peace from our talk. Our bond is more than sex. My release comes from my mind as well as my body. I look at the handsome, sweet man next to me and for the first time since I learned about needing a mate, I think I feel a little closer to a decision than ever before.

13

CLINTON

The sliver blade glints when I hand it to Morgan. Her eyes widen and the surprise that graced her lips shifts into something different—the curve of a small smile.

"Damien made this for me?"

"Yes. For your training."

She looks up from the sword, her eyebrow lifting in question over her dark, curious eyes. "You want me to fight with a sword. Like a knight or something? Wouldn't it look a little weird for me to carry a weapon like this?"

"When—*if*—the Darkness succeeds, Morgan, the ways of the present will fall away." I press my hands over hers, feeling the magic in the sword rush from the hilt through her skin and then mine. "The enemies you'll fight won't go down easily. This will help you win."

"So to beat the Darkness, which we don't even know exactly how that will present itself, I need physical training, runes painted on my body, magical charms," she glances at the ring on her finger, "and now this? You're scaring me, Clinton."

"Good."

I slip behind her and maneuver my hands around her hips and

back onto the blade. Her body molds to mine and I inhale her sweet scent. "You'll want to hold it like this."

I show her but it quickly becomes apparent that her innate abilities are strong. She holds it perfectly, cutting through the air with precision. Her hair is pulled back but wild tendrils curl around her face, and her cheeks are bright with excitement.

"How does it feel?" I ask, taking a step back.

"Good," she says with a hint of surprise.

I walk across the room and grab my own weapon, a similar sword off the rack on the wall. When I return to the mat, we square off. "Are you ready for this?"

"Strangely," she says, gripping the handle, "I think I am."

I'm skilled in the art of warfare. The gods created me from the ash of the strongest, most cunning soldiers in the Morrigan's war. I know her moves as well as I know my own. I've shadowed her from the sky and the ground. I've slept next to her soul. But today I have height and weight on her. I have experience she hasn't even begun to unravel—yet she stands before me with the darkest glint in her eye and I know I should be careful.

The tip of her sword shines against the light and she smiles wickedly before lunging to the left and then spinning, throwing me off balance. I straighten and tilt my head.

"It's like that then?" I feel the surge of adrenaline between us and can't take my eyes off the way her chest heaves with excitement.

Her only reply is to lick her lips before she goes on the attack once again, her blade slicing toward me.

I bring down my sword and we duel.

14

MORGAN

The tip of the blade points at Clinton's throat. In a blink, he could be dead. One slice and his blood would spill. I'm reveling in my skills when he moves beneath me, sweeping my legs, sending me tumbling to the ground. He moves fast—quick as lightning—and before I can think he towers over me, clasping a hand around my wrist. The sword stays tight in my grip, the magic coursing from the metal, but Clinton squeezes with a mighty force. I grunt bitterly before finally dropping the blade.

The heavy metal is replaced by Clinton's hand and fingers and in seconds I'm pinned to the ground, not with a sharp sword but by the overpowering man.

"Well done," he says. His hair falls over his ears and I long to brush it back. "I think you've retained some of the Morrigan's fighting skills."

"That's crazy. How could that even be possible?"

"The same way we all cling to memories, rituals, and understanding of the past. It's in our soul, Morgan. It's instinct."

I look up at him, paralyzed by the gray steel of his eyes. The rush of the fight boils beneath my skin—a conflict of desire. I'm finding that I love a fight. I revel in it, the way my body and mind feel when they're pushed to the brink. But along with that comes the Darkness that has only one cure. "Right now my instinct tells me to kiss you."

Clinton licks his lips and dips his head to mine. My hands are still bound and although it makes me a little edgy and out-of-control, I like the way it feels. I like the way he feels. He's big. He's unpredictable. And I've come to trust him completely.

His mouth lands hard against my own and I sink into the mat. I'm sweaty and slick from the workout but so is he. Unlike Dylan and Bunny, Clinton isn't shy with his affection, but even though he'll kiss me there's a firm line and I know soon we'll have to cross it.

Unlike the others though, something about Clinton scares me. His size maybe, or just his presence. He's powerful and I've felt the hardness between his legs.

Dylan warned me off but it only took a second for him to become putty in my hands. Clinton? I don't have the same confidence.

I blink and take in the man hovering over me. He releases his grip and cups one hand behind my head. His kisses are perfection. Soft when they need to be, hard when I want it. The dark energy from the training drains with every touch and I want to inhale him.

I lift up on my elbows trying to reach him and his hands move down my sides, sending a ripple through my body. The runes heat up; I feel them under my skin and I desperately want to feel that way all over, inside and out.

I bite down on his lip and grab for the front of his pants. Murmuring in his mouth I say, "I'm ready for this too."

He responds greedily, raising his hips so I can get better access. I don't have artist's fingers, and I fumble, missing the button on his pants. Instead I tug at his hips, feeling the hard length beneath the fabric. Fear swallows me again. But it's the kind tinged with adrenaline and anticipation. I cling to him, needing his body next to mine, and just as I'm about to reach my hand down his pants I feel Clinton stiffen slightly, a split-second of hesitation.

"What?" I say, barely above a whisper.

He rolls over and I straddle his lap. I grind down a little with my ass.

"You have an appointment."

My eyes flick to the clock over the door.

"I can skip it."

"No you can't."

I frown. "Why not?"

"Because..." He lifts me off his body, biceps bulging. He grimaces and shifts his pants. "We're not doing that now. Not here."

I laugh. Like a burst of hysterical laughter. "Wait, you're rejecting me?"

Because we both know I was ready to finally go for it. Like *do it* do it. My eyes catch the sliver of my sword and Clinton's hand comes down on it. He wordlessly moves it aside.

"I'm not rejecting you." He brushes my hair aside. "When this happens between us—any of us—it won't be on a smelly mat in the basement. Or in ten quick minutes before your critique partner arrives." He leans forward and kisses me with a gentleness I didn't know he possessed. "It won't be fast. It will not be quick. Trust me on that."

A chill runs down my spine at his words. My nipples harden and my lower belly tightens. He's not helping me turn away. I only want him more. Regardless of my desires, he helps me from the floor, holding the sword.

"I'll store this down here."

I nod, feeling light on my feet. God, Clinton does something to me. He has since our first encounter. I start for the door and he grabs me by the arm. He kisses me again and whispers in my mouth, "This isn't over."

I don't reply but I feel it in my bones. No, it isn't.

15

MORGAN

An ornate wood and gold clock sits on the mantle above the fireplace. The *tick-tock* echoes through the room, accentuating the awkward quiet between me and Anita.

We sit across from one another at a small, square, game table. We've swapped questions. It's a testy process—it's hard not to feel under attack as a writer during any sort of critique. I do see the value in Christensen linking us up. I feel my skin is getting tougher—unlike the exposed rawness I felt in college when people like Ryan questioned my work. Don't get me wrong, I'm still ridiculously connected and protective of my story. I know that it's part of my larger history now—the Morrigan and the Darkness—but I still have the same compulsion to get it down on paper. I want to get it right even if I can't help but feel defensive.

Anita; with her sapphire blue eyes and long, straight blonde hair smiles at me from across the table. "Do you want to go first?"

No. "Sure."

She reads from her copy of the questions. "Why does Maverick follow the cat to the woods even though the ravens are freaking out?"

I tap my pen against the paper. The feeling of being in the woods with the cat swallows me whole. I take a breath and say, "Simple curiosity I guess."

Anita's smile slips. "That's not good enough. Maverick is your protagonist. Your main character. She has to have some motivation other than just curiosity."

My fingers tremble and I snatch them off the table. "Maverick has a feeling—like a gut intuition—she needs to follow that cat. She has to. Just like she communicates with the ravens she has a connection to the cat. It feels natural."

"But the cat is bad, right?"

"The cat is..." I search for the correct word, "alluring. There's something about him that's different. That makes her ignore the ravens. Unfortunately, Maverick has an irrational response to a bad character that leads to deadly, tragic results."

Anita watches me, her eyes slightly narrowed, as though she knows I'm holding something back. "You'll have to convince the readers about that. You're close, but I'm not sure if you've sold it yet."

"Good point," I say, swallowing back my annoyance. She's right.

Turnabout is fair play and I get to go after her characters next. It feels liberating—yes, I'm a little vindictive. I almost laugh because if the Morrigan truly resides in my soul, 'a little' is probably the understatement of the year and I'm actually doing really well with restraint.

The thought makes me feel lighthearted—maybe I am beating the Darkness—and when Anita asks me a question on the way out the door I surprisingly consider it.

"I'm going to a concert tonight and have an extra ticket. Do you want to come?" I do consider it—for a split second—but then hesitate because my days and nights revolve around my routine at the house. Anita notices and says, "I think it would be a great way for us to get to know one another better. Build some trust and camaraderie."

Leave the house? On a Thursday night? I run through my schedule in my head but I know the evening is free. I just have a session with Damien in the afternoon.

"Come on, Morgan. It could be fun." She gives me a flirty smile and bats her eyelashes.

She's quite persuasive. Alluring, even.

"Okay. Yes, let's do it."

Anita hops in excitement and squeezes my hands. "This is great! I'll text you details, okay?"

When the front door closes behind her and I take moment to breathe, I wonder what I've gotten myself into. If anything, maybe it will give me a little credit from Professor Christensen for making an effort.

16

MORGAN

Dinner is a quick affair. I dodge the sultry looks from Clinton, still in a heightened state from earlier in the day, and excuse myself before dessert. Anita instructed me by text to meet her at nine. I don't dress until after dinner and even though I'm not intentionally hiding anything, I don't inform the guardians of my plans. They seem hesitant about anything outside The Nead, and although they are my protectors I don't actually need their permission to leave the house.

I stand before my closet unsure of what to wear. I've been in New York for over a month and I haven't actually been out yet. I pull out my phone.

Suggestions for what to wear?-M
Something fun. Dressy but not too much-A
That doesn't make sense-M

My phone vibrates and an image pops up. It's a picture of Anita wearing a sexy red dress with tiered ruffles from the knees to her hips. The front plunges to a deep V between her breasts and has small capped sleeves. Her hair is loose around her shoulders and it's not straight—she curled it in loose ringlets. The only noticeable makeup is the bold red lipstick.

Got it-M

I stand back in front of my closet and push the clothes to the side. I've got nothing comparable to that dress in here. Except...

I dig past my winter jacket and find the plastic-covered outfit against the back wall. I tug down the zipper and smile at the contents.

Yes, I think this will work.

17

DAMIEN

Bed. That's all I want.

Bed. Maybe a thick piece of Sue's chocolate cake from the kitchen.

It's been a long day—a long week. Forging the sword for Morgan had taken a lot out of me. The magical pieces like Morgan's ring and sword require a huge amount of physical and mental energy to create. I need sugar and sleep.

Sue and Davis have cleaned the kitchen when I stop in for a hunk of cake. I carry it out on a plate, licking the icing off with my finger. As I head toward the front stairs I notice someone by the doors.

My jaw drops.

"Have mercy," I mutter. Morgan spins in my direction, making the fringe on her black dress swing.

"Damien," she says. "You scared me."

"Sorry." I swallow the piece of cake that has suddenly become lodged in the back of my throat. "Damn, you look, fuck, Morgan. I've never seen you like this."

A primal urge crashes over me like a wave.

Aware of the way I'm looking at her, Morgan bites down on her upper lip and something in me nearly cracks in two.

"I'm just waiting for my cab," she says.

"A cab? You're going out?" *Like that?* I almost add, but don't.

"I'm meeting Anita, my critique partner." She looks at me defiantly and God, I want her even more. Lights flash out front and the cab horn blares its arrival.

"Have fun."

She flashes me a smile. "Thanks."

I reach for her and grab her by the arm. I tilt my head and she does the same and we kiss, slowly. "You look fucking stunning."

"Thank you," she whispers.

"Be careful."

She nods and kisses me once again, her lips hot with fire against mine. She slips out the door and I'm left standing in the foyer with my cake in hand. I look up and Sam stands at the top of the steps.

"Does he know?" I ask.

Sam nods. "Already gone."

We haven't told Morgan yet that she can't leave the house alone—it's not that we don't trust her—we don't trust the Darkness, which will take any opportunity to slip through the cracks.

"Did you see that dress?" I climb the stairs.

Sam nods vigorously. "Holy shit, yes."

18

MORGAN

The cab stops outside a busy strip of road. A deli, a bodega, two pawn shops, and a boarded-up storefront line the sidewalk. I look at the address Anita gave me and wonder for a quick second if she's pranking me. When I glance back at the street I spot her next to the abandoned shop, waving.

The dress isn't easy to miss on the litter-strewn road. The bright red draws looks from pedestrians. The minute I'm out of the car Anita pulls me into a tight embrace and says, "I'm so glad you came."

"Exactly where is this concert?"

"I've been reading about this new thing. Secret clubs. From the outside it looks like an abandoned building but the insides are supposed to be amazing."

"Like a speakeasy?" I ask, referring to prohibition bars.

"Yes!" Her eyes light up. "But each one has a theme and they only last a few nights. I managed to get three tickets."

"Three?"

She points to the boarded-up wall. For the first time I notice a familiar-looking blond. He has striking features—a narrow nose and strong chin. He looks as apprehensive to be here as I feel. His eyes burn the same color blue as the girl standing next to me and I say, "Are you related?"

"My brother!" She drags me over. "Morgan this is Xavier. Xavier this is Morgan."

His face relaxes and his eyes drink me in. "Nice to meet you, Morgan. I've heard a lot about your project."

Typically, my defenses rise. I'm never a fan of discussing my book, particularly with strangers. Xavier must notice because he tilts his head and says, "Only good things, of course."

"Your sister is very talented," I reply. "But I'm sure you already knew that."

He smiles and it's breathtaking. "I have heard that once or twice."

"Hey!" Anita cries, tugging at his sleeve. He grins down at her and wraps an arm around her shoulder. "I'm not braggy."

"Never," he says with a wink in my direction. "So, are we ready for this adventure or what?"

"I'm ready to get off the street," I reply. The night air is still warm and hopefully there's air conditioning inside.

Xavier offers me and his sister the crook of his arm. It's weird but what in my life isn't lately? I link my arm with his and he leans in and says, "I'll buy you a drink to cool you off."

Anita directs us down a small alley and takes two steps down to a rusty door. She bangs twice, smiling back at me and her brother. I glance up at him and with the street light behind his head his hair glows and I get the strangest feeling I've met him before.

The door opens with a creak and a well-dressed man with flaming red hair stands in the entrance. Anita hands over three tickets and he nods for us to enter.

I follow Anita down the steps and just like she said earlier, we step into something amazing—a whole different world.

"Wow," I say, freezing in the doorway. I take the whole place in. The bar to the right, gleaming with a glossy shine. Three bartenders in bow ties and starched white shirts work behind the counter, mixing cocktails. A cluster of men and women surround the bar and small tables fill the floor space. A small stage sits at the front of the room, with a single chair in the middle. A heavy black curtain hangs behind the stage. I have no idea what sort of concert to expect, but before I can say anything Xavier has bolted for the bar and Anita is dragging me toward a table with a reserved card on top.

"This is really neat," I tell her when I'm settled in my seat. "I had no idea places like this existed."

"One of the perks of living in the city. So many cool things to do. After seeing that amazing historic house you live in, I thought maybe you'd like it."

Xavier returns with three martini glasses. I don't waste time taking a sip of mine.

"So who's playing?" I ask.

Anita shrugs. "That's part of the surprise. You never know. Sometimes it's someone famous or like, undiscovered but incredibly talented. One time it was a rapper singing show tunes. Another, a Broadway star playing hard rock. It's always something unique."

"And after a few days they'll close it down?"

"Yep," she says. "And then move somewhere else."

While we wait for the show to start I learn a little more about Xavier. He's an investment banker—doing things that make zero sense to me even when he explains it in explicit detail. "Working on the stock floor is sheer pandemonium. I love it though. It's a rush. The clock is ticking—numbers are flying. It's like mental marathon every day."

Even though Xavier is very attractive there's something about him that rubs me the wrong way. Maybe it's the ego or smug confidence. He's exactly *not* my type, which after a month of living with five amazing men is a little refreshing. Honestly, just being out of the house feels good. There's so much energy and tension between me and the guardians. I didn't even realize how much I needed a break.

"Thanks for inviting me," I say to Anita. "I've been a little cooped up."

She gives me a sly grin. "Not sure I blame you. I've seen a couple of those housemates. Yowza."

Xavier makes a face but the lights dim, keeping him from any comments. The chatter in the club comes to a halt and even the people by the bar quiet. A spotlight arcs over the ceiling and lands on the chair, which, to my surprise, is now occupied.

By a familiar face *and* body.

Clinton sits in the chair, his cello angled between his legs. His hair is loose, swaying by his jaw, and his muscular biceps strain against the fitted, black button-down.

The crowd applauds at the sight of him, seeming to know or recognize him. They only settle back down when he lifts his bow and begins playing a deep, haunting melody.

It's certainly not the first time I've heard Clinton play. His music lured me from my room weeks ago. The vibrations creep over my skin and into my soul. I may be in a packed room filled with other people but instantly I'm transported. It's like the club around me disappears and it's just Clinton and me. Watching him now, I remember the way his mouth feels, the way his body lights mine on fire.

His gaze isn't on anything in particular. His jaw is tense. His fingers are deft and precise. A heavy weight moves across the room, something I now recognize as magic. Ancient and powerful. I lean forward, feeling the energy rising in my body.

Xavier shifts next to me, his arm brushing against mine. Heat tingles across my skin—fiery and alive. A powerful need—a want—shocks through my system. It's the music. The crowd.

It's the Morrigan.

I glance over at Xavier, who's staring at me with hungry eyes. The Queen wants to respond, but I push her back down, calling on the lessons of the last few weeks.

I focus back on the stage. I focus on Clinton, who has the crowd so enthralled they never notice when he lifts his eyes and stares out into them. Our eyes lock. I know they do. I feel it when the runes flare. In the twist of my stomach. He can't see me in the dark—not with human eyes—but the guardians are not exactly human and I know for certain he's aware of my presence.

I blink and bang my elbow on the table, knocking into my glass, sloshing the contents across the top.

"I'm sorry," I whisper, breaking the magic of the moment. Anita looks at me in annoyance. Xavier stares. I stand and mumble, "Excuse me."

I push through the tables, stepping on toes, issuing apologies. The bartender points me to the small hall in the back and I find the doors leading to the bathroom and one that has a broken exit sign overhead. The door sticks but I slam my shoulder into it and the hinges give, tumbling me into the alley.

I take a gulp of air.

"You don't control me," I say to the Goddess inside. I understand it now. She wields her power with an iron grip and if I don't find a way to release the energy she'll come forth. How? That's the scary part. I don't know.

The back door opens and slams into the brick wall. The energy in the air spikes and I turn, thankful that Clinton's performance is over.

"Thank God," I say, spinning around but it isn't Clinton, it's Xavier.

He understandably misinterprets my statement and lunges for me. He doesn't wait, pressing his lips to mine. The Goddess roars, eagerly consuming the energy of the man before me. I tug the hair at the back of his neck and bite his bottom lip. He pushes his hips into mine, pinning me against the wall.

This is how it should be done, the Morrigan whispers in my ear. The rune painted over my heart flares. *Feed from him.*

I could devour him. I lick his tongue and absorb the energy. He's not like my guardians. He's different. Raw.

Dark.

The Goddess inside me cries, wanting to tear him apart.

Xavier hikes my skirt up my hips, the brick of the building cool against my upper thighs. The rough texture scrapes and I grab for his belt.

Be done with your purity. Here. Now.

"Shut up," I tell her, knowing it's the wrong thing to do. My brain knows this. My body—

"What?" Xavier says.

"Nothing." I reach for him but jump when the door slams against the alley wall and a massive hand drags Xavier off of me.

"It's time to go home," Clinton says to the other man. Xavier looks miniscule next to him. Clinton's steel gray eyes rake down my body—assessing me for injury.

"Hey man, back the fuck off. This isn't any of your business."

A dark shadow crosses Clinton's face. The Morrigan whimpers back into her shell. Morgan takes back over and I feel the heat of the rune on my chest fade. "Xavier." I swallow. "You should probably go."

"What?" He looks between us. "You're the cellist? You're leaving me for a musician? Fucking tease."

Clinton makes a move but I step forward, pushing him back. I grab Xavier by the chin, my nails digging into his skin. "Don't talk to me like that."

"What? I can't call you a tease? Please. You wanted it."

"Maybe I did, but I don't anymore." I release my grip, which I can tell he notices is stronger than expected. "Just go."

"Whatever," he stays, stepping back. He rubs the spot on his chin where I touched him. A fiery red mark remains. "You're not worth it."

Clinton holds the door for him and slams it once Xavier steps back into the bar. I straighten my skirt and say, "I'm sorry. I don't know what came over me."

Without speaking, he walks me out front and waves down a cab. One appears immediately and he swings open the door, letting me in.

From the street he tells the cabbie our address. I realize then that he's staying behind.

"You're not coming?"

He shakes his head with a small jerk, the knot in the back of his jaw twitching.

He slams the door and walks away.

19

CLINTON

From the doorway of the club I watch the cab drive off. It took every ounce of strength not to get in the backseat with her. Morgan was scared and confused. I was aroused and about to take her in public.

That wasn't how this night should end.

In fact, none of it should have happened in the first place. How she ended up here? In this club, listening to my music? It can't be a coincidence and I enter the building to find some answers.

The crowd is still in full swing, the tables near the stage having been cleared for a dance floor. My act was planned to be short—it's up to the artists' discretion how long they want to perform. The simple fact I'm creating the music—me, a guardian—means magic is involved. It's volatile and with the right trigger, explosive.

There's no doubt Morgan was the perfect trigger.

I push through the crowd, towering over most of the other men. Many look up and recognize me from the stage. I don't stop, hoping to catch up with the two that brought Morgan here.

I spot the red slinky dress of Morgan's friend and the male with her. I can only assume they're related. The guy notices me before I get to the table and he holds up his hands. "Listen man, I don't want any problems. Okay? Misunderstanding. The girl said stop and I stopped."

"What did you do?" Anita asks suspiciously.

Xavier coughs. "Nothing. We just had a moment. Then this guy broke it up. No big deal."

"Where is she now?" she asks.

"She left," I say. "How did you know to bring her here?"

"Know?" the girl asks. "I just lucked into some tickets. Thought it would be a fun night out."

I don't believe in luck.

"Who gave you the tickets?"

"They were just delivered to my apartment. Said I'd won them."

Xavier coughs again and I notice a thin sheen of sweat on his forehead. I nod at him. "You may want to get him home. He's not looking too great."

"Not feeling so great either," he replies.

I walk away, realizing the girl doesn't know much, if anything at all. I head to the back and grab my cello before making my way back out to the street. Hailing a cab, I think about that moment during the concert between me and Morgan. I knew she was out there the minute I walked on stage. I sensed her. Smelled her. I felt the heat of her body and the powerful runes etched onto her skin.

When the magic spilled from my bow, igniting a fire in her soul, something happened. She left. The man, Xavier, followed.

I don't know how. I don't know why, but the Morrigan was summoned. I could hear her voice through the strains of my music. I heard her as clearly as I knew Morgan did. That's how it starts. That's how the Darkness takes over.

A yellow cab pulls over. It's a van—big enough to transport my instrument. I hop in the backseat and give directions. The street lights flash out the windows.

A smart man would cool off for a bit before going home after a night like this. I may be strong. I may be powerful, but no one ever told me that I'm smart. I am cunning, a warrior, and I have a feeling I'm about charge into battle.

20

MORGAN

The door is unlocked when I arrive home. Thankfully no one greets me. My lips are still hot with shame, my mind a jumble of the Morrigan's whispers. Want and desire and need and yearning war in my mind. They tug at my body. I close the heavy wooden door with a click of the latch. Carrying my heels I run up the steps, past Clinton and Damien's rooms to the third floor. Sam's light is off. I enter my room, dropping the shoes with a too-loud thud against the hardwood floor.

My skin crawls. I think of Xavier and the way his body felt. The way the Morrigan responded to him. I'd never heard her before. Not like that. Not off the page.

I cross the suite and enter my writing study. On the window seat is my notebook with the last chapter I'd written. I'd been struggling to convey what happens to Maverick when she opens the gateway between one world and the other. What happens when the Darkness crosses over?

The fair-haired prince stands next to her. His eyes glint with deceit.

"What is this?" she asks.

"Your destiny," he replies. His teeth are white and sharp. A gust of cold air passes through the gate, the kind that chills a person to their bones. Maverick feels it deeper than that. In her soul. Black smoke wafts into the green forest. The ravens caw overhead but it's hard to hear them.

The cold air turns warm—hot, even—blistering her cheeks. A voice calls to her, "Join me, Goddess of War. Unleash your powers from this world to the next."

She turns and faces the prince, who continues to smile. Maverick takes his hand and tugs him down with one hand. The other is heavy with a surprising weight. But she knows. She knows what to do with those that are disloyal. With her lips close to his she leans in to steal his breath, while raising the other hand and stabbing him with the tip of her blade.

He jerks back—the smile vanished—but he knows. He knew. As does Maverick.

In every story this is how it happens. This is how the Darkness begins.

A hand lands on my shoulder. Startled, I drop the book and spin, using the moves from my training. I land a punch in Clinton's gut.

"Oof," he grunts, taking a step back.

"Mother fu—" I clench my fist. It's bruised for certain. "Clinton!"

"Sorry." He takes my fist and kisses the bridge of knuckles. "I called your name."

"What are you doing here?" The twist of fire in my belly from the concert is still there.

He holds my gaze. "It's time."

"Time?" I'm confused by his statement but the warmth in my belly gives me an instinctive clue. "Because of tonight?"

"The Darkness is too strong. You're running out of time to pick a mate. But I also think you're scared to choose between us. That if you lose your virginity to one of us, then that's it." His eyes search mine.

"It doesn't work like that, Morgan. You're free to make the choice. Having sex with one of us doesn't bind you forever. That energy needs a place to go—you felt it tonight. You felt her. She'll only get stronger."

"So you think it should be you?" He's right. I've been afraid of this moment for weeks. Particularly with him. It seems ironic yet strangely accurate that he would be the one to push me on this.

"It can be any of us, sweetheart, but it needs to happen soon."

He stands before me and waits. I know in my heart I can dismiss him and he'd leave. I could ask for any of the others and they'd come. But the consuming energy from the concert is still live and charged between us, and the fear that has knotted in my chest for weeks slowly dissipates.

I take a step forward, closing the gap between us.

"I'm scared."

He frowns. "Of me?"

"No. Of how things will change from here. I mean, my life has already changed a lot. Living here. The Morrigan. The magic." I swallow. "The sex."

"You're right. It's another step, but a necessary one. I don't think you'll regret it." His eyes search mine. "It doesn't have to be me, Morgan. I can walk out that door."

I consider how earlier I'd wondered if Sam would be the one. So kind and a good friend. He'd take care of me for sure. And Bunny? He would be gentle. I knew that. Damien would treat me like a princess. Dylan would give me a night I would never, ever forget. But Clinton? He'd been the one I was afraid of from the beginning.

Which may make him the perfect one.

"Maybe nothing about tonight was a coincidence? Maybe we're meant to do this."

He ghosts his hand down my shoulder, his fingers linking with mine.

"Maybe," he agrees.

I nod and lick my lips and a switch flips between us. All of the talk and worry and craziness of the night disappears. Clinton pulls me into his arms, his hands grappling with my backside, pushing up the hem of my dress. He lifts me up and I straddle his hips, happy to be face-to-face with him since he's so tall.

He walks quickly toward the bedroom, holding me like a treasure. I kiss his forehead, cheeks, nose, and mouth. He tastes like liquor from the club and when he stops at the edge of my bed I can't believe I ever hesitated.

"Tell me to stop at any time. Don't do something you'll regret."

"I regret that scene at the bar, Clinton. I never wanted to be with him. I wanted to be with you. You were magnificent up there on the stage. So strong. So sensual. I thought about your mouth. Your lips. I thought about your cock and what it would feel like inside of me. It was too much—too intense. That's why I left. Xavier just got in the line of fire between us. Stupid boy."

A shift takes place on his face. Something feral and less constrained. When I mentioned his cock I felt him tighten between my legs. With one hand he gently lays me on the bed. He stands over me, pants tented with arousal. He places two hands on my bare legs and pushes my skirt over my hips. I rise up and his eyes turn glassy at the sight of my black, lace panties.

The next few minutes are a blur. I lose my dress, the black fringe falls to the floor. Clinton's shirt follows, revealing the hard lines of his chest and abdomen. I eye the ladder of muscle that flinches at my touch and I can't look away from the hair that travels from his navel to the waistband of his pants. When I tug at the button and he quickly shucks them off. I can't help but stare at his throbbing erection.

It's big like the rest of him.

My stomach tightens in anticipation and the space between my legs grows warmer with desire. I should be afraid but I'm not. I desperately want his weight and warmth on top of me and I pull him down.

The contrast between the two of us—hard to soft—is a glorious feeling. His arousal pushes against my core, each of us slippery with excitement. His mouth meets mine and he kisses me hotly. Hard. His hands move to my breasts and he explores them with the same precision he uses playing the cello or teaching me to fight. When there's a gap of space between us I lift my hips, wanting, wanting and wanting to feel him against me—*in* me.

He doesn't need my permission but when he stares down at me I realize that he's waiting. This is my choice. Everything about this is my choice. My mate. My guardians. The fight between good and evil.

"Please," I beg, reaching between our bodies. I touch the velvet tip of his cock in invitation.

He's quick, entering me with a swift motion. I cry out in surprise, feeling the spread of pain. The intrusiveness of warmth. My eyes are shut when I hear his voice, "Breathe, sweetheart," and I do, unclenching my teeth and exhaling long and shuddering.

I open my eyes and find him staring at me, checking on me, but I'm fading into the feeling of him inside of me, marveling at the way my body reacts to him. I slip my hand over his bicep and squeeze. He moves his hips, just a little, circling them in a way that causes me to gasp, "Oh!"

It's in a good way. A very good way.

Clinton realizes the shift, the way I've relaxed to his movements, the way the sensations adjusted from pain to pleasure. He pulls nearly all the way out before slipping back in. The move triggers a wave through my body. I can't help but smile when he does it again.

He smiles back.

I plant my feet next to his hips and he grunts with approval. Satisfied I'm okay he sinks deeper—faster—speeding up gradually. The change makes my breasts bounce rhythmically, slapping against his chest, igniting another, different wave of sensations. I moan with approval, eliciting a pleased grin from the man over me, and when he dips his fingers between us, brushing against the desperate bundle of nerves, I cry out.

He sets a rhythm, his long hair swaying with each thrust. At first it's awkward and off kilter but soon it's our rhythm, our place in time. Our skin slick, our nerves frayed. *Our. Our. Our.*

I wonder for the slightest moment if it's just Clinton and I or something larger. Do the others feel it? Do they feel him pounding between my legs? Do they feel the coil tensing and tightening? I wouldn't be surprised. Magic courses through this house. Through my limbs.

My mind slips away and my body takes over. Clinton seeks my mouth and kisses me desperately, panting raggedly. I think he's going to come but then his fingers find that spot again I close my eyes and I'm the one that can no longer hold back. With the tweak of his fingers I'm sprung, riding the wave of euphoria.

As my body shudders, I slip into the wild. The walls creak and the rafters sway. I think I hear a muffled caw outside the window and swear I feel the charm burn against my chest. Brightness engulfs me and I shut my eyes, spinning, spinning, spinning. The energy, the Darkness lurking inside releases, bathing me in adoration.

My nails dig into his back and that's when he comes, riding the crest of my own orgasm. His shoulders tense, his abs constrict. He grunts into my mouth, long and ragged, mimicking his hips.

Clinton collapses, his massive body heavy against mine. I like the way it feels. I love the sticky warmth of his seed pooling between our bodies. I don't want him to move, but I know that this is just the beginning. There's more. So much more.

As soon as he catches his breath he rolls me over, switching our positions. I'm on top, relaxed and truly satiated for the first time in weeks. The Morrigan is quiet. The energy quelled. For once I don't feel the Darkness lurking at the edges. I hadn't realized how close she had been.

When I look down at Clinton, his cheeks red and his eyes glassy and distant in a way I've never seen before, I feel a mixture of emotions. Slight embarrassment—wondering if I did it right and if it felt as good for him as he presented. Pride for taking this step in my life. I'd been fearful—of Clinton the most—but I beat that. I owned it.

I claimed him more than he claimed me and that feeling burns in my chest.

"What are you thinking about?" His finger criss-crosses over my bare body. He's mimicking the runes painted on by Bunny. The burning from earlier with Xavier—on my chest—is gone.

"How I shouldn't have waited so long."

He laughs, a rare sight on Clinton's face.

"Do you think the others know?" I ask.

His face loses a hint of its humor. "They know."

A new feeling settles in my chest.

Dread.

"I'm going to have to choose now, aren't I?" Because I'm still not sure. Even after all that, I'm not sure.

He brushes a curl of hair behind my ear. "Yep."

I sigh and slide off his lap. I'm sticky and need a shower. A dull ache has replaced the euphoria. I don't hate it. It's a reminder—a good one—but a signal of how I've changed.

Clinton catches my hand and squeezes it just as a loud knock raps at my suite's door. A thin line forms between his eyes and he says, "Get dressed. I'll see what's going on."

None of the guardians have come to my room this late before and the worry on Clinton's face sets me on edge.

"Is something wrong?" I ask. The rapping happens again. Louder this time.

He doesn't answer, just tugs his pants up over his hips. Shirtless and barefoot, he walks down the hall and I grab a blanket from my bed and wrap it around my body, following him.

The door opens and Dylan stands on the other side. His eyes land immediately on me from over Clinton's shoulder. If he's fazed by our state of undress or intimacy, he never reveals it.

Like Clinton said, he knows.

"We have a problem," he says, shifting his gaze back to Clinton. "Meeting in the library. Ten minutes. Everyone will be there."

I walk down the hall, gripping my blanket at my chest. I push past Clinton and ask, "What is it. What happened?"

    Dylan pins me with an ice blue stare. "Xavier is sick."

    Something inside me cracks, a jagged edge that cuts to the bone. I sway and Clinton draws an arm around my shoulder. Terrified, I ask anyway, "With what?"

    "You infected him, Morgan. With the Darkness."

21

DYLAN

Earlier That Night...
Gifted with intuition and instinct, I know the minute dinner is over that Morgan has plans. She leaves the dining room quickly, declining dessert. We stare at one another for a moment and excuse ourselves. We all have work to do and mine, first and foremost, is to make sure Morgan is safe.

I'm aware she's longing to leave the house. I'm also aware of Anita's visit earlier in the day. I'm not surprised when she exits her room after dinner, dressed to go out.

I am stunned by her beauty.

Her legs.

Her hair.

The curves of her hips and the swaying fringe of her dress as she walks down the stairs.

I watch as Damien speaks to her. I watch Sam watch her. The second she touches the doorknob, I'm gone, shifted into my original form. Sleek feathers. Sharp beak. Wide wings.

I alight from the window in my room.

I'M the only guardian that has retained the ability to shift from raven to man. As the sentinel, it's my job to keep a close eye. I trust Morgan. I have faith in her, but the Darkness is powerful.

It will take a champion to resist the Morrigan's tests. They'll come in a variety of forms. Money. Success. Beauty. The Darkness will take any slip to work her evil and since Morgan is not fully reinforced with the help of a mate, a breach is likely.

I follow the cab through the city streets, landing on a water tower when it stops. Morgan exits the car and meets with her friend. There's a man with them—I sense a familiarity with Anita. I also feel Clinton nearby.

From my perch above the city, I wait.

THE DARKNESS ROSE while Morgan was inside the building. Now, she's on the street below, in the shadows of the alley. Her lust and desire are amplified. I expect Clinton to follow her outside—he'd triggered something—but it isn't him. It's the blond.

I'm about to shift when the door opens. Clinton performs his duty and sends Morgan home, following soon after. The other man? The one she kissed? Something has transpired. I feel it.

Pushing off the ledge I fly through the city, following a different cab to a different place. There, the man is helped inside by his sister. I can smell the death on his skin already.

It's familiar.

It's ancient.

It's the Darkness.

22

MORGAN

The guardians are already in the library when I arrive. Clinton shuts the door behind me and I make uneasy eye contact with each man before finding my seat.

"What happened?" I ask, feeling the dull ache of concern in my chest.

"The Darkness jumped the barrier."

"I felt her," I confess. "Something happened with Clinton's music and it's like I just slipped. I could hear her speaking to me. It was like she was there. Xavier and I got caught up in it. She disappeared when Clinton arrived."

"When you were in the alley with Xavier you scratched him on the neck. It seems that was all it took to infect him with an illness."

"What kind of illness?" I ask. The blood drains from my face. "Is it the plague? The flu? Ebola?"

"We don't know yet."

"Has it spread?" I look around the room. The guardian's faces are strained with worry. "Can it spread?"

"We just don't know yet but we'll make every effort to contain it,"

Dylan replies. "This can't happen again, Morgan. You've got to fight harder."

His words hit me like a slap. "Do you think I'm not? That I'm slacking off?"

"You snuck out of the house!" he rages—raising his voice in a way I've never heard before. "You risked everything for a little play time. Some leisure. Not to mention hooking up with another man."

"Dylan!" Sam says, rising from his chair. "She didn't do anything wrong."

I stand and push Sam out of the way. Bunny sits on the couch, looking as though he'd like to disappear. "Don't you dare suggest I'm not committed. It's all I do. I train. I study. I balance and expend my energy trying to keep the Darkness at bay. I have other obligations. I had a life before I came here. I have friends, or at least I'm trying to. And I never would have gone to that club if you'd been honest with me and told me Clinton would be there. It's like I walked into a fucking landmine. I stepped on a mine and the whole place blew up. Don't blame that on me."

To my surprise it's Bunny who stands up and makes an attempt to diffuse the situation.

"This isn't helping," he says. "There's a man dying and he could be patient zero. Fighting about it is not going to fix this."

"What do we need to do?" I ask, thankful for a little logic.

"Damien and I go over and try to help Xavier," he says, and Damien nods in agreement. He looks at Dylan. "Go do what you do best—research the hell out of this. See if we can stop it."

Dylan reluctantly nods.

"Clinton, fortify the armory. We may need it."

"Got it."

"Sam, get on the street. Start taking photos. Make sure we aren't missing something big coming our way."

"Good idea."

"And what about me?" I ask.

"You need to rest. Recharge. Your mission hasn't changed—it's only sped up. You'll have to choose a mate, Morgan. Now." His copper eyes hold mine. Clinton said it earlier. I know it in my heart. It's time.

They file out of the room and I should follow—go to my room and rest—but I don't. I sit back on the leather couch.

I feel a tickle in my ear. A soft whisper. There must be a way to figure out who is my match. Who is my one. The voice makes a suggestion, like a thought popped suddenly in my head.

My eyes scan the books around the library. The answer must be in here. I touch the rune over my heart. It must be in *here* as well.

As though I'm guided by an unseen spirit, I walk across the room to a thick book with a black, peeling spine. I pull it from the shelf and take it to the table. On the cover in faded gold is a woman surrounded by her five crows.

I open it up and read.

BLACK MAGIC

1

MORGAN

The smell of antiseptic assaults my nose the instant we step into the hospital. The nurse spots us before we get to the desk. There is no wait and Sam and I are ushered quickly through a swinging door and down a long hallway. A police officer stands with his back to the wall. I feel the tightening squeeze of Sam's hand against mine as the officer steps aside, opening the door.

"Thank you," I say, looking up at the officer's face. He stares straight ahead, making no eye contact.

As we step through the door, Sam whispers in my ear, "You've got this."

The room is small, with a glass window separating a larger, secured room with a patient lying in a hospital bed. Xavier.

Anita, my academic partner and Xavier's sister, stands at the window, eyes focused on her brother. I'm not sure she's even aware we came in until she breaks the silence without warning. "They say they don't know what it is." She turns and glares at me. "What's killing him. It's some weird virus they've never seen."

"They told me," I say. I'd been tested, prodded and poked for six hours the day before. My blood came back clean. I had none of the mysterious illness that was ravaging Xavier's body.

Neither did Anita.

Anita told the doctors that I'd been with her brother just before he fell ill. That we'd kissed and it was likely I had either passed the infection on to him or he gave it to me.

I adamantly explained that this was untrue. We never kissed. We'd merely spoken in the alley. I'd gone home early. If Xavier ever said differently, then he was confused. Hallucinating. I mean, it's not as though he could literally become sick in minutes, could he?

The lies came easily. I'd like to blame the Morrigan for how quickly I adjusted to covering up her carnage, but I know better. The lies belong to me and me alone.

Once cleared, I decided to go visit Xavier. It seemed the right thing to do. Sam came with me for support and I suspect a little bit of protection. Protecting me from someone or protecting someone from me, that's the real question I have. Are the Guardians afraid of me? Clinton surely wasn't when we were in bed together. Sam's gentle touches don't express fear.

Anita looks back at the window, through the glass at her brother. Xavier doesn't look good and it's difficult to see him like this. The last time I saw him, when we did kiss, he was very handsome. Animated and full of life—lust even. The infection ravages his body from the inside out. He's pale but feverish, a slick sweat clinging to his face. Splotchy gray marks blemish his arms and neck. He looks one step away from being a corpse and I realize with sudden clarity that it's not the only time I've seen someone looking like this.

The gray sky parts and Maverick runs from the forest back into the safety of her yard. The cat is gone. The prince is dead. Her ravens flew to the sky, never to be seen again. The cold crept through the gateway and she ran. She'd never run so hard—so fast. Until she saw the grassy yard, the little swing, the blanket stretched over the grass with a book on top.

The sun beat down here—but the chill lingered and quickly the warm light vanished, like a front had pushed through. Maverick grabbed her book and blanket and raced into the house like a mouse with a cat on his tail. She bursts through the back door, the knob crashing into the wall behind it. The girl freezes, waiting for the sound of her mother's reprimand. For her father's annoyance. But nothing came.

Dread fills her heart.

She drops her book and her blanket. She walks up the small flight of stairs.

"Mom?"

Silence.

"Dad?"

The air feels frozen as she walks down the hall. The door is open. She spots her father's shoes first. Then her mother's hair—wild like her own—twisted beneath her cheek.

They look—

"Morgan?" Sam's voice brings me back to the hospital room. Anita glares at me with a heavy dose of bitterness.

"Sorry." It's the only thing I can say and even then my voice is shaky and quiet. "I'm sorry, Anita. I truly hope he gets better. Call me if you need something." I turn quickly, unable to look at his body, unable to look at Xavier one second longer. It's weak. I'm weak. But we know that. It's why we're here. The Morrigan overpowered me. She took a life to feed her desperate, awful soul.

Sam follows me back past the officer, down the hall, through the waiting room and into the street. It's hot and muggy out here but it's preferable to the cold resting in my heart. I haven't gone two feet away from the entrance before Sam grabs my arm and stops me.

"What's going on? Are you okay?"

I look at this man. So handsome. So kind. Fierce just like the others. He'd do anything for me. I see it in the depths of his blue eyes.

"No, I'm not okay."

"Tell me what's going on then. What happened back there?"

"I've made a decision." He raises his eyebrows, encouraging me to continue. "The Morrigan doesn't own me. She doesn't get to take away the good and torment the living. I'm not willing to be her puppet anymore."

A crease mars Sam's perfect forehead and he says, "We just have to keep working to control her. Help you get stronger. You'll have to pick your mate."

"I'll do that too but I found something, Sam. A book in the library. I think if we use the information correctly we can stop her for good."

He looks at me like I'm crazy. "How are we going to do that?"

"We're going to kill the Morrigan."

2

MORGAN

I ask Sam to gather the other guardians and have them meet me in the library in an hour. I'd found the book the day Xavier got sick. It was just hours after I lost my virginity to Clinton and found myself under increasing pressure to pick a mate from the five men in the house.

I know I'm not ready for that. As awkward and selfish as it sounds, I like them all. Each feels like a piece of the puzzle I've been missing in my life. Every time they push or suggest I make a decision, any ability to do so slips from my grasp. They would say it's the Morrigan trying to keep me weak, but increasingly I feel it's more than that. Much more.

Sleeping with Clinton is the primary reason for my view. I'd held off for so long—afraid of something—but when we made love it's like the world crumbled and not only did I want him with me at the end, I wanted the same experience with the others too. I want to feel their bodies on top of me, naked and hot. I want to feel them inside of me, come in me.

Now that I understand, I'm less willing to concede to just one until I've had a taste of them all.

Sam with his kindness and understanding—supporting me unconditionally—he's helped me find the "me" in a battle against ancient evil. He's sweet and sexy. Mischievous under that adorable, handsome grin.

Bunny guides me spiritually—grounding me to this place and to the powers I carry. He shores up my soul and finds the strength deep inside to keep me going. I long to run my fingers through his hair, feel his hips against mine.

Clinton, my trainer, keeps me fit and ready for the physical war headed our way. He pushes me. Tests me.

Damien provides my weaponry and outfits me with charms and symbols designed to keep me safe. He's quiet and likes his independence—his solitary space out back behind the house. But when we're together I feel the magic of our bond.

And then there's Dylan. My sentinel. He carries the knowledge of the past and he has an eye on me—*always*. He's afraid of his own strength and together we're breaking one another down. His passion knows no limits. And I'm here to tempt as well as test him.

I remove the ancient book from under my bed. I'd hidden it, wanting some time to study it in private. The gold image of the Morrigan on the cover, embossed with five ravens in various states of flight, sings to me when I touch the peeling leather spine.

The pages are filled with drawings and short stories—an odd historical account of the Morrigan's mythology. They come from various stages in her life. Before she went mad with rage, when she was just a young goddess wanting to find her true love. There are alternate stories, including the tale of the Morrigan being split into three. Sisters. An old woman. No story is the same, although they all carry similar themes. War. Love. Betrayal.

It's fascinating and I've neglected my work to study them.

The raven's stories are my favorites. The book is littered with little snippets of their lives. I try to connect the mythology to my housemates but it seems too fanciful. Too made up. I'm not convinced anything in the book is real, but tucked in the final pages is a spell that catches my eye and after two days of dreaming about it, seeing Xavier has made me want to believe it can be done.

Killing the Morrigan.

The concepts are tricky, it involves splitting her soul from mine and then destroying her, but with the help of the Guardians (who are skilled in the magical arts) I think it's possible. And really, it may be our only chance.

I grab the book and head for the door. The others should be assembled by now. I cross my fingers and prepare to tell them my plan.

3

DYLAN

"Absolutely not."
"No fucking way."
"I can't, Morgan. I just can't."
"Sorry, sweetheart."

Clinton does nothing more than cross his arms over his chest and shake his head once.

Morgan, who holds a book I'm not familiar with in her hands, narrows her eyes and looks...pissed?

"Morgan, there is absolutely no way we're performing magic like this with or much less *on* you," I finally say.

"Why not?"

"Why?" I take the book from her and study it for a moment. "Because I've never even seen this text before, but on first glance it looks like this magic is dark. Darker than what any of us are comfortable using. And if it doesn't work you'll be the one that's dead."

"I'd rather be dead, Dylan, than hurt someone again. Do you understand that? I won't be responsible for any more deaths!"

"He's not dead," Sam says, but Morgan shoots him a glare.

"He will be soon. We both know it. We *all* know it," she spats.

"I'm not living like this. I don't want to be a conduit for death. Not anymore."

"I don't even see how that's an option," Damien says. "Do you plan on kissing a lot of guys? Outside of this house, I mean?"

"It can happen anywhere," Morgan cries. "And don't judge me on kissing Xavier. That's the whole point. I didn't have control. She's stronger than me!"

Clinton stands and approaches Morgan, who is standing near the back windows. He touches her cheek and says, "It's too dangerous."

She sighs. "Can we at least think about it? Have it as a backup?"

Bunny walks over and peers over my shoulder, flipping the pages of the book. He runs his fingers down a long list. "The ingredients look complicated. It may take months to find them."

I snap the book shut, nearly taking off Bunny's finger. I glance at him apologetically. "It's off the table."

"Why do you get to make that decision?" Morgan asks. Her voice carries a different edge. "Did someone put you in charge here and not tell me about it?"

I open my mouth to speak but think better of it. I rest the book on the table and slide it to the middle. Morgan watches with interest and then assesses the others. They too are silent until Bunny steps forward. I fight an eyeroll. He's always first to cave.

"We can collect the ingredients," he says. "We can store them in the basement with a stipulation that we do nothing unless we all come to an agreement." He looks at Morgan as he emphasizes the word 'all'. "Like I said before, it may take a while to gather them all, if we even can."

I fight an outburst. I rest my hands on the back of an armchair, bracing myself. "Morgan already has obligations. She has her training. Her studying. Her book to write for the University—which is still a priority. She has to pick a mate. That is paramount. Every delay, each distraction is just falling into the Morrigan's hands." I hold her gaze. "Do you realize that this sort of endeavor is exactly what she wants?"

"Then she'll get it," she declares, unwavering. "I'll work with each of you to gather the supplies needed to complete the spell. I'll also use that time to get to know each of you a little better—fulfilling my promise to select a mate quickly."

After a beat, Clinton speaks up.

"I think that's acceptable." He looks at me to challenge him. But I've said my piece. I do nothing but shrug. The Queen has made it clear she doesn't want my opinion. Damien picks up the book. "I'll divide these out into our specialties. Sam, you make a schedule, okay?"

Sam nods and Morgan smiles. Everyone seems to be in agreement but me.

I leave the room first—as always—and contemplate that it's just another day at The Nead.

4

MORGAN

A schedule is set by dinner and much to Dylan's obvious dismay, lessons and training will be on hold—other than what I learn on my outings to procure the spell ingredients.

Damien and I agree to meet at ten the next morning and at quarter 'til, I'm looking for an appropriate outfit to wear to a 'magic shop' when my phone rings.

It's Professor Christensen.

I haven't spoken to him since Xavier fell ill but I have no doubt he's been in contact with Anita. Ironically, he's the one that tipped me off to the type of underground club that the guardians were performing in—the one that we were at when Xavier got caught up in the Morrigan's Darkness.

"Hello," I say, looking for my black jeans. That seems appropriate for a magic shop, right?

"Morgan! I'm so glad I caught you. Is this a good time?"

No, I want to tell him, but he's my graduate advisor and I can't do that. "I have a few minutes."

"Good, good. Well, I'm aware that you've been told of Anita's family circumstances."

"Yes, sir. I've been to see her."

"Excellent. It's always good to support a fellow student and colleague during a time of need." He coughs away from the phone. "Anita has requested a leave of absence for the remainder of the semester. Obviously we granted it. She's the only family nearby to take care of her sibling. We want to give her as much time as she needs."

"That's very considerate of you, sir." With the phone in the crook of my neck and shoulder, I tug my pants over my hips. "How should I proceed?"

"I considered giving you a new partner but really I think it may be best for you to work independently for now. Hopefully Anita can return after a short break and you can get back on track. I'd love for you to consider spending a little bit of your former critique time visiting with her."

I doubt that's what Anita wants. I got the explicit feeling she blamed me, rightly so, for Xavier's illness. But that's between the two of us, no need to involve the professor, who, frankly, is already nosy enough. "I'll do that. Thank you for taking the time out of your day to let me know all this."

"You're welcome. I'll still expect weekly updates on your progress and I'll have my secretary make an appointment for our next review."

"Sounds great." I grit my teeth and pull my boot on over my heel. "Talk to you soon!"

I hang up before he can say more.

Taking one last look in the mirror I assess my outfit. Black jeans with a tie instead of buttons or a zipper, black tank with thin straps at the shoulder. My bra criss-crosses dramatically over my back. My boots are also black leather, with thick, chunky heels. I grab my bag and head to the door, thinking how I have no idea what I'm getting into but at least I look like a badass.

Damien meets me in the foyer. He's wearing dark jeans and a tight, gray T-shirt covered with a black, leather vest. The tattoos that mark his biceps peek from under his sleeves just like the ones at his collar. The hoops in his ears glint from the chandelier. When he walks toward me his heavy boots echo off the marble floors, and he looks me up and down appraisingly.

"I see you got the memo about what to wear."

"You sent me a memo?" I blink dumbly. He raises his eyebrows and it clicks that he's joking. "Duh. Yeah, I didn't know what to wear to go to a magic shop."

"I don't think there are any formal requirements, but you nailed it anyway." He offers me his hand. "Got everything?"

"Yeah. Are we taking a cab?"

He smiles and directs me down the hallway, away from the kitchen. "No. I've got my own transportation."

The Nead is full of wonders. I know that. The historic mansion has a rooftop garden, a magnificent porch, and a lush yard. Add that to the various studios and suites we live in, the dining room with its historically accurate mural, and the vast library. There's a training room and gym in the basement as well as other doors that lead to rooms I haven't been in yet. I didn't even know the hallway Damien takes me down existed. But soon enough, we're going down a new flight of stairs and at the bottom he opens a basic door and flips on a row of lights.

The fluorescents brighten one section at a time with a loud, echoing click. The lights reveal a row of sleek vehicles. Cars and trucks shine with a glow. While I take each one in with a sense of wonder and delight, Damien passes them all and stops in front of something smaller but possibly even more powerful.

A motorcycle. The glossy, black paint gleams under the lights, showcasing the perfectly curved and understated pinstriping on the gas tank. Chrome polished to a high shine punctuates the beauty of the entire package, and it automatically makes me hear the roar of the engine in my head, feel the vibrations between my legs, and I have a sudden desire to wrap my arms around Damien's waist, hugging his back in a mixture of fear and exhilaration. It terrifies me.

My heart lunges into my throat because I have no doubt Damien wants me to get me on that thing. I stop in the middle of the garage, frozen in terror while Damien unhooks two helmets and turns to hand me one.

"What's wrong?"

"I can't get on that."

A small smile tugs at his lips. "You've never ridden one before."

"No and I don't plan on starting." I glance over my shoulder at the sports cars and luxury sedans. "Can't we take one of those?"

He takes a step closer and runs his hand through my hair. His lips are close to mine and the fear is replaced with something else entirely. "I don't like to drive. I like to fly. It's all I dream about. It's all I crave. I'd give almost anything to have my wings back." He looks down at the cycle with soulful, violet eyes. "This is the closest I get. Come experience that with me."

How can a girl say no to something like that? I'm not a dream crusher.

I nod. "But you'll be safe. Like, nothing crazy."

"Nothing crazy, I promise." He lowers the helmet over my head. He swings his leg over the bike and gestures for me to do the same right behind him. The leather seat is soft and I instinctively wrap my arms around his waist, even though we haven't moved an inch.

He clasps his hand over mine and squeezes them tight against his rock-hard abs. "You hold on, okay?"

"Yeah, no problem. Got it."

He turns and smiles at me. "Relax. You'll have more fun."

Damien secures his own helmet and I already miss his face. He grips the handlebars and in a blink the engine revs, echoing off the garage. My whole body tenses against the vibrations and I cling to his back as he eases out of the parking spot.

Like he promises, he starts slow, exiting through a sliding garage door into the back alley near his studio. The hum isn't so bad and I think I can handle this. I loosen my death grip just a little as we come to a stop near the main road.

Damien revs the engine again and shoots out into traffic. I yelp, retightening my grip. I squeeze my thighs and feel the heat between us. Fear races through my limbs, I hate being out of control and this proves it. But as much as I hate to admit it, Damien is a skilled driver, deftly moving in and out of traffic, skimming the curbs on turns. My heartbeat is drowned out by the hum of the engine, the vibrations strangely soothing my nerves. Damien's back is lean and strong. He feels at home, like he said; he's flying, not driving, and my unease slips away into something else.

Pressing the side of my helmet against his back, I close my eyes. There's nothing I can do but trust him to get us there in one piece.

When I open my eyes we're in a part of New York I've never been in before. The streets are narrow and lined with gray buildings. Apartments stack to the sky while dingy businesses squish close together on the street level. Packs of kids roam the streets wearing baggy shorts and at least two walk vicious-looking dogs in metal-studded collars. My fear of the motorcycle has shifted to something different—apprehension about where we're going. I thought I'd dressed like a badass for the magic shop. I didn't realize I needed to be a badass to just get through the door.

The bike slows and Damien directs it to the curb. The feeling of warmth from his body and impressive skills distracted me from being concerned about where we're going. He takes off his helmet and shifts to assist me with mine. When it's over my head I say quietly, "Nice neighborhood."

He looks around. "It's a bit unique."

"Are you sure this is a good idea?"

He narrows his eyes at me. "You're not usually so timid. What's going on?"

I shrug. "I just feel out of my element here."

He touches my chin. "Sometimes I forget you're more suburban girl than terrorizing ancient goddess."

"Yeah, just like I forget you're an epic warrior molded by the hand of a god."

He pecks me on the cheek and the warmth that came from the motorcycle's vibrations flares in my belly. "Come on. You're going to love Tran."

"Tran?" But he already has me by the hand and we pass a group of boys admiring the bike.

A sign hangs from the building with an arrow pointing down. The words are in Chinese so again I can do nothing but trust Damien as we take the stairs to a below-street-level shop.

The door is glass but covered in a thin layer of plastic, making it hard to see in. Damien pulls the handle, gesturing for me to go first. I step into a claustrophobic's nightmare. The shop is messy, dirty. Baskets and boxes and bins cover every inch of available space. The counter is a collection of bottles, jars, and containers. Murky items fill each one and there's a faint, fishy smell in the air that reminds me of the exotic farmers' market back home.

Chimes on the door clang as we enter and a small man pops out from the back. He moves to his spot behind the counter. I can barely see him behind the clutter but I spot the flash of a smile when he locates Damien behind me.

"D!" he shouts. "Nice surprise!"

Damien moves around me but links his fingers with mine, keeping me close. I trip over a box that squeaks in reply.

"Tran, good to see you. I'd like to you meet my friend, Morgan."

Tran looks me up and down with small, concentrating eyes. "We've met before?"

A strange chill rolls down my spine. The kind that comes with déjà vu. A tiny voice replies in my ear, "*Yes*," but I ignore it and shake my head. "I doubt it. I just moved here."

"Ah," he says, but his eyes never leave mine. "I hear the accent in your voice. Not from around here."

"The South," I confirm.

"Well, welcome." He looks at Damien. "What can I do for you today?"

"We're looking for a few items," Damien replies, pulling the list Bunny wrote out of his pocket. "Thought I'd stop here first and see what you've got."

Tran takes the list, his face blank as he goes over the ingredients we need. I know the list—I read it in my book—and even though this is my idea, the fact the man didn't flinch at the words 'dragon tears' or 'powdered ox testicle', rattles me.

The man turns away and begins rummaging around the wall of jars and tiny drawers behind the counter. He hums as he works, weighing and measuring items. Damien bends over and studies a jar full of what looks like rocks.

I take the time to look around a little myself, although I do avoid the box on the floor that squeaked at me. The shop carries a world of mysteries and a strange feeling settles in my bones. It's probably just the magic, I tell myself. I'm getting used to the feeling, the constant push-pull of various energies trying to take control. I haven't a clue what most of the items are or what they do. I pick up a dark glass orb that fits in the palm of my hand. The ball hums in my hand as I hold it up to the light. Shadows flit inside and I squint, wondering if I made it up.

"You found my WishMaker orb."

"WishMaker?" I ask, turning to find the small man right behind me.

"Yes. It's very old—Romanian. You look inside to reveal your true desires."

I stare at the glossy surface, trying to catch the shadows again. "Like a Magic 8 ball?"

Tran laughs. "A little bit. But the WishMaker, like all magic, can reveal things you never knew about yourself. Things you possibly never wanted to know. The orb knows your heart. Your truth. You can't hide from it."

"Yeah, I'm not sure if that's a good thing or not." I set the orb back on its stand and look over his head at Damien. There's a box of supplies on the counter next to him and I wonder how we're going to get that back home on the motorcycle.

"Get everything?" I ask, suddenly ready to leave.

"Most of it. We'll have to track down a few other things. Between me and Bunny, I think we can find everything." He rests his hand on the box and says to Tran. "You'll deliver this?"

"By this afternoon."

We step out of the dark shop and into the warm daylight. Feeling bold and like I need to the shake the weird feeling I got in the shop, I squeeze Damien's hand and ask, "Think we can take the long way home?"

"You want a longer ride?"

"Yeah," I say, looking up at his curious face. "I think I do."

∽

Damien takes the scenic route, giving me a tour of parts of New York I never knew existed. Bridges and side roads. Perfect views. I grow comfortable leaning against his back and revel in the intimacy of the moment rather than the fear.

The magic I felt at the shop flickers under the surface. That kind of place seems perfect to lure out the Morrigan. Ancient power is her lifesource. Touching that orb gave her a tiny taste. She wants more and there's only one real way to satiate her.

These feeling are still churning when Damien slows his bike and turns into the alley behind our house. He eases it next to the shop instead of the garage below, killing the engine.

We remove our helmets but I keep my body pressed against his. I wrap my arms around his waist and feel his muscles tighten. He hesitates, just a moment, before twisting to see my face. He's curious. He feels it. Me. All of this is written on his face.

He licks his lips and his eyes flare with heat. "You're not going to get games from me, Morgan."

"Games?" I ask, genuinely confused.

He cracks a smile. "The others? They all have their standards. Codes or morality. Personal hang-ups. I'm here to do a job. My sworn duty is to protect you, but I'm no angel, darling, not in this life or any other. If you need to blow off a little steam, I'm ready."

His words, no matter how blunt, are exactly what I need to hear. The Morrigan makes me feel dirty around the honor of these men. Her ways are wicked. She's a killer and her darkness already lashed out and took a victim. I need a man right now that will be nothing more than a release. Someone with a little dirt on his hands, and after weeks of playing guessing games with the others and losing my virginity to Clinton in a steamy night of tragic passion, I need someone to just take the energy I have to give.

"Good. Because that voodoo shop gave me the willies and riled up the Darkness."

His fingers twist in mine. "Come on. I've got just the thing."

The thing turns out to be a small room off the back of his studio. There's a bed, a small table and chairs, and it's clean. Like, immaculate.

"What's this for?" I ask, relishing the feel of the air conditioning on my hot face.

"I sleep back here sometimes. The house may be big but it still feels crowded on occasion." He unbuttons his leather vest and tosses it on the chair. "Lately it seems more so than normal."

"Because of me?" I ask.

He walks over and tugs at the straps of my tank. "The energy you carry? It's no joke. With my sensitivity, it sends me over the edge."

I'm already acquainted with Damien's body. I've tasted his mouth, his skin, and his cock. Right now though, from the way he licks his lips, I get the feeling he's ready to get a taste of me.

He doesn't mess around, and my shirt and strappy bra are on the floor before I can blink. His hands push the skintight jeans over my hips to my feet, where I have to hold on to him to get them the rest of the way off. I take him in when he pulls his own shirt over his head, revealing the carved muscles of his chest and the tattoos that I've never seen up close. Silver hoops hang from his nipples and when I touch one on impulse he shivers in reply.

I stand before him and touch the raven just above his heart and trace the ink around his biceps and onto his back. Realization dawns and I gasp. "It's our story."

The whole thing. The lovers. The battle. The ash and bone. God's hand dropping from the heavens. The hurricane, and around to the other side there's a girl with dark hair and five ravens swooping low around her.

"You carry the burden of the Darkness," he says, touching my chin. "We carry the burden of the past."

I brace myself for his kiss and when his pants drop to the floor, it's no surprise that he's already hard. It's also to my pleasure that he's bare beneath his jeans. We stand naked with one another, skin skimming skin, heightening the desire.

His hands move to my breasts, kneading the tips into hard points. His mouth falls to mine, lips warm, tongue sweet. No, Damien doesn't play games. He gets right to the point, right to my want and need. His fingers do not stray. His mouth never loses focus and within minutes I'm putty in his capable, agile hands.

He falls back on the bed and pulls me over his hips, while spreading my thighs wide. His manhood stabs eagerly at the air between us.

"Okay?" he asks because we both know it's only my second time. I nod vigorously and together we guide him to my center. He allows me to set the pace, taking him in inch by inch. When he's inside I close my eyes and exhale, the stress from the shop dissipating with each second. Damien's hands clench around my hips and with his hungry guidance I begin to move.

It's different like this, I think as I rock against him. Different than Clinton, who hovered over me like a protective blanket. In this position I feel the power surge in me, similarly to when I knelt between Dylan's legs.

Power comes in many forms. Each of my guardians helps me understand that. It's about balance and control. It's about maintaining a level of objectivity and strength. Damien's jaw clenches as I move above him, his abs flex and the ravens on his chest twitch as if in flight.

I lean over and bite his lip, smiling into his mouth. I'm going to enjoy this while I can.

5

CLINTON

Dylan arrives in the training room a few minutes before my spontaneous session with Morgan. It's a rare evening workout —and we're going on a field trip. Both ideas brought a smile to her already-pleased face at dinner. I'm in the middle of packing a small bag to take on our outing when I spot him in the doorway.

"Good evening," I say, slipping the leather gloves in the bag. Dylan watches me closely. He's aware of where we're going. "What are you doing down here? Another workout?"

"Just dropping off the ingredients Damien and Morgan picked up in the lab. The box was delivered before dinner."

"Everything there?"

"We're missing a few things. Damien and Bunny think we can locate the few we're missing."

"So you're down with the idea of the spell?"

He shakes his head. "No. I think it's risky and stupid, but Morgan is right. We don't get to tell her what to do. We assist her. If she wants to try it then what choice do we have?"

I cinch the tie on the bag and toss it over my shoulder, not believing that he's remotely okay with this for a minute. Or that he'll simply step down. But that's between him and Morgan. After watching how quickly the Darkness took over with Xavier, I know we have to do something.

"You're sure this is a good idea?" he asks, gesturing to the bag. Of course he asks. He doesn't trust the rest of us. It's not in his nature.

"She has to be tested."

"It's too soon."

I snort. "Tell that to Xavier Cross. I'm sure he won't agree."

We both know Xavier can't agree or disagree with anything. He's bed bound and dying, the life slipping out of him like sand in a sieve. I doubt he'll last the week.

I leave the gym and head up the back stairs. Morgan is waiting in the foyer. She has on tight, black, workout pants and a hoodie with NYU on the front. I expect her to start for the door but she looks toward the hallway that leads to the garage.

"You've got a car down there, don't you?"

I raise an eyebrow but nod.

"Well, let's go. May as well get this ass-kicking over with so I can come home and get in an ice bath." She walks off.

A small smile twitches at the edges of Dylan's mouth. "You didn't tell her?"

"No. Not yet."

He laughs and the sound echoes off the marble floors. "Good luck, brother."

I leave him to his humor without another word because I know he's right. When Morgan finds out where I'm taking her she just may kill me.

6

MORGAN

Clinton's preferred vehicle is a massive black pickup truck that sticks out on the streets of New York like a sore thumb. It's top of the line, with every bell and whistle offered in a custom package. The truck is a beast—just like him.

I press the buttons on the dash, adjusting the warmth of my seat. Who knew there were seat *coolers*? Not me.

"Were does all this money come from?" I ask. "You know, for the cars and weird spell ingredients and everything else."

"It comes with the house." His eyes remain on the road. They better. These narrow streets were not made for a monster like this one.

"And who pays for the house?" The question brings out a tic in his jaw and when he doesn't answer I stop pressing. For now.

I look out onto the street and I recognize a bodega and then an electronics store. So much of the city looks the same to me but when I see a kid with baggy pants and a gold tooth hanging on the corner I say, "I've been here before. Today. Are we going back to the Magic Shop?"

"No, but we are nearby." He drives past the stairway that leads to

Tran's shop and turns a corner. There he directs the car into an underground garage and parks. Opening his door, he nods at the floor and says, "Get that bag."

I'm already dressed for a workout. Athletic tights. Hoodie with a workout tank underneath. My hair is pulled back into a ponytail and I have trainers on my feet. I grab the bag off the floor and sling it around my shoulder.

On the way out of the garage Clinton finally explains. "You've made a lot of progress in our sparring sessions, but if the Darkness crosses what you'll encounter will be a totally different situation. You'll not only fight physically but mentally and against magical forces. A simple punch won't kill anyone."

"Kill?" I ask following him across the street.

"This isn't about getting the upper hand. It's about stopping the apocalypse. The Darkness will not stop—not this time. It's hungry."

On the sidewalk, I stop Clinton with my hand. He turns and looks down at me. "Aren't you afraid you're just teaching the Morrigan how to be a better fighter?"

He shakes his head. "The Morrigan already knows how to fight, sweetheart. She's the Goddess of War. This is about me teaching you how to fight back. If you're serious about separating away from her you'll need to be strong and ready."

"But who am I supposed to kill?"

"You'll know when the time comes."

I hate him for being vague but I know he doesn't care. This whole thing is crazy. Apocalypse. Goddess of War. Sometimes I'm sure I've lost my mind. That this is just another fantasy I've slipped into like my books and writing.

But the smell of the asphalt is too strong and the smarmy skin of the guy at the door is a little too memorable. And when we step into the gym there's no need to pinch myself. My imagination isn't this creative.

There's a crowd packed around the square ring in the middle—much like a boxing ring, with ropes bordering the edges. Seats are on an incline for better viewing and the stench of alcohol is strong. Curiosity licks at my brain and a strange energy pulses behind it.

"Clinton—what is this?"

"The fights."

"And we're here to watch?"

A thin line appears on his forehead. "No, you're here to fight."

I spin on my heel. No freaking way. I've barely made it three feet toward the door when I feel a huge hand wrap around my upper arm. Clinton has stopped me in my tracks. "You can't make me go out there."

"No, but it's what you need to do. Take it to the next level."

"Suicide? In front of a crowd? No thanks."

We stare at one another for a long moment. Finally he blinks. "We'll watch. Maybe you can at least absorb some of the strategy and when you gather enough courage we can come back."

That little jab goes nowhere. All I want is to get out of here. Away from the lure of magic and the blood-thirsty crowd, but I'm curious enough not to walk out the door. The magnetic pull of clashing forces drags me back.

"Two matches," I say.

"Three?"

"We'll see."

He graces me with one of those rare smiles, followed by a brief but toe-curling kiss. I follow him to a sliver of bench with a good view of the ring and the crowd around me. After a moment I lean into him and ask, "Who are all these people?"

"It's probably not a surprise to you that if gods and goddesses and ancient magic exist, then so do other supernatural beings."

I stare at him for a second. "This actually does come as a surprise."

"Really?"

"Well, yeah, I guess?" But of course that's stupid. I've seen enough in the last month to know that my grip on what's normal is flimsy at best. The raven friends I'd made and forgotten as a child were real. They're my guardians, assigned to me because I carry a smidge of the ancient Goddess of War in my soul. I narrow my eyes. "What are we talking about here?"

"Various beings. Angels, demons, demi-gods, Nephiliam...a little bit of everything."

"Angels."

He nods. "Yes."

"What's a Nephiliam?"

"Fallen angels...back in ancient times, they bred with the daughters of man and created Nephiliam. Basically, a human-angel hybrid. They're vicious warriors."

I glance around the room trying to figure out who is who, but everyone just looks like regular people, just like Clinton and I. Other than some incredibly attractive people, with striking features and intimidating physiques, I can't find identifying markers. "And you all come here to fight?"

"Sure. It's no fun to fight a human. Not fair either. It's a good way to blow off some steam." Clinton's hair falls over his ear and I reach up to tuck it back in place. A shadow falls over us and we both look up to find a woman with braided blonde hair standing before us. She wears a flirty, dangerous smile and holds out a bottle of beer in Clinton's direction.

"Brought you a drink," she says, eyes never acknowledging me. "I owed you one for last time."

I notice the way his eye brow lifts, just a little, and the way his eyes take her in. I can't be sure it's out of interest. He's a Guardian after all, his job is to assess those around me, but I'm not sure how I feel about the tone of their exchange.

"Thank you," he says taking the drink. "How have you been?"

She raises her arms over her head, flexing her muscles and lifting her ample breasts inches from his face. Good grief.

"Pretty good. I haven't seen anyone interesting sign up tonight. It will probably be pretty lame. Unless you're fighting." Her blue eyes flare. "Will I see you in the ring?"

"No," he says, taking a sip of the beer.

"No? One of your brothers?"

"Not tonight. We just came to enjoy the show."

At last her eyes skirt over me when he says 'we'. The blue is so cold I nearly feel the air shift in temperature. "Oh well, I guess you'll have to settle for cheering me on. I'm up in a bit."

"Good luck, Hildi, but I doubt you'll need it."

She smiles at the compliment and walks off.

"Uh, what was that all about?" I ask, noticing he's put the beer on the floor.

"That's Hildi. She's a Valkyrie. If she offers you a drink you take it."

"And if you don't?"

He laughs. "She's a little like you. Blessed with the power of a Goddess. She also thrives on war. And in ancient times traveled with Ravens. It gives her an affinity for me and the others, although I don't think she really knows why."

I tilt my head. "And do you have an affinity in return?"

He slips his arm around my back and pulls me close. In my ear he whispers, "It doesn't work that way and you know it. You've claimed our hearts, bodies and minds. You dictate our whims and in return we protect you from the Darkness that lurks at the edges. Don't question our loyalty."

I turn and our lips are nearly touching. I feel his breath. I see the determination in his eyes and I don't doubt him for a second. Jealousy has no place in our relationship and I understand his conviction. I lick my lips and I'd claim him for real right here and now but a bright light flashes over the ring. He brushes my nose with his, breaking the moment. "It's about to start."

I have no idea what to expect but I focus on the ring. The lights dim around us and the rowdy crowd settles—a little. A tall man strides to the middle, a spotlight glaring off his smooth, brown skin. His teeth are white, and from my seat, appear sharp.

"Welcome ladies and gentlemen! Are you ready for the Monday night free-for-all?"

"What's the free-for-all?" I ask.

"It's when anyone can throw their names in. Other nights have organized fights. Sort of like regular boxing or wrestling."

"And you thought I'd toss my name in? To fight angel-hybrid-Valkyrie warriors?"

He smiles and shrugs.

I can't even with him.

Two more spotlights click on, one zooming to opposite corners. Two men stand on each side dressed like a mixture of a MMA fighter and possibly a ninja. I have no idea what is even going on down there.

"Watch these two. You'll learn a lot. That's Diamond Dave and Rocky Boa."

"What kind of names are those?" I ask, but Clinton's eyes are glued to the scene below. I expect a little fanfare but there's nothing but the sound of a buzzer announcing the start of the fight. Both men move to the center of the ring, circling one another. I'm not sure what Damien wants me to learn and I'm about to tell him so when what happens on the stage nearly forces me to my feet.

"Oh my God," I say, rising up. Damien tugs me back down in my seat.

Black tendrils slither down one Rocky Boa's arms. It looks like smoke but I blink and realize they're snakes.

Snakes.

Dave doesn't seem remotely surprised and he flicks his wrists, revealing a series of blades. They glint in the bright light and a wicked grin appears on his mouth.

"Blades?"

"It's legal. Anything goes in there."

Dave slashes through the air, cutting off the head of one snake. In reaction, two more appear. The smile slips and he goes for Rocky's body. Clinton leans in and says, "The snakes are a protection. The more he cuts them the more they'll appear, eventually wrapping Rocky in a body of armor. Dave needs to go for throat."

"The throat?" I watch as the fighter does just that, taking a sharp swipe at the other man's neck. He misses but the snakes hiss in fear and as the snakes grow they slither along the canvas ring, growing into something larger, scarier.

"All Dave has to do is nick him and he'll go down. Those blades are dipped in poison." Sure enough. Dave goes after him again, this time tearing a hole in Rocky's shirt. The snakes circle around and around, zeroing in on Dave.

"They're going to get him," I say about Dave, covering my eyes. The sound of the snakes hissing echoes in my ears.

"Don't be so sure."

I take a peek just in time to see Dave perform a pretty fantastic acrobatic move, jumping over the snakes and using the corner post of the ring as leverage. He flips in the air, slicing so fast I can't see his movements. Snake heads roll and the smoke conjures more but Dave has Rocky on the ground with a blade against his pale neck. The snakes continue to circle but blood is drawn, spilling from Rocky's neck. The serpents offer one last hiss before fading into thin air. Rocky's body lies in a pool of blood. The crowd is on their feet, shouting in a chorus of cheers and jeers, depending on who they wanted to win.

"He's dead?" I ask, feeling sick to my stomach.

"In the real world? Yes," Clinton says. "But the ring is enchanted. Rocky will survive—other than his ego."

"The ring is enchanted?"

"Yes. Those skills? The blades and the snakes? These people can't use those powers on Earth. Somewhere else? Wherever they came from? Sure. But here? The laws don't work that way. Just like how I can't shift into a crow anymore, and how you can't infect people with the Morrigan's death. Not normally, at least." He looks down at the ring. "But down there? Like I said, anything goes."

I stare down at the body, which definitely seems to be dead.

Rocky's neck is limp and twisted. Dave struts around the ring, declaring and owning his victory. The referee (if you can call him that) ushers Dave off the stage and for a few, awkward moments Rocky's pale, graying body lies alone on the floor.

The referee returns and stands over the body. He waves his hands and a flash of shimmery light hovers over the ring. The man's mouth moves, reciting an incantation. No one around me seems to notice. They're talking and drinking and behaving the way any event-goer would during an intermission. Not me, though. I can't keep my eyes off the man on the stage—the body on the mat. The magic swirls over Rocky and enters him quickly through the mouth. A moment later the fighter's eyes pop open and he inhales a gulp of air. He fumbles for a moment but the man helps him off the ground, pats him on the back, and sends him out of the ring.

I look at Clinton and say, "That was fucking insane."

"That guy is a Shaman. He monitors the games—makes sure everyone plays fair."

"Fair?" I shake my head, feeling like I'm in an alternate reality. I mean, maybe I am. Suddenly the room feels too crowded. Too tight. I stand up, seeking air.

"You okay?"

I wrinkle my nose. "Just going to the bathroom. Be right back."

His gray eyes narrow in concern but I squeeze his hand and work my way through the people on our row, down the walkway and toward the sign pointing to the restrooms. I get to the bottom floor, turn the corner and sigh. Even the supernatural have a long line for the women's room.

I lean against the wall and wait, glancing at the woman behind me and giving her a sympathetic smile. She simply glares at me in return.

Okay then.

The crowded line moves slowly and the casual chatter of the women turns to whispers. I'm staring at my feet, wondering if I should go get a pedicure tomorrow when I hear a girl near me say, "Can you believe he showed up with her? That scrawny thing?"

"Seriously. He turned me down last week."

"Same but two months ago. I stopped trying after that."

"I've never seen him with anyone. Never. And then bam, he's got a date. He fucking kissed her when they walked in. I saw it with my own eyes."

Someone snorts. "Date? Let's call a spade a spade. That girl looks a one night stand. Like he found her down at the sorority house or something." That voice rings louder than the others.

"Did you see his last fight?"

"I saw his body. His muscles. That's not a six-pack, girl. I counted at least ten."

"He's hot but I'm sort of into the other one. The broody one," the girl behind me says. I peek over my shoulder and see a spark in her eye. "I bet he's wound up so tight. I want to be the one to loosen the spring."

"I'll admit it's hard to pick. The men in the Raven Guard are all fucking epic. I can't wait to sink my teeth into them, one-by-one."

There's an explosion of giggles and when I look up at the name "Raven Guard," the girl who said it is staring straight at me. It's Hildi with her white blonde hair braided tight around her skull. She's very tall and when she talks her hair flows down her back like a mane. Her Norse genes stand out among the other women in the line, including my own dark hair and skin. Tiny tattoos decorate the sensitive skin behind her ear and even if Clinton hadn't told me she was powerful, I would instinctively know.

"What?" I ask, because I'm slow as molasses.

"You seem interested in listening to us so why don't you just join in? Tell us what he's like."

"Who?" Okay, I'm not that dumb, but I'm also not sure where this is going. Hildi grins. She knows she's got the upper hand. I bite. "Clinton? He's just an old friend."

"An old friend?"

I step out of line to meet her. The other women fall back, watching the scene unfold. "Don't play games with me. Clinton and the others? They need a real woman to take care of them. Not a little girl like you. Someone who can handle their strength—their passion." She strides forward and places a hand casually on her hip. "Do you even know what you're playing with here?"

"I have an idea."

The same buzzer I heard before cuts through the air and her eyes flick over my head. "Clinton deserves a warrior, not a filthy human or whatever fairy hole you crawled out of. You should stick around. Watch a real woman in action. We'll see who he leaves with when this is all over."

It's a foolish threat on her part. Weak and pathetic. She's the one that has no idea what she's dealing with and laughter echoes deep in my mind.

There's one way to bring out the Morrigan. Threaten to take her man.

～

I PUSH THROUGH THE CROWD, not back to my seat like I should, but toward the ring in the middle. The next fight is in full swing and it looks like a goblin of some kind is battling a man with sleek black wings. It takes me a few minutes to find who and what I'm looking for: the Shaman. He's standing at the edge of the ring. A list of names is on the table next to him. I walk up and see Hildi's name and pick up the paper.

"I need to get added to this list," I shout, trying to be heard over the roaring crowd. The black winged angel swoops overhead and I hear the disturbing sound of crushed bones. I reach for the Shaman's robe and yank.

"Hey," I say, when he finally looks down on me. His expression is more curious than annoyed. His dark eyes take me in. Unlike Hildi, I suspect he knows exactly who I am. "I want to fight."

"The slots are full."

"Make room." I point to her name. "Against her."

He lifts an eyebrow. "You want to fight the Valkyrie?"

"I do."

The Shaman's eyes flick to the crowd, to where I know Clinton is sitting. I don't turn around. "Yeah, I'm here with him. He brought me here to fight. I'm ready and this bitch needs to be taught a lesson."

"Revenge?"

"Let's call it a lesson in making assumptions."

He nods and slashes his finger across the name of Hildi's opponent, causing it to disappear. "So who is going to fight tonight? You or the Goddess?"

I pull my hoodie over my head and the charm heats at my neck. "Probably a little bit of both."

7

MORGAN

I'm whisked to the side, only catching a glimpse of Hildi's hair as she goes to her own corner. The Morrigan whimpers deep in my chest, clawing at her irrational jealousy and need for bloodshed. If I didn't know better I'd think Clinton set this entire thing up as a test. Who will win for control in a duel to the death, me or the Morrigan?

Two handlers wait for me, tugging at my hair, twisting it into a knot. "What are you doing?" I ask, slapping at their hands.

"First time in the ring?" the woman asks. She has a gold tooth and glitter swirled over her eyes.

"Yes."

"You'll want your hair back. Close. Otherwise she'll rip it right off."

"I thought the ring was enchanted?"

She smiles, the cap glinting back. "You won't die in there but you can still come out snatched bald."

I touch my curls and nod, giving her permission to fasten it close.

The other handler checks my shoes, running his hands over the edge. "Looking for something?"

"Blades. Spikes. You can't have weapons in the ring."

"But what about the others? The snakes. Diamond Dave had those blades on his hands…"

"Magical," he says. "Those are part of him. Just you and your abilities go in the ring. Nothing else."

I eye Hildi across the ring. She's removed her jacket and beneath the tattoos covering her arms I see the lean, hard muscle. She reaches above her head and stretches. My female handler notices my interest. "She's good. Fast and strong."

"What do Valkyries do…mythologically speaking?"

"They choose which warriors will live or die in battle. The ones that die will go on to Valhalla."

I stiffen. "So wait, she can determine if I'm going to die?"

"Not today. That will be up to you and your skills."

The buzzer sounds and the lights flash.

I'm up.

It's then that I notice how big the crowd is around the ring. The lights are bright as I climb onto the canvas mat. I can't see the spectators—I only hear them—roaring like a giant beast. I look over at my opponent and note the surprise on her face. She didn't realize I'd be here.

"Since when do they allow little girls in the ring?" she asks the Shaman.

"She'll prove her worth," he says, then shrugs. "Or not."

The strange thing about this moment is that I'm not afraid. Not of Hildi. Not of the possibility of enchanted death. I take deep breaths, attempting to calm the beast rising under my skin. She wants out. She wants to play.

Most of all, she wants to feed.

I use all of my concentration to keep her at bay. I'm going to beat her. Morgan, not the Raven Queen.

Me.

The second buzzer goes off and the Shaman vanishes. It's just the two of us and it doesn't take Hildi long to make a move, springing from her spot.

My training has prepared me for this moment. The hours Clinton pushed me to my limit. I dodge her fists, her feet, her sharp elbows, and manage to land one of my own in her kidneys. She bends and I take a breath, glancing up at the seats. A shadow moves and all I feel is pain, sharp and excruciating as her fist slams against my chin.

"Dammit," I curse, feeling my teeth wiggle. I kick her in the knee and then the stomach. I duck, avoiding another punch and then I take the offensive, lunging at her waist and knocking her off her feet.

We stumble and I scramble fast, pinning her to the mat. To my surprise she doesn't fight back, instead staring at me with wide eyes. "Stronger than you look," she says, her voice sounding far away. I drag my eyes from hers but they're magnetic. I can't look away.

"You have no idea," I say, but I blink and when I open my eyes I'm on the mat alone—Hildi gone. The crowd roars, amplifying my confusion. I glance behind me and feel her fist before anything else.

I fly backwards, held in the ring only by the barriers. My feet wobble but I steady myself. I'm ready when she comes at me again. I grab her by the neck, getting her in a messy headlock. "You tricked me."

"Did I?" She laughs. "Show me what you can do—he wouldn't let you in here if you didn't have the receipts."

But that's the thing. I don't know what I can do. I can fight—hold her off. I can release the Morrigan and kill everyone in here. But what can I do? What magic do I really possess?

I flip Hildi over and again I'm in a position of dominance. I avoid her eyes and I think of the last time I was like this in a fight. What would I do if she were Clinton or Dylan or one of the others? How would I over power her?

The answer comes in a wave of hungry emotion.

I lift her by the shirt, focusing on her mouth not her eyes. She cries at my strength.

Yes, the Morrigan begs.

No, I shout back. Fucking no. I fight the desire. The want and hunger, but I succumb, pulling her face close to mine.

One kiss. Just one. Kill this bitch who came on to your man. Who talked about his body. Spoke of what and who belongs to you.

I look into her eyes hoping Hildi will do whatever it is she did before, but all I see is blatant desire in return.

Fuck.

The shimmer of silver catches my eye just to my left and I can taste her breath she's so close, so very close, but the glimmer flashes, the reflection blinding me and I blink.

"Do it." Hildi breathes into my ear but I'm looking at the mat and the object that suddenly appeared. "Do it."

I don't know what she want me to do; kiss her or kill her when both are the same. And isn't that what I'm supposed to do anyway? This is a game to the death.

But I push her back and reach for the shiny sword. The one that fits perfectly in my hand. The crowd gasps, wondering where it came from. How did it appear? And I have the very same questions but Hildi has picked herself up off the ground and charges at me full force.

I swing the blade, slicing it across her arm.

I flip it over, smashing her along the jaw with the hilt.

She falls, knees first, and the auditorium grows silent. I stand over her and step on her hand with one foot and her stomach with another.

"Remember this day," I tell her. I look up into the crowd. "The Raven Queen did not do this." I stab Hildi through the heart, her blue eyes shocked until the blue drains to a pale gray. "I did."

I leave her body on the mat and walk back to where I'd entered. The handlers are there, eyes wide and faces pale. The sword is heavy in my hand and in a quick motion I slash the ropes off the ring and they fall quickly to the floor. I step down, searching the crowd, the faces, finally feeling relief when I see his face.

"I fought her," I tell Clinton when he's pushed through the crowd.

"I know." He takes the sword from me and catches me when my feet falter. "You did good, Morgan."

His words warm my heart and my head spins. His gray eyes are the last thing I see before the world turns black.

8

DYLAN

Sam and I are in the middle of a game of chess in the library when the front door bursts open.

Davis runs past the doorway shouting, "Hurry, it's Mistress Morgan." The chess pieces fall as Sam and I both leap from our seats.

Footsteps thunder down the staircase and Damien appears, brandishing a sharp blade, but drops it when he sees Clinton carrying Morgan in his arms.

"She's okay. I promise. Just worn out." He moves to the staircase. I step in front of him and hold out my arms. He twists away like a child refusing to hand over a treasure.

"I told you it was too much. I told you it was too fucking soon."

"She's fine!" he roars and his voice echoes to the top floors. Surely Bunny has been drawn from his attic studio. Sam touches Clinton's arm and gives him a short nod. He inhales and reluctantly hands her over to me. I feel a tiny bit better with her safely in my arms, able to feel the warmth of her body and beat of her heart. She's bruised along the jaw and her pants are torn. Raw scrapes line the top of her knuckles and I push past the others to get her up the stairs.

Bunny meets us at the third floor and opens the door to her suite.

I carefully enter, making sure not to bang her head on the door frame, and lay her on the bed after Sam pulls down the linens.

She takes a deep breath the instant her head hits the pillow, followed by a small sigh. Her dark hair fans out like a halo. The bruise on her cheek only makes her look stronger—like the warrior we all know she's meant to be.

Sue appears and shoos us out of the room. She'll clean and dress her.

I look at Clinton and ask, "What the hell happened?"

He walks across the bedroom and out to the sitting room. There he finds a bottle of whiskey and takes a gulp straight out of the top. He hands it to Sam who does the same and before he speaks we've all had a drink. "I took her to the fights. I was going to enter her—match her up to someone she could easily beat. Just to test the training. But she went to the ladies' room and, fuck, I don't know what happened. Next thing she's in the queue and on the mat squaring off against Hildi."

"Hildi," I repeat, thinking of the blonde, incredibly dangerous Valkyrie.

"Oh boy," Damien mutters. "Bet that Viking was pleased to see her in the ring."

"She was jealous when she saw Morgan with me. I let it pass. Took her drink in good will. Offered her good luck in her match." He looks over at Morgan sleeping in the other room. "Somehow those two got into it."

"Morgan or the Darkness?" Sam asks. There's a difference.

"I think a little bit of both," Clinton replies. "The Morrigan was looking for a victim. I thought she was going to take her and I don't think the enchantments would have held against her kiss of death. But our girl, she held strong. Conjured up her sword and beat both Hildi and the Darkness."

Damien raises his eyebrows. "She beat the Darkness?"

"Yes."

"And conjured her weapon?" I ask. The implications are huge. It may mean that Morgan is strong enough on her own to do this. She may even be strong enough to survive the spell she's so determined to cast.

"Yes," Clinton says again. "She's weak, obviously. It took a lot out of her. But she made it off the mat in one piece and slayed the Valkyrie. The entire crowd was stunned."

"So they know she's here," Bunny asks, pointing out something we'd all been avoiding. "Everyone in the community is aware that she's alive and what that means."

"I suspect they've known for a while," I say. "Although now they'll know for sure and not everyone will want the same outcome we do."

The five of us stand over her bed, watching her sleep. Thing are going to get harder before they get better. I glance at Sam and say, "Stay with her," knowing it's likely she'll need comfort and sustenance before the night is over.

9

MORGAN

I wake swaddled in warmth but achy and filled with a hunger that burns deep in the pit of my belly. The room is dark but I know it's mine, the twinkly star lights I hung when I arrived blink over the window. I shift but the cocoon tightens and in my ear I hear, "Slow. You're injured," in Sam's soft, comforting voice.

Eyes closed, I stay in my spot, knowing he's right. The last thing I remember is killing Hildi, then Clinton's face. I feel the ache in my cheek and down my ribs. There's another sensation, the soft caress of fingers along my jaw and fussing in my hair.

I shift just a little, realizing I'm not in the clothes I left in. I feel the soft cotton of a nightgown from my drawer.

"Sue changed you." It's as though he's read my mind. "And cleaned you up." With my eyes still shut I sink into the sensation of his lips along my ear. "Is this okay?" he asks, gently wrapping an arm around my waist. We're spooning. He's the big and I'm the little and relief stretches and groans in my muscles.

"Yeah, that feels nice."

Sam. Beautiful Sam. With the strong jaw and Jolly Rancher green eyes. With the gorgeous face and kind smile. My friend. The man who has fingers that make my blood boil. Whose kisses bring me peace.

I need him now.

I want him desperately.

I'm hungry.

I'm wounded.

I need *everything* that he can give me.

"I heard you slayed a Valkyrie," he says. Some of the pain dissipates when his hands run over my skin.

"She made me mad."

He laughs. "I bet."

"And the Morrigan?" he asks.

"I told her to fuck off." I push my backside closer to him and he snuggles in just the same. I feel the hard length pressing against my back and my belly screams with need.

He lifts my hair and peppers hot kisses along my neck. Each one sends a flare of energy through my body. I'm learning every day the connection between my health, magic, and sex. If I want to be strong I need to be with my Guardians. Right now I need to heal and I'm quite certain he's aware of my condition.

His hands bunch the nightgown around my waist and his fingers wander down my stomach and between my legs. I reach behind me, feeling for him, and it's not difficult to find his enlarged cock. He's clothed and I fumble for the buttons, wanting his skin next to mine.

"I need you to get undressed," I tell him. "And get back in the bed."

"Yes, ma'am." There's a hint of amusement plus desire in his murmured reply.

He vanishes for a moment, slipping off his clothes. The bed cools behind me but when he returns I'm rewarded with the heat and impact of his body. Sam doesn't wait and I don't want him to. He eases me on my side, pushing my top leg over just a bit.

"This is...this position is new," I confess.

He pauses. "Too much? Would you rather?"

But the spot between my legs is already wet and I crave the feel of him inside me. I lay my hand over his and encourage him. Without pause he enters me slowly from behind.

"Oh," I cry, not only from the sensation of our bodies joining, but from the surge of energy flowing through my limbs. The bruises numb and my ribs cool while everything else is centered on Sam taking a tentative rock.

"I won't break, you know."

I feel his smile against my neck. And he pushes in before pulling out. I sink into the motion. Again and again and again.

He moves in quick, even thrusts, perfectly timed, and one hand holds my ass while the other is looped under my body, kneading my breast. The spot between my legs aches and I move my own fingers down to relieve the pressure.

To my surprise he slows dramatically. His kisses, his hips, slowly moving in and out. I pant from desire wanting more, faster, but with every excruciatingly, intense thrust my muscles turn to jelly. He feels so good. It feels so good, I bite my bottom lip and let him lead.

I'm drifting into the all-consuming sensation when I hear him whisper in my ear, "I've spent my life waiting for this moment. To share such intimacy with a goddess of such strength." In and out. In and out. "I'll never leave your side, Morgan. Not in a fight. Not on the battlefield. Not in your bed when you need my touch to heal."

I cry out, because of his words and because I'm not sure how much longer I can hold on.

His mouth is on my neck and I turn to meet his lips with mine and it provides the greatest twist of pleasure below. "Harder," I command, barely able to stand it. He grins and bites my lip, gladly picking up the pace, moving with increased speed. I no longer feel the pain from the fight, just him. Just his hands. His cock. The magical warmth of healing.

His hands dip between my legs and our bodies are melded into one. His breath coats my neck and the little grunts coming from his chest sound feral and wild. I've stopped listening, only feeling, only aware of my body aching in a different way. The coil deep in my core twists and twists, my legs lose their ability to stay apart, I scream when I finally come, a long, satisfying groan. Sam shudders behind me and his teeth clamp into my shoulder. I feel every twitch, every pulse, and we slump together in a mass of worn-out exhaustion.

Moments pass and the haze clears. I hear Sam's breathing even out and I slip from his arms. Walking to the bathroom, I flick on the light over the mirror. My hair is wild, my eyes bright. In a quick movement I pull the nightgown over my head and stare at my reflection. The injuries fade—healing with passion and shared energy.

I've learned much tonight about my body and its abilities. Things I hope will be of use in the future. But one thing I know for sure, I think as I slip back in bed. Once a night may not be enough.

10

SAM

I've got a mouthful of eggs when Bunny walks into the kitchen the following morning. He grabs a cup of coffee with his good hand and sits across from me at the table.

"She doing okay?" he asks.

I nod and grunt, swallowing the food. I'd woken up an hour before, with an empty stomach, a raging hard-on, and Morgan snuggled against my side. She looked a thousand times better than the night before and I didn't want to wake her so I showered, rubbed one off, and came down to eat.

"She just needed to rest and to heal."

He arches his brow on the word 'heal'. "So she took to the healing?"

"Like a champ." Again his expression is more annoyed than anything else. I sigh and rub my chin. "What do you want me to say, Bunny? That we fucked and she healed and then we fucked again because we wanted to?" Because that's exactly what happened. An hour or so after we'd made love the first time she woke me up to do it again. No healing wounds. No magic. Just sex. It was nice and felt more like bonding than I could have imagined.

"I'm just curious about the process, that's all. If her runes are still protecting her. If she's really holding the Darkness back."

"You don't think she is?" I ask.

"I think the Morrigan is a tricky bitch and we all need to be careful."

I stand and walk over to get more coffee. I mix in cream and it turns the perfect shade of brown. Leaning against the counter I take a sip and say, "I'm not letting my guard down."

"No?"

I sense something. A twinge of jealousy or misplaced anger. I understand what it's like to listen and feel Morgan being intimate with the other guardians while you have to wait your turn. I get that. That was me until hours ago, but patience is key and Bunny knows this. I'm not going to give him that speech.

"We're going out today," I say, changing the subject. "I'm taking her to the park where I saw the anomaly the other day while on a shoot."

"What do you think it is?"

"Maybe an opening," I say. "I want to see if she has a reaction to it."

He nods and reaches into his pocket and pulls out a scrap of paper. "Will you swing by and pick this up? It's for the spell."

The paper has an address not far from Times Square. "Yeah, we can stop there."

He smiles, the tense expression from earlier gone. "Thanks. I think we're pretty close to getting all of the ingredients."

"And then we'll try it?" I'm hesitant. The book and magic are strange and carry a hint of darkness. It's risky but I'm not here to assert my opinions. It's Morgan's choice. I do know that not everyone agrees with that position.

"I think we should." That's all he says because we both know who the hold out will be: Dylan. Even if he's stepped aside now, he'll fight her about it in the end.

I'd be willing to pay for seats to that showdown.

11

MORGAN

"It's nice to get out of the house." I follow Sam down a winding path. We walked out the front door, across the road and entered the park. "I miss trees, you know? We had so many back home."

"I remember." He grins. "I miss them too."

I think about that. "Do you miss being a raven? Damien said that's why he rides a motorcycle—for the sensation."

"We've had many forms, but I think I like this one the best." He squeezes my hand and I get a little flutter in my belly. Last night with him was amazing. Sex is one level of intimacy but the way he healed me...now that I know angels are real, I think Sam may be part one. My cheeks burn thinking about it and I can't help but watch the way he moves.

He glances over, linking his thumb in the camera strap over his shoulder. "What?"

"You." I watch a flock of pigeons fly overhead. "That was unexpected last night."

"Which part?"

"All of it. You, the healing. The way you felt..." I swallow, "inside me. Can everyone do that? The healing part?"

He nods and it's not nearly as awkward as it should be to discuss my increasing sex life with his co-guardians. "It's just like how we absorb the Darkness. We're here to serve you."

We reach a bend in a wooded section of the park. Sam steps off the path and guides me to follow. We leave the bright sun behind for the shady trees. "What are we looking for again?"

"There's a clearing on the other side. This is a shortcut. I wanted you to get a good view."

"A good view of a possible gate?" Goosebumps rise on my arms and down my neck at the idea. I don't like it.

"There's something over here. I saw it the other day. Here, look."

He stops and holds up his camera. Photos flip by as he presses the button. He slows and I see a series of shots that look similar to the area we're in. He stops on one in particular and hands it over. I peer down at the image.

It's a simple patch of grass, and picnickers are spread here and there. A few children and a dog are in the scene. In the back corner though I see a slight variation. It looks almost like a smudge but when I run my finger over the screen it's still there.

"You think that's it?"

"I can't see it with my bare eye. Just the camera. I thought you may have a different reaction."

I step over a large branch. "Why me?"

"If the Darkness is really on the other side of that thing it's going to want to check you out."

I freeze. "You want me to bring out the Darkness?"

"No." He frowns. "Well...we've got to get a step ahead of this, Morgan."

"So is this just another test, like Clinton taking me to that fight last night?" I don't want to be a pawn. Not like this. Not by these men.

Sam must sense my shift in attitude. He reaches out and touches my cheek. I jerk back, not wanting to be consoled. "Hey," he says, reaching for me. I pull away again but he fights back, wrapping his hands around my waist. "These aren't tests. They're reality. Are we going about them in a systematic way? Yes, because look what happened when you stumbled upon it on your own?"

"Xavier."

"Right, Xavier. So, call it what you want, but I'm just here to check something out and have you help me. Sounds like a partnership to me."

He releases me and walks off, hurt that I'd been suspicious. The farther he goes the more embarrassed I am at thinking badly of him and his motives. I give myself a moment to shake off the attitude but when I look up he's gone. I start moving through the woods going in the direction I thought he'd taken. I step to the right and a voice in my head whispers, *wrong way*.

I know the voice. It's the voice that urged me to kiss Xavier. The one that taunted me in the fight with Hildi. It's the Morrigan, and fear ripples down my limbs.

"Sam!" I call, picking up my pace and chasing him down. As much as I want to ignore her I follow her directions, pretty sure he's going to the place she wants me to be. I catch up to him at the edge of the field. He's still in the shade when I reach him but I'm nearly struck down when I feel the blast of cold air blow through the clearing.

"Did you feel that?" I ask, running my hands up and down my arms. It's still late summer. It's hot out and everyone in the area is wearing shorts and T-shirts, including me and Sam. But that's not what I feel and I shiver when another gale rips through the trees.

"No, what?"

"The cold air? The breeze? It feels like the arctic out here."

His green eyes widen and he pulls out his camera, the shutter clicking even before he's got it pointed in the right direction. I scan the field and I realize quickly I don't need his filter to show me the gate. It's clearly visible to me in the middle of the field. Dark and shimmery. Part this world and part another.

I open my mouth to speak but nothing comes out. My feet move, stepping from the woods and in the direction of the gate. The click of the camera fades, the voices of the children playing disappear. The grass crunches beneath my feet, brittle from the cold. I ignore the burning sensation of the charm around my neck and the ring on my finger.

Step inside little sister, she coaxes. *See what the Otherside has to offer.*

I do take a step forward. Not intentional but more like my feet are being pulled like magnets. There's no hesitation, just a strong, insistent pull. I don't fight it. I can't.

Do I want to?

The air grows colder, harsher. My eyelashes freeze. The sky is the color of coal and smells like dry, charred ash. I feel the grit on my skin, taste it on my tongue. But then, the strangest thing happens. I feel warm under my skin. A deep energy that crackles with the twitch of my muscles.

Welcome home, the voice says.

I blink and gray slithers beneath my feet, heading out the gate and into my world. The worlds battle, a hazy fight over space. A weight tugs at my hand and I lift my arm and see the glint of my sword. Leather creaks and I look down to see my outfit has changed. I'm in warrior dress. Sleek leather skirt and leggings. Bone-crushing boots. The sword hums in my hand and the incessant voice murmurs in my ear, "*That sword belongs to you, Morgan. To this world. It's the weapon for a warrior—a goddess. It was created to take the life of your enemies. It pierced the heart of Cu, after he ripped yours out of your chest. Still beating. Still bloody. Still loving. Do you really trust these Guardians with their weak magic and secretive ways? Their tricks and seduction. Are they any different than Cu? Will they allow your righteous place when the gate falters? Will you lead them in battle or will you fight against them?*"

"Shut up."

"*What makes you think they're any better? That they won't betray you? Use them to gain your strength, to further your knowledge, and then fight with me. Unleash the rage deep in your soul. My soul. Together we can conquer your world as well as this one."*

I stare out into the desolate landscape and notice a dark spot on the horizon. I wave my sword and the sky clears, still a slate gray but less sand and wind. I take another step forward and squint. Unless I'm imaging it, imaging all of it, there's a castle in the distance.

"Morgan!" a voice cries in my ear. Feeling an intense pull, I take another step, wanting to see the castle. In a blink I realize the lure isn't the gate. No, it's the castle.

"Morgan!"

I'm jerked physically, but dig the heels of my boots into the dusty ground. I swing an elbow behind me, at the hands tugging me away. Away from this world. Away from my destiny. The sword glints and I clench my hand around the hilt.

Kill them.

"You don't own me!" I shout, raising it over my head in a lethal swing. The blade slices between the worlds, the sunlight offering a blinding reflection before it comes back to me in the gray of the Otherside. The hands reappear, four of them, and I use my feet as well as my hands. Into the cold air I shout, "No!" only wanting to get to that castle. Only wanting to get home.

My feet are swiped beneath me and I land hard on my back. The sword falls when my elbow strikes the hard, frozen ground. I struggle. I scream. Words of anger and rage passing over my lips. And when the air turns from bitter cold to scorching heat I'm sure the world has ended.

My world has ended.

Two hands hold me by the thighs and other by the shoulder. I squint into the too-bright light. "How dare you," I breathe, but the words sound foreign and the faces that appear belong to the men sent by the gods to protect me.

Sam and Dylan.

Their muscles strain and I realize I'm still fighting. Who? I don't know. Why? I haven't the faintest, other than it's important. Very important.

"Morgan!" Dylan shouts, his voice carrying an edge I've never heard before. I clench my jaw and swallow back the pain, the voice inside.

Another set of hands touches my face. Glasses and copper hair. "Morgan? You with us?"

His thumb, dipped in something slippery and wet, makes a mark on my forehead. The mark burns, so hot I start screaming, then a hand covers my mouth and I see rather than hear Bunny say, "I'm sorry," before the pain is too much and I pass out.

12

DYLAN

"Hurry," Bunny says, kicking the door open. We're at the entrance of my suite and the plan is to get Morgan in a contained space.

I turn and say to him and Sam, "I've got this."

Sam frowns. Bunny looks outright distressed. He glances at Morgan, who is not exactly passed out. More like in a trance.

"Are you sure?" he asks, pushing his glasses up his nose. "I can wake her up."

"I want to talk to her."

Not Morgan. *The* Morrigan. We need to have some words.

"Put her in that chair," he says. "Sam, find some ties. She'll have to be restrained."

I start to argue that, but Bunny cuts me a non-negotiable look. I sigh and say, "There's rope in that top drawer."

I place Morgan in the armchair as gently as possible. Sam disappears into the entry and I hear him opening and closing drawers, before slamming one and reappearing. I take the ties and nod to them both.

"I'm good. Thank you."

"Are you sure?" Bunny asks again.

"Yes. I'll call you if I need you."

He slips me a small pot. Inside is the mixture he used to activate the trance and subdue her at the park. Morgan is 'wired' with an intricate security system through the runes Bunny painted on her body. They're meant to keep her and everyone else safe. "Use it if you need to. It won't hurt her."

I rest the container on the table. "I will."

The Guardians leave and I hear the door latch behind them. I quickly bind her wrists to the chair, making an effort to keep them tight but not painful. I need the Morrigan to appear. I need to see her strength. I touch her chin and lift it upwards, placing a gentle kiss to her pink lips. Energy flows between us and I pull away quickly. It's enough to wake her and she licks her lips, eyes fluttering. I wait to see who will appear. The wicked smile that greets me clues me in.

"Your Highness," I say, bowing before her. The act makes me feel dirty.

"The Sentinel." She looks me up and down. No, she's not at full strength. If so, she would have ripped my throat out in greeting. "Where are the others."

"I wanted some time with you alone."

"Did you now?" She laughs. It's Morgan's face, her voice, but her eyes are cold and dark. She's in there but somewhere deep beneath the surface. "Why? To kill me?"

"Why would I kill you?" I ask standing with my hands behind my back. "I'm your guard. As I have been for a millennium."

"You're a man." She slinks back in her chair, crossing her legs. She makes no notice of the binds. "It's in your nature to betray. You have an attention span of a gnat. Once something more interesting comes along, you'll walk."

"Just because one man betrayed you, Your Highness, does not mean we all have such nefarious desires."

Her eyes narrow. She's gorgeous, of course. And the look of evil doesn't take away from her beauty. Her lips are pouty and red, her cheeks flushed with anger. The curve of her breasts is always alluring and I know if I took her right now I could banish the Morrigan back to her tiny corner of Morgan's soul.

But my job isn't to fuck the devil. It's to protect the angel that houses her. We'll consummate this relationship when she's ready. Today is not that day.

"Why have you summoned me?" she finally states more than asks. The mark on her forehead shimmers.

"That little stunt you pulled today? That can't happen again. Our job is not only to protect Morgan, it's to protect this realm. You're not going to start the apocalypse here—not again."

"That wasn't a stunt. I was simply showing the girl her home. Where she's from." She flexes her hands. "She has a right to know her history. Is that so wrong?"

Her eyes twinkle with amusement, as though I'm nothing but a speck. I keep my emotions close but make my intentions clear. "We'll kill her before we allow your evil to spread. One victim is enough. It will stop at two."

"Then why not just do it? Just take me out right now?" She looks me up and down. "You can't, can you? Not before you've had your taste." Now she laughs and a cold edge rolls down my back. "Men. So typical, always thinking with your cock. Why do you think it's taking her so long to pick a mate? Why do you think she's prolonging this entire affair?"

"She's making a conscientious decision. It's a mate. Forever."

"She's playing you for a fool." She sighs. "You learn nothing. Nothing! But whatever, dear Guardian, let the girl have her fun while she pussy whips you all into submission. All the better for me."

"Shut up."

Her eyebrow arches and her she licks her lip. "Why do you think she's holding out on you in particular, dear?"

"I'm not the only one."

"You mean the cripple?" She snorts. "She's only kind to him out of guilt. She doesn't need his power—too weak. My minion took care of him years ago. You? She just likes toying with you. You'll never truly get a taste of her. She knows what you are—what you've always been."

A rush of anger boils over me and I reach for her throat. My hand clasps around the thin column of flesh and I say, "You won't divide us. Together we are strong. We're here to expel you and the misery that you bring to this place." Her eyes bulge and I detect a hint of fear. I reach for the blade strapped to my leg and hold it against her temple.

The door bursts open and both Sam and Bunny run down the hall. Each take a side but I step back and drop the blade. Bunny takes the pot from my pocket and rubs the mark, making it shine in a fresh coat of gold. Morgan blinks, recognition flaring for just a moment before she slips off to sleep again.

"Fucking bitch," I grumble, kicking a chair and toppling it to the side.

"She's evil, Dylan. It's what she does. She plays mind games and tricks people. She gets in your head, causes doubt," Sam says, picking up the chair.

I glance at Bunny and see the pain in his eyes. He heard her. He heard her and no matter how quickly he looks away, I know he believes what she said. I want to say something but no words come out. Storming out of the room, I can't help but think that I may believe the Morrigan too.

13

MORGAN

I wake, slumped in a chair with my hands bound to the arms with black leather ties. My neck aches from being at an awkward angle and I stretch, feeling the burn in my muscles.

"Feeling better?" Dylan asks. He's sitting in a chair directly across from mine. His eyes are narrow and wary.

"I guess." I jerk my wrists. "What's this about?"

"She took over. Fully."

"Who?" I ask, but I know the answer. I still feel the Morrigan lingering in my veins. I wrinkle my nose. "Was it bad?"

"You fought us at the park. It took three of us to bring you in and Bunny knocking you out with a spell."

I search my memory. It's hazy at best. I remember Sam and the park. Getting angry with him and then chasing after him. I remember the gate—it was there—it's real, but beyond that I recall nothing but the sensation of cold air and the sound of the Morrigan in my head. I tell this to Dylan and the crease on his forehead only deepens.

"So I fought you?" Oh boy. One of them I could take. But three? That seems foolish even for the Morrigan. "How did I do?"

"Bunny has a black eye. Sam sprained his wrist."

Ouch. "And you?"

"I nearly throttled you."

That one hits home and wariness creeps up my back. "Why, exactly?"

"Because the Morrigan has a mouth on her and it was the only way to get her to shut the fuck up."

Ah, right. I take a deep breath. "So what do we do about this?" I pray he doesn't say that I need to be tied up from now on.

"Two things. You need to pick a mate. Seal that up and gain the strength that comes with it." He flexes his wrists. "Then, you were right, we need to do the spell. Split you into the three parts of the Morrigan."

"I'm not ready," I say. "I can't choose a mate yet."

"You have to."

"It's too fast. What if I choose wrong? What if this is just another test I'm going to fail. Like the one in the park or the fight with the Valkyrie?"

He frowns and leans forward. The shadows of the room make his cheekbones look sharper than normal. "Those weren't tests, Morgan. This is all real. Do you understand that? It's real. This is our world. Where magic prevails. Where battles and death are around every corner. Where destiny dictates our future. You don't get to change those rules. You may have a goddess in your soul but that doesn't mean she can override what must be done."

He rises and crosses the room, stopping before me. He carefully removes the binds from my wrists and I rub the sore skin. I stand beneath his towering frame and he thumbs the column of my neck. A jolt of electricity shocks my system. "I hurt you. I'm sorry."

"Sounds like I had it coming."

"You?" he grimaces. "No. I let her get to me. I always do."

I tilt my head at that comment, thinking. "You remember her from before?"

"Vividly."

I consider this. I consider what that means and how shaken he seems to be. How controlling he has been during this entire situation. Fighting me on every step. Is he fighting me or the Morrigan? Or both.

He's using you.

The voice is crystal clear.

No. I reply. That's wrong, I'm using them. They give me the strength to fight back. Fight you.

Is that really any better? I hear the genuine curiosity in her question.

"Morgan?" Dylan asks, lifting my chin. His eyes are so blue, like deep pools and I'm struck with instant clarity.

"I'll pick a mate. Once that is...accomplished I should be at full strength."

He hesitates slightly before asking, "When do you plan on making this decision?"

"I'll decide by tomorrow night."

"Do you really think we have more time than that?" I can still feel the chill from the Otherside. I also sense something larger. Looming. A power I can't help but fear and desire at the same time.

"Not much. I think we should have the spell ready by tomorrow," I say. "If you'll let the others know, I'll go back through the book and find out if there's anything else I need to do to prepare."

I move past him but he grips my waist. "You know this could go badly. It's complicated magic."

"I don't think we have any other choice, do you?"

He leans down and kisses me. It's fiery hot and I feel it deep inside where my soul meets my spirit. His mouth is perfect, his tongue titillating, and the shadowy Darkness lingering at the edges recedes with every push and pull. There's something else and when a knock at the door interrupts us and we separate, I see it in his expression, the same way I felt it in the kiss.

Desperation.

Loss.

Dylan walks away to open the door and I know one thing for

sure. He thinks that's the last time he'll get to do that. I fear deep down that he may be right.

∼

I STAND in the lobby of the apartment building and wait for the elevator to arrive. The doorman let me in, my name on a list of approved visitors. I'm not sure if it was added from before, when Anita and I were critique partners, or today. Today seems unlikely as Xavier just died and why would his sister be thinking about names and visitors and such.

I press my damp hands against my skirt and try to quell my nerves.

Xavier is dead.

I killed him.

He's dead.

The Morrigan slipped. I slipped.

"Excuse me," I hear a familiar voice. My stomach turns from nervous to something more unpleasant. "Ah, Morgan. I see you got my message."

"Good evening, Professor Christensen." I offer a polite smile. I haven't seen him face to face since he'd made me angry in his office a few weeks before. "I was devastated to hear the news. I barely knew Xavier but he seemed like a nice person."

The words taste bitter coming off my tongue. I really am no better than the Morrigan. I lie and betray. She's becoming part of me and I hate it. I stare at the elevator door as we rise to the top floor, the penthouse, and pray I get through the next few moments.

"How is your writing coming along?" the professor asks.

I glance over at his expectant expression. "Honestly, I haven't gotten much done."

"Oh." The disappointment is clear. "I hope you don't find yourself off deadline."

"It will be fine. Just a little stress right now." I look down the hallway as the doors slide open.

"Too much distraction at home?"

"No," I snap. "With all due respect, Dr. Christensen, why are you so worried about my living situation?"

He pauses outside the large, wooden, front door. "I worry about all of my students. You've won a coveted spot in our program. It's my obligation to the university to make sure it doesn't go to waste."

"So you keep track of the others the same way? Ask the male students about their roommates? Fish around for personal information?" I feel on the edge of a breakdown. I rub my eyes. "This isn't the right place. If you have concerns about my progress I can make an appointment at your office."

I press the buzzer. Before it opens I feel warm breath on my ear. "You should know from your *story* that not everything is as it seems. Our friends are not always our allies and our allies are not always our friends. Be careful where you tread."

The door opens before I can reply but I spare a glance back at Christensen who is staring at the person greeting us, as though he didn't just make a threat. I'm ushered quickly into the apartment and separated from the professor into a mingling crowd of mourners. Anita sits in the middle, red-eyed and pale. The guilt, along with every other emotion from the day, overwhelms me and I spin on my heel. I look for a room, any room, where I can take a breath.

The hallway is crowded. The kitchen packed. There's a door off the hallway and I slip into it. I find myself in a small office or study. What I do see is a small array of liquor bottles on top of a cabinet and quickly pour myself a drink.

"Get your shit together, Morgan," I mutter, taking a gulp of the fiery amber.

My nerves settle just a bit and I'm fully aware of my problem. It's been over twenty-four hours and a major altercation since I've last been intimate with one of the guardians. I'm in a weakened state. My mind is a mess thinking about which man to choose for a mate. Tomorrow.

I take another gulp.

Something else is bothering me. It's more of a feeling than a fact. Something happened when I went in that portal—and it wasn't all bad. I have a flicker of interest—that same sense of intrigue that I write about in my book. There's a draw to the Darkness and I'm not convinced it's just the Morrigan pulling me. I think it may be *me* pushing me.

The thought is chilling.

And exciting.

A photograph across the room catches my eye. I walk around the massive desk and pick up the frame. It's of Xaiver and Anita. Probably around high school graduation, with their arms wrapped around one another. They look like fair-skinned porcelain dolls.

On the shelf next to the photo I spot a small box. It's made of dark, carved wood, the edges smoothed with age. The carving matches the one on my necklace and an eerie chill creeps up my neck. Curiosity gets the best of me and I open the box. To my surprise I recognize the contents. With two fingers I pluck the shiny ball out of the case. A shadow flits across the orb.

It's a WishMaker.

What had Tran said? It shows you your truest desires. I peer into the ball and make out the faintest of figures. It could be my imagination but I think they're waving at me.

A noise breaks my concentration and I slip the orb into my pocket. I flip the lid on the box and spin, realizing I'm no longer alone in the room. Anita stands with her back pressed to the door.

"What are you doing in my father's office?" she asks in a quiet, accusatory voice.

"I just needed some air. I apologize if I shouldn't be in here." Something in her attitude shifts and her eyes narrow. Blame. Anger. "I wanted to tell you how sorry I am about Xavier. I really liked him. It's impossible to understand what happened. It was so fast."

"Wasn't it though?" she replies. Her voice is shaky. "He was fine when he walked out of the club that night."

"I thought so too."

"But when he came back he was angry. Embarrassed a little. The cellist from the concert approached him." She tilts her head. "Do you know him?"

"Yes. He's one of my roommates. I had no idea he was playing that night."

She walks around the room and picks up the photo of her and her brother. The one next to the wooden box. The orb feels like a ten pound weight against my leg. "We were best friends, you know. We did almost everything together until he went to business school and I started writing more seriously."

"I'm so sorry, Anita."

She flashes me a sympathetic grin. "Don't be sorry for me, Morgan. We've always known we would be the conduit. The beginning. Remember, the prince always dies right after the gate is open."

"The prince?" My blood runs cold. "What are you talking about?"

She steps forward and there's an instant warring in my mind and body. Alluring. That's the word that continues to pop in my mind. Anita is alluring....just like, "The cat."

"Yes?"

"You took me there on purpose. You just led the way, to the club, to your brother. You knew Clinton's music would ignite something in me." The ramifications rock me. "He was a sacrifice."

"There always has to be a first one. And it's always Xavier." She bares her teeth. "Always."

Anita reaches for me, grabbing my top. She's strong, more than I would have suspected, and my back is pressed against the wall. Weakened from the events that led to this moment, my attempts to fight back are lame and useless. I've no idea what she's doing or how to get out of her grip, and when her mouth crashes to mine I'm stunned. I'm confused. But most of all the Darkness rears up and I'm only one thing. Hungry.

Her lips are hot against mine. Softer than any other I've ever felt. Her hands grip around my waist and through the haze of desire, I realize she's not just kissing me—she's feeding—much like I do with the Guardians. Much like I did with Xavier.

I struggle to get away, biting down on her lip with my teeth. She hisses and I've drawn blood. I taste it on my tongue.

"You don't get to do that," I tell her, spitting on the floor.

"Don't I?" she laughs. Oh god, she laughs. Long and hard, bent over and hysterical. "You're nothing but a fool. A stupid, stupid fool that thinks she can fight fate and overpower a goddess. You're a vessel, Morgan. A vessel. Nothing more." She rests her hands on her hips. "It's too late. The process has begun. There's nothing you and your little minions can do to stop it. Dark will prevail and soon you'll really have to decide which team you really want to be on."

"I'll never be on the side of evil." But I'm hungry. So very hungry, and I know I need to get out of here before things get worse.

I push past her and she doesn't try to stop me. Leaving the apartment is a blur but soon I'm down on the hot, busy street. I feel the shadow of wings pass over my head and the ache of loneliness in my chest.

The Morrigan is winning and there's no doubt that I've allowed it to happen.

14

MORGAN

I make it home and to my suite without notice—or at least anyone stopping me. The Guardians, Dylan in particular, always seem to know my coming-and-goings. As much as I know that I need their support right now, I also need a minute alone. Just a second to breathe and get my head on straight because I expect a call at any moment. The battle is looming, there's no getting away from it, which means it's time for me to make my choice. Pick my mate. Gain the strength that I need and perform the spell.

That's it.

There's just one problem.

I still have no fucking clue who to choose.

I walk into the room and notice the heavy weight of the orb in my pocket.

The WishMaker.

I pull out the crystal ball and hold it in my hand. It's cool against my skin and the shadows that make it seem alive flicker back and forth. If there's anything I need right now, it's clarity. But I've never used something like this, I don't possess the ability to perform magic, and the longer I sit with it in my hand the dumber I feel.

"*Like a Magic 8 ball?*" I'd asked Tran in the magic shop.

I lay in the center of my bed, knees bent. My head is balanced on two fluffy pillows and I hold the orb up to the light. Feeling like an idiot, in the most reasonable voice I can find, I ask, "Who should I pick for my mate?"

Knowing no clever words or phrases will appear, I shake the ball anyway. The dark mist inside swirls around but nothing happens. Not even the figure I think I saw earlier appears.

"Too good to be true. Thanks, Tran," I mutter, resting the orb on my bedside table. Like I was going to get out of making this decision on my own.

My phone chimes. Ten minutes to dinner and for a brief second I consider backing out. Just claiming I'm too tired from everything going on, surely they'll give me a break? But a tug in my lower belly tells me I want to see my Guardians, that perhaps I *need* to see them.

∼

THE FIRST SIGN something is weird is that Sam doesn't come to escort me to dinner me like he normally does. The second is that the dining room is empty. No food, no Sue or Davis, and no Guardians.

I'm one second from panic when I hear laughter a few doors down. I'm in the odd hallway toward the garage—away from the kitchens and library—and I stop before a door I've never entered.

I hear Clinton's booming voice and turn the knob. What lies before me is instantly intriguing. The room is magnificent; wood-paneled walls, gorgeous leather chairs, and soft-looking couches provide an intimate setting. A massive, roaring fireplace is on the far side of the room, but it isn't hot and I suspect there's magic at play. In fact, the more I look around the room, the more I get the sense I'm one step out of reality.

"Morgan," Sam says with a breathtaking smile. He steps forward and links his fingers with mine. "We've been waiting for you."

"What happened to dinner?" I ask, taking in the men. They're dressed in their nicest clothes, looking dashing and handsome, so much so they are a little hard to look at.

My friend and lover stares back at me with smoldering green eyes. "Uh, well," he looks at the others. "It seemed like we could all use a break from formality tonight."

It's an odd statement since they all look so nice and I certainly didn't get the memo to dress up. I'm wearing the same dress I'd had on earlier that day at the visitation. It's not unflattering but even so, the way each man looks at me appraisingly causes the strangest sensation in my belly.

They want me.

All of them.

Now.

I'd had the thought once—the fever dream on the bus—and even in my imagination the experience was overwhelming. Five sets of hands. Their lips, mouths, and cocks. I feel my cheeks heat at the idea. Everything else in my body sets on edge.

Damien walks over and offers me a drink. I take it and swallow the liquid fast. There's a feel of expectation in the room mingled with anticipation, but as usual, I'm in control. I know this. I love this. It only heightens my arousal.

I look around the room, taking in each of my Guardians.

Sam with his perfect face and insight.

Clinton with his solid strength.

Damien, independent and bold.

Bunny with his charm and amazing skills.

Dylan, intelligent and reserved. A silent ally.

I've been with each of them, one way or the other—Clinton, who ushered me into womanhood. Sam, most intimately due to our bond of friendship and his healing my wounds. Damien showed me sex can be fun and exciting. I set my eyes on the other two. Although I've yet to consummate my relationships fully with Dylan and Bunny, that doesn't lessen what I know and feel about them. They've touched my soul.

But tonight is about something different. I feel it in the air. I feel it in my bones. I have to choose, and what we experience in this room will last with us forever. It will help me make my decision.

I turn and shut the door behind me and then face the men of my past and future.

"It's all led up to this, hasn't it?" I ask the room.

They each nod their approval in their own way.

"Then let's do this." I take a deep breath. "This is about souls. About mating. Not just about sex. That's off the table for tonight, understand?"

They all offer agreement, although some more reluctantly than others.

"I want to taste you. Feel you," I explain. "Let me touch you, if that's all right?"

I sound brave but I have no idea where to start. How do I do this? I was a virgin weeks ago and now I'm ready for a semi-orgy? My hands shake and I settle them against my side. Sam, always my Sam, senses my hesitation and wraps his arms around my waist. He pulls me close and says in a whisper against my lips, "Anything you want. Anything you need. Got it?"

"Got it."

He kisses me and at first all I can think of is that the others are watching. I feel the hard length in his pants pressing against my lower belly. I feel the soft pads of his fingers as they stroke the bare skin on my shoulders and arms. Goosepimples rise on my arms. I feel the energy churning beneath the surface, the hunger and need I'd pushed off now for days.

I exhale, feeling a sense of relief. "Thank you."

"You're very welcome," he replies and spins me around. I stumble into Clinton's massive arms.

His hands palm my back, tugging at the fabric of my top. He drops his head, his tongue seeking mine. His kiss exemplifies everything I know about him. Strength and confidence. I touch his stomach and feel the hard muscle beneath his shirt. My belly clenches. My core aches. It's as though my head is spinning and spinning with each deepening kiss and when I stop to catch my breath he says, "I know you'll choose wisely, my Queen, never doubt our loyalty."

Before I can reply, he picks me up with those bulging arms and carries me across the room. The act is silly and sweet for such a dominating presence. I wonder for a brief moment if he's going to simply carry me from the room, toss me on a bed and ravish me. For a quick second I almost ask him to, but instead he eases me onto Bunny's lap, my skirt hiked up around my thighs. We're on a wide, square ottoman, an island in the middle of the room. The warmth of Clinton's hands releases me but I feel the elegant touch of Bunny's fingers in my hair and his copper eyes boring into my soul.

"Hi," I say to him, completely unaware of the others. His gaze holds me tight. The hard length of manhood presses against my leg. My resolve to only kiss these men—feel them—wavers, especially when Bunny kisses my throat, then shoulders. He presses his lips to the center of my chest, right above my breasts. My nipples harden. My panties wet. I kiss him hard and shift against the steel in his pants. I'd said this wasn't about sex but the hunger in me doesn't agree. I need friction. I want more.

Bunny pulls me forward with his one good hand and the move presses hard against my clit. In my ear he says, "Every day is an honor. Every breath is a gift. I love to see you laugh. To see you fight. To watch you come."

Bunny, good lord, Bunny. He has this way. He has such an incredible intensity. I desperately want to feel him inside me. He kisses me hard, the strength rolling through every inch of my body. I climb on top of him. I lick his jaw. I only stop when he pushes me back gently and says quietly, "Not now, love."

"But," I start to argue, but he slips from underneath me. I'm suddenly on my knees and Damien is inches away, crawling over the leather. I perk up and meet him halfway.

"This is hard," I confess. "Why do you all have to be so beautiful?"

He touches my cheek. "Because a Queen deserves the best. The most powerful and strong. The brightest and intuitive. Someone to make you happy in bed. Someone to fight next to you in battle. Someone that will protect your kingdom and your heart."

His kiss is wild and brings out the feral animal in my chest. I want to run free with him. I want to strip off his clothes and mine and fuck until we've got nothing left. My body heats, my mind spins, and my blood boils. And just when I think things are taking shape in my mind, I feel a body behind me. I feel hands on my hips. Damien looks over my shoulder and winks at the person behind me. I hear a grunt in reply.

Dylan.

I haven't kept track of the others when I'm with one of the Guardians and even now I find them hazy around the edges. It's like when I'm with one, the others vanish. I sense them, but can't see them. A veil separates us. It makes me bold.

I press my ass into Dylan's body, finding his cock hard and ready.

He hisses this time and he steadies my body. Each of these men allows me to take control—all but this one. It's in his nature. He'll fight me to the end. Like Bunny, I know he won't push it all the way tonight. He's too proud. He wants me to make the decision based on merit—not physical prowess.

Tonight though, under the circumstances, he caves. Just a little.

I can't see him but I definitely feel him as he pushes my hair over my shoulder. There's the heat of his breath against my neck, followed by slow kisses over my shoulders and back. A chill runs down my spine—not the bad kind—the very, very good kind. Every nerve in my body sets on edge.

His hands run down the curve of my sides, grazing over the edge of my breasts. He grips my hips and bends me forward, until my palms are flat against the surface of the ottoman. I feel him behind me, the weight of his cock, the calculated control. I shift my ass, begging, begging for him to take me like this. I know it's futile, he's playing games, fucking with my mind as much as my body. The crazy thing is that Dylan knows that I like it. I want it like this as much as every other way the Guardians tease and taunt me with. I want it slow and powerful like Sam. I want it sweet and doting like Bunny. I want it carefree and fun with Damien, and I want the glorious skills Clinton has mastered.

And I want Dylan. Hard and rough. Dark and commanding.

I feel his hand twisted in my hair and he pulls me off my hands. In my ear he says, "You're close, Morgan. So close. You feel it in your bones. In your heart. There's one true way to break the Darkness. Only you can choose."

I think he means that he's caving. That he's going to take me here on the ottoman. But his warmth vanishes and his shadow is gone. I blink and I'm alone in the room. Just me and the crackling, magic fire.

15

MORGAN

It's Sue that slips me the note the next morning, telling me to forget my normal schedule and meet Dylan at the front door in an hour. My head is pounding in a hangover kind of way. My memories of the night before are hazy, like a ghostly, erotic dream.

I take a gulp from the coffee Sue left on the table and a bite of the gooey cinnamon roll that lured me from my room in the first place. I watch the older woman clean up from her baking. "Sue, can I ask you a question?"

She turns and the wrinkles in the corner of her eyes deepen as she smiles. "Sure, dear."

"How long have you and Davis been married?"

"Oh." She thinks for a minute. "Feels like an eternity, but it's been about forty years this fall."

"Forty years. Wow."

"Yes." She wipes the counter with a cloth. "I suppose that does seem like a lifetime for a girl your age."

"How did you know he was the right one?"

The woman turns and leans against the counter. Her face takes on a faraway look and she says, "Truth be told, I'm not the most patient person. I've always been like this, particularly when I was younger. People annoyed me. Grated on my nerves. When I met Davis, I kept waiting for that to happen—for the part of him I disliked to come forward." She grins like a schoolgirl at the memory. "It never did. That's how I knew."

"Basically he's the guy that didn't annoy you?"

She laughs. "Pretty much."

I shake my head and think about the decision in front of me—the decision that has to be made today. I groan and drop my head in my hands.

"Are you having a problem with a young man?"

Make that five, not-so-young men. "Sort of. I just need to make a decision and I'm having a hard time."

She crosses the space between the counter and the table. She reaches for my hand and squeezes. "Follow your heart, Morgan, but also your brain. You're a smart girl. I can tell you're wise."

I laugh. "I'm not sure wisdom will help me here."

"Wisdom always helps. It's when you follow other body parts that things get tricky."

I feel my eyes widen at her boldness, partly because it's so true. She doesn't seem remotely embarrassed. Her eyes carry a wisdom of their own.

I stand and take my cup to the sink, washing it before she can. "Thank you for that," I say. "I just needed someone to talk to."

"Anytime, dear."

I pause for one more moment in the cozy, peaceful kitchen. Once I leave this room I'll have to face Dylan and the reality of the day. I'll have to tell him about Anita and the truth behind Xavier's death, prepare for the spell, and finally choose a mate.

16

DYLAN

"Slow down."

I glance over my shoulder and see Morgan in a half-run, trying to keep up. I slow my stride, annoyed with her short legs.

She evens up with me, breathing heavily. "You should be in better cardiovascular shape—with all the training."

"Dude, don't blame me for your tree-trunk legs."

I snort, but hold back a reply. We're both on edge. I'd already known it was possible Anita and Xavier had greater roles in Morgan's life. Each interaction could be the one that tips the scales. The Darkness always has a reach into the world she wants to conquer. Xavier was a sacrifice—a blood offering to a hungry goddess.

"Tell me again about the kiss," I prompt. She gives me a suspicious look. "Not in a perverted way. It's just very odd."

"It was odd," Morgan replies. "She seemed very desperate and the Darkness was needy too."

"So you—or rather, she—liked it?"

"She did." But the expression that ghosts over her face tells me Morgan enjoyed it too. Not sexually. The energy exchange, which is definitely more alarming than sexual exploration. No, despite our best efforts, the Morrigan is growing stronger. We have little choice but to act immediately.

I direct her up the flight of marble stairs, lingering just a bit to get a long look at her ass. Her legs may be shorter than mine but they're exquisite, and although I'd held back the prior evening, my willpower is close to snapping.

It all depends on who she chooses. If it's me? I'll relish breaking her in. Feeling the tight warmth of her body around mine. If not? The gods did not intend it to be.

"Dylan!" she hisses from the top of the stairs. Her hands clench around the straps of her backpack. The book with the splitting spell is inside. I've stopped moving completely, absorbed with my thoughts. "What the hell are you doing?"

I don't bother with a reply, but climb the stairs quickly and lead Morgan through the entrance, past the front desk, and to a small elevator obscured by a long row of books.

"Seriously though," she says, eyes lingering over the stacks of books. "Where are we going?"

We're in the New York public library. The smells of paper and the inevitable layer of decay that comes with so many in one place. The elevator arrives and I follow Morgan into the lift.

"There's a special collection upstairs reserved for sensitive topics." I press the button for our floor. The elevator begins to rise. "The occult, magic, witchcraft, ancient supernatural histories."

She frowns. "Wait, so the library knows about this stuff?"

"Some of the librarians do. Not everyone. Not that clerk at the front desk."

"And these librarians think it's real?"

I shrug. "Some are probably skeptical. These books do exist and they deserve a place in the library." The elevator lurches to a stop and the doors open. We step into a small hallway. A small sign directs us toward "Special Collections" and I lead Morgan down the hall to the unassuming door.

A small keypad is mounted on the wall and I punch in a code.

"How did you get that?" she asks.

I shrug again. "It's my job."

The lock springs with a loud click and I open the door. The room is a spectacle. Rows and rows of dark leather with cracked and faded bindings. Parchment mounted behind plexiglass cases, alongside artifacts that carry mysteries we may never unlock. The librarian sits behind a large desk, flipping through a book. Her hair is blue and the glint of light reflects off the hoop in her lip.

Morgan tugs my hand and says, "This is crazy, you know that right?"

"As crazy as a portal gate opening in the middle of Central Park two days ago. Or a mystery virus killing a man, spread from nothing more than a kiss. Or you using the WishMaker last night, bringing an entire guard to their knees—"

"Right. Got it," she cuts me off, apparently not wanting to go into the details of the night before. She definitely pulled a fast one on us all. I'm not even sure where the magic orb came from or how she came to possess it.

We approach the desk and I take a request slip from the stack. I write down the name of the book I'm looking for and slide it over.

"One second," the librarian says, her eyes sliding between me and Morgan. She looks at Morgan appraisingly and a flare of jealousy ripples under my skin. I'm willing to share the Queen, but even I have my limits.

Five.

That's where it ends.

The librarian returns, handing over the massive book. I lift it from the counter and nod my thanks. "Can we use one of the study rooms in the back?"

"Sure." She fishes a key out from under the desk. "Let me know if you need any other assistance."

"Thank you," Morgan says. The librarian winks in reply.

As we walk away from the desk I look down and notice a red tint to Morgan's cheeks. "What? You're embarrassed by her attention?"

She grimaces. "I know this may be hard to comprehend from a guy with a face and body like yours, but until I moved up here no one ever paid me the slightest attention."

"I find that hard to believe. You had other boyfriends."

"Nothing serious, and none of them seemed inclined to drop everything just to be with me. More like the opposite."

The study rooms are along the back hall. They're private and quiet. I slip the key in the lock and we step inside. I place the book on the table and the key in my pocket. I turn to face Morgan, cupping my hand under her chin.

"You're beautiful. You're strong. Any suitor in your past that didn't understand the gift that you are wasn't man—" I glance to the desk—"or woman enough to see it. And if they did, they were terrified of the power you possess. I won't pretend I'm sorry you didn't find love with another before it was time for you to come here. You weren't made for other men. You were made for one of us."

"Is that your way of trying to convince me to pick you?"

I laugh. "Sweetheart if I wanted to convince you, I wouldn't use words."

To prove my point I kiss her on the mouth. I know she feels it across every inch of her body, down to her toes, because that's where I feel it too.

17

MORGAN

One kiss is all I get because Dylan has willpower made of iron and is focused on the books on the table. He scribbles occasionally on a notepad while I go over the spell in the book I found weeks ago, making sure I'm prepared.

The spell seems complex; a combination of the ingredients we've been collecting, a series of runes, and then the incantation. Dylan assures me it will be fine, but I see the hint of worry in his eyes. He's still not convinced.

"Did you see this?" I ask, pointing to a particular passage. *"The Morrigan often comes as a trio of three sisters, each with their own power and authority. Combined they create the Goddess of War, separate they prevail over different imagery: Land and livestock, fertility, and of course, war."*

"I'm aware of the mythology," Dylan replies, studying the passage.

"Do you think it's possible to remove her soul from mine? What if there's another?"

"It's a risk we have to take. But the myths are always vague. The Morrigan probably hoped future generations would fear her more by thinking she had triple the power." He grimaces. "As though we need to fear her more than we already do. She's quite the threat as is."

He finishes his notes and closes the book. I pack up my own book but pause when I find him staring at me. "What?"

"Are you sure you want to do this?"

"No, but I don't think I have a choice."

"We'll remove her soul and destroy her. The spell isn't that hard. Bunny and Damien should be able to handle it easily."

I nod. "I have faith in them."

"And you?" He studies me carefully. "You're ready to pick your mate? You'll need strength before the ceremony."

I swallow. "I'll be ready."

~

WE WALK BACK to The Nead, traveling through parts of the park and along the street. I'm wary after the situation with the gate, but Dylan assures me it will be fine.

I've developed a theory about Dylan's habits and as we walk down one of the more populated paths I ask, "Why have I never seen you in a vehicle?"

"Excuse me?" he asks.

"You always walk or you know, fly," I add quickly. "Are you afraid of driving?"

He stares straight ahead. Dylan pretends he isn't interested in me but I know better. I'm aware that he watches me when he thinks I can't see him and that his commentary with me is always calculated. I wait, giving him a chance to answer and he finally says, "I'm not afraid of much—particularly cars."

"Then why are we walking?"

"Because it's healthy. And good for the environment. And it makes us stronger and keeps our hearts pumping."

We cross a bridge that takes us to a more isolated side of the park and I tap my hand on the iron railing. "How conscientious of you."

A flash of white comes from the side and before I can blink I've been hit. I fall to the ground, stumbling to my knees. I catch myself and recover quickly—my reflexes faster than before. Standing over me is Hildi, the Valkyrie, her white blonde hair blowing in the summer breeze. She still has a bruise on her cheek from where I clobbered her.

Dylan steps between us.

"Move, you fool," she grinds out at him. Her eyes are dark as night. She'd come for payback. "This little girl and I have a score to settle."

"Not here," he says.

"I'm not a little girl, bitch." I'm now on my feet and I press a hand to my guardian's back. "Yeah, move."

He glares at me with ice blue eyes. "Not a chance. Not now."

Of course we have important things to do, but Hildi brings out the fire in me. The Darkness flickers to life, wanting a fight. The Morrigan always wants a fight.

Dylan holds his hand up to Hildi and she looks like she may just bite it off. He turns to me and says in a low voice, "If you do this it has to be you, Morgan. Just you. You can't cave to the Darkness this time. Are you up to that?"

I think about what he's saying. Can I do it? The look of skepticism on Dylan's face makes me even more eager to prove myself. "I think this is one of those times you don't get to tell me what to do, Sentinel."

There's a flicker in his eyes, a cross between anger and desire. He nods and steps out of the way. "At least move under the bridge. The last thing we need is a crowd."

Hildi smirks and leaps over the railing. I hear her feet land quick as a cat on the ground. Dylan raises his shoulders as if saying, I warned you. I take a deep breath and mount the railing. The ground looks so far below and I hesitate.

Kill her.

I blink, mentally swatting the Morrigan out of my head. I take one look at Dylan and jump, feeling the sharp twist of my belly but land on both feet—way more gracefully than I expected. Although not as skilled as Hildi.

Hildi waits for me at that bottom, her face made of stone, like a warrior. Her muscles are lean but developed. Her abs tight. She clenches her fists and I drop to a defensive stance. Dylan lurks in the shadows silently watching—assessing. I don't wait for her to make the first move, instead launching myself at her.

Her fist clips my chin and her foot cracks against my knee. I manage to punch her in the side and it's hard enough for her to recoil. She aims for my nose and I catch her fist with my palm. Her eyes widen in surprise at my reflexes but I'm in the zone and kick her hard in the gut, with more strength than I knew I had.

Hildi flies backwards, hitting a stone pillar under the bridge. Her head cracks against the hard surface and her eyes narrow. She's pissed. Super pissed, and I need to think fast. Spotting a small ledge I race toward the wall, jump up with one foot and flip back toward Hildi, who is coming at me full force. Coasting through the air I feel free for the first time in ages, my mind completely zeroed in on the moment. When my feet land hard, punching the Valkyrie in the chest, I instinctively know what to do next.

The fight is quick, a series of kicks, punches, and jabs. I taste blood in my mouth, feel the ache in my side. I also hear silence in my head. I'm fighting Hildi—not the Morrigan. The realization of this clicks in the Valkyrie's head when I sweep her feet from under her.

I'm breathing heavy and bend over. She squirms on the ground but the fight is over. "Are we square?" I ask.

"Yeah." She winces. I offer her a hand and she takes it warily. Dylan comes out of his hiding place as I'm helping her off the ground. He assesses my body for injury, but his eyes hold mine, searching for the Darkness.

"We're done," I declare, brushing my hands together. "You're a worthy opponent, Hildi. We'd be better on the same team than apart."

She studies me for a minute. "You think you need a team?"

"I hope not, but if I ever do, I'll give you a call."

"You do that," she replies, squaring her shoulders with pride. She wipes the blood from her lip and walks away.

"Are you okay?" Dylan asks.

Instead of telling him how I feel, I push up on my toes and kiss him. Heat fires between us but not the desperate kind. Nothing dark.

His fingers skim my cheek and I feel the warmth of his healing touch.

"What just happened?" I ask Dylan, who has pushed me back up the hill to get on the path toward home.

"I think that actually was a test," he says. "And you passed."

18

MORGAN

Back in my room, I feel better than I have in weeks. Maybe since I arrived in New York. The sense of balance that started the night before with the WishMaker and proceeded through the day until my fight with Hildi makes my head clear and my heart at peace. The lustful hunger that normally taints my every move seems to be soothed, even if I haven't had sex with my Guardians in the last few days.

Something has changed.

There will be no skipping supper tonight, despite the fact our after dinner activities include splitting my soul. Sue made it clear with a message left in my room. I assume the others received a similar one. Dinner will be ready at seven sharp.

I'm changing when my phone rings and I'm pleased to see it's my friend Shannon from back home.

"Hey," I say, holding the phone between my shoulder and ear. "I've got ten minutes before I have to be at dinner."

"So you're still doing that roommate dinner thing every night?"

"Mandatory. Well, other than yesterday."

"Ooh, what happened to break the rule?"

I sit on my bed. The WishMaker is on the bedside table. Crystal clear at the moment. "The last few days have been really weird."

"Weird? What's going on?"

In a moment of honesty I tell her the truth—well sort of. I tell her about Anita and her brother's death and how I'd been with him right before he fell ill. I tell her about going to a fight club with Clinton and spending time with Sam in the park. I go into detail about Dylan taking me to the special collections room at the library. Without the death and darkness and magic it all sounds pretty normal.

"So seriously," she says. "It sounds like you're dealing with five amazing men."

"Truly amazing."

"But five? I can't imagine juggling all that. One guy is enough for me."

One guy.

One mate.

Shouldn't that be enough?

"Yeah, but..." I stop.

"But what? You want them all?" She laughs.

"I mean, do I really have to choose?" I say the question to her, but the words resonate in my mind—my heart.

"Okay, Morgan, if that's the game you want to play. What do they think?"

They want what I want. They want me to be happy. Safe. Powerful. I think about how I've felt since the night before when I had a taste of them all. I've been more balanced. More controlled.

I can't tell Shannon that so I just say, "They think I need to choose. And believe it or not, they're like really cool about the whole thing. But yeah, I need to choose."

"You're just a girl that wants it all." She's quiet for a moment. "You know that's not a bad thing—not really. Don't settle until you're ready."

My phone alarm rings, giving me notice that it's time for me to head downstairs. I say goodbye and consider that after the decisions I have to make tonight, things will change. I hope when I see my friend face-to-face I'll have made the right ones. I pick up the WishMaker one last time and peer into the glass. This time there's no doubt about the figure staring back at me. At long last I know the truth. The one that belongs to my heart. It's been obvious this whole time and I'm a fool for not realizing it sooner.

I drop the orb on the bed and head to the door.

It's time for dinner.

19

BUNNY

I don't know why or what happened, but I am certain the moment a shift occurs in the house.

Morgan has made a decision.

I'm sure the change in energy is partially from the runes I'd placed on her body. An alarm and security system of sorts, but even so, we've all become so attuned to her emotions, her body, that it's not a surprise I felt it.

Nerves flare as I button my shirt, using one hand, as I'm used to. The gods blessed me with dexterity and precise skill—for working in paint as well as managing my disfigurement. Who will she pick? Me or one of the others? I'd heard the Morrigan the other night, spewing her hate and paranoia, but she's got nothing to lose and the truth always lurks in the lies.

Does Morgan feel guilt when she sees me? Pity? It wasn't pity in her eyes when I brought her to a violent orgasm on my work table. Nor when she saw what my runes could do.

I adjust my glasses in the mirror, touching my copper brown hair one last time before heading downstairs to find out my fate.

20

DAMIEN

The tremor hits and I cling to my workbench. An earthquake? No, I know better than that. I've survived hurricanes and tidal waves, erupting volcanoes and fault lines that cracked to the center of the earth. I look toward the house—up to Morgan's window. That wasn't an earthquake. It was a decision. The one we've been waiting for.

Respecting her wishes will be a challenge. Fighting in her army will not. We're bonded to her regardless, and my heart and soul belong to her no matter what her choice. When we rid the world of the Morrigan—tonight or in the future—that's when I'll take my leave, if she doesn't choose me.

It's hard to think she won't. The way our bodies work with one another. The fearless smiles she gives me from the back of my bike. We fit. We're good and I want nothing more than a lifetime of her body and mind.

The clock on the wall shifts toward seven and I grab my jacket.

It's time.

21

SAM

The clock says ten 'til seven, and I think I can process at least one more photo. I've been in the darkroom all day, looking over image after image. The future is changing and I'm not sure if it's because Morgan has chosen a mate or if we're going to be successful with the split.

Because the future looks good. Really good.

I hold up the photo I took this morning from the rooftop. The sky is clear. The park, bright green. The typical signs of the apocalypse are gone. Something happened during that encounter with us all the night before. She'd definitely used some kind of magic but whatever it was, it was strong enough for her to see more clearly.

I hang the photo to dry and exit the darkroom.

Between the experience with Morgan the night before, the photo, and the warm sensation in my lower belly I'm feeling good. Feeling right. I've come to treasure Morgan so much. I'd never want to lose her but I want her to fulfill her heart. That's what is most important to me.

I'm a Guardian first.

BLACK MAGIC

A friend next.
And a lover third.
And it's time to go face a brighter future.

22

CLINTON

After a long workout the steamy hot water from the shower feels divine. I like the burn on my skin, cleaning away the sweat and grime. My time is limited—dinner is in a few short minutes. Even though I'm in a rush, my mind wanders to Morgan. Her strength, her beauty, and gods help me, her body.

I'm a man of maximum control. I've been this way for centuries, since I was nothing but ash. But the woman upstairs breaks my resolve. Everything about her keeps me focused. I want to protect her. Fight her. Love her.

It must be the steam that's making my head spin—filled with images of the night before. My cock grows hard at the memory. My size may give the impression I'm a brute, but I'm skilled in many ways. Music flows in my blood. As much as I'm greedy over my time with Morgan, the way her skin feels against mine, she's just as alluring when she's with the others. I like to watch her move. Her face is a mystery as she struggles against each of us.

A mystery I hope to have an eternity to unlock.

I run a hand down my growing length, thinking of the way her lips taste, the way her ass curves. My hand presses against the tile as I recall the gentle swell of her breast and the scent that is uniquely hers.

Tonight is important. She'll make her choice. I feel it in my bones as well as deep in my loins. I close my eyes and think of her, stroking myself into a heightened ecstasy.

There's no room for distraction tonight. No time for lust. I groan under the blast of the shower, preparing myself for the next step in the battle.

23

DYLAN

Sue sets the table. Soups and salads first. She's aware tonight is important. An evening to memorialize. How much she truly knows, I haven't the faintest idea, but along with the secrets of this house, the Guardians, the magic, the history, she and Davis seem to be part of it. They may be pawns of the gods as well. I'm not privy to all things. It's my job to be on the lookout.

Which is why I'm first here, waiting for the others to arrive.

We spent the hour before dinner preparing for the separation spell. The ingredients have been mixed. The incantation is ready. Once Morgan announces her mate, we can begin.

I feel the tension growing in the house. The Guardians are aware that what we've been waiting for—training for—is finally coming to fruition. One of us will be chosen. The others will focus on the spell—the battle ahead. It will be an honor to serve Morgan in either capacity.

I hear the first footsteps on the stairwell and brace myself. I may be the only one that is hesitant to become her mate. I may be a man of conviction but I've known from the beginning this woman could destroy me. If I win her heart it means she will consume mine—and if I let her inside will I be able to fulfill my duties?

On the other hand, if there's one thing I detest, it's losing.

24

MORGAN

We dine together like a happy household. Everyone in their seats; Dylan across from me, the others flanking the sides. Conversation is light—we talk about the gorgeous weather. The fantastic meal. I hold each of my Guardians' eyes, letting them know I hear them. I'm with them. No matter what happens at the end of the night.

When the chocolate soufflé has been consumed and our plates are bare I pick up my glass of wine and say, "I'd like to make a toast."

I stand, making it a dramatic moment—shouldn't it be? I'm changing all of our lives. Holding my glass high, I begin. "I won't bore you with a long speech about what tonight means. You all know—probably more than I do. I never dreamed this is where my life would end up—okay, maybe I dreamed it—wrote it in my journals, but I did believe that was a fantasy. I had no idea there was truth and history behind my words."

I gaze at the men. "It's been an adjustment," I confess. "And frankly some would say I adapted too easily. That I fell into insta-lust and easily in love with my handsome roommates. But it was never that simple. I knew in my heart that we had something different. A bond. People outside this house would never understand. But we understand each other."

"That we do," Sam says, his green eyes twinkling.

The lustful desire I carry for these men grows in my belly. I'd been at peace all day but the more I talk about it—them—the more restless I become.

"I won't drag it out any longer. I've made a decision."

The men lean forward, all but Dylan, who looks a little ill.

"I've decided not to choose." The words hang in the room. "I want you all. Each one of you. In my bed. In my heart. I know it's the right thing to do."

Clinton's eyebrows rise to the top of his head. "All of us?"

No!

"Yes." The feeling grows in my chest. A sharp twist. The flicker of a whisper in my ear. "You each bring me something equally important. But most of all, it's exactly what we need to fight the Morrigan. At least right now."

My final statement is accompanied by a sharp stab to the temple. I'd wondered if this would happen, when she would appear. I'd beaten her down but this was too much. I drop my glass, the wine spilling across the white table cloth, and clutch my head.

"Morgan?" Damien cries; he's closest and gets to me first.

"Prepare the spell," I direct through gritted teeth. "She's coming."

Bunny hops from the table—he and Dylan already in motion. The Morrigan screams in my ear.

You fucking idiot. All of them! What are you trying to do? Shatter my heart times five? This won't work. It won't keep me away. One. One is all you get. You may not share the power of five. You cannot beat me down with love and lust.

Sam crouches next to me and holds my hand. "Stay with me, babe."

"With only one of you she can control me. Manipulate me," I say through the pain. "But not all of you. She can't penetrate me when I'm bonded to you all. I realized that last night. Ah!" Another stab of pain. It's like she's clawing at me from the inside. "Today was much better. Calmer. This is all she's got and we need to kick her out for good."

A thunderous crash brings my attention to the table. Clinton has cleared it in one dramatic swoop. Bunny and Damien carry the ingredients for the spell. Dylan, the parchment for the incantation.

"Ready?" I ask, feeling the Morrigan squirm inside. She doesn't want out—she wants to take over.

If you let this happen, you'll never get to that castle. You'll never meet your destiny. You were born to rule worlds! The Otherside and this one! Don't be a fool.

Sam brings me to my feet and I feel unfamiliar hands on my back, tugging at my skirt. With a pounding headache I spin and find Sue and Davis stripping me of my clothes.

I start to argue but Sam presses his lips to my ear and says, "Stay calm. It's okay."

It doesn't feel okay—yet none of my Guardians stop them. In seconds, I'm naked and lifted from the floor on top of the mahogany table. Flashes from my fever dream return. All five men surrounding me, loving me. It had been a vision—not a dream.

Last chance, the Morrigan hisses, *before you lose it all. You need me to access the castle. You need me for power.*

"Shut up!" I cry, swiping at the shadows creeping in the edge of my vision.

I feel the hands on me now. I look up and see Dylan speaking in a deep voice, the words a confusing language. I feel Bunny's paintbrush slide across my breast. I feel Clinton's hands on my belly. Damien's calloused fingers on my feet. Sam holds my hand and whispers words of love warring with the Morrigan's awful barrage.

There's a battle in my soul, fighting, pushing, punching and I get loose, taking a swing at Bunny. I tag him across the cheek before Clinton can subdue me. I fight. I cry. I scream.

And the Morrigan does the same.

Her face hovers over mine—a mirror image of my own. Her eyes are darker and filled with hate. I break free once again, slapping her across the cheek.

She smiles with pleasure at the pain.

You're foolish, don't you know? she asks in a calmer voice. *There's so much more out there, so much I can offer you.*

I don't want your destruction.

You think that's all it is? We're the Goddess of War, Morgan. We didn't create such a thing—we clean up the mess. We conquer the weak. You realize that in many cases, we're heroes.

No, I tell her. I don't believe that.

Images flash before my eyes. Kingdoms. Conquerors. Rebellions. The stench of smoke clogs my throat. The symbols are familiar, filled with hate and a history of violence. I want nothing to do with it.

But her pull is strong. Her tentacles deep.

You're so stupid, don't you know that? So very stupid. You'll rip me from your side but that won't stop me. You're not the only one. Contingencies have been made. You slipped through my grasp once before. If you spit me out the regret you'll have will make the angels weep. I don't need you, mortal, you need me.

Dylan's voice rises above her threats and my body is pulled in a million directions. My hands. Feet. Fingers and skin. My scalp burns, my hair stretches, pulling flesh away from my body. I scream and scream and scream until my voice is swallowed by hers and we're screaming all at once. Her nails scrape down my arms, gouge my cheeks, until the sound of a soaring bomb splits my eardrums like glass cracking. My eyes burn with a sudden flash of light, much like a nuclear detonation. I'm blind. I'm ash. I'm nothing more.

25

BUNNY

Three weeks later

The scabs are healing.

The bruises faded.

The visible wounds, at least. Internal? I'm not convinced. I know Dylan isn't either. So we wait and watch.

"What is she doing?" Clinton asks. We're sitting on the rooftop enjoying one of the final sunsets before summer.

"Cartwheels?"

"I think that's called a somersault." I have no reason to know this but I do.

"Ah right."

She jumps from the ground, hair springing around her. She looks like the sun—bright and beaming.

"And things are progressing? She seems okay?"

"Dylan says so," I reply. "He's always the most skeptical, so if he thinks she's better then I trust him."

The spell worked, although with some consequences. That's normal for magic though. There's always a price to pay.

He looks at me for a long moment so I ask, "You don't?"

He doesn't reply, just glances back across the rooftop, staring at our girl.

Sam approaches her with the camera. He takes a series of snapshots, getting her to smile in at least one. His face never betrays him, but when he thinks no one is looking I catch the frown as he looks at the pictures. He doesn't like what he sees.

"She went to Damien's workshop last night," Clinton says. His gray eyes follow her every move. I straighten at his revelation. I didn't know that.

"Did she?" I'm dying to know what they did behind closed doors. We all are. We aren't ruled by sex, of course, but ever since the spell we've been careful, letting her heal.

Our bond is based on friendship, love, and intimacy. It's only become stronger since that night.

"She wanted to ride on his motorcycle. He took her around the city until dawn."

My muscles relax. "Good. The fresh air should help her."

"I agree."

Damien comes and sits next to us. Dylan a few moments later. The sun slips to the edge of the city, casting us all in a pinkish-orange glow.

I feel like there are so many unanswered questions. What do we do now? How do we proceed with our duties? I know I'm not the only one but no one wants to rock the boat. Not yet.

She links her hand with Sam's and they walk over to where we're sitting. He takes a seat on the ground and she nestles in the middle of the bench. Clinton tosses a protective arm around her shoulder and I wrap my hand around hers, relishing her heat. Damien leans against her thigh and she strokes his head. Dylan, like always, stands just above all of us.

Watching.

Waiting.

And that's what makes me nervous.

OBSIDIAN FIRE

PROLOGUE

There's something about freedom that heightens life's experiences. I'm sure ice cream in prison tastes sweet, but licking a double scoop of chocolate fudge swirl on a warm fall afternoon in the middle of the world's most amazing park is a different kind of pleasure.

That's what life feels like, I think, looking over at the naked man next to me. His back is broad and taut with carved muscles. His waist narrows and dips to the most perfectly curved ass I've ever had the opportunity to fondle. Sex with the Morrigan screaming in my head was good—epic; it thrived on a form of hunger and desire not known to most humans. A sort of insane, magical lust.

But it wasn't me. Not exactly.

It was part of me. My body. My conflicted mind. My tortured soul. She tainted my heart and my spirit. She made me do things I'd never consider while making me regretfully reconsider many of the things I did.

But not anymore, I think, brushing a small piece of hair out of the face of the beautiful guardian sharing my bed. He stirs and reaches a sleepy, wandering hand over my bare hip. The Morrigan is gone. Morgan is fully in charge.

And I plan to enjoy life to the fullest.

1

ONE MONTH AFTER THE SPELL

The kitchen smells delicious, like cinnamon, and when I peek inside Sue is standing over a massive bowl of peeled apples. Thin dough is rolled out on the table and there are four pie pans floured and ready. Quietly, I slip into the room and dip my finger along the gooey edge of the bowl. I've just tasted the most heavenly, sugary-sweet concoction when she turns and catches me.

"Shoo! That's for dessert!"

"It smells so good." I reach out my finger and this time, she swats it.

"It's hard enough keeping those men fed. I don't need to have to monitor you, too."

"It's not our fault you're an amazing cook."

She wipes her hands on her apron and says, "You had a visitor while you were out."

I frown. "Who?"

"Someone from your advisor's office."

I sigh and sit down at the table. "Again?"

Between Xavier's death, Anita's weird threats, and everything going on in the house I'd had a hard time focusing on writing my book. The book that got me acceptance into the NYU graduate writing program. When I'd arrived in the city that book was all I could think about. It haunted my dreams. I thought about it all day—every day. But then I learned about my fate—my destiny—and the book seemed less and less important.

And now?

I haven't written a word in weeks.

What have I been doing? Honing my fighting skills, tracking down ingredients for a dark and powerful spell, choosing which of the Guardians would be my mate (spoiler alert: I didn't choose. For now, it's all five) and expelling the Morrigan from my soul. Things have been a little busy.

I thrum my fingers on the table.

"You better keep up with your work, Morgan, or they'll kick you out."

"I know, I know."

"I've seen it happen before. All you students think you're special, but trust me, there's another to replace you in a heartbeat."

Of course I *am* special. Aren't I? I carry the Morrigan, The Goddess of War, in my heart and soul. Well I did, until recently. That's just another one of the distractions lately, losing the familiar power I'd become accustomed to. I consider what Sue is saying. Maybe I'm not special anymore. Maybe I'm just a woman who needs to focus on keeping her scholarship.

"Did they say anything in particular?"

"Left a package. Davis took it up to your room."

"Thank you. I'll make sure to read it." She gives me a stern look. I add, "Right away."

Her eyes soften and she says, "I know things have been challenging for you lately. Just stay focused. Sometimes it seems like our journey has changed but really it's just a different path. Stay the course, Morgan. Finish what you came here to accomplish."

She walks over to the oven and opens the door. Using a thick pot holder pulls out a tiny, perfectly baked pie. She places it on a plate and brings it to me with a fork.

"Let it cool."

"Thank you."

She grins. "Don't let the boys see, okay? I already kicked them out once today."

I return the smile and on my way out the door say, "I won't. I promise."

∽

I NEVER PLANNED on hiding the pie. I go straight upstairs, past the second floor and my suite on the third, heading straight to the attic. I needed something to lure him out. Something irresistible. Something sweet.

Bunny's been hiding from me.

I secure the plate behind my back and knock on the door. It takes him a few minutes but when the door swings open, Bunny stands there looking adorable with rumpled clothes, messed-up hair and askew glasses.

"Hey Bun, did you just wake up?"

"Uh, no." He rubs his eyes. "I've been working on a painting all night."

"You've been really busy lately. I've hardly seen you."

"Yeah." He sniffs. "I really should get back to it."

"Okay," I say, fully aware he's been avoiding me for weeks. He's been sweet of course. Gentle and kind, but unless he has to talk to me, he vanishes. I'm ready to find out why. "I thought maybe you'd like a sneak peek of dessert tonight."

"Dessert?" Even if he's able to resist me, he's unable to fight his love of sweets.

I hold the pie up, right under his nose. The warm scent wafts between us. "Smells good, right?"

He nods.

I pick up the fork and press it to my bottom lip. "I thought maybe we could share."

He swallows. "Now?"

"I know eating dessert so close to dinner is a little naughty, but why not?"

His eyes are all over. On the pie. On my mouth. Lingering over the tiny hint of cleavage showing under my neck. He licks his lips and I hold the pie higher, thinking I've finally got him.

Hook. Line. Sinker.

His eyes dart behind him and he clears his throat. "You know, I'm just really busy. Like totally in the middle of this piece. I can wait until after dinner." He begins to shut the door but stops abruptly. "But thanks, though. That was sweet."

The door shuts with a harsh click.

Okay then, it's going to take more than pie to lure Bunny out of his funk.

2

BUNNY

I shut the door and lock it—providing a safe barrier between us. Me and the pie. Me and Morgan.

I walk away, rubbing my hands through my hair. I'm exhausted and wound tight. My mind is a hamster wheel of creativity and motion. Painting after painting, an endless cycle. I wake up and paint. I eat, then paint. I try to sleep but the images won't stop, so I paint. And paint. And paint. My brain is trying to tell me something. Something I'm not sure I want the answer to.

I stand before my latest and concede that the "what" of my paintings, I get. I know it's a castle. I know it's in the Otherside, but what confuses me is the way it changes shape, color, and style. Some days it's dark and dangerous. Others, it's light and full of wonder. The sky is often black with clouds—a never-ending darkness. But then I'll catch a few minutes of sleep and wake up to the most vivid imagery of blue, cloudless skies, and lush green grass. I paint them all, hoping that at some point it will make sense.

It has to—before I go mad.

With the Darkness gone and the tensions in the house abated, I thought my mania would curb. It's been the opposite though. My desire for Morgan is tainted with guilt and shame. She doesn't need me anymore, if she ever did. She tries to corner me. Talk to me. I know she feels pity for my disfigurement. I don't want her to feel like she owes me something. A debt. An offering.

I stare at the painting, at the sharp spires that jut to the sky. At the heavy gate that divides it from the barren landscape. It doesn't look right. It's wrong. Clutching the paintbrush in my hand, I dab it in a mixture of black and gray oil paint before attempting to fix what's wrong. I work quick—fast motions through the sky and along the tallest spire. The sound is what makes me stop. The jagged ripping sound. The ear-splitting tear.

I blink and realize it's not a brush in my hand but a blade. The castle is ripped into shreds. I drop the knife on the floor with a loud clatter and stare at the destruction for a long moment.

Then I reach for a fresh canvas.

3

MORGAN

Before I split from the Morrigan I'd declared I wanted all of the Guardians as my mates. That act of rebellion, of refusing to choose, helped me fight off the Darkness and regain complete control of my mind and body. After that I went through a small period of transition. I needed time to heal. To find some peace. I did ask the Guardians if the agreement to mate would end now that I didn't need them. The response was a universal 'no'. None of them are sure what will occur after the split, but they do know that the Morrigan isn't dead. I know it, too. It's not a fact as much as a feeling. No one killed her after the spell. Her spirit is alive—somewhere—and it's unlikely she's through with me, or them.

"Are you her guardians or mine?" I asked Dylan that day. He was pouring over history books like nothing had happened.

He didn't reply for so long that I wondered if maybe he didn't *have* an answer, but eventually he looked up from his book and said, "We're bound to you, Morgan. You. This body. This soul. That was part of the need to declare who your mate," he pauses, "mates, are. Once you made the announcement there was no going back."

"So if I hadn't picked you all then you would have been free to go with her."

He touches his chin in thought. "Possibly. We'll never know, because you did the right thing."

Now I sit in the window seat of my writing office, the empty pie plate on the floor and my journals around me. The pages are blank—my creativity blocked since the night of the spell. Maybe even before. It's like when the Darkness left it took a small part of me with it. One I've continued to fill in one of two ways.

Both physical. Both I use to distract my thoughts and exhaust my body.

I peer out the window, down at the expansive park below. It took a few weeks but slowly I've begun training and having sex with my Guardians again. Clinton, Sam, and Damien are all ready and willing partners. Even with the short break, we never skipped a beat. We're good together. We spar. We learn and we love with a renewed passion. Less anger. More fun. I like it.

But something's off.

That rejection from Bunny isn't the first one I've had. He's withdrawn and nothing I do seems to lure him out. And Dylan? Fuck if I know what's going on in that man's head. He, too, has put up a wall. A physical barricade between us. They both claim to be my mates, that they're here to fulfill their roles as my Guardians, but neither is attending to all of my needs. And they're certainly not allowing me to attend to theirs.

My alarm chimes, giving me a warning that it's time for our mandatory dinner, which I always enjoy, but tonight I'm more excited about what's happening afterward. Sam is taking me out, like he's promised. Where? That's a surprise. I leave the notebooks, the pie plate, and my aimless thoughts and head to my bedroom to change.

DINNER PASSES UNEVENTFULLY with the highlight being Sam sending me teasing texts.

Ready for tonight?

Yes, I reply under the table. *Where are we going?*

You know I can't tell.

Can't or won't.

His response is a shrugging emoji. I roll my eyes.

Give me a hint?

Wear something nice.

A dress?

Something that shows your legs.

The shorter the better.

And forget the panties.

I give him a hard look across the table and he winks. The other men are involved in a discussion about the fights later this week, oblivious to our flirting.

After a second piece of pie at dinner, it's a good thing I'd planned on the dress because there's no way I'm getting in a pair of skinny jeans. I check out the gray dress in the mirror, liking the way it clings in all the right places. If these men have done anything for me, it's boost my self-confidence. They treat me and my body like it's something to worship. They crave the parts I consider my biggest flaws. At the last minute I do as Sam directed and slip out of my panties.

He'll probably never know but if he does? That will make the evening even more fun.

4

SAM

I look twice when Morgan walks down the stairs in that slinky gray dress. The fabric hugs the rounded swell of her breasts and the curve of her hips.

"Damn. I should tell you to dress up more often." I walk over to the steps to greet her, taking her hand and pulling her close. I breathe in her scent and consider that maybe we shouldn't go out at all.

"You look pretty good too." She straightens my tie. "I've never seen you so dressed up."

We definitely shouldn't go out.

"Any chance you'll tell me where we're going now?" Her eyes carry a spark of excitement—something that's been sorely missing lately. I'm not going to let her down, even though we could have just as much fun at home.

"Nope, not yet. But we should go." I offer her my hand and she links her fingers through mine. She heads toward the front door but I tug her in the direction of the garage.

"Oh, we're driving?" Another flare of interest. She loves the cars in the garage.

"Yep." We walk down the long flight of stairs and I flick on the lights. Each section brightens, revealing two rows of magnificent vehicles. I pull her in for a kiss. She's hungry for it—like she's been waiting for it all day. She tastes like the sugary sweet pie we had for dinner and her engine is revved high as one of the cars in front of us. I run my hands down her back and over the arc of her ass.

No panties.

This girl is gonna kill me tonight.

I step back and adjust my pants, trying to calm myself before I really do ruin the night. Morgan laughs at the tight grimace on my face. Her awareness of how she affects me—affects all of us—only makes her hotter. She doesn't exploit us, nor us with her, but the mutual appreciation we have with one another makes nights like this similar to walking on the edge of a knife.

"You pick," I tell her.

"Pick what?" she asks.

"The car. Which should we take?"

There's zero hesitation as she walks between the rows, stopping in front of a shiny white Tesla. "I've always wanted to ride in one."

I open a cabinet on the wall and pull out the key. I hold it up. "Want to drive?"

She laughs. "No way. Walking in the city still freaks me out."

"Fair enough, but sooner or later you'll have to learn to drive up here."

She makes a face and I open the passenger side door for her. Her hand is warm on my shoulder as she holds on to me to get in the low car. I kiss her again before shutting the door and quickly get behind the driver's wheel.

Fall is coming and when we exit the garage, it's already dark. Morgan covers my hand resting on the gearshift with hers. Her touch is like a spark of fire. I'm overwhelmed by her scent filling the small, enclosed space. Everything about her pulls me in and my reactions to her have only increased since she declared that I, along with the others, would be her mate.

"How's your work coming?" she asks.

"Good," I say. "Different."

"Less apocalyptic?" she says with a small laugh, but I know she doesn't really think it's funny.

"Maybe? I've had some interesting images. I'll show you soon." I haven't been sharing my work with her lately. The photos are off. I'm seeing things that shouldn't be there—but they're also not as disturbing as they were before we performed the spell. I can't quite decipher it. I glance over. "What about you? How's the book?"

"Slow," she admits. "I'm having some writer's block."

I flip our hands and squeeze hers. "You'll get past it. Things have been weird lately. Change is hard on creativity."

"I just stare at the page and nothing comes out."

"Then I'm glad we're going out. Sitting around and dwelling on it only makes it worse. Trust me, I've been there."

I speed through the city, taking shortcuts and trying to avoid traffic. The Tesla runs smooth and when I change gears Morgan moves her hand to the back of my neck and runs her nails up under the band holding up my hair. I lose concentration for a moment and turn left a road too soon.

"Shit," I mutter when we're trapped in a narrow, dark alley. "Wrong turn." I turn to look out the back window and like a tragic destiny an 18-wheeler rolls to a stop, blocking the alley. "Dammit."

"What happened?"

"We're stuck. I guess I can go ask the truck driver to move." I check my watch. It's going to be tight.

I glance over but stop cold when I see the wolfish grin on Morgan's lips. Her fingers tighten around my neck. She pulls me closer.

I ask, "What?"

"I think your mistake just became the best decision you've made all day." I raise my eyebrows in question but she unclips her seatbelt and leans over. "I don't know if it's how handsome you look in that suit or this sexy as hell car, but I'd think we'd be remiss to not make the most of this moment."

She licks her lips and reaches for the ever-present hard-on in my pants.

"Here?"

"Do you have a problem with that?"

I shake my head. "No. No, I really don't."

I adjust the seat to recline and Morgan leans over to kiss me. Her hand runs along the outside of my pants, taunting, teasing. I touch her hair and neck. I kiss her mouth. Her hands and fingers explore and before long I'm straining against my pants.

"You know," I tell her as she unbuckles my belt and frees my cock from the confines of my pants. Have mercy. "This wasn't what I had in mind when I said no panties."

She grins. It's nice to see her carefree smile. "I like to switch things up. Plus you can repay the favor later."

She kisses my lips once more and then bends over my hips, enveloping me in her hot, warm mouth. I clench a hand in her hair and stare at the ceiling of the car, murmuring a promise, "Don't worry, I will."

5

MORGAN

An hour later I can still taste Sam on my tongue as we arrive fashionably late for the reservations he made at a club uptown. The valet takes the car and Sam, red-cheeked and eyes slightly glazed, grabs my hand. He's a contrast of sexy looks; a nice fitting suit and tie along with the for-once tidy bun at the back of his head.

I hear the music before we enter and stop short. "You brought me to see Clinton?"

"Yeah, I thought you'd like to see him play again." He didn't add *under better circumstances*, but it's implied.

"Are you sure this is a good idea? Because last time..."

"Last time you had the Darkness fucking with you." He pulls me close. "You don't need to be afraid. You're tough as nails and different now."

I can't help but think this is just another test. A way to see how I'll react under pressure. My guardians are smart, even if they are huge pains in the ass sometimes.

"Does he know we're coming? Because he may be mad we're late because, you know." I'd sucked him off in the car. That's also left unsaid.

"We're late because we got stuck in an alley. What we did to bide our time is no one's business." He flashes me a grin as we follow the attendant across the crowded club. Patrons ignore us though, eyes transfixed on the performance. We slide into the circular booth tucked in the corner of the club. "Even though I'm pretty sure Clinton would understand."

Unlike last time, Clinton isn't alone on the stage. A full section of strings accompanies him and the magical sound of their music reverberates through the building. I'm so used to the strains of his music filtering up the stairs that it's almost like a pulse—a heartbeat. I focus on the concert, not the complicated feelings being here brings up.

Sam orders drinks and I'm relieved when he wraps his arm around my shoulder and pulls me close. My heart races as the melody intensifies. I think about the last concert I attended with Xavier and Anita. Clinton's music ignited something in me—it brought out the Darkness and allowed the Morrigan to cross from her world to mine.

"She's gone," I whisper to myself. *Remind* myself.

"Did you say something?" Sam says, leaning close.

I shake my head and he squeezes my shoulder, his fingertips warm on my skin.

The waiter brings our drinks and I quickly take a sip. The liquid burns but it also fills my nervous belly. Sam moves my hair and speaks into my ear, "I know this is hard for you, but you're safe. The Morrigan is gone. You can relax."

Clinton's eyes connect with mine from the stage. Without breaking contact, I nod in reply to Sam. "I'll try, I think I just have PTSD or something."

I don't know exactly why but Clinton's music tugs at the threads of my soul. Even though the Morrigan is gone, I slip into the same heated trance as the last time. I watch his movements, the way his biceps flex while he handles the long bow. My eyes skim his legs and the way he straddles the cello. It makes me think of being in a similar position.

Suddenly the room feels too warm and I shift in my seat.

"Hey," Sam says. "Are you okay?"

"I, uh," I blink, trying to focus on him. The room is foggy. "I feel a little strange, that's all."

"Talk to me, Morgan. Do we need to leave?"

I shake my head and look back at Clinton. He's still playing but watching us like a hawk. "No. I feel like last time. Which is impossible, isn't it? What if I hurt someone?"

Sam pulls me into his chest and I feel the heat of his mouth on my ear. "You're tied to each of us in a unique way. Clinton's music must trigger something powerful inside. I know you have an effect on my photography. Before, those binds connected to the Darkness. What do you think it connects to now?"

I hadn't thought of it that way, that maybe there's more inside of me than just a normal woman left with a hole from the removal of magnificent darkness and destruction. He's right, I feel an itch deep down—something that needs to be scratched. I turn to face Sam and the same compulsion that took over when I was in the alley with Xavier grips me.

I want to kiss him but I don't. I'm scared. Heart-pounding fear. Maybe Clinton's music is evil. Maybe I'm evil. Maybe the Morrigan isn't truly gone. Sam holds my face with his hands. "What's going on in there, babe? You look terrified."

"Help me not be afraid."

He nods and gives me my drink. I swallow the rest in a gulp. "Focus on Clinton," he says, slipping his arm around my waist. "Think about the joy his music gives you. The life. Think about how no matter what happens out there, we've got each other."

With my eyes locked on Clinton's, I feel Sam's hands on my sides, rubbing little circles to keep me calm. He moves lower, stroking my arms underneath the table, playing with the hem of my dress.

My breathing calms. My heartbeat shifts. It doesn't slow, not exactly. The fear subsides but Sam's touch has me on edge. I'm about to turn and tell him to take me out of here when he runs his knuckles down my inner thigh, urging me to spread my legs.

I do.

We're out of view of the rest of the crowd; everyone's eyes are focused on Clinton and the other musicians. His attention hasn't left me for a second. I lick my lips in anticipation of Sam teasing, what he's threatening to do and where his fingers are traveling. I have zero doubt Clinton is aware of everything happening in our little corner booth.

"Is he watching us?" I ask, feeling a little thrill.

"Who do you think told me to remind you not to wear panties tonight?"

The admission turns the heat between my legs moist. Sam laughs quietly in my ear while rubbing his thumb over my most sensitive parts. I rest my hands on the table, palms flat to keep myself centered —at least where people can see. Clinton's eyebrow arches just as Sam spreads my center wide and pushes a finger in. My breath catches.

"Breath, babe."

I nod and exhale.

"He likes to watch you come, you know, just as much as I want to feel it on my fingers, or Damien on his cock," Sam murmurs in my ears. My cheeks heat at the confession.

"What about the others?" I ask in what probably sounded like a breathy whisper. Sam spreads my moisture around and inserts another finger. My legs widen beneath the table. My skirt strains against my thighs. "I can't get the other two to seal the deal."

"All the Guardians have their hang-ups, Morgan. We're far from perfect, but I have no doubt they'll cross that line with you soon."

I grip the table as he moves in and out, his thumb swiping over the bundle of nerves at the top. I know my cheeks are red. I know I'm not nearly as quiet as I should be. The orchestra (under Clinton's urging) changes direction, beginning a melody with an ever-increasing pace.

Oh, boy, he knows what he's doing. No doubt about that.

"They'll come around," Sam says, but his words sound muffled and far away. As do the voices of the other patrons and the clinking of glasses or the music up on the stage. "Until then the three of us will take care of your needs, whenever you need it. However you want."

The orchestra reaches a fevered pitch in time with the movement of Sam's hand. Faster, faster, faster. My knees wobble and I lose control of the muscles in my legs. Tighter, tighter, tighter. The coil springs at the crescendo, sending shock waves through every inch of my body. Sam wraps his arm around my neck. I bite down on his forearm, stifling the orgasmic groan just as Clinton hits his final note. He winks at me from the stage.

The crowd jumps to a standing ovation while I use the reprieve to catch my breath. I turn to face the man behind me and say, "You planned that didn't you? All of it. The date, the outfit, the music."

"To be fair, I didn't plan the blow job in the alley. That was all you."

We stare at one another for a moment and I wonder how in the world I came to this place of sex and lust and absolute, uninhibited courage.

"My life is really weird."

"Maybe." He wraps his arm around my shoulder. "But do you feel better?"

It's with slow realization that I know that I do. I fought through the moment, the fear, and the trauma. I'm going to be okay. I'm sure of it now. I give him a quick kiss and say, "Yeah, I think I do."

~

OUR MOOD IS light after the show. Clinton takes us to a late night diner he and the other musicians frequent after concerts. He's in a surprisingly good mood, being that his go-to demeanor is cranky, and I watch with fascination as both men consume large amounts of bacon and eggs before digging into massive stacks of pancakes.

"Where do you put it all?" I ask, knowing both men hardly carry an ounce of fat on their ridiculously fit bodies. "If I ate all of that, I'd be big as a house."

"Doubtful," Sam says through a mouthful of pancake. A drip of syrup runs down his chin and I swipe at it with my finger. "All that energy pulsing through you—it burns off everything but muscle."

I study my reflection in the diner window, noting the lean, developed curve of my arm and the thinning around my jaw. It's true that ever since I arrived in New York, at The Nead, I've become stronger. The result is a faster, leaner body and a ravenous appetite myself. I think of the two helpings of apple pie earlier in the day. "Do you think I still have it? The energy?"

It's something I think about all the time. Are my moods my own? Is something propelling it for me? Something stirred in me earlier tonight. Something greater than lust answered Clinton's call.

The men look at one another, Clinton chewing and Sam wiping his mouth. He pauses like he's ready to answer my question when all three of our phones vibrate and chime at the same time.

I reach for mine first and look at the name and message. The knot of worry I'd spent all night removing returns, tighter than ever.

"It's Dylan. He needs us at home."

~

THE WINDOWS ARE ablaze with light when Sam parks the car in front of the house. Davis, who should be in bed at this late, late hour, opens the door before we reach the top step. "He's waiting in the library. For Ms. Morgan." He holds my eye. "He'd like to speak to her alone."

There's a noticeable shift between the men and it's clear they weren't expecting that news. I look at them both and give them a tight smile. "It's fine."

"Are you sure? He's not actually the boss, you know."

I laugh—this time genuinely. "Oh, trust me. I know."

My attitude lightens the mood and Clinton gives me a kiss on the cheek before heading up to his room. Sam hands Davis the car keys.

The older man nods, closes the door and heads out to the car, likely to put it back in the garage.

Sam squeezes my hand and we part, him going upstairs and me down the hall to the library. A feeling of déjà vu rolls over me. No good conversation has come from being asked to speak to someone alone. It's how I learned my parents were dead. I hesitate outside the door and take a deep breath.

The door opens before I gather my nerves and Dylan stands in the opening. He's imposing—devastatingly handsome and undeniably strong. His shoulders are broad and although his body is lean, there's no doubt about him being a physical threat.

"Thank you for coming," he says, stepping aside so I can enter. There's a fire burning in the fireplace, giving the room a feeling of warmth.

"Sure. Is everything okay?"

Something in his eyes falter. "Yes, well, I'm not exactly sure." That's better than someone is dead—or at least I think it is. He gestures for me to take a seat and continues speaking. "I apologize for interrupting your evening out. I hope you had a good time."

"I—we—did. It was a lot of fun. You should come next time."

He sits across from me and I tug the hem of my dress slightly lower over my knees, suddenly acutely aware I'm bare underneath. "That's kind of what I wanted to talk to you about. You and me. Our relationship."

"Okay." Now?

"I've known my whole existence that I'm here to perform a job. A duty. I'm here to protect this world from the Morrigan and her Darkness. We've failed before but not this time. You held firm and fought unlike any other vessel before. I'm very proud of you."

I literally have no idea what Dylan is going on about but the fact he's called me here and is talking instead of brooding up in his rooms must mean it's important. I wait to hear more.

"I do think that choosing us all as your mates was key in the destruction of the Morrigan. She thrives on lust and the wicked side of men and women. You turned that on her by refusing to cooperate. You fulfilled your destiny and then some." His eyes falter. "I cannot say I've done the same."

"Dylan, what are you talking about?"

He stands and walks over to the fire, resting one hand on the thick mantle. "I've failed in my position with you. I've been jealous and covetous. I've been arrogant and dismissive. I've allowed you to service my needs while failing to reciprocate."

A heavy pause lingers between us and I finally ask, "Wait, are you talking about sex? Or power or magic? I'm confused."

He turns to face me and there isn't the slightest hint of irony on his face. "Sex. Obviously."

I'm completely confused and have no idea where to even begin but I take a stab at it anyway. "You haven't failed me. Not at all. You've been with me every step of the way. Steadfast and true. You've protected me and trained me for the biggest moment of my life."

I walk across the room and take his hand. The fire has made his skin hot. I force him to look at me with those intense blue eyes. "I'm a solider, Morgan. A warrior. Not a lover. Do you know why I'm the only one that hasn't stopped shifting?" No, but I've been wondering. I just haven't had the nerve to ask. I shake my head. "Because the gods needed a link between worlds. I've always been bound to many things—people—and souls."

I touch his chin. "Because you're the best, the bravest. They chose wisely."

"Those days are over. When you split from the Morrigan, I was cut off. That is how I am here to protect you and only you. But even so, I'm not sure you need my protection. And without that, what am I?"

I frown. "You can't shift anymore?"

He shakes his head and a deep sense of sadness fills his eyes. I wrap my arms around his waist and pull him close. He buries his face in my neck and for a moment we cling to one another.

I consider the past few weeks. The change in Bunny. The distance from Dylan. Their life changed as much as mine. The others threw themselves into their art—into pleasing me—but these two... Sam was right. They all carry their own weight. It's my responsibility to help them the way they've helped me.

I lean back and tilt his head toward mine. "What you're forgetting is that I do need you, and in more ways than as my Guardian. When I declared you as one of my mates we moved to a different sort of relationship—one that you may not be used to—hell, I'm not used to it either, but together we'll work through this."

A small smile tugs at the corner of his mouth. "I should have known you'd have the answer."

"I may not be the Goddess of War anymore, Guardian, but I'm still the Queen around here."

His hand clenches around my neck and in a quiet whisper just above my lips he replies, "Yes, my Queen," and I know that even though Dylan may have centuries of conditioning to undo, it's going to be fun being the one to unravel him.

6

MORGAN

With the idea of starting fresh and facing reality, I wake determined to deal with my writing. There's one thing that has always helped me get my creative juices flowing, so I lace up my sneakers and head out to the park for a run.

I cross the busy street outside the house and continue on the nearest path. It's early, but the weather has cooled enough that it feels nice outside. I plug my earbuds in, hit my playlist and pick up my pace.

The world slips away as I try to focus on my story. What started off as a story about a girl and her ravens ended up as so much more—something that mirrored reality in disturbingly sharp clarity. Maverick's ravens are lost when she opens the gate to the other world. One is injured, the others vanish. She kills the prince and the cat disappears. I know now that the story was really my history—or parts of it. The ravens are my guardians. Xavier, the prince. And Anita, a girl I considered a friend, was the cat that lured me that fateful day.

But what happens next?

I know what happened in my life. Nothing good. Nothing interesting, either. My parents died. I moved into a group home for my senior year and then on to college. After that I moved here and my entire life changed.

But none of that—at least prior to moving here--is book-worthy. Maybe I'm really not supposed to finish. I run over a bridge and past a playground with children zipping down a slide. The more I think on it, the more I consider that maybe I shouldn't be in the graduate program anymore. It was all a ruse to get me up here anyway, wasn't it? I know Dr. Christensen will be upset—he seems to be the only one not part of a larger plan, even if he is nosy as hell. *But*, I think, running around a fountain, *if my story is finished, it's finished.*

I get to a more populated area of the park and I spot what I think is a familiar, long braid of hair. In a pair of nearly non-existent running shorts and a tank top that accentuates her well-defined physique, Hildi stretches her calves against a bench.

Our last fight ended so oddly, with me winning a second time and her handing it well, I decide I've got nothing to lose by approaching the Valkyrie. I slow my jog and stop at the bench, taking a minute to catch my breath.

"Hi," I say to the woman as she glances up. The lack of surprise means she'd probably already spotted me.

"Morgan, how are you?" She straightens her laces and then stands. She's about three feet taller than me.

"Okay. I'm just trying to clear my head, you know? Make some life decisions on a run." I laugh, hoping she'll think it's a joke and not a pathetic revelation about my life, but again her steel blue eyes give me the impression she knows more about me than I'd like to admit.

"Exercise is good for the mind and body." She looks me up and down. "Are you ready for another round in the ring?"

"Not yet." I try my best to keep my face straight. So she doesn't know I've been split from the Morrigan. I'm sure I've retained my basic fighting skills, but the magic needed in the ring? I suspect those left with the Darkness. I'm definitely not willing to try it in an environment that may get me killed—or reveal to the entire supernatural world that I'm nothing but a mortal.

"But you'll be there tonight, right?"

"Tonight?" Fuck. If Clinton signed me up again I'm going to kick his ass.

She smiles, finally realizing I'm clueless. "The Raven Guard is the main event, did they not tell you?"

"No, no they did not."

"They're keeping secrets. One of their gifts, I think." She sighs and shakes her head as though this isn't a big surprise. I wonder again how well she knows my Guardians.

"I'm sure they forgot. Things have been a little hectic around the house lately."

"The Raven Guard are the fight's biggest draw. Watching them is a testimony to the ancient ways of war." Her whole expression lights up as she speaks. "You should definitely come and witness the spectacle. The whole arena has a different vibe. The pure energy is raw and everyone ascends to a higher level."

Ah, that could be the issue. Me versus the raw energy of my guardians? None of us knows what I am anymore—or what I can do. I'm a liability in a magical environment like that. They'd never risk it. Hildi studies me intently.

"What?" I ask, uncomfortable under her gaze.

"Come with me tonight. Be my guest. I think you'll be interested to see this side of the Guard." I'm tempted, because I would like to see them in action. But what if I lose control? Hildi nudges me further. "We'll go in the back door. They'll never know you're there."

A flock of birds flies over head, alighting from a massive tree. They're smaller than ravens, but still dark-feathered. I watch them take off against the bright blue sky, their wings flapping fast and hard.

I'm quitting school. Dropping my book. Helping Dylan conquer his fears. It's a day for change and being afraid of myself or anyone else is stupid. A total waste. I smile at Hildi and say, "I'll meet you at nine."

7

DAMIEN

Through the window of my studio I spot my girl walking in the back gate. Her hair is damp with sweat and her cheeks are flushed pink. A wet spot spreads across her chest from sweat. I'm in the middle of a project but I'm drawn to her anyway. I put down my tools, grab a water from the refrigerator, and head out into the sun.

Her eyes light up when she sees me and a thrill runs through me.

"Good morning," she says, shading her eyes from the sun.

"Hey, babe." I go in for a quick kiss before I give her the water. I want to taste the salt on her lips.

"Ugh, I stink," she says, shying away. I grab her anyway and wait until she finishes a gulp of water.

"I don't mind." She shakes her head but there's a look of interest in her eyes. An idea springs to mind. "If it would make you feel better you could take a shower—there's one in the back of the studio." I run a hand down her sticky back. "I could join you if you want?"

She presses her forehead into my chest and groans. "I'd love to. I would. But I promised myself that I'd go into my advisor's office today. I've been avoiding him for weeks."

"What's another day?" I skim a finger down her neck and

between her breasts, tugging at the edge of her top. I raise my eyebrows, looking for permission, but her jaw is set with determination. I give it one last shot. "I'm not really sure why we can't do both? Shower then meeting?"

She laughs. "Nice try, but I know you. We'd get in there and you'd get all soapy and I'd get all soapy and I think we've learned that you like to take your time."

Damn, this woman knows me well, and the idea of her being soaped up isn't helping her argument. I sigh and rub my head. "All right, go shower and I'll give you a ride to your advisor's office, okay?"

"Thank you," she replies, pushing up on her toes to kiss me again. I clench my hands around her waist and fight the urge to toss her in the shower anyway. "I'll be back down in an hour."

"I'll be ready."

She pulls away slowly, her fingers lingering in mine. With a tilt of her head she says, "And that shower idea? I'll keep that in mind, okay?"

She walks off and I head back into the shop to take a cold shower of my own.

8

MORGAN

I don't release my grip around Damien's waist until the motorcycle comes to a complete stop. Even then I'm reluctant to let go, as I like the way his body feels against mine and to be honest, I'm not looking forward to speaking to Christensen. I have a feeling he's not going to take my announcement well.

Damien squeezes my hand and then lifts off his helmet and then mine. "You okay?"

"Yeah, I'm just dreading this meeting."

He frowns. "What's going on?"

"I'm quitting the program."

Okay, what I saw before on his face wasn't a frown. The expression on his face is an actual frown. "You're what?" he asks as though he didn't hear me. He totally heard me.

"I'm quitting the program. I never should have been in it in the first place. That story wasn't my creative mind, it was a memory—sort of--and a painful one at that. Now that we're caught up to the present I've got nothing left to tell. My writer's block is not going away and I realized today that it's not a block. It's that the story is finished."

Damien is my wild Guardian. Free-spirited and independent. He doesn't care about rules or feel bound by the same internal struggle as the others. But he touches my chin and holds my eyes with his strange, intense, violet ones and says, "That story is far from complete, Morgan. The day your parents died and we changed to human form is another chapter entirely. The things we did. What we saw. It's a story for Dylan's history books."

"But it's not my story. It's yours. It's not Maverick's, my main character. None of this makes sense."

"Give it time and I think it will become clearer. You've been through a lot. Think about when you first got here and how the gates of your memory opened. You received a wealth of detail."

The simple fact Damien knows all of this and cares enough to say it rattles me. "I'll consider it, but even so, I have to go in and talk to him."

He nods. "I'll wait here."

I slide off the bike and he grabs me by the jacket, giving me a powerful kiss. The Morrigan may be gone but I still feel a burst of hunger from his touch. Even a mortal can't help but get a boost from Damien's raw sexual energy.

I take a deep breath and walk away, hoping I can figure out my next move.

The professor makes me wait.

I suppose I deserve it after forcing him to follow up on me for a month. I sit for twenty minutes in the lobby before the receptionist escorts me back to his office. Even then, he's not there. I'm instructed to wait a little longer.

Alone, I glance around the room, realizing I've never been alone in here before. The wall behind the desk is covered in certificates and three large, framed diplomas. A bookshelf flanks one wall and photos line the other. Curiosity grabs me and I stand, looking over the pictures. Professor Christensen seems to be quite the world traveler.

There are images of him all over the world, mostly at ancient ruins. Egypt, Rome, Greece, among many others. My eyes skim over his desk and land on a file with the name Anita Cross on the edge.

Anita.

I'd assumed she'd also left the program after her brother's death and the bizarre announcement that she'd been part of the plan for the Morrigan all along. Xavier was nothing but a sacrifice to the Goddess of War. But again, all of that was shut down when I split from the Darkness. What would Anita do now?

As much as I wanted to hate the girl, I still felt guilt for taking her brother's life—planned or not. I'd let the Darkness win and it will go down as my weakest moment.

I slip a finger under the edge of the file, desperately wanting to know what's inside, but I hear voices down the hall, followed by quick footsteps. I step back and move to my seat. My heart races even though I've done nothing wrong.

"Morgan, what a surprise." Dr. Christensen walks into the room behind me and circles the desk. He lays a stack of papers on top of the file folder and pushes back his chair to sit across from me. "I'm glad you came in."

"I apologize for my behavior lately. It's been incredibly unprofessional."

He looks back at me with kind eyes. "I know Xavier's death hit you hard."

"It was a shock, yes."

"And then Anita disappearing. I never expected that but you just don't know what people will do in a period of grief."

I sit up in my seat. "Anita did what?"

"You didn't know? I thought she must have contacted you. It's one of the reasons I needed to speak to you so desperately."

"No, she didn't. Why would she?"

He shrugs. "Professional courtesy? Friendship?"

"I don't think we really had much of either of those, sir."

I'd like to say he looks surprised at my comment but he doesn't—

more resigned. He shuffles the papers on his desk and I see my incomplete manuscript on the top. I feel a pang of sadness and confusion. Do I quit or is Damien right? Is there more to the story?

"I regret that this has been an odd start to your program, Morgan. There are always little bumps in the road but this is extreme. I've spoken to the board of directors, they're willing to overlook the critique portion of your assignment for the rest of this semester as long as you continue working in good faith."

"No more partners?"

"No."

"To be honest, Dr. Christensen, I was planning on coming here today to leave the program. I've been struggling with my writing."

"I'm not surprised. The chaotic events of late are not conducive to creativity. But I would be against you quitting entirely." He picks up my book. "This is stellar work. You have me hooked. This isn't a book that will go on a shelf for three weeks in a bookstore and then disappear. This is a book that will become a classic and reside on important desks for future generations."

"Seriously?"

"Absolutely. Take your time. Rest your mind and when you're ready the words will come back."

"Are you sure about that?"

"Positive," he says without missing a beat. "I have faith in you, Morgan, and you have work to complete. Some events in life are not an option. They're an obligation. Remember that."

The comment is strange but coming off the heels of Damien's thoughts I feel a little more confident that I can get my writing mojo back. "I'll do my best," I say, standing up. "So you haven't heard from Anita at all?"

"No. Not since the visitation."

Shortly before we performed the separation spell. Maybe she felt it and left. Or maybe her role in all of this is over. Either way, I'm not sad she's gone.

9

MORGAN

After an uneventful dinner, I patiently wait for the men to leave The Nead. They don't make a fuss about it and if I hadn't been warned I never would have noticed them slipping down to the garage.

Davis doesn't question when I ask him to call me a taxi, but the glint in his eye tells me he's no fool and already knows where I'm headed. Maybe it's my casual outfit. Not quite workout clothes, but jeans and a t-shirt.

"Stay safe, Ms. Morgan."

"I will, Davis. Have a good night."

Hildi sent me the address and I ask the driver to take me around back. The alley is dark but there are people milling around. I hop out of the car and am happy to find the Valkyrie waiting for me. She's also dressed in normal clothing—she's not fighting, either.

"You made it," she says, giving me a smile. Somehow we've become friends, I think.

"I snuck out after the guys left."

She raises a perfectly sculpted blonde eyebrow. "You're not allowed to leave?"

"Oh, no. I can, but they like to keep track of me. You know, guardian stuff, but they still never told me they were coming tonight. I decided I'd surprise them."

Her grin widens. "I like it. Sneaky. And they deserve it."

The bouncer watching the back door lets us in and we're immediately engulfed by the massive crowd. It's way more crowded than the last time I was here. And just like Hildi said at the park, the Raven Guard is definitely a draw. A huge banner hangs over the ring with an image of a black crow, talons extended.

I can't stop staring at the banner and Hildi tugs on my arm. "What?"

"I guess I didn't realize they were that well known."

"The Raven Guard?" she laughs. "They're legendary. Literally. Legends are written about them." She winks. "You, too."

Of course I know this, I've read the lore—the myths—there are books about it back at The Nead, but it's weird to know that others know about it, too. I squeeze down a row of spectators and sit next to Hildi. When we're settled I ask, "So tell me what you know about them? What makes them so special?"

"Their sheer power for one thing," she declares. "You'll see that tonight. The fights will be epic, I assure you. But beyond that it's the mystery, I think. It's well known they were created by the hands of gods, molded to protect the earth from the Darkness that lurks beneath the surface."

"You know about the Darkness?" I ask, feeling a little exposed.

"Everyone in here knows about the Darkness, sweetheart. We know who you are. What those boys are doing for you." She nods toward a door on the far side of the room. I see a glimpse of Clinton. "You realize every woman and a few men in here have tried to lure them into bed?"

"I gathered as much last time I was here. Before our fight."

There's a moment of silence and I sense that Hildi has something else to say. Finally she blurts, "Is it true? That you've taken them all for mates? Not just one as intended?"

"How do you know this?"

She laughs. "There's more gossip in the supernatural world than in the human world. News travels fast. Especially when it has to do with the fates." I must look confused (as well as a little horrified) to learn that everyone in here knows about me and the Guardians so she says, "There are decisions in our world that can affect everyone. When the Morrigan chooses five mates instead of one, people notice."

"I'm not the Morrigan anymore, everyone knows that too, right?"

She watches me closely but says nothing. The lights flicker overhead and the loud buzzer sounds, signaling the beginning of the events. Hildi leans in close and says, "Another time you'll tell me how they are in bed. I assume they're legendary in that respect as well."

"Uh, okay," I say, wondering what she would think about me not having sex with two of the Guardians yet. I suspect that news would travel faster than a bolt of lightning.

The shaman/referee strides across the ring carrying a microphone. His voice is deep with a slight accent when he begins to speak. "Welcome to our main event! The night you've all been waiting for! The return of the Raven Guard!"

The crowd jumps to their feet, cheering and shouting for my Guardians. A light flashes over the audience and that's when I see many are holding up signs—each declaring support for one of the men.

I lean into Hildi, "So when you said this was a big deal, you meant it was a big deal."

"Oh yeah. These guys are so quiet and elusive that when they finally come out of that hidey-hole you've got, the community loses their minds."

A woman two down from me starts chanting Bunny's name. I glance down and realize that she's wearing a headband with bunny ears. I see what Hildi means by lost minds.

"This is surreal," I say, more to myself than to Hildi. My eyes are trained on the ring where the shaman is announcing each of the men. Clinton, Bunny, Sam, Damien, and Dylan all step forward when their names are called. They look oddly blasé, as though this is a normal day for them. Who knows, it probably is.

"For those of you that are new to the fights tonight, I'll explain the process," the shaman says, his voice echoing through the crowd. "Each Guardian will fight a beast from another realm. They do not know what or who they will encounter. Each fight is to the death. The survivor wins."

"Magical death, right?" I clarify. I'd killed Hildi in our own battle in that ring. As long as you're in the ropes the death is only temporary and symbolic.

"Yes, but I don't think you have anything to worry about."

I know what she means. It's impossible to think of them as losers in any fight, but I also know that they would not step into a ring without a worthy competitor. Whatever happens below will be brutal and the feeling in my stomach urges me to leave before it even begins. The thought is fleeting. They've each watched me fight my own battles and it's time for me to do the same.

There are no further announcements but the men do shake hands. Clinton steps forward and the spectators scream and shout their support. A figure steps into the ring across from him. In the light he looks completely normal—not like a beast at all—and definitely physically comparable to Clinton.

"He's fighting that guy?"

"He's just a vessel—once the fight begins, the beast will emerge. It keeps the guards on their toes. They have no idea what sort of opponent will appear, but I did hear a rumor that they'll be fighting their biggest fears."

"Their fears?"

"The shaman does a spell and he's able to figure out what the Guardians fear the most. That concept is incorporated in their opponent."

Clinton, who is wearing nothing but long, black pants, clenches his fists as he waits for the signal to begin. His upper body is bare and even from up in the stands I can see the rippled muscles that cover every inch of his arms, chest, and back. He's shoeless and from the glint in his eye I know he's dying to get started.

It only takes a moment for him to get his wish. The buzzer sounds and his opponent steps to the middle of the ring. He's a scrawny man, with pale skin and an excessive amount of hair on his chest and back. They circle one another and Clinton bides his time. I've fought him enough times to know he'll never make the first move.

Turns out he doesn't need to, as the man flinches and cries as though he's already been hit. His back arches. His teeth clamp shut. He falls, knees buckling as Clinton, ever alert, stands by and watches it happen.

"What is this?" I ask, totally confused.

"He's transforming," Hildi replies. I can nearly feel the energy vibrating off her. She obviously loves this. She points to the ring. "Keep watching."

The man rolls around the floor, painfully crying as his body spasms and jerks. There's a final crack, like the sound of his back breaking, and I think maybe he died on the stage. That the fight was a bust, but no, something happens, a transformation like Hildi said. His hair lengthens, darkens, growing thick across his entire body. His face alters, turning into a longer, hair-covered snout. Rows of sharp, jagged teeth are revealed when he opens his mouth. It only takes a minute but the man is gone and an animal—or beast—takes his place. He growls and the sound reverberates through the building, echoing off the high, metal ceiling.

Clinton grins when the beast notices him waiting and I swear his body has grown in the last minute. Clinton's biceps and calves are cut and massive. He appears taller—broader. The snaggle-toothed animal pushes back on his hind legs and pounces. Clinton meets him in the air.

Their bodies crash together and as much as I want to look away from the sharp teeth and tearing flesh, I can't. Clinton is poetry in motion—pure athleticism. It feels like we're watching them fight for hours but when I hear the final snap of the beast's neck and the buzzer chimes, the clock says two minutes. Two was all it took.

Clinton raises both arms over his head, his chest coated in a slick spray of blood, and is declared the winner. His smile is proud. His fans ecstatic.

"So?" Hildi says, jabbing me with an elbow. "What did you think?"

I watch as the carcass of the beast is removed from the ring.

"We have four more to go?"

"Yep."

"I think I'm going to need a drink."

~

I HAVE THREE. Drinks, that is, as I watch the Guardians battle beasts I now know are from the Otherside. They're disgusting. First, there was the wolf-monster that Clinton demolished.

Then Damien clashed with a lizard-skinned beast with a tongue that acts like a whip. That fight goes on forever—twenty minutes— until Damien is covered in forked lashes all over his tattooed skin. Venom coats the amphibian's saliva, making welts rise, but the Guardian cuts the tongue off at the throat and then ties it around the lizard's neck, choking him.

Yeah, that's when I order drink number four.

I'm less sure when Sam swaggers into the ring, his pants slung low around his hips. His muscles are lean beneath his black t-shirt, the color matching the short fur of the six-eyed, eight-legged, spider-thing that spews a greenish-yellow slime when he guts him with a blade that appears in his belt mid-fight. He tears off his shirt after the spider is dead, wiping the blade on the cotton. The women in the crowd swoon at the sight of his body and even I smile when he flexes and makes a show. I can't deny that I'm impressed by his skill and speed. It's a side of him I'm unaccustomed to.

Hildi leans into me and whispers, "Is he this arrogant in bed?"

I smile. "No, quite the opposite."

She shakes her head in amusement.

Although I've never seen Sam fight, I'm not surprised he does well. Sam is the kind of man that lives life with easy success. His stunning good looks are an easy cover for him being a brilliant solider. But when Bunny steps into the ring with his limp, useless arm, I grab onto Hildi out of fear. Bunny, my sweet, gentle artist. Surely, he's adept. But he's also suffered greatly. I am both filled with dread and eager anticipation to see what he can do.

"Tell me he'll survive," I plea.

"You don't have faith in your own Guardian?" Hildi's incredulous expression says it all.

"I do, I just..." I swallow. "He got that injury protecting me while I was being a fool. If he fails out there it's my fault."

Her blue eyes are hard. "If you learn one thing tonight, Morgan, it's that you should never underestimate these men. Never. Not for a second. They're smart, savvy, and made from a sense of commitment and passion that no injury or mere disfigurement could destroy." She grips my hand. "But I will tell you one weakness they may have."

"What is that?"

"You."

A roar ripples through the crowd and my attention is dragged back down to the ring. Bunny no longer has a limp arm. Instead a sharp, pike-like weapon is attached to the end. He slashes it at the the man across from him that has transformed into a rabid, drooling zombie.

Just like in my battle with Hildi, the ring provides fighters with weapons and attributes they'd have in an alternate universe. But also like my fight, Bunny doesn't need the weapon. I see the blood thirst in his copper eyes as he fights off his attacker. Or rather, *attackers*. The one man that entered the ring splits into six zombies that may be brain-dead but they're fast with dirty claws and sharp teeth. Hildi tells me they roam the barren lands of the Otherside looking for flesh to eat. Bunny moves with a speed I never could have imagined. Leaping, kicking, and easily taking down the shuffling horde. A chill inches up my spine as one gets too close to Bunny's bare shoulder, his teeth perilously close. Again, it's a foolish moment because it's the final gain the zombie has in the fight. Bunny knocks him to the ground and stabs him in the temple with the end of the pike. I watch in fascination as my delicate artist-turned-savage-warrior rips the head off the body and holds it in the air on the tip of the steel pike.

Hildi gives me a knowing look and I say, "Point taken."

"You must have confidence in them," she tells me as the attendants at the ring clean the mat. "It's paramount."

"I do," I say, annoyed that she keeps bringing it up. "They're my mates, Hildi. I chose them based on their merits—without even seeing this side of them. These men are complex, complicated creatures. You tell me not to underestimate them—you shouldn't underestimate me, either."

A moment of tension sits between us but the final buzzer rings. Hildi can't hide the look of excitement. I know that Dylan is her preferred Guardian and if he showed a sliver of weakness she'd consume him greedily. This shouldn't be much of a surprise. He's dark and broody, incredibly elusive, and even I haven't managed to get him into bed.

Yet.

The other Guardians stand by the edge of the ring, each in various states of disarray. Their injuries healed the instant they stepped out of the ring but they're filthy, covered in slime, dirt, and blood. Damien and Sam both drink from bottles of liquor. Women push through the crowd to get to them but security keeps them back. I hear their names shouted through the arena. As a group, they too only have eyes for their Sentinel. Who will he battle?

"I've heard the game masters have something special set up for Dylan this time," Hildi says over the increasingly energetic crowd.

"Something special? Worse than the spider or lizard thing?" I don't even fight the shudder inching down my spine.

The lights flicker and the buzzer sounds. Dylan makes his way across the ring. He's wearing tight, black pants and thick-soled boots. He pushes his hair back, revealing the taut arm muscles under his gray T-shirt. The difference between Dylan and the others is that all of his emotions are kept low under the surface. Only a few times have I witnessed them bubbling to the forefront. From what I've seen so far, I suspect the game masters know this, too, and will do whatever they can to push him to his limits.

The crowd has started something different, a rhythmic stomping of their feet against the metal bleachers. After a moment the sound overtakes everything else. The entire arena is a wave of unified sound. I can't keep my eyes off the man in the ring. He rolls his shoulders and faces the opposite side of the ring.

The overhead lights flash across the ring and land on a very small person. A gasp ripples through the crowd and the stomping slows. I frown and ask Hildi, "Is that a child?"

The Valkyrie tenses. "The game masters aren't just toying with him physically but mentally as well."

"What?" I ask, but Dylan is walking toward the child—it's a she— a girl, with dark hair and a flared skirt. A barrette glints in her hair. An unsettling feeling unfurls in my chest. "What is he going to do?"

"What do you think?"

The girl turns her head and my blood runs cold. I look over to the Guardians and see their faces drain, their complexions paling. I push past Hildi, past the others in my row and race down the stairs.

There's no doubt in my mind who that girl is.

She's me.

Even while running, I can tell that he recognizes her—me. There's a falter in his step as he flicks his wrists blades, shooting from the back of his hands like feathers on a wing. I reach the sidelines and the security guard holds me back.

"Damien!" I shout, as he's the closest. "Damien!"

He turns, a deep line across his forehead, clearly confused about me being here. But he waves for security to let me pass and gives me a hand up to the edge of the ring.

"What are you doing here?" he asks, looping an arm around my waist. He squeezes me in next to Sam, who also does a double-take when he realizes I'm here. On the other side of the rails I spot Dylan circling my tiny doppelganger.

"Hildi invited me." I point over his shoulder. "What the hell is that all about?"

Before anyone can answer, the mini-me, wearing a dress I distinctly remember, opens her mouth wide and unhinges her jaw like a snake. Her teeth jut forward, dripping with venom, and any hesitation Dylan has vanishes. He slashes across her body with the blades and I yelp, covering my eyes. Damien squeezes my side and I look up to see black smoke in the place of the girl. I stand straight and watch in horror as the form sweeps into a swirling tornado, spiraling up in the air. The whole arena is frozen in fascination as the mist takes shape. I notice the hair first. Then the lips. Damien inhales next to me and Sam's hand slips into mine.

The Morrigan, looking very much like me.

Dylan retracts the blades and the sound echoes through the silent room. He reaches into his back pocket and pulls out a small, oblong object. With a sharp twist it unfurls into a coil of leather. It's a whip.

"What's happening here? Why is he fighting me?"

The crack of the whip cuts off my questioning. Dylan circles the mocking form. She licks her lips and rests a hand on her breast. She speaks in quiet voice that I suspect only he can hear. Whatever she says hits him like a ton of bricks.

He stares at her for the longest time and I think for a moment that he won't kill her. His eyes grow cold, dark blue sapphires. She smiles mockingly and steps forward. "She can't hurt him can she?" I ask.

"She'll do damage," Damien says. He taps the side of his head before leaning over the barrier. "Destroy her, Dylan!"

I can't take my eyes off of the figment. She looks so like me. Her eyes, her face and hair. She's a perfect replica. I spot the slightest wavering in his eye, a confusion. What is it about the Morrigan that has him so tied up in knots?

"Dylan?" I shout. He looks over, blinking once. "Slay that bitch!"

He jumps out of his calm and lunges for her. She punches back, many of her moves reminiscent of my own. I can predict each swing, each step. I know before she does when she'll kick or duck. She and Dylan fight hand to hand, her dark eyes lit with fire following each hit. He clips her chin and her head snaps back. To my surprise, blood drips from her lip. She licks it and grins.

He moves quickly, swiping her feet from under her legs. Bending down, he reaches for her throat and holds her in the air. The crowd jumps to their feet and the chorus of feet stomping begins again. The figure shifts again, right between his fingers, turning to smoke. Again it whirls through the air but this time over his head. Out of the mist, feathers stretch, creating a wide span of wings, followed by a beak and beady, dark eyes. The crowd gasps, crying out at the figure—we all know what it means. When the Morrigan sends her Raven, her enemy is dead.

Dylan stands beneath the Raven, its shadow covering his face. Massive wings flap and I think he's about to drop—surrender to the power of the Darkness. The bird coasts through the air, wings spread in victory, and I feel Sam's fingers tighten in mine. Dylan moves just an inch—barely that—clenching his fist. The coil of his forgotten whip slithers across the canvas mat. He spins on his heel, the black tail flying overhead, ensnaring the Raven by the feet. He yanks hard, muscles bulging, pulling the bird back to the ground. It lands with a thud, no longer bird. No longer a body. Just the fading mist of magic that has just been defeated.

The buzzer rings over the cheering crowd and the lights flash, signaling the end of the fight.

Damien pulls me into a hug, clearly relieved the event is over. I release him quickly, pushing past to get to Dylan who shoves through the barrier to get off the ring. He doesn't look at me or the others. His eyes are hard and tortured—focused on getting out of the arena.

"Let him go," Clinton says, holding me back. "Just give him a minute."

Any other night I would, but not tonight. Not this time.

I ignore him and slip away, following Dylan's wake.

10

DYLAN

The crowd parts, fully aware they need to stay out of my way. I keep my eyes focused on the door against the far wall. If I can just get there, I can lose it in private.

Even though they give me space, the spectators scream my name with such ferocity I feel it in my bones. I'm propositioned. I'm revered. There is no higher ranking in this arena than Guardian and after that spectacle they all want a piece of me or my brothers.

A dark shadow flits across the corner of my eye and I clench my fist, looking for the handle of the whip, but of course it's gone. So is the shadow.

I'm losing my mind.

The door is five feet away and I ignore every voice calling my name. Four feet. Three. Two...

I slam my palms against the metal door and step into a blast of cool air from the prep room. I tear off my shirt and throw it on the floor.

The door opens right behind me and I spin. The shaman stands between me and the door.

"Get out of here," I tell him.

"Dylan, I did that for your own good."

I reach for a towel and wipe my face. "Are you fucking kidding me? I know I signed up for it, but that was brutal. You didn't do that to the others."

"Yes, I did. I didn't do anything to you. I perform the spell—you're the one that willingly revealed to the world what your biggest fear is, and it turns out that it's a little girl."

Something in my brain snaps and I charge toward the shaman. He holds up his hand, palm out, and an invisible barrier appears between the two of us. I slam into it full force and bounce back, crashing into the wall.

"Get your shit together, Dylan. This war isn't over."

He opens the door and leaves, engulfed in the sound of the crowd. I stagger to my feet and pick up the nearest object, a long metal bench. I throw it down the hallway where it slides until it crashes into the far wall. I punch the locker, slamming my fist into the metal, over and over and over, until the skin breaks and blood drips down my hand. The fight flashes before me. Morgan as a little girl, The Morrigan as an evil temptress, the symbolic raven.

The shaman is right. The war isn't over no matter how much I want it to be.

I kick over a trashcan and face the wall as the door opens once again.

"Get out. I don't want to talk to anyone."

After a moment the door closes and I exhale, trying to clear my mind. I'm just so fucking angry and so unbelievably scared. Not just for me but for the other Guardians and for Morgan the most.

I hear a footstep and spin, fists clenched and ready. The real Morgan stands before me, hands up in peace, looking just as beautiful in tight jeans and a hoodie as she does in a fancy dress. I take a step back.

Her eyes dart to the destruction I've caused in the room and down to my bleeding hand. "You're hurt," she says, closing the distance between us.

"It's nothing," I grunt, wiping my knuckles on my pants. "You should leave."

"I'm not leaving, Dylan." She reaches for me and I flinch. Adrenaline still runs through my veins and one false move and I may snap her like a twig.

Again, my fears are festering and open tonight. I look away from her face but can smell her hair and feel her heat.

"If you won't leave, then I will." I start to move around her but her hand clamps on my arm.

"You're not going anywhere and neither am I." I glance at her hand and think of how easily I could get away, but then my eyes skim up her body to her face and I know that's nothing but a damned lie. "Tonight is the night you stop running from me. You stop being afraid of me."

I laugh. "And how do you propose doing that?"

She pushes up on her toes but I'm already leaning down, drawn to her like a magnet. "You're my mate, Dylan, no more running. No more excuses. It's time to get that bitch out of your head and your hands on my body."

The internal fight is strong. So strong, and I've resisted for so long, but the image of that Raven overhead broke something in me. If the sign is true then I don't have long to wait.

I place my hands on her hips and give in.

11

MORGAN

Dylan's lips are hot and his chest is sweaty, fresh wounds marking his skin. He kisses me eagerly and I want it this way, raw and unrelenting. He's worked so hard to bring himself to my level that I now realize that will never happen. Dylan is a warrior. A fighter. He carries the burdens of the past and future on his shoulders.

He guides me to the wall, my back pressing against the hard surface. With one hand against the wall and the other skimming my side, I tug at the waistband of his pants. I'm relieved there's no hesitation—no fighting back. He keeps kissing me while he slips off his pants, then the skintight boxers he wears underneath. There's no denying his arousal. Standing back, his eyes follow my hand as I unzip the hoodie and he brushes it off my shoulders. He dips his head, first kissing between my breasts, then sinking his teeth into the soft flesh in the crook of my neck. My nipples harden and I release a hiss of pleasure.

"Don't stop," I tell him, even though nothing implies that he will. Every inch of my skin tingles in anticipation.

"I've waited an eternity to prove my worth as your mate," he declares. "I couldn't stop now if the gods themselves ripped me from this realm."

My stomach tightens when his cock brushes against me. The spot between my legs dampens as he twists his fingers under my panties, the fabric ripping in a hard yank. Our bodies bump and again he claws to get the bra off my back, impatient with any barrier between us. The elastic snaps under the pressure and the scrap of lace falls to the floor with the rest of our clothing. When we're both bare and his mouth has found mine again, he lifts me under the legs, pushing me against the wall.

His cock slides between my legs—not in me—not yet. I'm thankful for his strength, the way he can hold me up, the way I can feel his body. I like the way it feels to press against his lower belly. The way his skin rubs against mine. I like the sticky tip of his cock against my backside. I press against him. My breasts, my clit, my ass.

I'm assured by the low groan in his throat that he likes it too.

Biting his bottom lip, he growls in return, but I only want proof this is real—not another dream or slip from reality. No magic. Just us. The pain does nothing but spur him on. The noise is deep and trembles in his chest. With strong hands he positions me the way he wants me, the way that it feels so, so good.

I'm slippery wet. He's hard with want. Just before he enters me, he pulls back and stares at me with eyes that cut to my soul. I toy with his hard, brown nipple and he swallows hard.

"Take me," I whisper against his lips. "Fuck me."

His eyes are pinned to mine and he licks his lips. In a reverent tone he says, "As you wish, Your Majesty."

I throw my arms over his neck as he enters. I feel him in every inch of my body. I feel his passion. His loyalty. Digging my nails into his back, I hold on for dear life when he begins to move. Dylan isn't just mating with me. He's exorcising demons.

He isn't gentle. He isn't slow. There's no patience or courtesy like with the others. No, Dylan fucks me righteously, hips thrusting so hard my breath comes in shallow gasps. I weave a hand into his hair and force his mouth against mine. His jaw tenses and I feel rather than hear the words coming off his lips.

"Oh god," I cry.

His moves grow frantic, the coil in my lower belly tightens and twists, bringing me to a shuddering, panting halt. Me, not him, because as my walls quiver and I groan my ecstasy, he pounds into me with unrelenting need.

My knees bend and I'm almost curved against the wall, when he comes to a fast and sudden halt, dropping his forehead to mine and spilling everything he has into me in several exaggerated thrusts.

I brush the hair off his forehead and he looks at me with dazed eyes. "Better?" I ask. He's still in me. Warm. Bonded.

He blinks and a slow, relieved grin graces his beautiful face. "Yeah. Yeah, that's better."

As much as I hate it, I separate from him, enough to get down on wobbly legs. He's barely moved, keeping close, and I touch him on the stomach. "I need you to tell me what that was all about."

"I know. I will."

"You can't protect me forever." I look up at his face.

"I can," he says. "And I will, but you're right, we need to talk. All of us."

He wraps me in his arms, the anger and angst he's been carrying a fraction of what it's been over the past few weeks. I know we need to leave the room and find the other Guardians, but right now I want to just have a final moment of peace. From the weight of Dylan's arms around me, I know he feels it too.

~

We take the long way back to The Nead, walking hand in hand down the long, busy streets of New York and then cutting through the park. The rage that consumed him back at the fight seems to have dissipated, although it's replaced with something different.

It's nearly dawn and the house is quiet when we walk up the

front steps. I'm not ready for whatever it is that Dylan has to say to me and the other Guardians. When we reach the landing between the floors of my suite and his, I lift my chin and say, "Come to my room."

I'm surprised when he says yes with a kiss and allows me to lead him to my bedroom by hand.

This time we take it slower. We're both clean from the showers at the gym. The blood has washed away and Dylan smells fresh, like soap. His blue eyes pulse with energy as he takes his time unzipping my hoodie, brushing his fingers over the swell of my breasts. He kisses down my body and I lean back on the soft cushion of my bed, lifting my hips so he can remove my jeans. From there I watch him lift his shirt over his head, revealing the impressive stack of muscles that line his stomach. When he lowers his pants I don't hesitate to reach for him, taking the hard but soft rod of velvet in my hand.

His stomach caves at my touch and he climbs over my body. Warm to warm. Wet to wet. His tongue tastes minty and the pads of his skilled fingers feel rough. When he rolls on his back and adjusts me over his hips my whole body goes on alert. I ride him slowly, rolling my hips at my own pace. I plan to make it last as long as I can because when we get out of the bed, I have a feeling our lives will no longer be the same.

꩜

HE'S GONE when I wake. His side of the bed cool is to the touch, but there's a note that simply says to meet downstairs at nine.

I check the clock. It says 8:54.

Scrambling, I race to the bathroom to wash my face and brush my teeth. I'm dressed in the clothing from last night when I walk into the library. Everyone is waiting, except...

"Where's Bunny?" I ask.

"I tried his room. It was locked," Sam says, making space for me on the couch. I walk past Dylan and catch his scent. My knees weaken and I think about his face, hours ago, lost in ecstasy. When our eyes meet I have no doubt he's thinking of the same thing. I realize that I've had sex with every man in this room. I should be scandalized by this. I'm not.

"Can we meet without him?" I direct this question to Dylan.

"We'll have to," he replies, shutting the door and walking to a leather armchair. I'm surprised when he sits down. Dylan rarely sits at these meetings. "We're running out of time."

"What's going on?" Clinton asks from his spot across from me. Damien sits in the chair next to him.

"You all witnessed my fight last night. The shaman plucked a fear out of my head I hadn't been able to recognize on my own." He glances at me. "Well, not all of it. I've conquered a few demons since then."

"This is about the Morrigan, isn't it? She said something to you," Damien says. He leans forward in his seat. "What was it?"

"Wait," I say before anyone goes further. "The fights aren't 'real', how could she say something to you?"

"It's real enough," Sam says from beside me. "It's a magic that channels energy from an alternate universe. Like how your weapon showed up in the fight against Hildi. It's real, but not real."

A rock forms in my stomach. "So you're saying that was the real Morrigan?"

Dylan swallows and nods. "Some part of her, yes."

"So she isn't dead."

"No."

I start to stand but Sam tugs me back. I yank my arm away, glaring down at him. "You said she was gone?"

"We said she split from you. There was no evidence she'd been eliminated entirely."

I shake my head, refusing to believe what they're saying. "That's rubbish. I'm evidence. I'm not hearing her voice anymore, or having mood swings or you know, off on a horny bender of sexual energy swapping like before."

"To be fair," Clinton says, "I think your sexual appetite is being satisfied on a more consistent basis now that you've declared your mates."

"What about the voices? They're gone. In fact, I'm creatively dry. Whatever the Morrigan was feeding me for my book has stopped completely."

"I don't think you understand," Dylan says. "The Morrigan was split from you. In the myths there are often three incarnations. You may just be one."

"Why would you say that?"

I don't like the set of his jaw when he replies, "Because she told me the Darkness was still in this world. People are going to die—if they haven't already."

"I haven't hurt anyone."

"That you know of," Damien points out.

"Are you saying you suck so much as Guardians you've let me wander around the city infecting people? Because that sounds like more your problem than mine."

"We may have been a little lax," Dylan admits. "But not anymore. Not until we figure this out."

"What you're saying is that you don't trust me."

"No. That's not what I'm saying. I'm saying we don't exactly know what is going on. I did warn you it was possible to have fallout from using dark magic," he says, holding my angry stare.

"So you don't trust me *and* it's my fault." I'm being irrational. I know this, but that's the thing about irrationality. It doesn't make sense. I move to leave the room and feel Dylan's large hand wraps around my arm. "What?"

"We don't blame you. But it's our job to stay on top of this. We've all been a little distracted."

I jerk away and head to the door. "Don't worry," I say over my shoulder. "I'm just going to my room. I can't kill anyone up there."

12

CLINTON

"Let her go," I say to the other three. "Give her a minute to calm down."

Dylan rubs his face and sits in the chair. "I knew she wouldn't take it well, but I didn't think she'd flip out like this."

"Really?" Sam says. "You didn't think she'd be upset to learn that more people are going to die and that the big spell we performed was a dud?"

"It wasn't a dud," I chime in. "We accomplished what we wanted—to get the Darkness out of Morgan so she wasn't killing people anymore. She's not."

Damien raises an eyebrow. "You sure about that?"

"Pretty fucking sure."

"Then who is the Morrigan talking about?"

"We need to check the hospitals," Sam says.

"Or the morgue," Damien adds. "If we find the victims we can find who's doing it."

Dylan stretches his legs. "At least we know that the Morrigan herself is in the Otherside—she revealed that in the ring. And if we assume it isn't Morgan…"

"Then there's a third," I say. "We'll have to find her. Shouldn't be too hard in a city the size of New York."

Sam hops up and walks around the room. "So what do we do about Morgan? How do we find out where she stands in all this?"

"We test her," Dylan says. "Like before. If she's carrying part of the Darkness inside of her or some sort of mystical power, we'll know."

I can't help but ask, "Will we?"

No one answers that question. After a moment I add, "So really, where's Bunny? It's not like him to miss a meeting."

Damien chimes in. "I haven't seen him since the fight. He disappeared after Dylan's round."

"Like I said, I checked his room. He didn't answer and the door was locked," Sam says. "But if his paintings look anything like my photos he probably already knew this was coming."

"You knew?" Dylan asks.

"Not specifically, but yeah, I knew something was off. I guess I just hoped I was wrong."

Damien rubs his chin. "Well, find him and we need to get a look at his most recent work." He looks at Sam. "Yours, too."

Sam nods. "Sounds good."

I look around the room. "And Morgan?"

Dylan grimaces. "We'll give her until tomorrow to rest. After that we've got to know what she can do."

"And what if she can't do anything? What if she's just a mortal?" Damien asks.

I glance at Dylan, who looks as concerned as I feel. "Then we're probably fucked."

13

MORGAN

Where there was warmth is a snap of cold, sharp and freezing across her brow. Maverick takes in her surroundings. Stone walls and floors. A torch-lit hallway. A moment ago she was in the forest behind her family home, fighting the gray cat and killing the prince. Now she's somewhere far away and unfamiliar.

She looks at her hands. Blood has stained her palms. The dagger from before is gone but a longer, more deadly blade hangs from her hip.

"Where the hell am I?" she says aloud.

No voice replies but she feels something—the deep thrum of magic.

Maverick notices her clothing has changed. She's no longer in the school outfit she'd worn into the woods. Her pants are a form-fitting black leather. Sturdy boots cover her feet. Her top is dark and made of thick hide. She realizes quickly that she must have been injured. Maybe killed, and this is nothing but a hallucination.

She takes a shaky step down the hall, figuring the only way out is to either wake up or figure out where she is. In the distance a loud explosion rocks the foundation. Cannon fire? Maverick isn't in the suburbs of Georgia anymore. She continues walking.

Footsteps echo in the distance and she presses herself in a shadow against the cold wall. At the nearest intersection a group of soldiers runs past, dressed in the darkest of blacks. A blood red patch rests on their breast. She's too far to make out the design.

Once she's sure they're gone she turns the way they've come from and works her way through the twists and turns of the hallways. She has no idea where she's going but a tug in the pit of her stomach guides her. Left, then right, then right again. There's no hesitation at the turns. Instinct leads her.

That is until she gets to a split in the hallway. Three different directions off the main hall. Her brain tells her to move forward but her heart tugs her to the left. Another sound bounces off the stone walls and she chooses the path ahead before she's noticed.

The corridor grows larger, taller and wider with each step. The décor is grand. Tapestries line the walls, each depicting a different bloody battle. Maverick pauses in front of one. In a rich black thread a raven flies across the sky.

There's little doubt what and who lies at the end of the hall. She takes a deep, nerve-settling breath.

The grand, arched doors are wide open. They're made of a thick, impenetrable iron. The activities in the room keep eyes directed away from her and she slowly inches her way into the crowded chamber.

Spectators press their backs against the edges of the room. The ceiling is high and vaulted. The center focus of the room is a throne and the undeniable queen perched in its seat. Two enormous banners hang from the rafters—ravens, naturally. Both carry skulls in their talons.

The queen has her own unit of guards but their faces are unfamiliar. One guard with wavy blond hair and a beard to match steps forward.

"Quiet!"

The entire hall falls into silence. Maverick inches her way behind a stone pillar.

"You're all here to learn of the fate of our mission," the Queen says, *her voice strong and confident.* "A sacrifice was made. The entry breached. They lost a man."

"But," a man across the room says. "What about the cannons?"

"Step forward," the Queen demands, but it's pointless because the guards, including the one that had spoken before, have dragged him from his spot in the crowd. In an even tone she asks, "Did you wish to speak?"

"The cannons," he says again. Fear shadows his expression. "There is fighting on the battlefield, correct?"

As if on cue another explosion rattles the lead-glass windowpanes.

"As this man has pointed out, a battle rages in the south side of the country. During the attack on the entry gate complications arose." Murmurs roll through the crowd. The Queen holds up her hand, asking for silence. Maverick hasn't moved an inch. "The Guardians are in our realm. They think they can keep us back, but we'll kill them, leaving the gate unprotected. It's only a matter of time before we obliterate it entirely."

She waves her hand and the bearded guard pushes the questioning man to his knees.

"I'm sorry," he apologizes but everything moves too quick. Maverick watches as a blade slices through the air and with a quick stab, releases the life from the man's body. He falls face first, cheek landing on the stone floor. It's only then that she notices the flash of gray rubbing against the queen's feet.

The cat.

I BLINK and stare at the words on the page, or rather, *pages*. I flip through the notebook, stunned at the volume. I haven't written a sentence in the past month and then, *wham*! All that tumbles out without a second thought.

A strange sensation overcomes me. A little out-of-body and a whole lot déjà vu. Just like with the first part of my book, the story feels close. Too close. But how? I know I wasn't ever in the Otherside.

I was here, dealing with the loss of my parents and surviving. I think back to what Dylan has told me about the past five years. That after the skirmish in the forest they transformed into men and went to fight a deadly battle against the Morrigan—keeping her out of this realm. Maybe that's it? Maybe I'm seeing their time in the Otherside.

A knock on my door makes me jump and I close my notebook, although not before I see the final line about the gray cat.

Anita.

I'd definitely like to have a conversation with her—if only I could find out where she's hiding.

From the fading light outside my window I see that hours have passed. Just how long have I been up here? Whoever is outside the door bangs again and I hop up, and shout, "I'm coming."

I don't run, I'm still annoyed from the meeting earlier. I feel like there's a tug of war on my body—my mind. Is the Darkness gone? The Morrigan? When they suggested I may have a little of her power left I can't deny I was excited. In a strange way I missed her. But I know she's an evil bitch and the last thing I want is her to control me.

I have a moment of clarity as I reach for the door. That's the thing. The Morrigan didn't really have control of me. When we were one *I* could control *her*. I turn the knob and Clinton stands on the other side, knuckles raised.

"Were you going to bust down the door?"

"If you didn't open it, I would've," he replies. He studies me. "You okay?"

"Just tired."

He frowns. "Well I hate to tell you, but we've got to go out."

"And do what?"

"We tracked down a few people with symptoms. I figured you'd want to go with me to check them out—see if they're infected."

Hell yes I want to go.

"Let me get my jacket."

"Shit," I say, looking at the man in quarantine. I've never seen him before. Never heard or seen his name. Clinton said something to the guard and got us five minutes of access. His gray pallor and glassy eyes look exactly like Xavier's before he died. "Who is he?"

Clinton shrugs but he takes a quick photo of the medical forms hanging on a clipboard. We move to the next room and there are two more victims. One female and another male.

"Shit, shit, shit," I mutter again. "What do we do? How do we stop this?"

"Find out where they got it—how or who is spreading it."

"And if we don't?"

For a moment I'm filled with relief that there's no way it could have been me. Quickly, though, the annoyance that with the Morrigan on the loose I have zero control over her. I rest a hand on Clinton's arm.

"I think I know who to look for."

"Who?"

"Anita Cross."

14

CLINTON

I'm not surprised to hear Morgan suggest we look for Anita, although I am pretty curious that it took her this long to make the connection. Anita and Xavier are both players in the Morrigan's game. I'm just not sure to what extent.

"Any idea where she may be?" I ask on the way down the elevator.

"None."

"Seriously?"

"She's wealthy, gorgeous, and lived in an amazing penthouse," she says. "Her brother was a banker or something. Other than our writing program, we had very little in common." The bell chimes, notifying us that we're on our floor. The doors open and I step out. Morgan hasn't moved an inch—her eyes narrowed in concentration.

"Morgan? You okay?"

"I think I know where we can get more information on Anita."

"Yeah?"

She steps forward and slips her hand in mine. "We need to pay a visit to my advisor."

"The professor?"

"Yeah, he said he didn't know where she went but he's a nosy bastard. I suspect he'll have an idea."

Every soldier has a crossroads, where they have to make a decision in a blink. Sitting behind the wheel of my truck with Morgan in the passenger seat, I have to make a choice. Risk more lives or reveal a secret that may send shockwaves through my home and life.

"Are you sure this is what you want to do?" I ask, giving us both one last out. "He may have questions."

"I think Anita is an important factor in all of this."

I nod and roll the truck into the street. At the first intersection I have the option to turn right or left. The university is to the right but I head left. Morgan isn't familiar enough with the city to realize we're going in the wrong direction until a few blocks later when the scenery changes. The streets become cleaner. The houses nicer. We're in a residential area.

I notice her fingers shift on the seat. She leans forward and asks, "Where are we?"

"Sutton Place."

"This isn't near the school."

"No," I agree, spotting the house ahead. It takes up half a block. Red brick and three stories high. "You said you wanted to talk to Professor Christensen. This is where he is."

She faces me. "What's going on, Clinton?"

I open the truck door. "You'll find out soon enough."

15

MORGAN

I'm filled with a mixture of confusion and dread as we walk up the steps to the grand house. Clinton refuses to tell me what we're doing here, and his jaw is so tight I think it may crack. The door is opened by a servant who doesn't seem surprised to see Clinton, but his eyes do hesitate on me for a brief moment.

"Seriously," I say to my Guardian as we stand in a small but ornate foyer, "you've got to tell me what's going on."

He opens his mouth, no doubt to tell me nothing important, but the servant returns. "Dr. Christensen will see you now. Follow me."

He leads us down a narrow hallway. The walls are covered in a thick, aging paper. I catch snippets of the images as we pass. They appear to be battle scenes from history. Some are quite gruesome.

I don't know what to expect, obviously, but I'm surprised when we're escorted to a large, modern kitchen. Everything in it shines. The appliances, the counter top. The pots hanging over the wide stove. The strangest part is Professor Christensen standing over the range in a black and white striped apron. Something sizzles on the flat surface and he flips it with a spatula. He glances up as we walk into the room and smiles.

"Now this is a surprise," he says, removing the food and placing it in a bowl. He turns off the range and wipes his hands before walking toward us. He offers his hand forward. "Clinton, it's always a pleasure to see you. How's the music?"

"Good, sir."

Sir?

"And Morgan. I knew this day would come." His eyes flash between us. "I'd hoped it would be under better circumstances."

The confusion I'm feeling merges with anger. I'm totally in the dark and I don't like it one bit. Unable to hold my tongue I blurt, "What the hell is going on?"

Christensen looks at Clinton. "You haven't told her?"

"Not a word. I felt like it may be better coming from you."

I grab Clinton by the shirt. It's a pointless move. He'd squash me in a second, but my mind is reeling from this moment and I look into his gray eyes and say something I know is true, "Start talking now. Or I walk out of here and none of you will see me again."

Christensen's eyebrows lift and in a controlled voice says, "Sit down, Morgan."

He gestures to a high stool across the counter. Clinton takes one and after a steadying breath I take the other. Christensen pulls another up to the end.

Clinton takes my hand and as much as I want to push him away I feel a comfort in his touch. He says, "Christensen is one of us. Part of the network created to keep the Darkness and Morrigan out of this world."

Christensen nods.

"We're part of a team that includes the Guardians, The Nead, Sue and Davis, and the Professor," Clinton asks.

"Anyone else?" I ask.

"Not specifically. There are those in the community that are aware of who we are and what we do. The shaman at the fights. Tran down at the magic shop."

"Hildi?

"The Valkyrie?" Christensen asks.

Clinton shrugs. "I think she has a feeling. She's very astute and is from the gods herself."

"We each have a role," Christensen says. "The men are the soldiers."

"And you?" I ask.

"I'm what mortals would call a General."

"You're calling the shots?" A feeling of dread bubbles in the pit of my stomach. "I don't understand? Are you not a real professor? Is my work pointless?"

"Oh no, Morgan. I'm historian and my job is to manage the writings and writers during the times of Darkness. Your work is priceless. Each incarnation of the Darkness must have a historian. Someone on the front lines to tell the myths and mythologies—the intricate side that human history will miss. They'll see the sickness, the disease, or wars. They won't see the game play from one realm to the other."

"Do you really see it like that?" I ask them both. "A game?"

"A deadly and precise one. To think of it as anything else is foolish. The Morrigan relishes war and destruction. You know that. We must always be one step ahead."

I think about what he's saying. It's a game. We're all just pieces or even pawns for the Morrigan's playing board. What confuses me most is who am I? What is my job in all of this since the split?

Clinton rests his hand on my shoulder. "We didn't end the battle when we split you and the Morrigan apart. We always knew it was a possibility that we would create another piece. It seems we created two."

"Two?" I ask.

"You know the myths often include three sides to the Raven Queen, each with specific qualities."

"I remember. Each goddess prevails over a different concept. Land, fertility, or war. Dylan thought they were exaggerated stories to make the Morrigan more intimidating. You think the spell actually brought on that manifestation?"

"Not at first. You seemed different. More at peace. I thought maybe we banished her but now that people are dying..." Clinton trails off and looks at Christensen.

"So you think I still carry part of the Goddess inside of me."

Christensen nods. "Yes."

"Which part?"

"Either war or land. Because fertility is already showing her hand."

I wish they'd stop talking in riddles but the intensity of their expression stops me from lashing out. "You're considering the spread of the virus as fertility—that's what's being created." They both nod. My mind races, thinking to the reason we came here in the first place. "Anita is the third piece. Is that what you're saying?"

Christensen leans over the counter. "She stole the kiss from you, Morgan. Took the Darkness right out of your body and has spread it across the city. The plague is here and I'm not sure how to stop it."

"Do you know where to find her?"

He shakes his head. "I don't, but Anita has always been bold, it shouldn't be long before she makes her move. The Morrigan is restless."

"Even if we do find her," I ask them, "how do we stop her for good?"

There's not an ounce of empathy behind Clinton's gray eyes when he replies, "We'll have to kill her."

16

MORGAN

I'm not angry after leaving Christensen's home, but I am tired. Exhausted really, and I know it's more mental than anything else. Between the writing binge, the confirmation that I'm still tied up with the Morrigan, and everything else Christensen revealed, I'm spent.

Clinton is smart enough to give me some space, and the spidey-senses of the other Guardians must be on high alert because the house is quiet when I get home.

I don't go to my room, instead I head straight to the pantry. We missed dinner and I'm starving. I don't want food and hope Sue has a stash of sweets in the cabinets. I cackle in delight as I find the motherload: boxes of cookies and candy. I reach for a huge container of fudge and shove a piece in my mouth.

"Drowning your emotions with sugar?"

Bunny stands in the door, looking just as tired as I feel. I hold out the container and he takes three pieces of fudge, popping them into his mouth one after the other.

"I saw you fight last night. It's the first time I've seen you like that."

He holds up his limp arm. "Magic helps."

"No. There was intuition and grace. The same skills you use on your paintings came out in your fighting."

His copper hair has flopped in his eyes and I reach out and push it aside so I can see his face. "You disappeared after—where did you go?"

"Nowhere," he says. "Here. I just didn't want to be there anymore. Too many people, you know? It's not my scene."

I nod and pick up another piece of fudge. I take a bite and then offer him the other half. He reaches for it but I pull it back, gesturing that I'd like to give it to him myself. He opens his mouth and I pop the treat in, rubbing my finger along his bottom lip.

Bunny chews the sticky fudge and swallows. He stares at me so hard that I squirm. To my surprise he asks, "Can I kiss you?"

"Of course."

I've been waiting weeks for him to do it again. A burst of fire ignites between us and I lick the sweet chocolate off his tongue.

"I've missed you," I tell him, linking my arms around his neck. "Why have you been hiding from me?"

His hand squeezes my hip. "I've just been in a weird place."

"You know I'm always here if you need something, right?"

"Yeah." His eyes move from my mouth back up to my gaze. "Right now I really need some more of that fudge."

I grab the box and then two more filled with other treats. "Come on. Let's drown our worries together."

~

WITH THE REMAINS of our gluttony surrounding us, Bunny and I snuggle on the couch. He reluctantly agreed to watch a cheesy movie with me and I'm full-out pretending the world isn't falling apart around us right now. Total denial about the sickness, Anita, and my role in the preservation of this world. I have a strong suspicion Bunny is hiding from something too, and for once I just let it go.

It's a quiet moment of peace for both of us. No expectations. No dramatic build up. I feel safe with him. Close. When I reach for him and press my lips against his pale throat, he doesn't resist.

His fingers push into my hair and I move to my knees so I can kiss him better. A box of cookie crumbs falls to the floor and I laugh. He smiles and his copper-brown eyes hold mine. "Don't you wish it was always this easy?"

"What? Life? Sex? Love?"

His head tilts at the word 'love' and his mouth crashes into mine. My stomach flip-flops at the soft strokes of his tongue. I reach for his pants, eager to touch him.

"Can I?" I ask, in the same way he asked me. It's a weird moment—after months of feeling like the less experienced one—the virgin—with Bunny, I feel like I'm the one leading him. He'd told me before that he didn't have confidence in this area—and then proceeded prove himself wrong in the most delicious way. I want to do the same for him.

He nods his approval, Adam's apple bobbing in this throat. I slide between his legs and unbutton his pants, shifting them over his hips and to the floor. His erection is hard beneath the cotton of his shorts and all it takes is a slight touch to get it to rise in response. I smile at his reaction and his cheeks turn red. I rest my hand on his length.

"I never meant for you to be last, you know that, right? It just happened that way. Fate, I think. Like everything else in this house. In the beginning I thought you would be first. You're so sweet and gentle, but we're in a war and I needed toughening up." He watches me carefully as I tug off my sweater and slip out of my jeans. I don't remove my bra and panties, though. Not yet. "I think this is better. I need you today. Someone safe. Someone solid. You don't play mind games with me, Bunny, and I appreciate that."

He responds again with his mouth and grazes my side with his hand. I continue to kiss him while pulling down his shorts. When I finally get a look at his cock, I stop and blink.

"What?" he asks in a soft voice.

"Uh, I don't have a lot of experience in all this, but your dick is huge."

We both look down at the swollen rod between his legs. I reach for the soft velvet of his skin and run my hands down his length. He shudders from my touch, shoulders slumping when I fondle his balls.

Kneeling between his thighs, I do what I can to make this day a little bit better.

17

BUNNY

The girl between my legs isn't the same as the one I'd painted on weeks ago. There's no shyness. No timidity. She's capable and strong. Confident and secure. Even though it's clear she had a hard day and is looking to hide from the world, there's no hesitation as she licks the length of my shaft.

I work my hand into her hair and cup the back of her head. My brain tells me to make her stop. My natural male instincts don't agree. Her lips are puffy and her tongue warm. Even though I'll regret it, I lean back in the seat and for once try to relax in the moment and not overthink.

Turns out, thinking is pretty impossible when her fingertips skim my balls and I feel the tightening of pleasure. I inhale sharply, fighting the urge to thrust my hips. Then she takes me completely, her head bobbing up and down. I curve my fingers in her curls.

The ecstasy of the moment rolls over me, making me forget the paintings and the dreams about the dark castle and what waits on the Otherside. I push aside the visions and the blackouts, because this is what I've wanted. What I've craved. Morgan wasn't rejecting me. I knew that. I wasn't last, no matter what the voices in my head said.

She swirls her tongue and then her finger around the tip. I swallow back a ferocious groan.

"Does that feel good?" she asks.

I nod vigorously. "Please. Please keep going."

She smiles, her pretty red lips widening around the girth of my cock. I can't help but move my hips now, wanting to feel the friction, the warmth along the length of my shaft. My hand leaves her hair and reaches for the satin of her bra. I feel the hard point of her nipple and brush my fingers over the raised tips before tugging down the fabric to feel the round firmness of her breast in my hand.

This time Morgan shudders, exhaling warmth around my cock. Up and down, up and down she bobs and I'm no longer able to hold back. She must feel my intensity because she increases her pace, sucking so hard that I'm sure she'll gag.

She doesn't. Not even a flinch, and she pushes one hand up my belly and another beneath my balls. I ram into her mouth, hitting her throat until the tight coil of ecstasy unfurls. I feel a click in my brain, a tug, and without warning I pull from her mouth, moving her hand to the base of my cock.

She frowns in confusion, her lips wet and red, but quickly changes course, sliding her hand up my shaft. I'm already on the edge and hot, gooey, pent-up cum streams across her chest. Her eyes are wide as the jism slides between her breasts. I fall back against the cushion, exhausted and a little lost.

"So that was—" she starts, but I cut her off. She's sticky with my cum when I reach for her and pull her mouth to mine.

"I've never done that before," she confesses, and an odd swelling of pride fills my chest. A tide has turned, something shifted. I feel it in my bones.

"There's a first time for everything." It's my duty to make her content so I pull Morgan on my lap even though we're both sticky with sex and sweat. I may not be able to cross that final line with her, I understand that now, but I slip my fingers between her legs and lead her down the pathway to oblivious bliss.

18

MORGAN

I'm standing outside Dylan's door but I haven't knocked. Bunny left my room a short while before and although our time together was amazing, something feels different.

I'm really not sure why Bunny and I didn't have sex. I wanted to and I thought easing him into it would help. He was nervous, but I also knew it was time. Each barrier broken between us brings us closer and tonight was no different. But it also revealed something—something I'd been fighting inside myself. With each of my Guardians, I've seen them at their most vulnerable. I can't get the image of Bunny's red cheeks and glazed-over eyes just before his orgasm. I'd had every intention of having him come in my mouth—I'd done it with the others—but at the last minute he'd pulled away. Why? What was he afraid of?

I don't want to see it as a rejection. But over the last few days something has awoken and it's telling me to be wary. This part of me resides deep inside, past the place where my soul ends and the goddess begins.

The Goddess. That's what I'm calling it. Not the Darkness or the Morrigan, they've both been banished with the spell. The anger and fear from before is gone, along with the frantic need to consume. I'm left with something different—something I haven't tapped into. Honestly, I'm hoping I don't have to.

My mates still have an important role in all of this, maybe more than I realized. My encounter with Dylan proved that to me. I need these men as much as I always have.

The Morrigan feels it. I have no doubt of that.

Which is why I've come to Dylan's room and why I have to tell him what transpired between Bunny and I, or rather, what didn't. I finally realized we're a circle. A group. There's no beginning and no end, except we're not whole. Not yet, and something—or someone--is keeping my final mate from fully bonding with me, keeping me from full strength.

I bang my fist on the solid wood door.

I just hope I'm not too late.

19

DYLAN

"Is something wrong?" I ask straight off. She glances over her shoulder, in the direction of Bunny's studio. The door is closed, I'd heard him go in not long before. "What?"

She pushes me into the room, hands flat against my stomach. Her touch sends flares through my body, but the wild look in her eye tells me she's not here for sex. If I had to guess from the sheen of sweat on her forehead and the scent coming off her skin, she'd recently done that anyway.

"Morgan." She shuts the door and I ask again, "What's going on?"

I've lit a fire in the massive, stone fireplace across the room, warming the drafty attic. Her eyes flick to the small tabletop covered in bottles. The first words out of her mouth are, "Can I have a drink? I could really use a drink."

Silently I walk to the makeshift bar and pour her a glass of amber liquid. I hand it to her and lean against the back of the sofa and watch her carefully. She swallows the whole thing in one gulp.

"It's Bunny," she finally says.

"What about him?"

She holds out her glass again and I grab the bottle by the neck, refilling it generously. "I need you to hear me out, just let me get this out, okay?"

"Okay."

"For the longest time I didn't exactly understand our mating. Not really." She holds the empty glass in her hands. "I just knew I didn't want to choose and that being with each of you felt right."

"Choosing one mate was locked in stone. There was never any altering that, but choosing all of us? That was totally you—and it was the right thing to do. It's how we fought off the Morrigan."

"Right. I know that now, but I also know something else. When you and I finally, you know..." I'm not sure why she stumbles over these words at times. She's not inhibited in bed. Or against a wall. But speaking freely about sex and lust is a stumbling block. I blame her Southern upbringing.

I help her along. "Yes, I know."

"I had another awakening after we were together. My words came back—they flowed. Then I learned the truth about Christensen, who he is and what he means to all of us." Her cheeks are red from the alcohol. "I didn't need to be told the goddess still resides in me. Even when I pushed it away, I felt her power. But she too is bound to my choice in mates and how you can help me fight the infecting Darkness."

"How?" I ask, but I already know the answer. She just needed to find it herself.

"We're a circle that will be forged in fire of our lust and combined energies." She walks over to the fireplace and stares down into the flames. "It didn't connect until he rejected me."

I frown. This I don't know. "Who?"

"Bunny. I was just with him and well, things were progressing, but at the last minute..."

"Bunny can be shy, you know that. He lacks confidence since the injury."

"No. I felt it. I felt the moment it shifted. The Goddess knew. I knew."

"He chose not to seal our relationship. On purpose, to keep me from fighting at full strength."

"That's a bold accusation." I'm standing behind her. "It amounts to treason. Bunny is sworn to your service, to your protection."

She spins, hair flaring over her shoulders. Her eyes narrow. She's beyond beautiful. "You don't believe me?"

"You're in charge here, Morgan. I'm your Sentinel. If you think one of the guards has gone off course, I will follow up."

"I know he has." She swallows. "I feel it in my gut. And with the Darkness spreading we can't have anyone going rogue."

"I'll check on him now and report back."

She grabs my arm before I walk off. "I won't allow any more infection or death under my watch, do you understand that?"

I nod in understanding and ask her to stay in the studio. She sits in my chair looking less shaken than when she came in. I walk down the hallway and consider that if what she's saying is true, we not only have a problem but a catastrophic event. Morgan's perception of the six of us is probably accurate—she needs all of us to solidify the power of the Goddess inside of her. If Bunny has stepped out of line, we're screwed.

I hear footsteps coming up the stairs and pause, bracing myself to face him. Instead I see Damien's shaved head and the glint of his earrings in the dim hallway light.

Our eyes meet. I ask, "Looking for me?"

He shakes his head and steps on the landing. "Nah, I've been asking Bunny for some indigo for a few weeks. I need it for a project. Figured I'd just come up and get it."

"He wouldn't give it to you?"

"Kept brushing me off. The one other time I came up, he was gone."

"When was that?"

"A few nights ago." Outside Bunny's door, Damien rests his hands on his hips. "His door was locked."

Bunny is notorious for keeping late working hours and sleeping most of the day. It's just about time for him to get up and it dawns on me that he'd been in Morgan's room when he'd normally be asleep.

I rub the back of my neck and Damien catches the grimace on my face. "What?"

I sigh. "We may have a problem."

"What kind of problem?" His entire demeanor shifts.

I raise my eyebrows. "Let's find out."

Damien raps on the studio door. After a moment's wait there's no answer, no sound from within. Damien jerks his chin up and before I nod my approval he's pulled a tool from his pocket and has inserted it in the lock. He fiddles for a moment but the spring triggers and the lock unlatches.

Before opening it Damien stops me and says, "Are you sure about this?"

"Morgan sent me. I'm just doing my job."

"Fuck," he mutters under his breath. He glances down at the tool and keeps it in his hand. The door opens with a soft creak, like all the old hinges in this house. I walk past him, getting the first look of his studio in a while. He'd been quiet lately. I didn't think much of it with things having calmed down with Morgan and, frankly, being involved in my own personal concerns. What I'd been was distracted and when Damien calls me over to look at the first of a dozen canvases, I realize what a tactical error that had been.

"What the hell?" Damien says, but I'm stunned speechless. The paintings tell a story. The Morrigan's story from the Otherside. Her dark castle looms in each one, sitting on a foundation of bone and ash. I'm struck by how real it looks. How I can feel the cold air. Smell the charred flesh. So many lives have been lost at the hand of this vindictive bitch.

Nearby are another series of paintings. Recognizable locations around New York. He's captured the same realism. They're an odd contrast of both worlds.

A sound captures my attention and I turn and find Damien at

Bunny's work table. He's picking through the tools and paints. He holds one up and shakes it. A powdery substance moves inside.

"What's that?"

"You're right. We have a problem," he says, grimacing. "These aren't normal paintings. Bunny's been playing with magic."

"How so?"

Alchemy is not my area of expertise. I'm the historian. "It's just a guess but this is elder root. When mixed correctly with compounds from this realm and the Otherside, it can be very powerful."

"How so?" I take the container from him and open it, taking a sniff. It has a dusty, woody smell.

"When he mixes it with his paints it fuses with the painting, connecting the two worlds." He walks over to a painting of the Otherside, a massive depiction of the decaying woods outside the castle grounds. Then he points to one of the modern, local paintings. A train station downtown. There's nothing notable about it other than Bunny's skill. "See these lines, the way they arch the same way?"

I do, now that he's pointed it out. "Yeah, I guess."

"If you enter here," he points to the station sign. "You'll exit in there."

"Seriously?"

"With a spell, yes, I think so."

I look around the room at all the paintings. There's an equal number of both. "He's created gates."

Damien nods. "All over the fucking city."

"Why?" The realization is almost too big to comprehend. "Why would he do that?"

"Because," a voice surprises us in the doorway. "The Morrigan can't do it without me. Not anymore. So she found someone new."

"Bunny?" I'm still shocked. He's always been the most steadfast. The most loyal.

"I suspect he had a little help."

"From who?" Damien asks, but the pieces are clicking into place.

"Anita helped him. She's the one spreading the virus."

Morgan nods. "The virus I spread to her. We need to find them and cut off the Morrigan's reach before it goes too far."

Damien and I share a look. We've never had to go after one of our own before and Morgan isn't at full force. I don't tell her this. He doesn't either. Our job is to protect her and keep the Darkness away.

"I'll get the others."

Morgan nods. "I'll meet you in the training room."

"Why there?" Damien asks.

"Because we're going to need weapons to kill them," she replies and walks out of the room.

20

MORGAN

All four of my remaining Guardians meet me in the training room. I'm dressed for battle: stretchy black pants, shin-breaking boots and a leather jacket Damien gave me to wear on his bike. The men watch me as I enter, four sets of eyes skimming down my body. I walk past them and go directly to the weapons case, pulling out my blade.

"You're taking that?" Damien asks.

"Yes." I slide it into the harness on my back, another gift, from Clinton.

Sam steps in front of me. "You do understand you can't kill anyone, right?"

"I understand I'll do what I have to." I tug the edge of my gloves higher. "Since we've been unable to find Anita, I called in a favor." I walk across the room and open the door. Hildi stands on the other side, dressed to fight. Her blonde hair is woven in a tight braid.

"Hello Morgan." She nods at the Guardians. "Boys."

Dylan stares at me so hard I think his brain may crack. Finally he clears his throat. "Can we speak for a moment? Alone?"

"Sure," I reply, following him into the hallway. He didn't dress for a fight but his shirt is tight enough to show the curved muscles over his shoulders. Intimidating to anyone that crosses his path. "Problem?"

"It's unorthodox to bring in an outsider for a situation like this."

"A situation where I've been betrayed by one of my own?"

He crosses his arms. "Yes. The outside world cannot know we're having this problem. It's a sign of weakness."

"Hildi is an ally. And is very knowledgeable about the activities of the community."

"She's a gossip."

"And my friend," I say with a touch of warning. "We need her help."

"At the risk of sounding disrespectful, Morgan, there are times you should defer to those with the knowledge and experience for handling the situation at hand."

"This is common? Traitors? Betrayal?"

He smiles and it's so glorious my knees wobble. "Have you learned nothing of the myths surrounding the Morrigan? Betrayal is her forte. Bunny learned from the best."

"Fine, but the Valkyrie comes."

He starts to argue again but Hildi interjects from the doorway, where she's clearly been listening. "I'm sent by the Goddess Freyja to choose the dead. I'm aware of your sickness and the looming battles. I can help you find the woman you're looking for. And the Guardian. Their stench is all over the city."

"You can sense them?" Clinton asks.

"The dead and dying? Yes. Normally mortals are not my concern but the Darkness and Morrigan are. I can guide you."

Dylan reluctantly agrees but corners both of us before we leave. "No one dies, do you understand? Not Bunny or the mortal, Anita."

"Why should we spare them?" I ask, the betrayal burns deep, more than I ever expected.

"We never abandon one of our own. That is the lesson the Morrigan's paranoia taught us. Bunny may be out of control but he's still one of the gods chosen."

"And Anita?"

"There's a chance we can perform the splitting spell on her and save her too."

I hold Dylan's eye and nod, but as I straighten my jacket over my sword I can't shake the tug of vengeance clawing at my soul. Even though I've showered and changed I can still feel the sticky heat of Bunny's cum on my chest. He used me. He betrayed me and now I must deliver justice.

21

MORGAN

In the garage, Hildi gives us two places to start. Dylan splits us into groups: me, him, and Hildi together. Sam, Clinton, and Damien pile into Clinton's truck and leave the garage first.

"Which one of these fine vehicles should we take?"

Dylan fidgets with his belt.

"He doesn't drive."

Her eyebrow rises curiously. "No?"

"No," he replies.

"Interesting." She strolls down the row of cars and stops before a shiny, silver-gray Mercedes. "I like this one. Keys?"

Dylan seems totally unsure what to do about a woman like Hildi. I pass him on the way to the key box. "She makes me seem like a piece of cake, don't you think?"

He grunts and follows us to the car. I concede and give him the passenger seat, due to his long legs. Hildi ducks in the driver's side and I grab him by the shirt. "It's a good idea."

He leans forward and kisses me, darting his tongue in my mouth. Hildi slams on the horn and the sound echoes through the garage, blasting our ears. "You owe me, got it?"

I nod, thinking about all the ways I'll repay him, before slipping in my seat.

∽

"Stop," Dylan says and Hildi slams on the brakes. We fly forward, my hands holding on to the seat in front of me.

"Holy shit, Hildi. Give us a little notice."

Hildi's driving skills were questionable. The scowl hadn't left Dylan's face the whole ride. To be honest, I'd checked my seat belt at least three times as she careened through the busy streets of New York.

We were following the scent of infection and decay—that's what she told us, at least. I trusted her senses but I'm surprised when Dylan tells her to stop the car.

"Over there." He's already out of his seat. I'm not sure what he's looking for but he hops out of the vehicle and dodges a series of cars to get to the other side of the busy road.

"Park the car," I tell her, following Dylan. I find him walking back and forth at a train station. "What are you doing?"

"I saw this in one of the paintings. There's a gate around here." He touches the signs, the bench, the curve of the guardrail.

"I could see the gate in the park that day. The air around it wasn't right. I don't see anything like that here."

Hildi races up, breathing heavily. She takes a deep breath. "Someone with the infection has been here."

"Anita?"

She shrugs. "Maybe."

Dylan continues his search but Hildi sniffs the air. She scans the people walking around us. Our whole group gets a few looks. Hildi looks like some kind of Nordic model and Dylan has a face that is almost too beautiful to be real. I try my best to seem normal, average, but my partners and their erratic behavior isn't making it easy.

OBSIDIAN FIRE

"I smell something," Hildi says, taking off in the direction of a small wooded park.

"Come on," I tell Dylan. "We can come back."

Again we cross the busy roads, Hildi unconcerned about traffic or cars. Dylan grabs my hand and leads me to the safety of the park. I feel a gust of familiar cool air roll in our direction.

"Do you feel that?"

"No, but I smell it," Hildi says. "God, it's awful." She retches, covering her mouth with her hand. Deep lines crease Dylan's forehead.

"There's a gate around here—you were right," I tell him, walking toward the grove of trees. A spot a wave of air and a discoloration. Hildi walks off, face scrunched.

I walk toward the gate and the familiar cold air burns my cheeks. I feel the draw, the lure, just like last time. Whatever exists on the Otherside beckons me, and I'm inches away when I'm jerked back.

"What?" I shout, coming toe to toe with Dylan.

"Last time they barely got you out of there. I can't let you get too close."

There's a crackle in the air and the coolness vanishes. I look over my shoulder and all signs of the gate have disappeared.

"It's gone," I say, pulling out of his arms. I search for Hildi. She's staring through the trees. "The gate closed, is the smell gone too?"

"No." Her eyes are locked on something across the park. I move next to her and grip her elbow when I get a better view. "It reeks."

The woman's blonde, wavy hair catches my eye. She's headed straight for us, or more likely, the closed portal. "That's her. That's who we're looking for."

I don't know what to expect but it's not for Hildi to charge toward her.

"Morgan, step back," Dylan says, balling his fists and stepping between me and the women.

I push him aside. "This is my wrong to right."

"I can't let you go over there. It's my duty to protect you." His hand wraps around my arm, squeezing tight. I jerk back and reach for my sword with my free hand. It glints in the sunlight.

"No, Dylan. It's your duty to serve and I started this with Anita. I let her get too close." Voices rise from in the trees. "Stay here. Watch the gate. Bunny may try to get through."

There's a look of cold rage on his face as he accepts my command. There's no way I'm letting him do this for me. I've trained. I've fought. I've studied for this moment. Anita may have a sliver of the Darkness in her, but I will banish her and the vessel she resides in to hell.

22

SAM

Click, click, click.

My camera snaps photos of the area. The pictures have a greenish-gray tint to them, but nothing unusual. Certainly nothing that looks like a gate from this world to the next.

"Come on, Bun, show yourself," I mutter. Damien is in the magic shop talking with Tran, hoping he's seen or heard something. Clinton walks up and down the street, scaring the locals with the scowl on his face.

Click, click, click

I sit on a cement wall outside the bodega and flip back through the photos. Bunny's paintings implied there would be a portal here, but I'm coming up empty. Damien exits the magic shop, his frown telling me what I need to know. He walks over and says, "He came in for some of the ingredients needed to make the portals. But he must have gotten the reactive stuff from the Otherside. Tran says if Bunny is using the area as a hotspot, he hasn't seen or felt it."

"Would he? I know the guy is like an elder of magic or whatever but the Morrigan? That's ancient level."

"Got anything?" he asks me.

"Not much."

Damien grimaces and scans the street. I point my camera in Clinton's direction.

Click, click, click

"So look, I think this may be a dead end," Damien says, scratching his chin. I look back down at the display screen. "There doesn't seem—"

"Fuck."

"What?"

"Fuck. Fuck. Shit."

"What the hell, Sam?" he grabs the camera and looks at the screen. His eyes dart up at Clinton. "Is that real?"

I glance at the photo I'd just taken. It's Clinton, but he's not in this world. At least, I don't think so. His hands are chained. He's shirtless with deep wounds across his back and chest. Dirt smears across his face and his knuckles are raw and bloody. I flip to the next photo, Clinton isn't in it but I do see something that wasn't there before. Black smoke rolls low on the street, like a tentacle.

"That's like the smoke in the ring the other night," Damien says. "When Dylan fought the Morrigan."

"We need to get out of here." I look up at Clinton, who makes eye contact with me. I jerk my head for him to walk over. "Now."

A blast of cool air rushes down the narrow street. It's then that I notice we're the only ones still out here. The sidewalk is empty. The stores quiet. I glance over at Damien but he's gone. "Dude," I say, "Damien?"

Another blast of cold rolls over me, this time like a freight train. I spin, feeling a presence at my back. There's nothing and no one there. I look back up for Clinton. Gone.

"Clint! Damien!"

With fumbling hands, I turn the camera around, the lens pointing at my face.

Click, click, click

The camera is still shooting when thick arms twist and coil around my legs. The last thing I hear, as I'm swept off my feet, is the crack of my camera as it hits the ground.

23

MORGAN

The glint of my sword announces me when I approach Anita and Hildi. We're deep enough in the grove of trees that people on the street can't see us. They haven't come to blows but Hildi has her in a tight grip. I notice an odd coloring on the Valkyrie's face and wonder if it's a reaction to the sickness.

Anita isn't a fighter and there's a contrast between the warrior stance of Hildi and the white, crisp jeans on the woman before me.

"You finally figured it out?" she says.

"I figured out you're a tool," I reply.

She laughs. "And you're not?"

I step closer and hold my sword at her midsection. "What did you do to Bunny?"

"Xavier taught me a little something about team management, from his work down on Wall Street. Never ignore the little person. Cultivate them the most. When a weakness shows they'll be the first to betray you."

"No one ignored Bunny."

"Maybe not, but with that disfigurement he's a liability. Or at least that's what I told him." I lunge for her with my hand, wrapping my fingers around her throat. Her bright blue eyes light up in fascination—not fear. "You gonna kiss me again?"

I release her and haul back and slap her across the face. "Fuck you."

She laughs again. I want to kill her. Plunge this blade into her belly and watch her bleed. I brace myself. I'm not a murderer. Dylan told me to let her live—we'll need her. I swallow back rage.

"So what's your grand plan? You infect the whole city? Start another plague? To what? Build up the Morrigan's strength so she can take over?" I ask.

"Well, yeah." Her eyes narrow. "And don't act like you don't want it—at least a little. I've read your book. Bunny even showed me your latest writings." She smiles at my reaction to that revelation. "You're curious about the Otherside. The power it holds. You should be."

Hildi tightens her grip and Anita winces before licking her lips.

"I'm a historian, Anita. Those writings are based on truth, not desire."

She tilts her head. "Since when are truth and desire mutually exclusive?"

"Come on," I tell Hildi. "We need to get her back to The Nead. Maybe once we rid of you of the Darkness you'll come to your senses."

Hildi moves her along and I glance over my shoulder at Dylan standing near the edge of the woods. He looks at me and then over to Anita.

"You realize he's the only one you have left, right? First Bunny and then the others?"

"Shut up, Anita."

Her footsteps crush the dried leaves on the ground. "Do you think the Morrigan would only want one? You know how she feels about being betrayed, particularly by men. *Her* men."

The threat rings true but I refuse to show it. "What are you talking about?"

"He was here. I felt him open the gate. You did, too." Her lips curve. "Where do you think he went when he realized you were here without the rest of the guardians? Three of her traitors?"

Dread fills my chest. She knows I need Bunny to complete my power. What happens if the others are gone too? "Dylan," I call. "Go back to the house."

"I'm not leaving," he calls back, stepping into the wooded area.

"Don't listen to her, Guardian," Anita chimes in. "It's too late anyway."

"Dylan," I turn to face him. "Go find the others and stop Bunny."

I sense his conflict. He asks, "And what about her?"

Hildi and I share a look before I declare, "We'll take care of The Third."

24

DAMIEN

The hard stone beneath my knees is cold as the frigid air. My skin chafes against the metal cuffs, the long chain linking to another around my ankles. Clinton shivers next to me, his face purple with bruises. Blood drips from the edge of his mouth. Sam shifts, causing the chains to clink. He's punished with the sharp crack of a whip lashing into his back.

"No moving!" the soldier shouts from the dark. I caught a glimpse of his face when they brought us in. Blond hair with a deep scar down his cheek. He carries the whip on his belt. It's similar to the one Dylan used in the ring.

Sam grunts against the pain, swallowing what he can. My knees ache from kneeling on the hard stone and I really need to piss, but I keep my eyes forward and my body still. Getting out of here will be hard enough without further injury.

I can only guess we got sucked into one of Bunny's portals—the Morrigan slipping out to drag us to the Otherside. That's where we are. I'd know this place anywhere. The cold haunts my dreams. The smell is burned to the insides of my nostrils. There's nothing here but death—and the same fate surely awaits us if we can't escape soon.

Minutes pass—maybe longer. I'm dizzy from the wait. Footsteps echo on the stairs. By now I'm sure we're underground and I wonder if we'll see daylight again, breathe fresh air, or taste the flesh of our goddess once more before we die.

The rustle of fabric—or is it wings—follows the footsteps. Then the sound of metal drags across stone. The temperature drops ten degrees and I hear Clinton swallow, either blood, rage, or both, next to me.

"Well, well, well look what the cat—or rather, bunny—dragged in," a familiar voice bounces off the stone. The Morrigan in a full pleated skirt and a corset made of leather walks into view. "Thought you'd gotten away from me? It doesn't work that way, Guardians."

She walks down the line, her fingers trailing over Sam's open lash marks, touching Clinton's chin to get a better look at his bruises. She stops before me and raises an eyebrow. "What? You didn't fight back?"

I grit my teeth to hold back a reply. She smiles. "You were always a smart one, Damien. But not as smart as Bunny."

"You manipulated him," Sam says. The guard from before steps forward and kicks him in the back. Sam nearly topples, but manages to hold himself upright. I hear the whip uncoil. The Morrigan's dark eyes flash to the guard.

"Thank you, Casteel. Your service is appreciated." She walks over to Sam and strokes his cheek. "But I can't have you scarring this face, do you understand?"

"Yes, Your Majesty." I hear the fear and anger in his voice.

"So here's the plan, boys, you'll be staying here until I round up your little leader and whore. Once you're all back under my command I'll determine if I'll let you live or not." Her eyes cut to Clinton. He's never been her favorite. "Until then you'll rot in the dungeons, so you better hope they get here fast."

She nods at the guards behind us and they move fast, dragging us up to our feet. Clinton makes a break for it, lunging at the Queen. Her eyes widen in delight when he comes up short, and then laughs boldly when a hard baton cracks against the back of his knees. Our feet are linked by chains and when he falls I crash forward too, using the momentum to swipe the feet of the guards. Sam jumps into the fray, swinging the chain over his head and wrapping it around the throat of a guard.

"That's enough!" Casteel roars but there's no way we're going down without a fight. It may be our last chance to cause any damage. I grab the blade off the nearest guard and stab him in the throat.

Blood sprays and the Morrigan says loud enough for everyone to hear, "When you're finished playing, clean up this mess," before she walks back upstairs to the sound of fist meeting flesh.

25

DYLAN

I shouldn't have left her.
That's the only thought I have as I run across the city, jumping over sidewalks, dodging cars. It's not until much later that I allow a few more negative images to push into my head.

I'll never see her again.
The others will kill me.
I'll kill *him.*

I race down an alley, passing by the areas the other Guardians had planned to visit. They're nowhere to be seen. After looking in two other spots depicted by the paintings I return home, hoping they gave up.

If only I could fly, I think, feeling the sharp pang of sadness and loss, I'd be able to see the city better. Find them. Those days are lost. My ties to the Otherside are broken. The Nead comes into view. The glass pane of my attic window glints and a shadow passes behind it.

Davis. Of course he knew I would arrive back home. I race through the back door, skidding over the threshold. I'm out of breath when I reach the foyer of my room. Davis stands near the fireplace holding a bottle of water. I take it from him and drink it all in a fast gulp.

"Are they here?" I ask, handing him back the water.

"No. The house is empty."

I called them the instant I left Morgan, but one look at my phone tells me they haven't replied. We never should have separated. I never should have left her. "I want you and Sue to stay downstairs, understand?"

"Yes, Master Dylan." The old man looks at me. "Be careful."

I make sure he's down the stairs before I enter Bunny's room. I feel the dark magic lingering in the room. How did we miss it?

Walking through the room I take a moment to look at the intricate paintings of the Otherside. My body reacts instinctively to the images, sheer terror. Nothing good happens in that place. The Morrigan has ultimate control over the living and dead—we'd barely made it out alive the last time. I'm not sure any of us would again.

An odd pop, followed by a blast of cold air occurs behind me, and I spin, blade already in my hand. My grip tightens when Bunny fully emerges from one of the paintings.

"Dylan," he says, shaking the dust off his boots. With his hair sticking up in matted spikes and dark circles under his eyes, he looks more frazzled than usual.

"I see you learned a new painting technique."

Bunny glances at the painting. "It's come in handy."

"Why?" I ask him. I shouldn't. He's a traitor to our mission and nothing but a criminal now, but I still want to know. "Why are you working with her?"

"We've always worked with the Morrigan," he says. "That's what we do—you're the one that changed sides and picked the new young thing."

"We work for the forces of good, Bunny. We keep the Morrigan in check and balance the powers. When the split occurred there was no choice which way we'd go." I study him. "At least, I didn't think so."

"We freed Morgan from the Darkness. That was the goal and I was behind getting her out of the danger zone. She should have gone on and lived her life in peace. She could have done that."

"While people were dying up here from the spread of the virus? Do you really think she could have lived with that?" I shake my head. "You don't know her very well."

Bunny reacts with laughter, disturbed giggles that he stifles behind a paint stained hand. "You're right, I don't know her well. Not like you. Not like the others. I haven't fucked her, you know."

"That was your choice."

"Was it? Or maybe I just repulse her. Maybe she's only with me because she feels the guilt from that day."

"That's the Darkness speaking, Bunny, not Morgan."

He shrugs and runs his hands through his hair, making it even more wild. "It's too late Dylan. The wheels are set in motion. The virus is spreading—"

"Morgan has captured Anita. That stops today."

He scoffs. "People are already infected—dozens of them. They're walking the city now. Flying on planes. There's no stopping the plague this time, Dylan."

"There's always a solution. Always."

"Not this time." Bunny walks past me and gathers a few things on his worktable, slipping them into a bag.

"Morgan may be weakened without you sealing your relationship, but she's still strong."

Bunny's eyes flick up to mine, curious amusement tugs at his mouth. "You don't know, do you?"

"I know that you're crazy."

"No, seriously, you don't know." His forehead creases. "I knew I could trick the others, but you? You're slipping, my friend. Probably too much pussy fogging that brain of yours."

Tired of the riddles and games, I lunge at him, pushing past the bottles and jars on the table. They shatter to the floor, smashing in pieces. I land hard on broken glass, the small pieces embedding in my skin. Bunny uses the commotion to avoid my grasp, racing toward the door.

I'm up in a flash, kicking his feet from beneath him. He falls and I lash at him with the blade, nicking him on the ear when I slam the tip into the hardwood floor. I'm on top of him.

"Watch your mouth, brother," I tell him. "And turn this around before it goes a step further. I don't want to hurt you, Bunny. But I will, and the gods will approve."

"It's too late," he says, squirming beneath me. "She has them all. You won't win this one, Dylan, but it's not too late to join us."

I must be stunned by his announcement—she has them all—because he wedges a knee between my legs and jerks upward. The pain is instant and he escapes from my grasp. I grab the knife but when I face him again he's fumbling with the lid on one of his containers. Flipping the cap with his thumb, he tosses it in my face. Powder rains and I cough and rub my eyes. He may be smaller than me but he's resourceful.

Through the haze I spot him shoving more items in his bag and then tossing it over his shoulder.

"Think of it this way," he says, inching toward the paintings. My throat is clogged with the powder. I spit, trying to clear my mouth, my throat. I struggle to breathe but I've still got the blade in my hand. "Now you'll have her all to yourself."

Cold blasts through the room and even though my squinted eyes I see the ripple appear in one of the paintings. Bunny steps one foot inside and I close my eyes, pulling my arm back and releasing the blade in a fluid motion. I hear the same pop from before and the stick of my knife, followed by a crash. I blink, expecting to find him on the ground but no, it's just his bag. The blade wobbles, sticking out of the middle of the painting.

I'm alone.

Grabbing a rag from the workbench I clean my face, wiping the powder from my eyes. Then I walk over and stare at the picture, holding my hand over the surface. I'm afraid to touch it—afraid of where it may lead me. If Bunny was telling the truth then the other Guardians are in trouble and I'll have to find them.

The knife entered right in the middle of the castle, the place I assume Bunny traveled to. Without touching the canvas I yank the handle and the blade slides out. There's now a huge hole gouged in the middle. I'm both worried and relieved that this may make the painting useless. At least no one can slip back through this one.

I hear footsteps in the hall and I brace myself, but I know the sound of her anywhere and it's no surprise when Morgan walks through the door. Her eyes bulge at the scene, at my powder-covered face.

"Are you okay?" she asks.

I can't answer that. "Are you?"

She nods. "Anita is downstairs. Davis showed me the cells."

"You didn't kill her. Good."

"I wanted to."

I sigh and rub my head. "I almost killed Bunny."

Our eyes shift to the painting. To the hole left by my knife. "But you didn't?" she asks.

"No, but I probably should have." The exhaustion of what's to come hangs over my head. I don't want to tell her. I've let her down—no, I failed.

Something about her expression tells me she already knows. Even so, that knowledge doesn't keep her from walking over, from resting her cheek on my chest and wrapping her arms around me.

"They're gone," I say over her head. I'm glad I can't see her face.

"We'll get them back."

I stare at the paintings. At the lunacy that had been running through Bunny's head. That's what the Otherside does to you. It makes you crazy. It makes you hard. I don't want to tell Morgan that even if we get them back they may never be the same.

ONYX ECLIPSE

PROLOGUE

BUNNY

Moonlight peeks through the arched windows, casting my studio in a dark shadow. The light is different here. The lack of electricity and the ever-present candles, torches, and fires give off a yellowish glow. The difference makes for a challenge when mixing the paint, because the process must be exact. The image on one side must match the other, regardless of lighting, toxins, or weather.

Closing my eyes, I bring to mind the scene that I want to paint, the one that will bring the two worlds together. I may as well paint lightning, an earthquake or hurricane. The result will be the same.

Over the past few weeks, the cold of the castle has settled in my bones. I wonder if that's part of the Goddess' magic, leeching the warmth from us slowly, methodically. Surely she feeds—Morgan does —Anita, too. I know Anita drank from Morgan's lips, taking the virus from her to spread across the city, stealing power from every victim. The true Goddess of War asks for nothing but blood and despair.

Maybe that's why it's so cold.

She's sucked the place dry.

I pass the shattered remains of the mirror, ignoring the reflective shards of glass. I can't look at myself now. I'm not sure if I ever will again. I am the betrayer of my mate, of my Guards and brothers. Even if I had my reasons, none will ever justify me to their eyes.

Or even my own.

Opening the container I brought from Tran, I sprinkle in a small amount of the powder, mixing it in with the indigo. If Dylan had stopped me...I didn't know what to think would be the result if I hadn't returned. I heard the blade connect with the canvas. He damaged the painting. A similar cut is slashed through the painting near the fireplace. It's useless now. I'll toss it in the fire.

I exhale and stare at the fresh white board before me and dip my brush in the paint. The process soothes me. It always has, but tonight the dungeons are full and the Goddess cleverly placed my studio right above them. Casteel, the brutish head guard handpicked by the Morrigan, normally stalks the hallways. Not now. She's finally given him playthings, and I easily hear the screams of my brothers echoing off the flat walls.

Do I feel the guilt of my transgressions? Yes, immensely, but it's chased by the frozen reach of my mistress across the barren castle floors.

I made a choice. The call no one else was willing to make. With another breath to steady my hand, I start on the canvas mounted on the easel before me.

The war isn't over. It's only just beginning.

1

MORGAN

There's little doubt in my mind that they're dead.

That's the thought that haunts my mind each and every day. The idea--no, the image of them alone with that malicious, spiteful, bitch worms its way into my heart, and I can't let it go.

Why would she keep them alive? Every breath they take is a danger to her. Every day that passes, a threat. That's what I tell myself, refusing to believe my Guardians--who are strong, ferocious warriors, created by the hands of powerful, ancient gods--would not have returned by now if they were still alive.

They have to be dead.

I cross the massive room and pass the stacks of newspapers on the table without looking down. I know the headlines.

Strange Sickness Baffles Scientists
Virus Overwhelms Local Hospitals
The Next Plague?

Surrounding the newspapers are books, dozens of books, all open, with smudged, worn paper. Dylan reads them over and over, desperately looking for the one thing that can open the gate to the Otherside from our realm.

I intended to do two things.

One, to bring the bodies back.

Two, to kill the Morrigan.

At least, that's my plan.

I push back the curtain surrounding Dylan's bed. The fabric creates a dark cave inside the expansive attic studio. He's asleep, a rarity in the weeks since Bunny betrayed us. The bed is massive, a king-sized sleigh bed made of the darkest wood. I stare down at the hard planes of his bare chest, my eyes lingering over his abs and the sharp cut V under his navel. His shorts cling to his hips. I zero in on the purple blemish at the base of his neck, the one I gave him two days ago, finally fading. I should do it again. Mark him. Make it known that no one is taking this one from me, and if they try, blood will be shed.

I'm not losing another one.

He rolls to his side, muscles tense even in his sleep. His jaw is locked, resulting in tight cords down his neck. Neither of us can relax, caught in an emotional hell of worry and rage. When the Morrigan took my guardians, my mates, she stole not only a chunk of my soul but the bright flame of my power. When Bunny betrayed me, he removed any chance of us fighting back. I must have all five of my mates to complete the circle of power. Something he knew and therefore distanced himself from me so we didn't physically bond.

Bunny.

I still can't wrap my head around his betrayal. For what purpose? Did he truly feel neglected? Had I pushed him aside?

Despite his actions, his absence leaves a cold hole in my frayed heart. I'd meant it when I claimed him as a mate. I didn't realize he was faking it all for a way to increase the Morrgian's control of the Darkness and the fall of our world.

I swallow back the rage and look down at Dylan, my only guardian. My only conduit. I needed five. I had four, one is lost and now only one remains. I am thankful for his strength, for his unrelenting service to my needs; his commitment to stoking the flames. My powers are nothing but a flicker in the growing Darkness.

I drop the curtain and step in the darkness of Dylan's sleeping chamber. I pull my shirt over my head and slip my pants over my hips. His arm is around me before I've hit the soft mattress. I steal his breath. He gives me his body.

Together, we survive.

∼

THE STAIRWAY that leads to the dungeons beneath the garage is dark, musty, and cold. Hildi stands at the entrance. Our only prisoner occupies the center cell. There's nothing in Anita's tiny alcove but a basic cot, a tray from her dinner, and a functional sink and toilet.

"How is she?" I wrinkle my nose at her scent. Anita needs a shower, but that's a privilege she hasn't earned.

"The same. Silent one minute, crying the next," the Valkyrie says. "In the end, she gives me nothing."

At the moment, the woman sits with her back against the stone wall and stares into space, her face emotionless.

"I can't thank you enough for this," I say. Somehow Hildi got caught up in our battle against the Morrigan. She helped capture Anita the day Bunny betrayed us and my Guardians went missing. Since then, she's taken over the role of watching Anita down in the dungeons.

"My Goddess does not approve of the Morrigan's ways. She's pushing her will and destruction on all of us. I'm at your service until this is resolved."

I smile. "Thank you. We're running short on people we can trust."

"Your home is comfortable. Your servants, Davis and Sue, have been very accommodating. It's not an inconvenience."

I take a side glance at Anita, uncomfortable speaking freely near her. She seems completely oblivious. "Are you sure you don't have family you need to attend to?"

"My partner is aware of my obligations."

"Make sure he's aware of the dangers out there—with the virus. No one is safe."

A smile ghosts over Hildi's lips. "*She* is aware. I've told her to take precautions."

I raise an eyebrow. "Oh, sorry, I shouldn't have presumed."

"It's okay. We did originally meet over my jealousy of your relationship with the Raven Guard." She smiles wider. "I'm not picky with the gender of my lovers, just that they are worthy of sharing my bed."

You learn something new every day, I think to myself, leaving Hildi and walking down the narrow hallway. I keep clear of Anita's reach. I'm not sure what her actual powers entail, but I do know she has been in and out of the portals, traveling between realms. I need to know how to open a gate that will take me to the Morrigan's castle in the Otherside. As much as I'd like to see Anita dead, keeping her alive seems like our best chance.

"Good morning." I approach her cell. Anita is a beautiful woman, one used to extreme wealth and luxury. Or rather, she was. I can see a glimmer of her beauty beneath the stringy, dirty hair and her blank, soulless eyes. Her nails are chipped. Her skin is ashy and dry. Her treatment may be uncivilized, but what is owed to a woman whose intent is to help destroy the world?

She doesn't reply, so I bang on the bars of her cell. "Hey, girl, wake up."

I'd been born as a human vessel for the Morrigan's earthly rise. Anita and her brother had the misfortune to be born as sacrifices to the Morrigan's dark plans. Xavier was already dead—the first victim of the new plague. Anita became a carrier, spreading the virus throughout the city. Dylan is sure there is only one way to stop the virus from becoming the apocalypse: opening the gate and killing the Morrigan. But there have been other plagues brought on by the

Morrigan in the past, other cures. I'm not willing to give up on any option.

The main problem is we do not have the abilities or skills to get the gate open, much less find one. The Raven Guard spent their lives keeping the gate shut, and although Dylan had crossed back and forth, it was in his shifter form, an ability he lost when we mated.

My patience has run thin and I drop down to a squatting position to make eye contact. Her gaze never changes but I start talking anyway, like I have every other day for the past two weeks. "Tell me why Bunny betrayed me."

Blank stare.

"Tell me what she did with my Guardians."

Nothing.

"Tell me your role in all of this."

Zero.

Rage consumes me. I know it's irrational. She's never going to tell me what I want, but I have no one else to ask. Nowhere to turn. I pull the key to the lock out of my pocket and shove it in the keyhole.

"Morgan," Hildi warns.

I fling open the door and step inside, yanking Anita's frail, limp body off the floor. I may not be at my strongest but I'm far more powerful than she is at the moment. When she's on her feet I raise my hand and slap her across the face. Nothing changes. Not even in the depths of her eyes.

"I know you're in there, fool, and you *will* help me. You'll stop this insanity and you will help me bring my guardians home, dead or alive."

The last sentence sparks something and her eyes narrow. There's a red mark on her cheek and her mouth splits into a deranged grin.

"What?" I ask, desperate for anything.

"You think she killed them?"

Grief wracks through me but I pull on it and use it to feed my rage. "I'm not afraid of the truth."

Again, she cackles, and I tighten my hands around her throat. She tugs at my wrists. "The Morrigan is the goddess of war—not death like your little friend over there." She nods at Hildi. "She loves the destruction. The pain. She wants a *fight*. She wants the biggest fallout this realm has ever seen, and then she'll preside over it for eternity."

"Blah, blah, blah," I mutter, refusing to listen to her nonsense. "If she wants a fight, she'll get one. But she'll have to show herself to make it happen."

I release her throat and push her back on the thin mattress of her cot. I leave and lock the door back with a loud, echoing click. Anita stares at me with the same maniacal expression as before.

"What?" I ask again.

"Ignore her," Hildi says. "She's gone mad."

Anita begins to laugh. First softly and then gaining in momentum. I walk away, unwilling to be an audience to her show. I need leverage to get Anita to talk to me. I need to find what she cares about. What she wants from all of this.

Hildi and I leave her alone in the dungeon, slamming the outer door and locking it with the enchanted keys. Hildi sets wards by drawing runes across the door.

"What do you think that was all about?" I ask as we walk up the stairs.

"I think she's crazy and probably always has been. That's what the Darkness does to people." She pauses at the top of the stairs. "What will you do with her?"

"I'm not letting her out until I know what the Morrigan needs her for. After that, you're welcome to take her back to your Goddess and drag her to the gates of hell."

2

DYLAN

The door needs a heave to get open, the warped wood sticks at the top. I use my shoulder to knock it loose and when the door finally opens, it slams into the wall, louder than I'd intended.

I brace myself for the response. I don't know what or even why. Everything in the house feels quiet now. There's no music from Clinton's second floor suite. No echo of laughter following Sam. I don't hear Damien's heavy boots on the stairs, or the roar of his motorcycle in the alley out back.

There sure as hell is no sign of Bunny roaming the halls at all hours of the night or stuffing his face with sweets in the kitchen.

Bunny. Damn, it still stings, like the wound of a rusty blade running through the gut. How could he? What is he thinking? We all have our weak moments; our pride or ego, our doubts and fears. But this? This was something much more and it hurt to even think of the consequences of it all. For him. For Morgan, and most of all, the world.

As suspected, no one comes from the sound of me entering the room. Even Sue and Davis have quieted—heartbroken over the situation. Food preparation is nothing but a whisper in the downstairs kitchen. Our mandatory dinner has stopped; what's the point with just me and Morgan? We're together constantly anyway. Working, sleeping, mating.

Even our lovemaking has turned quiet. Nothing but shifting sheets and the sound of our bodies moving together. Even if we do derive pleasure from our bonding, it seems wrong to celebrate. It seems a betrayal to my fallen brothers.

I enter Bunny's room and take a deep breath. The room smells a little musty—the stale chemical of his paints—closed since the day of his traitorous actions. I've had my nose stuck in books or obsessing over the news. Morgan goes to the dungeons to interrogate Anita. I've been unable to even walk down the hall and step foot in the place where I allowed Bunny's escape.

But now I'm at a loss. My books are useless against whatever magic Bunny conjured to pass between realms and shut us out. So now I'm here, hoping to find *something* that will help us.

I stop before the torn canvas—the one Bunny used as a portal for escape. I ripped it—ruined it—in my haste to stop him. It may have been our only way to the Otherside. For all I know, it may have been their only way back.

The Raven Guard.

I've no doubt they're still alive. Suffering, but alive.

Morgan thinks they're dead and I've allowed that for the time being. She hasn't said the words, but I see it in the dark shadows of her eyes, and in the tears that slip down her cheeks when she thinks I don't notice. It's better that she thinks they're gone. The alternative is worse. Being a prisoner at the hands of the Goddess of War is like standing in the fiery pits of hell. If she realized...if she understood...

I can barely think of it myself and push back the weight of guilt of knowing they're bearing it without me at their side.

Which is why I finally caved and came back to Bunny's studio. Why I'm searching, day after day, for a fucking break—just the smallest clue. We can't give up on the others. They're alive, at least physically, and it's my obligation to bring them back.

I've COMPLETELY LOST track of time when I hear her footsteps on the stairs. I've been staring at painting after painting, castle after castle, trying to see *something* in the imagery for what feels like hours, when Morgan enters the room. She has smudges of dark under her eyes, either from lack of sleep or losing her power. The sight guts me. Another failure to add to the others.

"Hey," she says, leaning against the door. Her arms cross over her chest and she watches me.

"How's the prisoner today?" I ask.

"Fucking deranged."

"So like yesterday?"

"Maybe a little worse. Now she's speaking in riddles or something." She sighs and walks over to where I'm standing. "What's going on in here?"

"Just trying to see if Bunny left any sort of clue on how he got the portal open." I pretend saying his name isn't a punch to my insides, and gesture to his worktable. "He took a bunch of stuff the day he left. Probably whatever I would need to figure out how to get the gate open myself."

Morgan steps closer and slips her delicate hand in mine. Just the sensation of her skin against mine sends a shock of energy up my spine. "We'll figure it out."

"We're running out of time. Did you watch the news today?" I ask. She shakes her head. "People are getting sick outside of New York now, it's spreading."

I hate the look of pain and guilt on her face. It probably matches my own. She squeezes my hand and asks, "What do we do?"

"I'm out of my league here. If," I swallow, "if Damien was here he could probably figure out the magic, but without some kind of lead, I'm clueless. We're going to have to find help."

"Where? Who can help us with this?"

I kiss her on her forehead. "Come on, I think I have an idea."

3

MORGAN

If I had to choose a guardian to fight with at the end of the world, I'm not sure it would be Dylan.

Not that I don't think he's worthy; he's strong and capable, quick and smart, confident and secure. But, he's also emotionally disconnected at times, making it a struggle for us to comfort one another. We're both a little lost, definitely on edge, and as we walk down the long, narrow hallway beneath Tran's magic shop, I really miss my other Guardians.

"Find a table," he says as we enter the seedy, underground bar. A flare of magic ripples over me and I give the bouncer a questioning look.

"Disarming wards. No magic in here," the burly man replies.

"I doubt I'm much of a threat."

He looks me over and I can't help but stare at the twisting rope of tattoos around his neck. They look like they're moving. "Sure, sweetheart, that's what dangerous ones all say."

Dylan nods as he steps through and I feel his fingers leave my back as I step into the room and he walks toward the bar.

Seriously, where's Sam or Damien when I need them? Ugh, scratch that. The despair that lives around my heart roars.

I know they'd have us in a quiet, unassuming corner already with drinks on the table. I glance back at Dylan, who's engaged in a conversation with the bartender, a girl with smooth skin and fiery eyes. More than one customer looks between me and Dylan, making some kind of connection. I forget that the Raven Guard is notorious. I wonder if they know what happened to the others—how fast does news travel in the supernatural world?

The place is packed and there's definitely an interesting vibe. An energy—disabled powers or not. Having never been here, I have no idea if it's normal or not, but I suspect everyone is aware of the virus ravaging the city and came down here to drink their worries away.

Probably like every other bar in the city.

A familiar-looking man catches my eye as I search for a table; he tilts his head my way. His eyes are so very dark, but there's a calmness rolling off his person and something that makes me want to go over to him. Even stripped of his magic, I can tell he's powerful.

"No," a voice says in my ear. Dylan's voice. He presses his hand against my back, steering me in the opposite direction. "Not tonight."

"Who is that?" I ask, feeling the tug as we walk away.

"You don't recognize him?" An open table appears against the back wall. I'd just looked over here. Did he conjure it out of thin air? I shake my head at Dylan's question. "That's the Shaman from the fights."

"Oh," I glance back. The Shaman is still watching me. "I thought he was a good guy."

Dylan laughs as he pulls out my chair. I sit and he scoots it in, like a proper guardian and gentleman. When he's in his own seat he says, "Everyone in here has various shades. The Shaman can feel your pain. He wants to cure it—but every fix comes with a price."

"How do you know?"

"Despite this form, I've lived a long life, Morgan." He looks across the room and locks eyes with the Shaman. "He is older than I am."

The concept is overwhelming. I feel childish and naïve. Which I probably am, compared to the others in the room. Yet, I sense their awe when they look at me. They must see past my body. Past my flesh and into my soul, where I don't feel young at all.

"So you bargained with him?"

A flicker of anger tics at his jaw. "Why do you think we agree to the monthly fights? Our talents, tactics, and weaknesses are not meant for display. They are for battles and war."

"What did you trade for?"

"We needed information." His jaw tightens. "On you. Just a hint about where you were. If you were alive or not."

I reach for him under the table, grappling for his fingers that are curled tight in a ball. A tiny shard of ice around my heart melts. "You feel shame over that?"

He looks away, and even though he doesn't answer, the truth is written on his face. A chunk of the despair I've felt over the last few weeks chips away as the need to make Dylan feel better, to feel *loved*, rises in my chest. He refuses to meet my gaze and just as I'm about to force the issue, he looks over my shoulder with interest.

"Tran," he calls. "Over here."

"Tran?" The owner of the magic shop upstairs approaches. The ancient (probably literally) man walks over. A heavy cloak covers his shoulders. He takes the chair Dylan offers and sits with a weary sigh.

"I wasn't sure you'd come," Dylan says.

"No. I wasn't sure I would." His narrow eyes skirt over me. "I try to stay out of the ways of the gods and goddesses. I've probably already assisted too much."

"I know, and I appreciate you meeting us," Dylan says. "I just want to know if you saw anything that day—heard anything?"

There's no question what day Dylan is referring to, but I lean in and press anyway. "The day my Guardians vanished. From everything we know, it took place near your shop, but our own canvassing has been futile. No one will talk to us." Damien would have gotten the men on the street to talk—he was friendly with them. "They're either afraid or don't care."

"Probably both," he says and sighs heavily. Deep lines crease his forehead. "It sounded like the world ripped in two; I felt the moment in the depths of my chest. The air turned to ice, coating my windows with frost. I heard the shouts of the Ravens and went to assist but my door was jammed tight. It was hard to see—thank the gods, because what I did see?" He shivers. "Tentacles of smoke. Long and black. Something dark from another world."

He stares at me. Dylan grips my hand. He fought those tentacles in the ring.

"The Morrigan?"

"Or part of her, at least. I fell to my knees and prayed." Tran reaches under his cloak and rests a crumpled paper bag on the table. "I found this on the street after it was over."

He slides the bag to Dylan and I hold my breath as he opens it. I don't know what to expect, but what he pulls out never crossed my mind, even though it seems obvious. Dylan's eyes flash to mine as he hands over the cracked black box that may hold a clue on what happened to the guardians and how to get them back.

It's Sam's camera.

"It's broken. I couldn't get it to work, but maybe there's a way."

"Thank you, Tran. This is very helpful."

I try to turn on the camera but it's pointless. He's right. I look up and find him staring at me once again. His hands tremble on the table. "I have a warning for you both."

"What kind of warning?" Dylan asks, but the line between his eyes tells me he already knows. I'm the only one left out of the loop here.

"Not everyone wants you to stop the Darkness. There are many others that have waited centuries, if not longer, for this world to fall to the demons."

"What do you mean?"

"Watch your back, young warrior. As the civilians fall to the sickness, the darker elements will arise. You're not just fighting the Morrigan."

I feel the hair on the back of my neck rise as I look around the room. Every person, witch, demon, and angel is focused on this conversation. "Do you think any of them helped Bunny betray us?"

"Nothing is off the table. The creatures down here? They're just the muscle and thugs. The gossips and traders. It's the ones that live in the world up top you have to worry about. They come in all shapes and sizes. Perform all kinds of jobs."

"Like what?" I ask.

"Doctors. Police. Those that will be called upon in a time of crisis."

I look at Dylan. Again, he's not completely surprised. "You knew?"

"You know the history, Morgan. Who do you think Hitler used as his commanders? As his closest confidants. It wasn't back-alley scum."

I think of the photos I've seen. He's always surrounded by a tight posse. Doctors. Generals. Educators. Which would be manageable if I hadn't just lost most of my own posse.

"Thanks for the information, Tran," I say, standing from the table. Dylan follows my lead, taking the camera from me and slipping it in his coat. "If you hear anything, let us know."

The old man nods.

I feel the eyes on us as we exit the bar. I don't miss the Shaman's nod. A simmering rage boils beneath the surface of my skin. I don't like not knowing the rules of this world. Who is an enemy or not.

Bunny has opened a wound that will not stop bleeding.

4

MORGAN

When we leave the bar, I can't help but notice the difference in the city. The streets are less crowded. Shops close early. People walk with scarves and surgical masks over their mouths and noses. The virus is here. It's real.

We return to The Nead and Dylan takes the camera to Sam's studio. He hopes to recover any image locked inside. Full of anxious energy, I go to the basement gym and blow off some steam. Hildi is already there, beating the shit out of a punching bag. She nods at the other gloves hanging on the wall, "Wanna fight?"

"Yeah," I say, yanking them off the hook. "I kind of do."

There's a white canvas sparring mat in the middle of the room. I've used it many times before, mostly training with Clinton. I've bled on it. I've made love on it, and that's when I realize that every room in this gigantic house has taken on emotional meaning to me. I blink back tears of nostalgia.

"You ready?" Hildi says, pulling me from my thoughts.

"Yeah," I tug on the gloves and square off. "Show me what you've got."

I've fought Hildi before, mostly just out of some kind of supernatural pissing contest to prove my worth. I won, and now we're friends. Or at least I think we are. What if we're not? What if she's one of the bad guys? Is that what Tran meant? Did Bunny leave her here to watch over us? Friend or foe, I won't take it easy on her, and when she punches me in the kidney, I know the same is true of her.

The workout tests my body. Hildi isn't exhausted or mentally drained like I am, but I keep up, dodging and getting in my own hits. We stay in the red circle, fighting for dominance. She has me on height. I have her on instinct. Clinton helped me cultivate a natural ability to remain two steps ahead. My feet and shoulders move faster than my brain. Her punches land hard. Adrenaline spikes in my blood when she swipes my feet and I land hard on my back, smacking my head on the mat. Black spots cloud my vision and rage climbs up my spine. I want them back. I want my guardians. My mates. I want my balance of power. I want serenity. But most of all I want to throttle Bunny and ask him why. Why would he do this?

"Why?" I mutter, the black spots clearing. Hildi hovers over me, concern on her face.

Is it real? Does she care?

"Morgan?" I use her distraction and kick the back of her knee, dropping her to the ground. I pounce, rolling on top of her and ripping off my gloves in the process. I punch her repeatedly, the skin of my knuckles tearing. She cries out, fighting against me, blood dripping down her lip. I wrap my hands around her throat and something dark unleashes; vines sprout from my fingers, coiled and black, twisting around Hildi's throat.

"Why?" I ask again, a choking sob caught in the back of my throat. "Why would you do this to us?"

"Morgan," Hildi grunts, using both hands to pry mine off her neck. The vines tighten. "It's me. Calm down."

"Who are you?" I ask.

"Hildi."

"No," I seethe. "Who are you really? What do you want? What side are you on?"

She stops struggling, her lips slack and turning purple. My vision finally fully clears and I take in the blonde hair and feminine features. I hesitate, and Hildi uses the opportunity to break free, kneeing me in the gut. Stunned back to myself, the vines retract, slithering back into my fingers. She tosses me aside. I lay on my back, breathing heavily, disoriented and confused.

The Valkyrie stands over me for a minute, flinging her gloves on the ground. Heavy feet race down the basement steps and I hear, rather than see, Dylan in the doorway. "What happened?"

"She's lost her fucking mind." Hilid rubs her neck. Red welts are starting to form.

"Go rest. I'll take care of her."

"She's out of control," she mumbles. "Her powers. She doesn't have control."

He absorbs that and says, "Take a break. We'll watch the dungeons. Go home. See Andi."

Hildi disappears and Dylan stands over me for a moment, assessing me. I can't stand the judgment on his face. "I just...I got paranoid."

"I know what Tran said, but we can trust Hildi."

"How do you know?" I rub a tender spot on my cheek where she hit me.

"Because even though the Goddess of War and the Goddess of Death sound like they would be on the same team—trust me, they're not." He touches my bruise.

"I'm fine."

"No," he says, bending over to pick me up. I fight against him, but he's bigger and in a second he's got me cradled in his arms. "You're not fine and to be honest, neither am I."

His words jolt me and fire boils under my skin. "What are we going to do? They're gone. People are dying. We can't trust anyone. We couldn't even trust Bunny."

He presses his forehead to mine. "We're going to get through this and we're going to do it together. Starting today. Starting now."

5

DYLAN

"You can't help me," she mocks. "You're nothing without them. That's why she took them and left you here. Because together we're a bumbling, useless mess."

I don't make it to the attic floor, not with her flinging words of poison every step of the way. I stop at her room, kick open the door, and toss her on her bed. Her white tank is covered in drops of Hildi's blood. Her dark eyes are lit with fiery pain.

As much as it kills me, Morgan needs that pain. She needs to feel the anger and hatred of the Morrigan and even Bunny. Sadness has gotten us nowhere. Wallowing in our guilt—that's what the Morrigan hoped we would do. My penchant for brooding. Morgan's guilt-prone humanity. The distrust Tran sewed this afternoon made something in Morgan snap and I plan to bring that rage and anger fully to the surface.

She sprawls on the mattress, propped up on her elbows. Her lip is puffy from taking a hit. I lean over her, hands on both sides of her hips, my mouth inches from hers. "I know you think the Morrigan left us here because we're weak, but that's not possible. She does not understand the reality of our bond, because in her mind what we have is twisted and perverse. She can't comprehend the strength we find in one another. Not fully." Despite her busted lip, I kiss her hard and she responds with equal ferocity.

Her nails scratch down my chest, tugging at the fabric of my shirt. I lift it over my head and then strip the tank off her body. She lands on her back, her hair a dark halo on the white quilt covering her bed. Her black, lacy bra contrasts with her pale skin. A dark bruise is forming on her ribs. Hildi got in a few good punches, that's for sure.

She lifts her hips and I strip off her exercise tights, taking the panties with it. I blink, having a vision of black wings spread across the sheets. *Dear gods*, I think, rubbing my eyes.

I drop my pants, kicking them off my feet, not hesitating before I grab her legs and pull her to the edge of the bed.

"She doesn't own us, Morgan. Not our minds or our bodies. She doesn't understand how, when I touch you here," I reach between her legs, eliciting a moan of pleasure. "Or if I fuck you like this," I flip her to her stomach, pulling her hips in the air, exposing her voluptuous, full ass, "that it brings us closer. Makes us stronger. Mentally and physically."

I slip between her cheeks, coating my shaft in the wet heat of her body. When she begs, I ease inside, pushing to the fullest—the farthest possible. Her fingers grip the bedding, mine grip her hips. The silence of the house is broken, filled with cries of passion, the release of anger and fear.

"Harder," she cries. "I want to feel you. Gods, I just want to feel more than the ache of loss."

I comply, thrusting in and out, and feel relief when her body moves in synch. But it's too distant, which, again, is what the Morrigan wants. I need to see her face, see the ecstasy tremble from her lips. I pull out and she rolls to her back. There's no hesitation, not a break in our movements. I lift her hips and lean against the bed, entering her once more. The anguish has vanished from her face, her eyes glazing even as they hold mine.

"She doesn't have this," I say, holding, holding, holding…

"She has them." Her breath catches, her body quakes.

Our fingers link and the wave crashes over Morgan like Thor's mighty hammer against a mountain. She shatters, her voice loud, her pleasure and satisfaction known.

I thrust into her, spilling the warmth of my seed and the keys to my soul. I'm still in her when I reply to what she last said. "No," I tell the woman lying beneath me. Our bodies are still joined. "She doesn't have them. She doesn't have their hearts—she sure as hell doesn't have mine—and that's what will break her."

6

BUNNY

Casteel arrives in my studio just past dawn. Hulking and demonic in the doorway, he makes no bother to knock. His rank gives him the privilege of coming and going as he pleases.

"The Queen wants to see you." He glances over my stained hand and paint-covered smock. I try my best not to stare at the gnarled scar at the base of his jaw. "Now."

I wipe my hand on a rag, leaving my paintbrush in a jar of turpentine. The painting behind me has begun to take shape. My mind is sharper in the Otherside—or at least, my magic is.

I follow Casteel out of my room in the tower and down the stairs to the main section of the castle. He wears a traditional uniform: black leather tunic, heavy pants with pockets and slits for hiding weapons. His boots are made from the hide of an animal I never want to see in person. Thick and bumpy, with soles made from the tar pits in the northern territory.

Even with the dark fabric I see and smell the blood splatters of my brothers. They are fierce warriors—the Raven Guard—and to elicit the screams of pain and misery that echo from the dungeons up to my rooms must mean Casteel has refined his level of torture.

Payback sucks, especially if you're not the one that committed the crime.

Casteel does knock before entering the queen's chambers, he's not that much of an arrogant fool. I lurk behind him, head bowed, counting the stones on the floor. A slave—The Morrigan does not pretend the people in her castle are anything but owned by her—opens the door and nods for us to enter.

"Reznick?" The Queen calls from the other room. It takes me a beat to recognize my given name.

"Yes, Your Highness."

"Come to me."

I spare a glance at Casteel, who is well aware he's not been invited to the inner chamber. He smirks, as though it may be my final act. It could be, but I don't think so. He's unaware of our relationship. How we work.

The Queen is still in bed, her cheeks unusually flushed. A sheen of sweat covers her overheated forehead and there's a look of hunger in her eyes. She grimaces as if a bitter taste is on her tongue. I have little doubt what caused the reaction. I too felt the echo of pleasure rattle across my bones. Even across realms, we're connected. Something happened with Morgan, something that increased her strength. I assume she mated with Dylan, just as she has every other day since I tore the Guardians away from her.

In this realm, the Queen pushes back the heavy, midnight blue covers draped over the bed. She swings her slim but muscular legs over the edge. She pauses, taking a moment to catch her breath. The pause implies an expectation.

I step forward and offer my hand. "Please, let me."

She smiles, white teeth against too-pale skin. Without the flush on her cheeks, she'd look like one of the hordes of dead that roam the Wastelands. "So sweet," she says, allowing me to help her off the mattress. "Tell me, Reznick, tell me about your dreams."

It's a trick question. If I tell her I don't have any, she'll know I'm lying. If I tell her that I do, she'll want my head for confirming

Morgan's strength and Dylan's virility. I hold her eye and declare, "I don't sleep, my Queen."

My words hold the truth, but not the reality that I feel the heat between Morgan and her Raven lovers regardless of where I am. It's a double-edged sword. I've never been able to contain my jealousy over her connection to the others, but I accept the flow of energy through our bond. It makes me stronger. It keeps my hands warm and my powers alert. From the way the Queen looks at me, I suspect she hasn't a clue to the lengths in which our bond travels.

The Morrigan passes me, entering the bathing room. The slave nods, encouraging me to follow. I step inside the room of marble and brass, observing her splash cold water on her face. The slave stands quietly in the corner, waiting for instruction. They're to wait. To predict. Never to speak.

I watch the Queen's reflection in the mirror, pretending not to see her flinch as she takes in the dark shadows under her eyes or the fine lines crossing her forehead. She hasn't aged like this in over a millennium, not since she took on the mantle of her reign, which implies something has changed.

I am not sure why she allows me to see her in such intimate moments. Her mind works in twisted and depraved ways. I stay alert while giving the air of innocence. She sighs, tugging at a wiry gray hair spiraling out of the thick, dark mane near her temple. She yanks out the offending hair without a hint of the sting of pain, dropping it into the sink.

"Tell me," she says, holding out her hand in the direction of the slave. The girl steps forward, a silver vial ready and uncorked. "Have you completed the next stage of our plan?"

"Almost. I just need a few more days."

She tips the vial into her mouth, swallowing in one gulp. Her tongue flicks out to get the final drop before tossing the vial back to her slave. She saunters past me, slipping her robe off her shoulders. The slave lunges for the robe but I catch it single-handed before it hits the floor. The Morrigan arches her eyebrow, either in amusement or displeasure that I'd interfered with the girl's work. It's impossible to know. I force myself to stare at the Queen's naked body as she lowers herself into the ice bath. It's expected. Looking away...it would suggest I don't find her attractive—a deadly move.

Do I find her attractive? I should, but despite my actions, my heart belongs to one woman. I don't find the Morrigan arousing, regardless of her beauty. I can't help but notice the wrinkles and sagging lines. Her hair hangs to the middle of her back, just above the twin dimples dotting the smooth flesh of her backside. Sinking into the porcelain tub, she exhales, clearly invigorated by cold. I know, and she knows that I know, that even from another realm, Morgan brings a fire through our conduit. The fire of lust that brags of her power, of the emotions that build against her flesh. She knows as well as I do exactly what Dylan does to Morgan, and it disgusts her.

The Queen will do anything to extinguish the heat, including submerging her body in ice.

She leans her head back against the pillow, the slave holding it between two hands. She cuts her dark eyes in my direction. "I need the gate reopened."

"Yes, Your Majesty."

"Don't make me wait much longer, Reznick, or your brothers will pay for your ineptitude."

I swallow. "Soon. I promise."

She waves me away with her hand and I bow before leaving the bathing chamber. Casteel waits for me, no doubt having heard every word exchanged between us.

I pass him, heading back to the hall. Casteel may know the Queen's commands but he does not know her wants, her pains. She's weaker than I thought, and I fight a smile as we walk back to my tower where I will continue my work.

7

MORGAN

Cool air wafts across my face and I snuggle against the warmth next to me, warding off the chill. I only want a few more minutes of peace before the day begins and I wrap my arms around Dylan, feeling something has shifted between us. We've broken part of the curse that the Morrigan chained us with when she stole my guardians.

Dylan rolls into me, tightening his arms. I feel the heat of his kisses across my shoulder, the hard length between his legs. I push back and raise an eyebrow.

"Don't even think about it."

"Good morning to you, too," he says with a smile. A bit of the angst he usually carries is gone for the moment.

His eyes look a different shade, a brighter blue, and I want to ask him what he's thinking—about his words the night before. His jaw clenches and I think maybe he'll say it—speak the truth--but he licks his lip and then licks mine.

I squirm beneath the weight of his body, loving the feel, loving this brief moment in the wake of war.

"Dylan," I say, successfully pulling away from him. "Do you really think we can beat her?"

"Yes. And we'll get them back."

My stomach knots, snuffing out the flicker of hope. "Don't make promises you can't keep."

His hand clenches around my wrist. "I never do, Morgan."

I brush my thumb over his lip and again the heat and intensity boils between us, the kind that fuels my power and makes me stronger. I'm realizing that I'll need all the strength I can get when the doorbell echoes up the marble floors and wooden stairway.

Dylan frowns. "Are you expecting someone?"

"No."

He groans and rolls over, taking the heat with him. "Then we probably need to go see who it is."

8

DYLAN

Professor Christensen stands in the foyer, looking every bit the part of University faculty. His suede jacket is only missing the patches on the elbows, and a pipe would make an excellent prop. His gray hair makes him appear distinguished as well as trustworthy.

I'm never exactly sure if he is either one.

"Dylan," he says as I walk down the stairs. I straighten the wrists of my shirt. "It's good to see you. I wish it was under better circumstances."

"Good to see you, too. If you're looking for good news, sadly we don't have much." I do tell him about Sam's camera and my attempt to recover the photos. "I haven't been able to access them yet but hopefully later today."

Christensen lowers his head and asks in a soft voice, "How is she handling all of this?"

I rub the back of my neck. "Twelve hours ago she was on the brink of a breakdown. Paranoia, rage, regret. She feels guilty and lost. She's overwhelmed by the loss of the other guardians. But we're working through it. I think we made some progress last night."

"She needs to be strong."

"I know. She does, too. She'll be ready."

We both look up when we hear footsteps on the stairs. Morgan slowly walks down, dressed for the day in jeans and a fuzzy blue sweater. Her hair is twisted in a knot behind her head. She's wearing boots, ones I know have a sheath next to her ankle for a small blade Damien gave her. Her cheeks carry a reddish blush, and pride swells in my chest knowing I helped put it there.

She's the opposite of the Goddess of War, yet just as lethal. I'm learning that. Heat makes her grow. It makes her strong, and I'll do my part to stoke the flames, but we've got to get the others back.

"Professor," she says, reaching the final step. "I didn't know you were coming."

"I got your message about your, uh, guest downstairs. Thought maybe I'd take a crack at her."

"You can try," she says, glancing at me.

"I'm going to get to work on the camera." I turn and head for the stairs. "You two have fun."

Morgan rolls her eyes. "Yeah, like talking to a psychotic bitch is going to be fun."

Christensen holds out his arm, offering to escort Morgan to the dungeons. It's a ridiculous pose, knowing what's downstairs and what we're dealing with. Morgan accepts and links her elbow to his. They've just rounded the corner when I hear him say, "I suspect this may be more entertaining than you may realize."

9

MORGAN

I still find it odd that the Professor is part of all this. That he's as old as the Guardians, if not older. His role is historian, documenting the Morrigan and her destruction through the centuries. He and Dylan hope that I will continue the trend by writing a firsthand account of the current attempt at evil taking over the world.

"Where's the Valkyrie?" Christensen asks as we get to the dungeon door. It's locked and I fish the key out of my pocket.

"She needed a break."

The look he gives me is questioning, but he doesn't say anything further. The door swings open and we're assaulted by the smell, the stench from Anita's cell. I flip on the exhaust fan built into the ceiling. An empty tray of food left this morning by either Davis or Sue sits on the floor. Anita's expression doesn't change when she sees her former supervisor, but unlike many other times I've been down here, she does speak.

"Came to see it for yourself? Gawk at me like a monkey in a cage?"

"I'm saddened to see it come to this. It didn't have to."

"No?" she asks. She bares her teeth. Maybe she is a little like a zoo animal. Is that what being caged does to a person?

"You could have told Morgan or Dylan how Bunny got the gate open. How you jumped from realm to realm."

"And what? They'd let me go?" Her eyebrow arches. "My secrets are the only thing keeping me alive."

"We're not killers," I tell her. "If anything, we're the opposite—trying to stop this bloody virus from spreading further."

She leans into the bars, clutching the iron with both hands. She glances between the two of us. "What if you could only get one thing from me? One secret, which would you pick?"

I sigh and rub my forehead. "What are you talking about?"

"You're right, I do know things. I know how to get back to the Otherside. I know where Bunny is. I know how to stop the virus." Her blue eyes skim over me. "I know where your precious guardians are being held."

I shake my head. "I don't believe you."

She shrugs. "You figure out what you want to know the most, and maybe we can make a deal."

Christensen has been silent next to me this whole time. I don't know what he thinks of his former student. Or even what he thinks of me allowing her to live in such conditions.

"What sort of deal do you want?" he asks.

"I want to go back to my mistress."

"Even though you've failed?"

Her body stiffens. "I'm bound to her—like you are to your little birds. In every lifetime, we find one another."

Christensen's eyes narrow, studying Anita closely, as though he's searching for a memory.

"Tell me what you know," I declare, "and I'll send you back—in a casket."

"You get one secret, Morgan. Only one. Choose well."

I shake my head. Why does this girl think she dictates anything?

Is it because she's a spoiled brat? Is she delusional? Maybe I need to let her shower—have a little sunlight.

"What will it be? What will you pick?" She begins, in a sing-song voice. "Save three and spare one. Save a million but lose them all. Cut off the head and kill the rest. Wings and fingers. Ash and bone. Mix them together for the elixir of life." She giggles, eyes glazed, and I sigh, gesturing for Christensen to follow me out.

Once we're outside and the doors are locked he says, "I assume that's why the Valkyrie needed a break?"

That and I tried to strangle her. "Partly."

"Keep an eye on her. She may admit some truth in her delusions." He stops in the stairwell. "I'm going to do a little research. See what I can come up with."

"We can't let her go back to the Morrigan. If she's part of the three, then we need to keep her far away."

He nods. "Her and you."

I lean against the wall. "I have a feeling there's little chance I'm avoiding a fight with the Morrigan, don't you think?"

"Anita may be right. Certain moves may always come into play. You thought you could hold the Morrigan back by splitting her in three. You accomplished keeping her in the Otherside, but she still managed to slip her virus through before that. To stop it all you may have to all be bound once again."

"And then what?" I'm trying to follow his train of thought.

He frowns, a sad expression that makes me not want to hear what he has to say next. "Morgan, you have to consider what Anita has already accepted."

"What? That I'm batshit crazy?"

"No," he shakes his head. I'm not ready for what he says next. "It's possible that to achieve success and beat the Morrigan once and for all, you may have to embrace the Otherside and the Darkness that rules it."

"You want me to join her?"

"No. I don't want anything but to stop her. You've just got to figure out the best way to do that."

He speaks in riddles—similar to Anita down the hall. I'm not sure what they want and I definitely don't know if I can trust either of them.

"How do I embrace it—her?"

Again he answers, but in a most unhelpful way. "I suspect you'll find out when the time comes. Do everything you can to be prepared for that moment."

10

MORGAN

When Hildi doesn't return that afternoon, I decide to go find her. I knew I'd been a jerk, (out of control, really,) but the Valkyrie is a fighter and it makes no sense for her to hold a grudge.

Dylan stays at The Nead, close to recovering the images on Sam's camera. He asked his friend Marcus, a security guard at the Empire State Building by day and underground demon fighter by night (Snakehead is what I've come to call him,) to watch over Anita. I told him about our visit this afternoon and enough of it unnerved him to make the call to keep her on closer watch.

I didn't tell him what Christensen said, about the possibility of my embracing the Morrigan and the Darkness in order to beat her. If I know Dylan as well as I think I do, he probably already figured it out.

They probably *all* already figured it out.

I have no expectations when I arrive at the address he gives me. These people live in a world beyond my understanding. From seedy bars to penthouses and mansions with secret dungeons, I have no idea what to expect when it comes to my new friends in the supernatural world. Where do they get their money? How do they survive?

When you've been around for eons, maybe you've got investment money in Swiss bank accounts.

I've got bigger things to worry about.

I take the train to Brooklyn, noticing the distinct lack of subway riders. More masks. One woman dumps a massive glob of hand sanitizer in her palm and nearly bathes in it. A discarded newspaper headline declares people should work from home until the experts at CDC get a handle on the sickness.

Even though I suspect I'm immune, it makes me paranoid and I shove my hands in my pockets and try not to touch anything—anyone—on the way out of the subway. Two blocks later, I double check the address to make sure I'm in the right place. It's a small, hipsterish community. Definitely not a mansion. I climb the steps and ring Hildi's apartment bell.

There's a buzz in return, the door unlocks and I step into the building. Hildi is in unit four, so I climb the first set of stairs. I knock, bracing myself for whatever anger she has after I lost my mind the day before, but when the door opens Hildi barely glances at me. Her brilliant blue eyes are rimmed with red. I can't stop staring at the bruises on her neck.

"Can we talk?" I ask. She nods and I step into the apartment. I'm barely in when I stop cold. Sniffing the air, I catch the familiar scent. I instinctively cover my mouth and nose with my hand. "Oh my god, Hildi."

"She's got it—the virus," Hildi replies, wiping her nose on her sleeve. "I came home from your place and found her like this."

"How? Do you know?" It doesn't matter. It's a stupid question. "How far along is it?"

"From what we've seen she probably has a few days. I'm not taking her to the hospital. I've seen the news, it's a cesspool there." She sighs, but it's more like a shuddering cry. "I don't know what to do."

She leads me to her room. The bed is centered in the room. I'm sure Andi is a knockout in real life. I can tell that from her dark, red hair and the angles of her face, but right now? She looks like death. Actual death. Ashy face. Sallow skin. Her lips are pale and cracked. She's asleep, or at least I hope she is. I notice heavy curtains cover the large windows and the lamps are all dimmed.

"Bright light hurts her eyes."

"Hildi, I came to apologize. I am so, so sorry about what happened yesterday." I reach for her hands and I'm happy when she doesn't pull away and punch me. "I'm working on this. Figuring out what to do—how to save these people. People like Andi."

"I'm not sure what you can do. It's spreading rapidly. Half the businesses in our neighborhood are closed—either out of fear or actual sickness. I think it's worse than what the news is reporting."

The sinking feeling I've had since speaking with Christensen churns in my belly. What it will take to end the spread of the Darkness is possibly more than I can give. It's a sacrifice. One after the other. It took one to get it rolling: Xavier, and it will most likely take more than one to get it to stop.

And if I go...Anita goes. We'll have to get to the Otherside together. There I can free my guardians, if they're even still alive, and we'll kill the Morrigan. Hildi watches me closely. "What are you thinking about?"

"How to stop this. Anita says she knows how, but she wants to return to the Morrigan's side. I'm going to have to take her." I tell her Christensen's theory about reuniting the three sides of the Queen to fully kill her.

The Valkyrie shakes her head. "No. There has to be another way."

"Splitting her up only gave us a little time." I glance at Andi, who takes a long, shuddering breath. "A slow spreading death instead of quick and total annihilation."

"What if you go and it's worse? What if she's too powerful to stop?"

"There's no good answer here. No good solution. People are

dying—people *have* died. I can't let fear hold me back from at least trying to stop her and find a cure."

Hildi sits on the bed next to her partner and takes her hand. There's no doubt that the look in her eyes, directed at me, is nothing but pure pity. "I don't wish the burdens you carry on anyone, Morgan. You'll have to make the decision."

"I feel like it's already been made. Do I even have a choice?"

"May the gods be with you." She stands and gives me a hug. "But if you succeed, bring me back the cure."

I squeeze her tight. "I will."

11

DYLAN

After hours of absolute frustration, tedious work, and three shots of whiskey, I'm able to download and print off Sam's photos. There's little doubt the Guardian documented his final moments in this realm so we would find them. There are dozens of shot with no organization, just a continuous shot of the grisly, dark scene.

My brothers didn't even have the chance to fight. The Morrigan slipped in from an invisible portal, one that simply merged our worlds together. I stare at the photo—a vision?—of Clinton, bound and beaten. I recognize the hard stone floor and the chains.

"Oh my god. What...what is that? Where is it?"

I spin and find Morgan in the doorway of the dining room. I've spread the photos across the long table. My heart pounds--I didn't want her to see them, but then again, it's her fight too. The truth will help us find them.

She snatches the photo from my hand. I pretend not to see the tears in her wide, dark eyes and reach for the final, erratic shots, stashing them in a pile. Her hand clamps down on my wrist. "Don't. I want to see them."

I hand them to her, each worse than the last. Whip marks, lashes, and bruises. Blood pooling on the cold, stone floor. "I don't think Sam saw them before he was taken or even had a clue what was coming."

"Does that make it better?" Her voice is hard.

"I'm just trying to piece it together."

"They walked into a slaughter. So the Morrigan—or at least some manifestation—was able to sneak through a completely invisible entrance and ambush them."

I point to one of the photos with the black, coiled tentacles slipping from one world to the next. "They're in the castle dungeons."

"How do you know?"

I roll up my sleeves and point to the scarred tissue around my wrist, then cut my eyes to a photo of Damien chained with his arms extended over his head. Iron manacles wrap around his wrists. "It's not the first time the Queen has taken a guardian prisoner."

She frowns and touches the marks on my wrists. "You? When?"

I look down at our hands. "When you opened the gate before."

"When my parents died."

I nod. Morgan looks like she may be ill. I pull out a chair and guide her into it. "Don't blame yourself for that one. It was all my doing."

She doesn't seem convinced, but drops it anyway. "How far in the future do you think these photos show?"

I've already studied the wounds. The scabs and reopened injuries. I see the gaunt thinning in their cheeks, the lost glimmer in their eyes.

"A few weeks."

"Weeks?" Her jaw drops.

"I suspected all along that they were still alive." I wrap my hands around the back of the chair. "It's not her way to make anything quick and painless."

Morgan stares at the photos, her mind running. I see the way her eyes move, the way her fingers clench. Her emotional reactions are why I hadn't told her. She's not the best at keeping in check.

She turns and lifts her chin. Her next comment catches me off guard. "Andi is sick—she caught the virus."

Another stone sinks. "And Hildi?"

"She's fine. Probably immune." She exhales and glances over the photos one last time before standing. "I'm going to bed."

"Do you want me to come with you?"

"No." She gives me a weak, tired smile. "I'm exhausted. I probably just need a little time alone."

It's not exactly a dismissal or even a rejection. I'm exhausted as well. Even if we bonded tonight, I'm not sure how much energy I'd have to give.

I grab her hand before she leaves, tugging her back to my chest. I do kiss her. I'm not letting her get away so easily, and the flare of heat still rises between us. "Find me if you need me, okay?"

She nods, licking the taste of me off her lips.

"Goodnight, Dylan."

"Goodnight."

12

MORGAN

I don't go to bed or even go to my room. Instead I walk up the four flights of stairs and enter Bunny's studio. The massive, high-ceilinged room is drafty and cold and I wrap my arms around my chest to stave off a chill. I hadn't been in here alone before. Not before or after Bunny's betrayal.

I had seen the paintings, though. Canvas after canvas of similar, haunting scenes. Most are of the castle. The Morrigan's castle. I've seen it in my dreams. Written about it. I know that in the realm where she lives it's cold and barren—a reflection of the soulless anger that resides in her heart.

I walk to the one with the tear and touch the jagged canvas edges. Dylan almost killed Bunny that night. It's a testimony to my confusion that I'm okay that he missed.

I walk down the long row of paintings and find a hint of obsession. What was Bunny trying for here? Some kind of perfection? Slight variations occur in each scene. A light in the castle window of one. The curved branch of a withered tree in another. Stopping at one set in the gloomy gray of the Otherside's day, I try to figure out what I'm missing. My eyes keep going back to the light in the arched window, a faint pale yellow. A slight blur mars the middle of the glass. A person? Someone watching.

A faint, cool breeze wafts over me and I blink, realizing my nose is centimeters from touching the canvas. I feel the tingle of magic, a faint reminder of the day I stepped between realms in the park. Narrowing my eyes at the two-inch window, I press a finger against the yellow glass.

Nothing.

Just hard, painted canvas, cast in the shadow of fading magic. Bunny must have infused it in the materials but how do I activate it?

I stare at the painting for a few more minutes, quite sure I can see something beyond the glass. If there's something in there, then I can hopefully get through there, like Bunny, Anita, and the other Guardians did. I'll need strong magic and someone to walk me through it—not Dylan. Someone more willing to take on the darker sort of magic required for this kind of spell.

I'm not exactly sure who can help me, but I have an idea where to start.

THE ZAP IS familiar this time as I pass through the disarming wards of the bar. Being so unfamiliar with my magic and abilities, I'm never sure what I'm losing—they've only been strong under spells or in the fighting ring—but I feel a specific loss when I step past the bouncer and into the shadowy room.

The music is loud enough to disguise conversations but not overbearing. The crowd is lighter than last time, empty tables are scattered across the room. I don't see anyone familiar but I decide to wait it out and find an empty stool at the bar.

"What would you like?" the bartender asks. I saw her speaking to Dylan the other night. She's got creamy brown skin and a shaved head. Her features are tiny, the tips of her ears slightly pointed. I try not to stare at her teeth, sharp at the canines, but fail.

"Whiskey," I reply, scanning the rest of the bar. I'd come to like the taste of it after being handed a glass so many times at The Nead. She pours the drink and slides it across the bar. "Thanks."

She helps another customer and I try to search the dark room. It's impossible, though, without looking nosy. The bartender wipes the counter and says, "You were here the other night. With the Raven."

I nod and take a sip of the fiery drink. "I was."

She lifts an eyebrow. "Where is he this time?"

I shrug.

"He doesn't know you're here, does he?"

"Why would you ask that? I'm an adult. I can go where I please."

She snorts. It's a delicate sound. She leans over the bar and I see her eyes, green with flakes of swirling gold. "Tell me, Your Majesty, why are you here? Maybe I can help?"

"Why did you call me that?"

"Your Majesty? Are you not the Queen of Ravens?"

"No," I say, but it feels like a lie. I look at my drink. "It's complicated."

"Not really."

Another customer approaches and she walks down the bar length. I consider leaving, but the woman may be able to help. When she returns, I take another sip of my drink and ask, "What's your name?"

"Cirice."

"Well, Cirice, I'm looking for the Shaman."

Her head tilts. "No, there's no way your Guardian knows you're here."

"Do you know where he is? The Shaman? I think he can help me."

"Oh, I'm sure he can," she laughs under her breath. "That's one bag of trouble you don't want to get into."

"Dylan warned me, but like you said, I'm the Queen and he's my Guardian, not my boss. I have to make the hard decisions—the tough choices. If the Shaman can help me, I have to take the risk."

The bartender hesitates but her eyes flick over my shoulder toward a darkened corner of the bar. There's a small booth tucked against the wall. I can make out a figure sitting alone.

"Thank you," I say, drinking the remainder of my whiskey and sliding the glass across the counter. I ease off my stool.

"Wait," she says, holding up a finger. I pause as she grabs a glass and a bottle of a dark liquid in a green bottle. I can't read the language on the label. "It's his favorite."

I reach for the cash in my pocket, but she shakes her head. "The Ravens have a tab. I'll put it on there."

Of course they do. Again, I nod my thanks, take the bottle, and start across the bar. I feel the eyes of the patrons watch me when I pass. There's little doubt they all know exactly who I am. That also means they know I'm responsible, at least partly, for the sickness raging outside. Tran mentioned not everyone was opposed to the Morrigan's war, but it's impossible to know what side anyone belongs to, so I keep my chin lifted and walk straight to the booth.

The Shaman sits with his back to the corner, focused on a small book. An empty glass sits next to it. I approach and hold the bottle out first, silently thanking the bartender for giving me an opening line. I open my mouth but without looking up he beats me to it, pushing his glass closer to the edge and saying, "Fill the glass and take a seat."

I screw off the lid and fill the glass to the rim. The liquid is so dark it looks like ink. I do as he says, sliding into the booth across from him. He closes his book, takes a sip of the drink, and smiles. "Remind me to tip Cirice generously. She's worked the bar long enough to know exactly what her customers want. Is that why she sent you here? Gift in hand?"

His skin is dark as midnight. His voice deep and smooth. There's no denying the confidence he carries, the lingering of magic even if the wards have him controlled—something I doubt as the seconds flip by.

"I thought maybe we should meet, personally."

He rests his hands on the table and I spot the tattoos and rings on his fingers. "I figured you'd be back. Your guardian doesn't know you're here, does he."

"By now? Probably." Whatever alarms and bells Dylan has in the little bat cave of his mind have probably been triggered. "Which only means we should probably get to it."

He smiles, and the simple act puts me at an unnatural ease. Another gift, I assume. "The Morrigan took my guardians. They're either dead or trapped in her realm, and we can't open the gate. It was damaged in Bunny's escape."

His eyes narrow for a moment. "You want in the Otherside. What about your traitor?"

"I'll be forced to deal with him, too."

"And you think you can just storm the Morrigan's castle? Get inside and do what you want?"

I shrug. "I don't have another choice."

"There are always choices, dear. Always. Suicide by the Goddess of War is one of them." He looks me up and down and I fight squirming under the gaze of his yellow eyes. "I've witnessed you fight in the ring. I saw your true powers emerge, but that was when you were complete—whole with the Morrigan." I hold his gaze and realization clicks. "That's what you really want, isn't it? Your full strength."

"I'll do whatever it takes to get my guardians back and stop the sickness." I swallow. "I know the risks."

He chuckles, flashing those teeth. "I seriously doubt it. But I'm not here to judge. I'm here to open pathways. I can give you what you want."

"What's the cost?"

The smile drops from his face and his expression is blank, like a slate. "There is no cost, because I'm interested in the results. Although, I can only offer you a limited return. One for the way there and three back for your Guardians. If you're truly up to the task of taking on the Morrigan, you can find a way back on your own."

He wants to trap me there, force the altercation between me and the Morrigan. He offers his hand across the table, waiting for me to take it or not.

I take a deep breath, knowing that if I accept, it's an oath I can't get out of. That's the price—losing control. I wipe my hand on my pants and hold it over the table, curling my fingers into a fist at the last moment. "I accept your challenge, but I'm going to need one more thing."

"What's that?"

"I need two entry tickets to the Otherside."

His hand wavers in the air. "They won't be able to return—not on their own."

I unclench my fist and slip my hand into his, shaking before he can ask any other questions. "Good."

13

BUNNY

I stare at the canvas, still wet with paint. The oil shines, malleable but firm, and I thought for a moment that the movement was just that—the oil—but when I peered closer, nose nearly touching, I know what I saw was real. Someone looking at me from the other side.

Not the Otherside. That's where I am, locked in my studio tower. But the painting is of the other realm, my former home and studio in the attic of The Nead. It's the opposite of here—the flip of the mirror. It's the way back and the way in, and gods almighty I think Morgan may have just been on the other side.

My fingers coil around the paintbrush, pushing back the desire to reach through and grab her.

Not that I could. Not yet at least, and what are the chances of it being so easy? The magic hasn't set, not from my side anyway. And the painting is one of many—hundreds—left to confuse Dylan or anyone else looking for entrance. I need to get back to The Nead. I must. If I don't bring the Queen what she wants, her wrath will rain upon the house. Not just on me—no—she never goes after her opponent directly. No, the Morrigan is methodical about her pain.

I cannot bear another night of screams from the dungeon.

What I have done to my brothers is unredeemable. Even if Morgan ever chose to look past my actions or if I can assist in her stopping the Queen, the Guardians, my brothers? They will torture me in the ancient ways.

I deserve nothing less.

Stepping back from the canvas, I exhale an exhausted shudder of relief. It's complete. I've worked day after day, night after frigid night, until my eyes blurred and my fingers cramped.

But the painting is a masterpiece, if not in subject but ability. My magic is so much stronger here. It doesn't take the layers and layers of infused ingredients to create the gate. Here, the magic is combined in every brush stroke, every drop. Runes mixed with images, stirred with spells and paint. But even then, there's nothing that can be done until the oil dries, which may take days with the damp chill of the castle. Glancing around the room, I spot the fireplace and the dry heat it emits. There's little wood—I'm only given a few logs a day—just enough to keep my fingers nimble. I stare at the other paintings. The rejects—or ruses. The wood backing would make acceptable kindling. The jar of turpentine, a decent accelerant.

The Morrigan's impatience for war has brought me to this moment. I toss the first canvas in, watching the painting melt with the heat of the fire. I watch the earth realm disappear into a puddle of goo, and direct my most recent painting toward the heat.

Soon I will cross back over, and with the gods on my side I'll earn the good will of my mistress. If not, I think, watching the canvas vanish beneath the flames, I'll brace for the future and the hellfire that will destroy us all.

14

MORGAN

I step out of the bar, feeling the faint tingle of my magic having been returned after crossing the wards. Again, my magic is faint—weakened by the split and being separated from my mates. Dylan is a pleasant boost, but not enough. I'm hoping what the Shaman and others have said, about magic being stronger on the Otherside, is true. It explains a lot about why the Morrigan wants me trapped over here.

I wait for the car to arrive—I'd been too chicken to drive here in one of The Nead's vehicles. There's little doubt that they are outfitted with trackers, anyway. Pulling out the phone, I check the app—the car is three blocks away, caught in some kind of traffic. It gives me a moment to go back over the final moments of my conversation with the Shaman, how I'll pass through the gate and where.

The instructions were vague. He'd told me to go to the last place Bunny had been seen. Look for the "cracks."

"The gate will still be there. It was created centuries ago. That house was built over the portal. You just have find the actual gate."

Bunny's studio makes the most sense. The magic is strong there. It always has been. I'd known it since that day he'd painted me with runes. The catch would be getting up there unnoticed. It's a long way from the cells in the basement of the house to the attic. I'll have to figure something out.

A block down the street buzzes, catching my attention, and I'm sucked into a strange sense of déjà vu. I step into the road, into a flicker of a memory—no, not a memory—a photo. One of the scenes from Sam's photos.

The street is empty except for leaves blowing against the curb. The air is cold, but it's nearing winter. It's not the icy fingers of the Otherside clawing through the realm, although in my mind I can almost make out the black tendrils of smoke, the vision of Clinton bound and beaten. I can taste the sulfur in the air. The image of him is superimposed—this world over the next—and I reach my hand out, wondering how far away he really is.

Leaves crunch behind me and I center back in this world.

"Well, well, well," a deep voice says. "Isn't it a little dangerous to be out here alone?" I spin and face a lanky man. His skin is pale. A heavy beard covers his chin. I don't know him.

I cut my eyes away from him, looking down the street for the car. "Why would it be dangerous?"

"Dark street, outside a shady bar. Three people went missing in this very spot a week ago."

Ah, so he knows who I am. He doesn't need to know that I'm aware. "I heard."

He eases closer. I feel the brush of his leather jacket against mine. The hair on the back of my neck prickles in warning. "Plus there's a nasty virus going around. You're not afraid?"

He doesn't wait for an answer, wrapping his arm around my waist. I rear back, jabbing him with an elbow and stomping on his foot. I spin, kicking him in the thigh and catching the glint of silver from a blade in his hand.

"There's only one reason for you to come back here tonight. You're going to try to stop her." He lunges, swiping the knife toward my gut. I jump back but he snags the front of my jacket, tearing the leather. "I can't let you do that."

I quickly move behind a parked car but he scrambles for me, sliding over the hood. While he's off balance I punch him twice in the face, slamming his wrist against the window shield. He struggles but my adrenaline surges, and like with Hildi, magic rallies. My nails grow long and pointed, stabbing into the thin skin of his wrist. He releases the knife with a surprised jerk. It clatters under the car.

"Stay away," I tell him, panicked at the nails, sharp as razors. He's frozen, and that gives me time to race toward the main road. The metal of the car hood groans under his weight but within seconds he's back on his feet, chasing me.

The color of his eyes darken as he runs, the hatred in his veins vibrates off his skin. He moves his hands together, creating a ball of visible energy—like fire but not quite. He tosses it in his hands before throwing it at me. I dodge and it crashes into a blue mailbox, knocking it to the ground.

With nowhere to run, I take a deep breath and conjure every lesson, every training session, every skill I've developed over the past five months, and add it to the rage boiling beneath the surface. We clash in the middle of the street, fist to fist, foot to knee, elbow to rib.

If I'm surprised at my strength then I know he is too, but the training has changed me and with every punch and jab I feel an increase in confidence. His moves grow sloppy, his punches miss. I lasso the energy and fling it at him and a rope lashes out, snapping him across the chest. He dives for me and I duck, forcing him to land on his back on the ground. I stand over him, wishing I had my sword, because I'd run it through him. My nails spike again, itching to draw blood.

"Stay out of fights you don't understand," I tell him.

He's dazed, probably concussed, but he still speaks. "You'll never beat her. Her legions are only just now assembling. War will come to this realm."

"As long as I am alive that is not an option. And when I kill her, death and destruction will end in her world, too."

I kick him in the side, hearing the snap of bone. Headlights flash on the street and a horn honks. I leave the broken man—or demon, whatever he was-- on the street and get in the back seat.

"Take me home," I bark, spilling the address.

15

DYLAN

I walk the foyer, pacing like an animal in a cage. At some point, Morgan slipped from the house while I studied Sam's photographs. She got past me. The Sentinel. Shame and disgust wracks through me. A time like this is not appropriate for me to forget my true mission.

I couldn't just run into the city chasing her down. I'd lost my wings—my ability to fly. Where would I even begin? Angry despair takes over and I wait. I'd give her an hour before I totally lost my mind. An hour or I'll tear the city apart.

Forty-six minutes later I hear the car pull up to the curb and Morgan's voice lilt up the front steps. Thirty-two seconds after that, she opens the door and I freeze in my spot.

"What the hell happened to you?" I roar. She's dirty. Covered in forming bruises and blood. My heart plummets at the same time as my blood pressure rises. "Who did this?"

She sighs with annoyance, taking off her coat. "Some minion of the Morrigan's, if I had to guess."

"He attacked you?" The thought is incomprehensible. I knew

there were loyalists out there but to actually attack Morgan on the street...

"Yes." She glances down at a broken nail and mutters, "Fucker."

"Morgan." I am seething. Beyond seething, but I need to calm down. Need to. Will try to. Failing miserably. "Are you okay?"

She finally looks at me—like really looks at me for the first time since she walked in. She takes in my anger—probably my fear—and her eyes soften. "I'm fine, Dylan. I'm sorry if you were worried about me."

Unable to handle her nonchalance for one second longer, I explode. "You don't get to walk out of the house like that. Not now. Not anymore. We're on the cusp of a great war, already in one, and your days of walking around freely are over. Do you understand?"

Her eye tics, a flash, and I wonder for a quick moment if I've stepped over a line. I don't care, though. Her life is worth more than ten of mine. She's the key to all of this. Always has been and always will be—until her final breath.

"I'm fine," she says, instead of a million other words that threaten to cross her lips. I watch her swallow them back. "I beat him, without magic, just using the skills you all have taught me. I thank you for that."

"Good."

I have ten other questions. Where had she gone? Who did she meet? How did the attacker find her? Where is he now? What secret is she keeping, because she has one. I see the shadow of it in her eye.

I don't ask any of them.

She yawns. "It's late. I really do need to go to bed now."

I nod and watch her go up the stairs. Once she's in her room with the door shut, I grab a chair from the dining room and carry it up three flights of stairs. There, I return to my duty. Watching over the Queen. She won't get past me again.

16

MORGAN

I do make time to shower and change, but otherwise my body gives out on me and I crash into bed. Tomorrow I'll go through the gate and find my Guardians. Beyond that I have no plan other than to kill the Morrigan and return home.

I have no delusions it will be that easy, and those are my final thoughts before I drift into an exhausted, anxious sleep.

The castle ripples with the angry chill emanating from the Queen's quarters. She's not who I'm here to see—not this time. I walk away from the throne room and turn down a side hall. I have an inkling of what I'm looking for. The castle tower with the bedroom window, like the one I'd seen in the pictures. Someone lurks behind the glass.

The halls seem endless, a continuous, twisting maze. Tapestries hang on the walls. Voices echo off the stone. I pause more than once in an alcove, ducking from the soldiers wearing all black. Their feet move in unison, stomping off the hard stone. Blades hang from their belts, polished to a gleaming shine. There's no doubt this is another dream, but everything about it--from the sound of feet on the ground to the chill in my bones--makes me hide. When they pass, I keep on my journey, finally making it to a stairway that goes up.

I take the chance, running up the steps. It feels warmer as I go higher—a slight break in the chill. I stop when I hear an angry voice, my heart pounding in my chest, both from adrenaline and exertion.

"Is it ready?" The man asks, his voice impatient and booming.

The response is said quietly—too soft for me to hear. I risk moving closer to the arched door that's not completely closed. "Her Majesty has grown impatient. Her needs are growing—surely you noticed that yourself when you were in her chambers. She requires you to fulfill your duties, which at the moment are only half complete."

The sound of the voice that replies rocks me to my core. "Surely having the Guardians here have kept the decline at bay. With Morgan not feeding, at least not at her typical levels, shouldn't that slow the regression?"

Bunny said that. Bunny is just on the other side of the door. I know it's just a dream but I want to lunge into the room and gut him with a sword. Watch him bleed out. Shake the truth from him. From the snap in the other man's reply, I think he feels the same. "You do not get to presume what the Queen needs or not, do you understand?"

"Yes," Bunny replies, his voice soft again.

"How long?"

"Tomorrow—maybe tonight. The paint is nearly dry. That's why I built the fire. Otherwise it's too damp and cold for the oil to set."

The response to that is a growl, low and menacing, and I truly fear for Bunny's life. I wish for the man to lose his composure and break him with a snap. He'd deserve it, but I need that gate open as much as anyone. I glance around for something—anything, and land on the tapestry hanging at the base of the stairs. Quietly I tip-toe down and yank on the cloth, bringing it and the iron bar holding it to the ground. I've started running before metal hits stone.

"Who's out there?" the man's voice shouts, but I'm gone.

This time I head down. Down, down, down. The warmth of Bunny's fire vanishes and I'm plunged into freezing temperatures. The *scrape of metal catches my attention. My feet stick to the floor and I glance down, looking at the dark, congealed fluid. A groan—low and painful—ricochets down the hall. A sick feeling lodges in my throat and I know, I know what is behind the bars at the far end of the wall.*

Footsteps echo down the stairwell, angry commands. I can't go down the hall—can't see what's waiting down there. I also can't go back up. I press against the wall and close my eyes, wake up, wake up, wake up....

My eyes pop open. It's daylight and my bed is a soft cushion beneath me. My hands tremble—fingertips cold. The dream was so real. More so than any I'd had before. I sit, feeling a presence in the room. Not human. Not Dylan. No, magic. Magic filled that dream. It was sent to me. By the Shaman? By the Queen? I don't know, but I now have a timeline. Tonight or tomorrow the gate will be open and Bunny will try to pass through.

I slip from the bed, figuring out how I'm going to get everything in motion. It's going to take a lot more than magic to make this happen.

17

DYLAN

I doze in the chair outside Morgan's room. Half in, half out of sleep. I'm tugged fully awake by what feels like a shift—magical in nature. I hold my breath and listen, but there's nothing and no one unexpected in the house.

I hear the click of the lock before the door opens. My main emotions lately have been frustrated and angry. Exhaustion outweighs both of those. But looking up at the tense, hungry expression on Morgan's face and the thin pajamas she's wearing catches my full attention.

"Keeping watch?" she says.

"I'm just worried." I sit straighter in the chair. "Something's building. Do you feel it?"

She nods and stands directly before me. Her T-shirt is so thin it may as well be a second skin. Her shorts leave nothing to the imagination. She's bare beneath both and if she's trying to knock me off my game, it's working.

Her lips are pink and her hair is a curly mess around her head. Energy vibrates off of her—the same one she's struggled with for months. She basically needs to feed, and my body reacts accordingly.

She steps forward, our knees touching. "Do you trust me?" she asks.

"Always."

"Even when I do things like last night—wandering off on my own?"

I touch her hip. "That's not about trust. That's about safety."

She licks her bottom lip. "Do you understand that sometimes I have to do things on my own? Make my own way in this battle with the Morrigan?"

She's asking a lot of questions, but her scent, her proximity, and that damn tight shirt are making it hard as hell to focus. It only gets worse when she tugs at the string holding up her shorts and they fall to the floor. Blood rushes from my brain, building to an ache between my legs. I swallow and skim my thumb over the flesh of her hip. "What are you trying to tell me?"

"The time has come for me to deal with the Morrigan. You've trained me. You've educated me. I'm as ready as I ever will be."

I shake my head, fighting through the fog of lust. "We need more time—we don't even have access to the gate."

Her hands reach for my belt. Mine go to her ass. I knead the skin as her fingers unleash me from my pants. A graze of fingertips sends a jolt through my body, I pull her on top of me, her legs straddled over mine, our bodies hot and wet against one another.

I push at the hem of her shirt, moving it over her head. I take her left nipple with my mouth, her right with my fingers. She exhales, resting her chin on my head.

She whispers, "When I get the gate open you have to stay here. Do you understand? We'll need someone on this side of the realm to keep watch—to be ready for our return."

She lifts up and my cock follows her like a magnet, angled up. She lowers herself quickly and I clench my jaw, feeling the most intense connection between us. I can't speak, I just listen as she tells me her plans in a breathless rush. "You're the anchor, Dylan. The rock that keeps us tied to this world."

I nod, even though my brain knows it's a fool's errand. There's no way she'll get the gate open any time soon. My research has come to a screeching halt. But she's got me mesmerized with the rocking of her hips and in her sheath of tight warmth. "You're the bond," I tell her, our lips touching as we move together. I will do everything in my power to keep her safe, to protect her role in the future.

Her dark eyes lock with mine, holding as the pleasure builds. There's no question in her voice as she says, "You'll follow my command and together we will shut down the Darkness. Shut the bitch down."

I'm not a weak man. I'm a warrior. I've killed and slayed, but as the ecstasy jolts between us, an intensity of magic, lust and power, a different kind of thrill overtakes me. My Queen is here. Commanding. Demanding even as she succumbs, crying loud enough to echo the bottom floors of The Nead. Shockwaves roll through her body. She bites my lip, trembling, and I cling to her like a lifeline from one world to the next.

I spill inside of her, our bodies twitching in kind. Warmth runs through my veins—her cheeks are red. I hold her face between my hands and say, "As you wish," although I have no idea what the next days will hold.

She smiles, regal and wise, a different look than I've seen on her before, and says, "Thank you, Guardian. Soon we will rule the world together."

18

MORGAN

He follows me to my room and I ask questions. So many questions.

"Tell me everything about the Otherside. Tell me about the Morrigan. How did you get away? What are her soldiers like? The dungeons. Describe the dungeons."

Dylan grits his teeth and answers, out of obligation. Hesitation tugs on every word—each answer. It goes on for hours.

"In her realm, the Morrigan looks like a woman. A queen. Her castle is where she spends the majority of her time as the lands around it are desolate and spoiled."

"Why is it so cold?"

He shrugs. "In general, I think she wishes it to be that way, but I have theories that go back to her relationship with Cu. When she was a young goddess falling in love. There's a heat to passion and when she shifted and embraced her title as Queen of Ravens, her blood ran cold. She thrives on it."

"So she's afraid of heat?"

"She's afraid of everything."

"Tell me about the dungeons," I ask, leaning forward.

"Do you want to know about the dungeons or about the prisoners in them?"

He can't say their names. I'm not sure I can, either.

"Both."

The dungeons are under the castle, he tells me. Deep in the belly, under the tower on the north side. There is no daylight. No plumbing or electricity down there. The air is a different sort of cold. "Although we reside in human vessels, we were molded into cold-blooded birds. The cold doesn't help. The inflicted wounds simply freeze. The blood hardens into ice. Because we can survive the conditions, it just provides more opportunity for torture."

I ask the question I've kept to myself for weeks. "Do you think they're dead?"

"I believe they pray to the gods that they were dead."

So no. Just like Anita implied.

"Why would she keep them alive—give us any hope to get them back?"

He reaches for me, taking my hand and resting it on his chest, above the heat of his heart. "We're bound. Connected. In all the ways we can help one another, we can also hurt each other. She'll use their power for her own gain. The longer they are away from you, the more damage it does." He chuckles. "I am a strong and virile man, Morgan, but even I can't fulfill your ravenous needs."

"But if I get them back," I say. "I can heal them, right? I can fix this?"

He gives me a hard look. "It's not so easy."

"What makes you believe I think anything will be easy? We don't even have access to the Otherside yet."

"If you ever, by a miracle of the gods, got to the Otherside, the Morrigan would capture you in moments. Her guards and soldiers are legendary."

I glance at the scars on his wrists. "You beat them."

"I had one chance and I took it. I have little faith that if I saw Casteel again I would survive."

"Casteel?"

"The Morrigan's Commander. She may have eschewed love, but if she has anything close to a partner, it's him."

"And he did that to you?" I point to the scars.

His blue eyes have become hard like sapphires. He stands and walks across the room. "I paid him back."

"So it is possible to fight back—and to escape."

He shakes his head. "Don't get your hopes up, Morgan."

"So you've just given up?" My anger flares.

"I'm doing what they would want me to. Keep you safe. Fight to stop the virus."

"Did they not come for you? Is that what this is about?" As soon as the words leave my mouth I know they are the wrong thing to say. He clams up and strides for the door. "Dylan, wait. Stop. I didn't mean it."

He looks at me sadly, neither of us happy or content. We're in a shitty situation. A mess that is drowning us both. But unlike Dylan, I refuse to sink any further.

∼

FORTIFIED on the strength of my guardian, I spend the afternoon preparing for my mission. I got Dylan's approval—at least for the moment. Sure, I know he basically agreed under the duress of magic and pussy, but it's the best I could do. I wanted him to know. I need his strength. Most of all, I must have his cooperation.

As afternoon nears, I ask if he'll visit Hildi and Andi and see if they need anything. While his jaw has the lax muscles of a man freshly fucked, his eyes carry shadows of concern. He'll try to stop me, it's in his nature and I adore him for it, but I need Dylan out of the way.

He leaves out the front door and I wait behind my closed door until he's gone. His keen sense of my whereabouts failed the night before—I doubt it will again.

When I'm sure he's off the property I slip downstairs, sneaking past the warmth of the kitchen. I take the stairway to the depths of the house, to the dungeon, where Marcus sits in the small lounge outside the cells.

"Hey," he says, rubbing his eyes. It's a boring job, but we set Hildi up with a computer and a comfortable bed. "What brings you down here?"

"How's she doing?"

"The same. How long do you plan on keeping her down here?" Marcus glances at the monitors, checking up on Anita, who is sitting on her cot with her arms wrapped around her knees. Her hair is a mess. Her clothing is wrinkled and dirty.

"It's been a week. I'm going to take her for a bath—see if a little reward will get her talking."

He snorts. "Unlikely. She hasn't said anything coherent since I've been here."

"Any incidents?"

"Other than rambling nonsensically, no. She's pretty docile."

I'd hoped he would say that. I give him the signal to flip the lock and he does, the metal bar clicking when it springs. I'm hit by Anita's stench the instant I enter. Marcus follows me in. "Maybe you can clean her cell while I've got her upstairs?"

"Upstairs?"

"There's no shower down here."

He rubs the back of his neck. "What does Dylan think about this?"

"It was his idea. He's waiting upstairs." I check my phone for the time. "He's probably wondering where I am."

Anita watches us as we approach her cell. She's sitting the same as in the monitor. Knees bent, arms wrapped around them. Her eyes dart between us with mild interest.

"Get up," I say, wrinkling my nose. She doesn't move. "I know you're used to your new digs but it's time to clean up. Come on."

She stands, slowly as though she's not fully coherent. I hope it will make her more docile on the way up the stairs. I don't have time for any of her bullshit. "Unlock the door, Marcus."

He holds the ring of keys. It's old fashioned but so are the cells. I suspect they've been down here way longer than the house above. Marcus hesitates. I get it. Anita is deadly. She's an active contagion. I hold out my hand for the key. "She can't infect you. It doesn't bother the supernatural—just humans."

Anita's eyes light up at that and she laughs, baring her teeth.

"Turn around, psycho." I fish the zip-tie out of my pocket. I'm not a fool. I won't take her upstairs unbound. Marcus sighs with relief when he sees my measures. "It's going to be fine."

I hate lying to him. Just like I hate the fact that I'm a betraying liar when I yank Anita out of the cell and shove him inside, slamming the door between us.

"What the hell?" he screams.

I get my hands back on Anita, moving her where I can see her.

"Sorry. I can't risk anyone coming upstairs right now."

Marcus swallows, his dark eyes watching me. "What about Dylan?"

"We'll be gone before he gets home." Anita starts giggling next to me. I'm not even sure if she knows why. "I'm sure he'll find you. Eventually."

He shakes his head. "He'll kill me."

"I'll tell him I was responsible. Don't worry—he knows I'm a loose cannon." I give him a sympathetic smile. "I'm not doing a bad thing. I'm trying to fix it, but I have to do it alone." I glance at Anita. "Well, almost alone."

"Whatever you're about to do, Morgan, don't. The Darkness is no joke."

I spin and stare at the man behind bars. I barely know him. He's an ally but to what extent? "I'm aware of the seriousness, Marcus. I opened that gate the first time. I let the Morrigan and her evil in." I walk back over to him and his yellow-green snake eyes watch my every move. He flinches as I lean in. "I'm taking Anita. I'm saving my men, and I'm gonna make the bitch on the Otherside pay."

He opens his mouth to speak but nothing, not a word, not a breath comes out when he realizes what's about to transpire.

∼

I TURN the shower on and shove Anita inside. She's still dressed. It's not like those clothes won't have to be burned anyway.

She shouts from the heat, getting a mouthful of water. I grab her hand and squeeze in nearly a full bottle of shampoo. "Clean up. I'm not spending the day next to you reeking like that."

I'd laid out my outfit before I went downstairs. I didn't want to tip Marcus off with the clothing I found in the training room supply closet. I'd been shocked when I found the sleek military pants with dozens of pockets and slits for weapons. The shirt is made of a durable material—halfway between summer and winter. Thin, but sturdy. It appears waterproof if not flame resistant. The boots are lightweight, good for fighting and running. I found my size amongst the much larger outfits clearly made for the Guard.

The fact I discovered them was no mistake. After breakfast, Davis asked me to find something downstairs—specifically suggesting I look in the closet for a length rope he needed. I found the rope, as well as the battle gear. He made no comment when I handed him what he'd asked for.

Maybe I'm not the only one that knows I need to make this move.

Anita showers and I slip into the outfit. The pants and shirt fit like a glove, seemingly sewn to fit my measurements. I look in the mirror, aware that the clothing alone makes me look like a badass. I feel like one, too. There's a sheath for the sword Damien made me. I fasten it over my back, sliding the sword into place. When the water stops and Anita emerges from the steamy shower, her eyes pop when she sees me.

"It doesn't matter what you wear," she says, water dripping down her neck. "The Morrigan is going to eat you alive."

I move quicker than lightning, clutching her chin with my hand. "I wonder what she'll say when she sees you? Nothing more than my prisoner and pet."

"The Morrigan loves me." Her voice is a squeak but I see the calculation in her eyes. "She needs me."

I laugh. "She needs me, too. And I'm going to be ready when she comes for me."

I toss Anita clothes and watch as she tightens the belt around her skinny waist. Everything is too big. Anita is a waif. But when she's finished, I tie her wrists back together, even though I know she desires going back through the gate more than I do.

"Why are you doing this?" she asks, genuine curiosity in her voice. "Why are you going to her? Because you can't win, you know that, right?"

I decide to answer truthfully. "She took the men I love. She poisoned one into betraying me. I have debts to pay and bridges to burn because she used me. Used me to take out people like Xavier. Like Andi and thousands of others around the city. I'm not waiting for another death, for her to make another move." I push her through the door before adding, "I'm not trying to win, Anita. I'm just trying to hold on and do what I can for the people I care about. Even if I don't make it back, I can assure that they do."

19

BUNNY

Casteel waits outside the door, just as he has for the last twenty-four hours. Obviously, the Queen wants me to know the pressure is on, that she expects the portal to reopen soon. I don't mind. I'm eager as well, but I have no control over the slow-setting oil paint or the elements of magic infused in every brush stroke.

The commander of the Morrigan's army doesn't trust me. I see it in his face, in the way he watches my every move. I trust it's both from his encounter with Dylan previously and the fact I betrayed Morgan. Sure, I did it for his Queen, but spies make people nervous and I know he'd have no qualms taking my life if it weren't for the value of my skills.

I press a finger against the canvas, feeling for the stickiness. The hardened fabric springs back—implying it may finally be dry. With a glance at the doorway, I mutter the words that will bring the portal to life, barely registering the shadow on the other side. The colors swirl, all my efforts in creating the perfect image now a mess of impressionism. The runes lift, interlocking with one another until they twist and separate. I feel the familiar gust of my former realm, the heat on my face.

I have one task on the Otherside and I plan to accomplish it today. I'll bring the third back to the Morrigan and seal the gate forever.

20

MORGAN

Even Anita can't hide her awe when I bring her into Bunny's studio. His work is amazing. Overwhelming, even. It's like being in the presence of a truly gifted master, and I know now that this gift is what doomed us all.

I drag her before the painting that called to me the last time we were here. Something in my gut tells me it's the right one. I don't know if the Shaman gave me that sense or if I had it all along. It doesn't matter now.

"This is your big plan?" Anita asks. "Taking me back to my Queen? Sure, sign me up."

"You're a means to an end," I snap back. "But I'm glad you're happy to be headed to the gallows."

She laughs, the same cackling, deranged one she's had since her brother died. "How much of your soul did you pay to access the gate? Fifty percent? All of it?"

"Shut up."

I step before the painting, already feeling the churn of magic. I put on a good face but I'm terrified. Petrified, really, of what's on the Otherside. But there's no other choice—not that I can see—not that

Dylan has given me. Christensen told me this would be the way. I would make the sacrifice; so even in my fear, I'm ready.

I'm ready.

The word the Shaman gave me is on the tip of my tongue when a cold gust blows through the studio. Frigid air tosses papers and tips over jars of brushes and tools. Canvases crash to the floor. I glance at Anita, but she's staring at the painting, a look of gleeful delight on her face.

I follow her gaze and see that the painting is no longer of a castle, it's a twisted swirl, shimmering and alive. Focusing on the tiny window, the one I'd seen a figure in days before, I watch as it moves from yellow to gold and widens larger and larger until the whole space is consumed by a gaping hole.

I step forward, dragging the still-bound Anita with one hand as I unsheathe my sword and hold it before me. Only the gods know what waits for us, but that cold air and dank smell make me think it's nothing friendly.

"Don't try anything," I say to Anita.

"Oh, you don't have to worry about me," the girl says, her blue eyes vibrant with life. "But I can't say the same about him."

∽

BUNNY STANDS IN THE PORTAL, copper eyes behind his askew glasses and hair gleaming. He looks drained and exhausted, but there's something else. Something dangerous, like a wounded animal or desperate man.

Something tells me he's both.

I hold the sword between us, the jewels Damien forged in the hilt glinting. "How dare you come back here," I say. "I should gut you."

"But you won't." It's not a question. The cold wind of the portal still rips through the room. "Give her to me. That's all I want."

"I'm sure it is." I shake my head. "You fooled me once, Bunny. You don't get the option to do it again."

"Give her to me," he says again. "It's how we end this."

"We?" I laugh. "You're kidding, right? Tell me, how are the 'we' living in the dungeons? Are they still alive? Do their hearts still beat? Or do you listen to their cries of pain and continue with the bidding of the Morrigan?"

He pales at the mention of the Ravens. "I'm giving you a chance, Morgan. Go, take Dylan and go. Leave this place. He can help you hide and you're both immune to the virus."

The reality of his words slam into me. "You're suggesting we run and let the world succumb to the Darkness? You think I'm a coward? You certainly know better than that about your fellow Guardian."

He glances around the room. "Don't pretend Dylan knows of this venture. He would agree with me."

"I doubt that." But Dylan had said it himself. The others wouldn't want saving. They would want me safe and protected. Is that why this has taken so long? Is he keeping me from going to confront and destroy the Morrigan? My head hurts from the confusion, the betrayal and deceit.

I take a step closer to Bunny. He doesn't budge and his hand coils into a fist. "Understand something, former Guardian. I'm going to save my mates. I am bound to them, I will heal them, and I will not allow them to be used by the Darkness as long as I am alive."

"You'll find nothing but shells," he tells me. "There is nothing to bring back."

"No. They are stronger than that. Dylan survived at the hands of the sadistic soldier, Casteel. They can too."

He flinches at the name of the soldier. "Do you really think so? Do you think Dylan came back whole?"

"Yes." It's a lie. A bold lie about my lover and guardian. My sentinel. Everything in Bunny's comment makes complete sense. Why Dylan's so guarded. Why it's taken so long to tear down his walls. Why his passion is so intense, much more than the others. Every moment with Dylan is a struggle, but we're making progress. We've *made* progress. "I will heal them. Each of them."

Something in Bunny's eyes falter. He looks like a man searching for a lifeline—a string of hope. I know what he wants, but I can't give it to him. The fear and rage built up inside takes over and I use his brief distraction against him, pushing him with one hand and dragging Anita with another.

Together we fall into the cold, heartless, dark.

21

MORGAN

Ice fills my veins, chilling me in a way I never knew was possible. It's not like the air is cold—the *world* is cold and bleak. I feel it in every inch of my body, my brain, and my heart. The stone floors do not give and Bunny's head cracks when we land. My sword clangs and skitters across the floor, buried beneath a pile of unused canvas. I'd go for it but I'm sprawled across Bunny's body and trapped beneath Anita. She jabs me with a bony elbow.

"What have you done?" Bunny asks, his voice a hiss.

"Fixing what you messed up."

His good hand wraps around my arm and he squeezes just as the sound of footsteps echo across the room.

"No, no, no, no, no," he mumbles. His eyes are more frantic than I've ever seen. I turn to see what scares him and see the dark leather boots and the black uniform. It's not the first time I've laid eyes on the man or the uniform, but it is the first time awake.

Casteel. I know him before he utters a word and there's little doubt he's aware of who I am too. His jaw is square, his shoulders massive. I eye the jagged scar under his jaw. I have a suspicion who gave him that scar.

I've no doubt there's demon blood running through his veins. Something inhuman, despite his good looks and expressive eyes. He looks over my shoulder and Bunny tosses me and Anita on the floor with a one-handed heave.

"Two for the price of one," Casteel says, looking us over. Anita quakes with excitement, like she's won the lottery. "Well done, Guardian. You've sped things up considerably."

I won't deny that I have no idea what to do from here. How could I? I didn't expect Bunny to try to stop me. I didn't anticipate anything about this situation. I'm off-kilter—not something you want entering a battle, so I do the only thing I can: pick a fight.

Bunny is close enough that from the ground I shift to my hip, swiping my legs to knock him off balance. He falls, allowing his useless arm to take the brunt of the landing. Without remorse, I punch above the cheekbone before lunging for the hidden sword. My fingers graze the hilt but massive hands pull me back. My entire body slides across the floor. I use the momentum and skirt between Casteel's legs, then kick the commander in the back of the knees, forcing him to buckle. I take two paintbrushes from the worktable and stab both into his neck.

Anita watches the fight happily and Bunny looks stunned. Too stunned, and I pick up a jar of turpentine and toss it at his face. He ducks and it hits the smoldering fire, glass shattering on impact. The combustion behind his back is furious and hot. I use the distraction to dart for the door. The stairwell I dreamed about is on the other side. If I follow it down, it will take me to my men. To my mates.

Even I know that's not going to happen.

Not now.

Casteel roars like a lion, pulling the shards of broken wood from his neck. I raise my hands to call on the magic I've used twice before, but he flicks his wrist and my vocal cords squeeze shut.

I grasp my throat with both hands. Within moments I'm deprived of air and fall to my knees. Casteel walks over, blood dripping down his black tunic. He yanks me to my feet and narrows his eyes.

Black spots fill my vision. Suffocation is close. Through the haze, I see Bunny's expression. It's made of stone.

I blink and smell the reek of his demon breath against my cheek. "Looks like you need a time out."

And then the world turns black.

22

DYLAN

The apartment smells of the final stage of sickness that soon will cross over into death. Hildi sits on the edge of the bed, holding her lover's hand. The Valkyrie doesn't look much better, but her heartbeat is strong, even if her emotions are weak.

"Do you know? Can you tell?" I ask, trying not to be insensitive.

"She's got a little time. The goddess hasn't asked me to bring her home. Not yet."

It's an odd position to be placed in—working between life and fate. Before Morgan knew her true destiny, I felt torn between the two; preserving her innocence while championing her future. From the look of Andi's translucent skin and gray lips, I don't see much of a future here.

"How's Morgan?" Hildi asks, obviously wanting to change the subject.

"She's struggling," I admit. "Probably more than I understand. She's carrying a lot of guilt and anger."

I don't reveal the details of our intimacy but there's no doubt what transpired between us earlier was an act caught somewhere between hunger and control. I'm attuned to Morgan's needs and I will comply with my duties as her guardian and mate, regardless of her motives, but I'm worried.

"She's impatient," Hildi says. "But she hasn't had centuries to understand that although today is a crisis, it's just one of many days to come."

I smile at the Valkyrie. Behind the beauty and brawn, she's wise.

"She cares for you a great deal, and Andi's illness is weighing on her. What can we do to help you?"

"I think there may be one thing," she replies. Her fingers tug at the hem of her shirt. "But it may be asking too much."

"There's no such thing. Tell me, and we'll make it happen."

~

With Davis' help, we move Andi from the apartment to The Nead. What Hildi needed was assistance. With the looming battle and hospitals being out of the question, she's afraid she will be called into service with no one left to take care of her partner.

Davis arrived in a windowless black van, often used by Clinton for his instruments. The unconscious woman is light as a feather and we gently carry her into the back. The neighbors watch, surely wondering if we're loading up a dead body.

Not yet, but it's a reasonable conclusion.

Sue waits at The Nead, directing us to a small suite on the main floor. The bed has fresh linens. The shades are drawn. Andi can rest here peacefully and Hildi can have the support she needs while remaining on the front lines of the war.

"Are you sure Morgan will be okay with this? That it won't just be another reminder of what's happening?"

I look across the room at the dying woman. Sue is fussing with her blankets. "Trust me, I think she'll be pleased."

"Maybe you guys can toss some of that healing energy down here."

I raise an eyebrow in question.

"Gods, don't even pretend like the whole place doesn't shudder when you two go at it. Even I get a little bit of a high."

"I don't think the healing powers are transferable."

She stares at me blankly and it takes a second for it to click that she's telling a joke.

"Oh, you were kidding. Well, right." I look down the hall. "I'm surprised she hasn't come up here yet. She went downstairs to relieve Marcus for a few hours."

"I'll go, if you want. I can explain why I'm here but give you all the credit for being kind and generous with your home," Hildi says.

"No, stay here." I frown. "Why would I need credit?"

Hildi leans against the door, her eyes skimming from my head to my toes. "Because you're made of stone and even though that girl has spent months chipping it away, there's a long way to go. Doing something like this? Even if it is just to make her feel better, it's a step in the right direction."

"What direction?" I ask, still a little confused.

"To becoming a real man."

23

MORGAN

I don't know what to expect when I open my eyes, but this isn't it. The room is still freezing, but it's a room, not a cell. I'm propped on a bed made of the softest down, a blood-red canopy overhead.

My throat aches, sore from whatever Casteel had done to me. Magic, I suppose, a level I'd never encountered before. He never hesitated—never even thought about how to use it.

Rubbing the tender flesh around my throat, I sit, taking in the room. It's opulent, like something out of a gothic fairy tale. Gilded mirrors, velvet fabric. Candles and lanterns cast the room in a shiny glow.

A movement catches my attention and I look to my left, both hands reaching for the blades stuffed in the pockets of my suit.

"I removed all the weapons," Casteel says from the chair next to the bed. His blond hair glints in the candlelight. Two bandages cover the wounds I'd given him on his neck. I'd suggest we're even, but from the angry spark in his eye I suspect he doesn't feel the same.

I swing my legs over the bed. "I don't need weapons to fight back."

"I'm aware," he says. His voice is a slow drawl. Not the harsh tone he'd used in my dream about Bunny. "You're quite resourceful."

I stare at the scar under his jaw. "I learned from the best."

The snarl in response is faint—but there—the beast is just beneath the surface. I have no doubt picking just a little will bring him out. I restrain myself. I'm not ready to fight him. Not yet.

"Why the finery?" I ask, gesturing to the room. "I thought I'd wake in a cell."

"Contrary to your beliefs, Morgan, you are not an enemy of the Queen. She's been trying to get you to come here for a very long time. She gave you the key as a child, she sent guides in the form of the cat and prince to guide you through the gates. She opened portals, giving you the chance. And you almost took them—all of them—but your little flock thwarted you every step of the way."

"You make it sound so peaceful. So easy."

"Ultimately, she had to get extreme. Take what you cared for the most to get you here." He smiles, two rows of perfect, white teeth. "It worked."

"If I'm not the enemy of the Darkness, then what am I?" The question is naïve and I know the answer. I've felt her tug for months—if not years. The way it felt to spread the virus to Xavier. The loss I felt after we performed the spell and split from one another.

Casteel doesn't answer anyway. He just stands and says, "You're to stay here. There's a servant here for your needs. Food, clothing, entertainment. She'll get it for you."

"And what if I don't?" I didn't come here to be a guest of the Morrigan. I came to find my Guardians.

With barely concealed restraint he steps forward and reaches for my chin. I bat his hand away, which raises his ire, and he clamps both of his hands around my wrists. "Dangerous things live in this castle, Morgan. I'm only one of them. Don't stray from your rooms, do you understand?"

It's a thinly veiled threat, letting me know exactly how much he would enjoy paying me back for the wounds to his neck. I'm not afraid of him; he's nothing but an obstacle between me and my mission.

 I nod anyway, letting him know I heard him, and watch him walk out the door.

24

BUNNY

Cloaked in the shadows, I listen to Casteel walk away from Morgan's room. I heard every word of their conversation—the small threats and the restraint in Morgan's voice. I, too, had been surprised when they brought her to the living quarters, far away from the dungeons below. Especially after attacking Casteel so viscously.

I stand outside her room for the briefest of moments, feeling the familiar longing—I may have betrayed her, but we are still bonded. There's only one way to cut the ties with a mate: death.

Casteel's boots echo off the hallway. I leave Morgan's door and follow him. I don't trust him not to turn around and make Morgan pay further for the wounds she inflicted. He's petty. Brutal, but weak.

He travels down the hall, turning at the corridor that leads back to my studio and the stairway to the dungeons. He passes the soldier at the landing, who calls out, "What happened to your neck?"

Casteel spins, quick and agile. His hand is around the soldier's throat. He squeaks, unable to breathe. This time it's not by magic but by sheer power.

"Mind your own fucking business, soldier."

"Yes, sir," he replies, gasping for air. I slink further into the wall.

"Get the prisoners ready," Casteel barks to unknown soldiers below. He vanishes around the corner but his voice echoes back up the stairwell. "I need to blow off a little steam."

25

DYLAN

It's not until I reach the observation room that I realize there's a problem. The monitors have been shut off. The room is empty. Keys hang from the lock.

My heart kicks into gear along with instincts and adrenaline. The instant I get the door open, I hear a voice.

"Dylan. Down here!"

My racing heart plunges into my gut and I run down the cells. Anita is gone and Marcus has taken her place in the filthy cell. "Where is she? Where's Morgan?"

"She left, man. Locked me up in here and took off with the crazy chick."

I look at my friend and try to process what he's saying. "She's gone? She did this to you?"

He nods. "Said the girl needed a shower and that you were up there waiting. I didn't think it was a good idea." He shakes his head. "I knew something was off."

Why the hell would Morgan do that? What was she thinking?

"Can you let me out?" Marcus asks. He rattles the bars. I slip the key in the lock and release him. "Thanks."

"Any idea where she was going?" I ask.

"No, but she took the prisoner with her. I don't think she lied about the shower, though." He waves his hand under his nose. "Start there."

I pat him on the back. "Go upstairs. Get Sue to give you some food. I'll be back."

"You need any help?"

"I hope not, but stick around just in case I do."

~

THERE's no sign of Morgan in her room, but her bathroom looks like a bomb went off. I step over a pile of towels, nudging the clothes Anita wore in the cell. It couldn't have been that long ago; the room still feels humid and the towels are damp. I exit the room, wondering where she could have gone.

Her bed looks in order but that doesn't quell the unease in my chest. I sit on the edge of the bed and close my eyes, hoping to catch her final scent, but the room is filled with too much *her* and a lot of someone else. Apples and fruit dominate the air—shampoo—Anita most likely. There's zero proof that they left the house. They aren't in the dungeons, kitchen, or first floor.

I decide to start at the top, in the last place I saw Bunny slip from one world to the next. His studio.

26

MORGAN

Under the watchful eye of my silent servant--who I suspect is no more than a slave in the eyes of the Morrigan--I check the room for something, anything that could be used as a weapon. Casteel did his job thoroughly and there is nothing useful I can pry, break, or twist for my own purposes. The room is a sham. Staged decorations to make me feel like a guest. It's just a different kind of cell.

I sit on the blood-red velvet chair and try to settle my emotions. Even if my entrance into this world was a bit rocky, I'm here, just like I wanted. Casteel poses a problem and I have no idea what to do about Bunny. Seeing him cut me to the bone...I didn't expect it. I was so focused on getting to the Morrigan and back to my guardians, I hadn't considered what seeing Bunny again would do to me.

I wrap my arms around my waist and feel the heartache and pain. Something I'd pushed aside, fueled by rage and anger. But seeing his face, his eyes, and his stupid hair...something cracked inside.

Better than ever, I understand the Morrigan's rage after Cu left her on the riverbank. I understand her raw pain. The bitter acceptance and the unrelenting wrath she fed on for an eternity.

But I'm not the Morrigan. Not fully, and I have four other guardians that need me. They need my love. And my compassion. They do not need me going off on a destructive bender. That won't help any of us.

I lean back in the chair, pulling a blanket over my knees. Part of me, the vengeful, angry part, wants to gut him and let him bleed out for what he did to me and our imperfect family. But another part, I don't know if it's my heart or my brain, tells me something else—that Bunny is a key player in all of this—and if I kill him it could hurt us even more.

∽

"What's your name?" I ask the girl holding a bucket over my head. Her expression is blank as she dumps hot water over me and I jerk up in the bathtub, howling.

"I'm sorry. Too hot. I'm sorry. Let me get something colder."

"No." I reach for her arm and she flinches. I release her. "No, I like it hot. This place is too freaking cold. It just surprised me."

The worry lines smooth by her eyes and she lowers the metal bucket to the floor. She lathers soap in her hands and begins working it through my hair. The smell of lavender is strong and I settle back against the tub, beneath the suds.

When no one returned to release me from the room, I decided to clean up. I'd started to smell a bit ripe. The name- and emotionless slave stood in the corner, waiting for my instruction, and she jumped eagerly when I asked her for assistance in the bath. The Otherside was definitely lacking in modern technology, or parts of it. The faucet ran, but only cold water. No electricity that I could see. It didn't make sense to me, but then again, this is a world of magic users, so maybe they don't need it.

I peel off my suit as the girl draws the bath, filling it with warm water and powdery soap heated over the fire. She keeps her eyes averted but modesty had been lost with me over the past few months.

My guardians had seen me in a variety of states of undress. They worshipped my body, built my confidence. I don't need a servant girl's approval of my figure. I know I'm strong. The lean muscles in my arms prove it. The tight dip of my belly is evidence of my change.

The water sloshes when I get in, spilling over the sides. The warmth soothes my aching muscles, my chilled bones.

She's just finished washing my hair when I hear footsteps on the stone floors and the bathroom door swings open. Casteel stands in the doorway. I glance at him, pretending I'm not annoyed at his presence in a private moment. I can't let him know I'm bothered or the slightest bit unnerved.

"Move," he tells the girl, and her eyes cloud with fear. I nod in agreement and she moves to the edge of the room, blending in with the walls. I'm aware that I have no control over the girl. That's the point of him being here, isn't it? Letting me know I'm nothing but a prisoner with no freedoms or rights.

"Hello, Casteel," I say, resting my arms on the side of the tub. There's nothing but the cloudy film of water between us.

"The Queen asked me to check up on you."

"Well, you can tell her I'm clean." I take the sponge and scrub my legs. "Anything else?"

"Tomorrow there will be a ceremony to bind you back together."

Interesting—so that gives me a timeline—less than a day to get out of here. "I won't pretend I'm happy about that."

"Once you realize your true powers, I think you'll come around. What you experienced in your realm is nothing but a blip of what it's like here."

I have experienced my full strength, in the ring at the fights. Magic is allowed and the rush I felt from fighting Hildi that first time still tingles in my veins. Again I felt it when Xavier kissed me, and then another time when Anita stole the virus. My instincts perk at the idea of such power, especially after being dulled recently.

In a move that is overtly casual, Casteel sits on the edge of the tub, fingers dipping into the heated water. The wounds on his neck are no longer bandaged, only red scabs remain. At this distance, the scars under his jaw are visible, deep and jagged. How Dylan didn't kill him, I don't know.

His tongue darts out and his eyes darken.

"She gave me full control over you until the ceremony tomorrow." I hear the clink of metal as his hand reaches for his belt. "She suggested I break you in as I please."

I swallow in an attempt to get the fear dislodged from my throat. And because royalty speeds through my veins I can't help myself when I reply, "Do you think that's possible? Breaking me easily?"

"What makes you think I want it to be easy?" Casteel reaches for me and I'm slippery and wet, nowhere to run and definitely nowhere to hide. I'm pulled from the bath, water rushing down my body. He eyes me greedily, unaware that the slave in the corner has run out of the room, panic and terror written on her face. This is surely not the first time she's seen the Commander take what he wants.

With my wrists clamped in his hands, he leans forward and says, "This one is for your Sentinel. Payback is a bitch."

27

BUNNY

Pacing the studio, I stop every pass and stand before the painting. Wondering. Wishing. Hoping.

I've fucked up. Worse than I thought. Morgan wasn't supposed to be here. Just Anita. My plan had been to kill the Queen and pawn, then restore the only survivor to the throne.

That was the plan, but now it's gone all to hell.

There's one thing I could do. It's worth a shot and the gate taunts me, beckoning me to go back through. Get help. Find Dylan.

He'll kill me, maybe before I can get him back here. And if he doesn't? The Morrigan and Casteel will string me from the rafters. A bunny caught in a snare.

Fuck. Fuck. Fuck. What have I done?

With a deep breath I focus on the painting, pressing my palm flat against the surface. I whisper the words, the ones that activate the runes built into the image. The center bends, swirling the colors from dark to light, light to dark, breaking down the barriers from this realm to the next. I feel the gust, the warmth from home, the smell of my studio on the other side, but a tug draws me back.

"Master! Master!" the voice calls. I look away from the gate, from my home, and see the girl in her gray uniform, eyes pleading. I yank my hand away and the opening shuts with a harsh, cosmic slam.

"What!" I regret my tone instantly. This girl—the slave—doesn't deserve my anger. "I'm sorry, what is it?"

"She's in trouble."

She. Morgan.

"What kind of trouble?" There's only so much I can do and even then it will never be enough.

"The Commander is in her room." Her hands shake. "He's going to hurt her."

I nod and thank her. I'm no match for the Commander—his magic or his strength—even if I had both hands. I kick the pile of canvases, scattering them across the room. The disruption uncovers metal, sleek steel with a bejeweled hilt. I lunge for the sword, recognizing a gift from the gods when I see it, and hope I'm not too late.

28

DYLAN

The painting parts before me, spinning like a tsunami. Paint and magic separate, splitting our worlds in two. I'd seen it before but not like this. Not so unexpected. I'd walked into Bunny's studio expecting to find little to nothing and instead I find this—an opening portal—just waiting for me to step in.

I hesitate. There's no guarantee the gate leads where I want it to. It could be a trap. Taking me straight to the dungeons. Maybe to the zombie pits on the south side of the realm, or to the darkest depths of the deadly, frozen sea. The Otherside is not contained to just the castle, but this could be my only chance to find Morgan and my brothers. It could be our only opportunity to take the Morrigan out, once and for all.

I step closer, feeling the rush of arctic air, my eyelashes freezing into stiff points. I pat my pockets for my weapons. I unsheathe the blade I always carry from my hip. Just as I'm about to take the leap the air softens, the gusts slow, and the gate shrinks before my eyes.

"No," I mutter, pressing forward. "No!"

I shove my hands into the gate and toss myself forward, forcing my way into the dark, praying to the gods I land safely on the other side.

29

MORGAN

Water runs down my body, slippery and wet from the soap. I've got no defense against Casteel's forceful, grabby hands. "It's going to be a pleasure breaking you down, little thing."

Desperate, I yank hard, using my soapy skin to my advantage and slip from his grasp. I fall backwards from the force but steady my hands on the tub. He doesn't care, I'm definitely not in any sort of dominate position. I'm naked and unarmed. He leers at me, taking time to unbutton his pants. The belt clinks to the floor and I look away.

"Don't act shy," he says, tearing off his shirt first. Black fabric falls to the floor. I fumble around the edge of the tub, touching the sponge, the soap, the shampoo. "Rumors of your lustful activity is legendary in the castle. Each time you fuck your guardians, the Queen falls apart—did you know that? Takes a little piece of her power. So much fucking over the last few months. Made the palace unbearable. So she figured she'd steal your guardians and strip you of that little bit of control you have over her."

He'd removed his shirt to make me see his strength. The broad, hard lines of his chest and shoulders. His muscles are massive. Bigger than Clinton. Bigger than any human man for certain. His hard length is visible underneath his trousers. His cock as much a weapon as any blade. I brace myself and wrap my fingers around the nearest thing. Something—anything.

He grabs me by the neck, pulling our bodies together. I recoil at the feel of him against me. He hardens and smiles, twisting his fingers in my hair. "The gods gave you beauty. I can't wait to see those sweet, perfect lips wrapped around my—"

I smash the soap in his eyes, spreading the lather with my fingers. He yelps at the sting—the lye burns—and I push him with both hands, slamming the bathroom door between us and then shoving a trunk in front of the door. It's only buying me a few moments. I try the main door—locked.

Frantically I look around the room, already knowing there are no weapons. I must defeat him on my own—using my powers. I fling open the closet door, rummaging through the clothing left for me. I toss a shirt over my head, aware that it barely skims my thighs, and pull the wooden hanger from the rack.

Casteel roars from the bathroom, banging hard against the door. Wood splinters and the force wrenches the door knob clear off. The trunk flies across the room, spilling the contents across the floor. I press my back against the wall, holding the wooden hanger like a lifeline, trying to gather a spark to fight back with.

He doesn't speak as he prowls toward me. His face has taken on demonic features. Sharp teeth, an elongated jaw. I blink, thinking I must be making it up, but I've seen the Otherside demons in the fighting ring. Casteel may have more than one form. And I have absolutely no idea how I'll fight him.

He closes the gap, ripping the hanger out of my hands and tossing it across the room with a clatter. I whisper a quiet prayer. To the gods, to my guardians, to Hildi's goddess, begging for this not to be my last moment and for the moments between now and death to be swift and merciful.

He flicks his wrist and I fling up my hand, protecting myself with an invisible shield. It only holds a second, flickering, but he's faster than me, casting power in my direction, and I'm struck with the same paralyzing sensation that he inflicted before. Amused, he smiles, and when he's close enough I feel his breath on my cheek, smell the sour stench of his skin. He's hard-packed muscle and as much as I don't want to acknowledge it, the length between his legs seems bigger, harder, and I shudder when he presses it against my lower stomach. Violence and fear turn him on.

"Don't fight, unless you want it to hurt more." His smile--the disgusting, awful smile--drops when a weight slams against the hallway door. "I saw the slave disappear. Who do you think is going to help you? There's no one here for you, Morgan. Not one person."

I was a fool for coming here so impulsively and I have no doubt I'll pay for my decision. Frozen under Casteel's power, I'm pressed against the wall and something or someone bangs against the door again and there's scratching against the lock. Shouting bounces against the walls and I dig deep inside, feeling the dregs of my own power—remnants from being with Dylan. A flare sparks, enough for me to wiggle my fingers. The commotion continues in the hall and I use the distraction to wedge my hand between our bodies. My nails elongate and spike. His eyebrow lifts when I wrap my hand around his cock, caught between confusion and pleasure.

The door crashes in and Bunny fills the doorway. I see the spray of blood on his face, the glimmer of my sword in his hand. I claw at Casteel, my nails ripping through the fabric of his pants to the flesh, and then I kick him in the gut.

"You came," I say, watching Bunny stride toward the bent over Casteel, who is howling in pain. He's down, but not for long.

"Always," Bunny declares.

The Commander stands, a beast compared to my smallest guardian. Bunny swings the blade in his hand like second nature. He glances at me before Casteel's fist makes contact with his jaw and my world turns upside down.

SHAKING OFF THE PUNCH, Bunny shifts into warrior mode, something I've only seen a few times. He always presented himself as the gentlest of my Guardians and it takes me a moment to reconcile the force in the doorway, that he came back to help me, and that no, I'm not alone.

"You do not get to touch her," Bunny says, voice laced with possessive venom. "You should not even look at her. If anything, you bow and grovel in her presence."

"Show me, weakling, what you plan to do about it." Casteel growls and lunges, the two men clashing in the middle of the room. I use the distraction to pull on pants and my boots. What else am I going to do, where am I going to go?

Bunny gives as good as he takes but he's smaller—and lacking the benefit of two functional arms. Casteel pummels him, slamming his fists into his face and kidneys. I lift my hand at a wooden chair by the vanity and by the power of the gods, I heave it overhead, slamming it down on his back. The wood shatters, barely stopping him, but he turns his back on Bunny and leers in my direction.

"Fucking whore. Gods dammed, fucking whore."

Bunny's on the ground but through swollen eyes we make contact, a brief moment of understanding, and he reaches for my sword and in a quick motion, slides it across the floor. Casteel turns at the sound of metal scraping across stone. He may be huge but I'm light on my feet and I dive for it, barely missing it. The tip of the sword lands in the fire. On my hands and knees I crawl toward it, getting my hands around the hilt.

It's heavy and my position is awkward and Casteel is hovering over me, breathing heavy. "What do you think you're going to do with that, little girl?"

I roll over, bringing the blade with me. My sword, the one given to me by Damien, infused with magic by Bunny. It feels light in my hands, the hilt curved to my dimensions. The sword moves effortlessly through the air, slicing down on Casteel's forearm. He jumps back, yelping, and I scramble to my feet. The rage on the Commander's face is unquestionable, and even with the sword, I know his wrath will be deadly. He lifts his hand, ready to use his magic against me again, but a presence appears in the door. Just as tall and twice as deadly.

The fighting stops as we all look up at Dylan standing in the doorway, ancient rage consuming him.

"Hello, Casteel," he says, withdrawing a blade. "Good to see you again."

30

DYLAN

I stare at my enemy and thank the gods that Bunny opened the gate. Did he mean to? I doubt it, but from the scene I find them in, there's little question it may have been fate and my link to Morgan that led me here.

Casteel snarls when he sees me, blood dripping down one arm. He's inexplicably shirtless, but I note the dishevelment of Morgan's hair. The anger and rage on her face and the heightened protective stance Bunny maintains tells me that something dangerous has happened here.

Morgan is savvy enough not to waste the distraction of my entrance. Her sword arcs through the air, aiming for his throat. He reacts quickly, jumping out of the way. Casteel earned his title of Commander for a reason, just as I earned mine as Sentinel.

His movement disrupts his use of magic—the forceful ability to manipulate another person—and I waste no time in catching Morgan's eye. "Go. I'll take care of this."

My wish for her to leave and go back to the safety of The Nead is futile. I know this without a word passing between us. She came here to complete a mission. The best I can do is give her the time to accomplish it.

Bunny follows her out the door and I stop him with an outstretched hand.

"You harm her and I will peel your skin off with a knife and leave it to the wolves surrounding the castle for feed."

"I won't hurt her." He swallows. "Not again."

It takes everything I have not to pierce him in the heart. But that is not my job to handle. Morgan will have the final say on the consequence of his betrayal and right now is not the time.

With them safely out of the room, I turn and face the soldier that tortured and held me captive the last time I was in this realm.

"I never thought you'd return," he says. "After you ran so quickly the last time."

I step forward, assessing everything about the room. The layout, the furniture, the scent of lavender shampoo in the air. Morgan's hair had been wet. And there are damp spots on Casteel's pants.

"Did you harm her?" I ask, unconcerned with his petty taunts.

"The little princess?" He runs a hand down the jagged scar. "Not yet."

"And the Morrigan wanted you to...defile her?"

"No, that was all on me." I hear the sharp click of metal and see he's found his own weapon, stashed away on his body. "I figured she could pay your debt."

"My debt?"

He laughs. "For letting you live."

I take him in. The weak point of his injured arm. His ego. The fact he doesn't even understand what's going on here and how much bigger all of this is than petty grudges. I let him laugh and then give him a smile of my own.

And then I launch my attack.

31

BUNNY

There's no hesitation when Dylan tells me to run. My behavior is out of instinct—out of the need to keep Morgan alive. Now that all hell is breaking loose and any semblance of control I had over the situation is gone, I have little choice but to get Morgan out of here alive.

At the turn leading to my studio—back to the portal—she stops, refusing to go further.

"Take me to them."

"To the dungeons?" I shake my head and keep an eye over her shoulder. "Not a chance."

Her grip tightens around my fingers and her voice turns cold. The glint of her sword, still tipped in blood, hangs at her side. "Fine. I'll go alone."

"Morgan, this is your chance to escape—get away from the Morrigan while you can," I plead but she pulls away, disappearing down the dark stairway that leads to the dungeons. In seconds her boots are nothing but an echo and I curse, chasing her down.

By the time I arrive on the floor, she's taken one soldier down by surprise and has another on his knees, her sword at his neck. "Hand me the keys," she says.

He spits in her face. She moves with efficient speed and indifference, smashing him in the head with the hilt of the sword and snatching the metal ring of keys from his waist. Her chin juts forward in defiance. Her are shoulders straight. I feel like I'm seeing a different side of Morgan—the one that wants her Guardians back. Someone who will stop at nothing to protect those important to her.

The magnitude of my betrayal rains down on me as she approaches the gate leading to the dark cells. She will do anything for her Guardians. Maim and kill. Travel from one world to the next. I'm terrified to think of how far her sacrifice will go.

And how in one defiant, selfish move, I endangered us all.

She fumbles with the keys and I step forward and take them with steadier hands. The stench from the cell is inhumane and it's so dark, I can't see any of my brothers. "Are you sure about this?"

I expect wrath. Rage. Anger or some smart remark challenging my question. She just says, "Yes."

"Okay, just...it may be...just be prepared."

She looks at me, searching for intent, but I have none other than to serve her. If she sees that, I don't know. The emotion reflected back at me is intense confusion and pain.

The lock flips, echoing off the rock walls. Morgan takes the keys back and steps over the threshold, peering into the dark.

"Hello," she calls in a nothing more than a whisper. "Damien? Sam? Clinton?"

The response is the clank of chains. The scrape of metal against the floor. She pushes deeper into the cavernous dark and I wait at the entrance, keeping guard. She doesn't speak but chokes back a sob, and I know she's found them.

I'm moving to help her when I hear footsteps on the stairs. I take a deep breath and prepare for another fight.

32

MORGAN

I see Sam first, his pale skin stained with so much dirt that it was hard to see him. He's curled in a fetal position and my heart nearly cracks at the sight. I fight back a gag at the smell, then the tears when I look at the sores on his back.

"Sam?" I touch his shoulder. He flinches but doesn't respond otherwise. "I'm here. I'm getting you out of here, okay?"

Again, no reply. I reach down and touch him, feeling for the cuffs around his wrists, and shove the key into the lock. Then I do the same for the ones around his swollen, stiff ankles.

"Hey," I say, pressing my forehead to his. The faintest energy pulses between us. "You've got to get up. I can't carry all three of you out of here." His eyes flutter and he blinks like he can't fully focus. I kiss his brow. Then his nose. My lips are wet from tears of anger. I kiss him on the mouth and finally, I get a reaction. It's nothing more than a sigh and a deep groan but he's alive. I kiss him again, pressing my warm lips against his chapped, cold ones.

"Stand up if you can—or at least sit. I'm going to get the others."

He nods, like a man coming out of a dream, and as much as it pains me, I leave him to feel around the dark crevices of the cell. It only takes a moment before I bump into something solid. I hold my hands out, palms flat and hear a hiss. He's chained to the wall, upright. He sways back and forth.

"Clinton?"

I feel his chin, his chest. A low growl rumbles in his throat and I say, "It's me. Morgan."

"Don't trick me, witch."

"What?"

"Kill me if you want, but don't put on the face of your enemy."

I touch his cheek and he flinches, turning away. "Clinton, it's me." I stroke his chest, feeling the bumpy, raw scabs that have recently healed over. He fights me but the energy burns between us—like it always has. He may think it's magic or the Morrigan fucking with his head but I push on, lifting on my toes and whispering in his ear. With every word his shoulders loosen, and he turns his face in my direction.

"Morgan?" His voice is a whisper—a hope.

"Yeah. It's me. We've got to get out of here."

I unlock his chains and thankfully he's stronger than Sam, able to move a bit faster, but I don't know how long it will last. What's happening with Dylan upstairs? Where are we even going to go? And Bunny? He said he would guard the door, but I sure as hell don't trust him.

"Damien's over there," he says, pointing toward a small window. It's dark outside but faint moonlight filters in the glassless, barred windows.

It doesn't take as long to find him. His body is lit by the moon. He's asleep on the floor but wakes seconds before I reach him. Dark rage fills his eyes but it shifts immediately when he sees me. "Babe?"

"Yeah."

"You came."

"Of course I came," I say, relieved I don't have to convince him it's really me. He moves slowly, but he too can move. Blood clots at the edge of his swollen, bruised mouth and I touch his head, feeling unfamiliar stubble from the weeks of growth. I nearly burst into tears when I see him. I'm just so happy to have him and the others back.

Or almost back.

"Bunny," Clinton says, his words slurring. "He..."

"I know."

"I don't know what happened. Why?"

"Me either," I say, walking back to the front of the cell and stooping to pick up Sam. I touch his hair, his face. He's weak and so skinny. Damien bears some of the weight. "But we'll figure it out."

Bunny is gone when we reach the front of the cell, but I hear voices and touch my sword, thinking I don't have anything left to put into a fight. I just want to get my men to safety. A shadow turns the corner and I muster the strength, lifting the blade before me and keeping the Guardians behind me.

Bunny rounds the corner and Clinton grunts and tenses when he sees him, but I hold up my hand. "I don't know where Bunny stands, but at the moment he's all we've got."

"He can't be trusted."

"I know," I stare him down. "I know what he did. But he saved me upstairs and we don't have much choice."

Bunny does nothing but gape at the Raven Guard, nearly shrinking at the sight of facing the men he betrayed.

"Who were you talking to?" I ask, keeping myself between him and Clinton. Before he can answer, I spot the smaller figure behind him. The form is familiar, slight, as though it's nothing more than a wisp. She steps into the faint light and I see it's the servant from my rooms.

Footsteps rumble overhead. Not Dylan. No, a group, probably the rest of Casteel's soldiers now that they realize the carnage in the hallway outside my room. I don't want to be here when they find the fallen men down here.

"We've got to get out of here," I say, fighting back the panic. I know I don't have the energy to fight much longer.

The girl steps forward, stepping between me and Bunny. "I can help."

"How?" The footsteps are closer, I hear Sam shudder behind me. He's fading fast.

"Come," she says. "Follow me."

It's not like we have a choice. The soldiers' angry voices echo at the bottom of the stairwell, discovering the body of their men. The girl walks in the opposite direction, toward the stone wall. I think maybe she's crazy, traumatized from gods know how long of living as a slave of the Morrigan. But a foot from the wall she turns, facing the side wall, and touches a stone. There's movement, the sound of stone grating on stone, and a small, narrow passage becomes visible.

I sigh, knowing that it's a risk. It's all one risk after the other. But it's for a bigger goal--stopping the Morrigan--and I can't do it without my Guardians, and there's no way any of us will survive another altercation. Dylan isn't going to save us, even if he's still alive.

I nod at the girl and make a decision that could either save or kill us, and climb into the passage.

～

THE TUNNEL IS long and incredibly dark. I blindly follow the sound of the girl walking in front of me, and listen to the labored breaths of my guardians coming from behind. The smell goes from musty to damp as we travel and the floor slants, taking us deeper and deeper beneath the castle. Just when I think we're going to have to stop and rest, the girl calls for us to stop. A hand grips my shoulder. I'm not sure which one of my guardians it is, but I feel the instant surge of power between us, helping him heal just a little bit.

I hear a series of knocks, light tapping on what sounds like a wooden door. Light seeps through a crack, then a long shaft down the tunnel, bathing us all in a yellow glow. I can't see what's on the other side, but it has to be better than where we are.

Bunny and I help the Guardians toward the exit, blinking as we acclimate to the light and the strange, humid warmth wafting our way. The girl waits for me and smiles as I pass. "You'll be safe down here and can stay as long as you need to recuperate."

"Down here" is a cavernous world beneath the surface, an entire community built into the ground. From the looks of it, a thriving community. For the first time since I passed through the gates, I feel safe.

"Thank you," I say, squeezing her hand.

With a glance behind me, she says, "Your men need help. Follow me."

33

MORGAN

"What is this place?" I ask Nevis. The slave finally agreed to tell me her name after she got my guardians safely to the medics. "Why are you helping us?"

We're standing outside a small cave dug into the black-brown earth. A swarm of men and women sprang into action the instant we appeared, following Nevis' directions to clean up and look over the wounds. I'd pushed to enter with them, but she held up her hand and told me to let them do their work. Bunny stood to the side, awkward and silent—too many questions surround him.

"My people built this community many centuries ago—when the goddess first went mad. When her heart was broken and she declared war on all people, there were few survivors. She scorched the land, turning it into nothing but barren ash and bone. The only place to survive was underground, in the caverns beneath the castle that had been in existence since the beginning of time."

"Does she know this place is here?"

Nevis shakes her head. "She's too vain to consider that life flourishes in her place of destruction—especially under her nose. We're protected down here and a few of us always maintain positions in the castle to keep an eye on things. It's a job traditionally carried down from one generation to the next."

I look around the open space. The air is warm, damp with humidity. For the first time in days, the chill in my bones disappears. Several small ponds of fresh water are fed by a stream coming from an outside source. Light shafts stretch from the high, rugged ceiling. It's gray like the sky above, but it reflects off the water and the gardens filled with plump, unfamiliar vegetables. Homes tuck into the walls; some natural crevices, others dug into the surface. People mill about, in the middle of normal daily activities. Cooking. Tending the gardens. Caring for children.

"You didn't answer my other question," I say, watching a small group of children run past. They're clean and look well-fed. "Why are you helping us?"

Nevis toys with the end of her braid, her hair as dark as my own. Her eyes are a deep blue and I notice this is the coloring of most of the people down here. Including much paler skin. "Legend tells us the tales of the Morrigan and how she came into existence. The stories of how her heart was betrayed. How she used her pain to wage war and wrath on Cu's armies." She leans closer. "There are other stories. Ones about the three sisters. That the Morrigan is only one part of the powerful Goddess that rules over this realm."

"I've heard the myths."

"My people have always believed in this version and have waited centuries for the reuniting of the three."

Embrace, the Shaman had said.

"You believe the myths."

"Yes, and you must know your role in all of this. I knew it the moment you crossed through the gate. Before, even. When the Queen brought the mythical Raven Guard here to torture and imprison, I knew you must be gaining strength in your own world. Enough for her to panic. I'm helping you because I know you may very well be the key."

The key.

I think back to my story—the one that haunted me for years—consumed my daydreams as a child. The cat and the prince and the ravens watching me from above. The key that opened the gate from one world to the next.

"What are you saying?" I ask.

"You may be the only hope we have to save this realm." She nods over to the structure that holds my men. "You and your Guardians."

I know enough that there could be truth to her ideas—that I am part of something bigger, but there are things she may not know. "She's doing a lot of damage back home, horrible things. I am here to stop that—to find what will stop the sickness back home."

"A virus?" she asks. I nod. "Tell me about this sickness."

I describe the symptoms. The way it sucks the life away from a person and the way it's transmitted, starting with two of her own minions using me as a conduit. "Not only are my friends in danger, the whole world is. The Morrigan has made her move to cross realms."

"So you didn't come here to save us."

I reach for Nevis' hand. "I didn't even know you existed. But that doesn't mean I don't want to help you, too. I'm just not sure I have as much power as you think I do."

Dylan and the others seem to think I'm the answer—this woman, too. But other than some mediocre fighting skills, a few magic tricks, and an unusual bond between me and four men, I'm not really sure what these powers are or how to use them.

Nevis doesn't seem as apprehensive. She smiles, revealing a chipped tooth that doesn't detract from her quiet beauty or the expression of hope filling her eyes. "Then let's make you strong and take the rest from there."

∼

Bunny watches me closely as I walk away from Nevis and toward the small hut. I want desperately to ignore him, but now that we're relatively safe, the emotions of the last few hours crash over me: Casteel and his assault; Dylan showing up to finish the fight; Bunny protecting me. I dare a glance and find him walking toward me. I push down my confused feelings.

"Are you going in?" he asks.

"Yes."

"Good." He shoves his glasses up his nose with one finger. "I know now is not the time—"

"No. It's not."

"It's not. I know, it's just that I'm sor—"

"Bunny." I cut him off. "If we get out of this alive and Dylan the others don't kill you first, we can talk. That's when I'll decide what to do about everything that's happened between us." I swallow back the rage building in my chest. I am not over what Bunny has done. Not even close, but I have bigger problems and some major healing to apply to my Guardians, and right now isn't the time.

"Take care of them," he says, knowing what I'm about to do. "I'll guard the door."

I nod and leave him to begin the healing process with Guardians and prepare them for the next phase in the war.

∾

A FEW MEMBERS of the underground community are in the room when I enter. Their clothes are shabby but clean. The building itself seems to be a very small clinic. Vials and bottles line the shelves on the wall. Wooden boxes filled with bandages and other supplies are stacked neatly.

The whole place seems surreal, but I have little option other than to trust them and to trust Bunny.

Calling it a hut is generous—it's basically a cave. How do these people survive down here? All three of my men are sleeping on a pallet of blankets and furs on the floor. Sam, looking weak and frail, is in the middle, flanked on both sides by Damien and Clinton. One healer remains, wiping down Sam's feet with a towel. Glasses of half-consumed, clear liquid are on the ground.

"Call for us if you need anything."

"Thank you." I look down at my men. They've been cleaned and their wounds tended to. I choke back a wave of emotion. "For everything."

The door closes with a click.

I undress as I walk toward the bed, kicking off my boots, lifting my shirt over my head, and dropping my trousers to the floor. I'm bare underneath—the battle upstairs gave me little time to dress. I feel the appraising gaze of eyes on me and look up to find Damien watching my every move. Dropping to my knees, I crawl to him while the others sleep.

He reaches for me with a rough hand. I take it, kissing the raw skin on his knuckles. Lifting the blankets, I slip beneath and snuggle next to his too-skinny body and run my hands up and down the tattoos on his chest. Skin to skin, we connect.

He presses his lips to mine and breathes, "Gods, I missed you."

3 4

DAMIEN

At first, I don't think she's real. I think it's another dream. Another fantasy I used to stay sane during the weeks of imprisonment and torture. I only thought of her face. Her eyes. Her body. I dreamed of her bursting through the door and snapping Casteel's neck. I knew she would come. I knew my Queen would not allow me to fester and die in his rotting cell.

Even so, her voice sounds so far away. Not real. Certainly not of this realm. But she says my name. She touches my skin and the charge of energy that only exists between Morgan and her Raven Guard bolts like lightning through my limbs.

I'm unsure how long ago that was. An hour? A day? But I'm clean and a team of strange healers tended to my wounds. And I'm about to slip into sleep when the door opens and she appears, back in my life like she'd never been gone.

She a goddess, stripping away her clothes and walking to me like a shimmering sun. The heat of her flesh calls to me and all I want is to quench my thirst, to drink from the well of her everlasting soul. I hate the tears that roll down her cheeks.

I will soothe her pain as she heals my wounds.

Once whole, I promise I will lead her down the path to victory, helping guide Morgan to her fullest potential. That is why I'm here—and why the gods chose me eons ago.

I touch her, feel her, and know that I will claim her--no, *we* will claim her--and triumph over the evil that dared to tear us apart.

35

MORGAN

"I am so sorry," I tell him. "I am *so* sorry it took me this long to get here."

"Babe, this is not on you. Not one bit." His fingers stroke down my arm and the energy between us flares, like a smoldering fire being stoked back to life. "I knew you would find us. I had no doubt. I bided my time and saved my energy for when you would arrive."

"You knew?"

"I knew."

I kiss his mouth. "Now that I've got you, all of you, I'm going to make everything better."

There's no coyness behind my statement, no doubt in what I have in mind even though my belly is filled with nerves, and I anxiously glance at the other two men. But Damien, even in a weakened state, is the least judgmental being I've ever known. He senses my apprehension and says, "Don't worry, we'll figure this out together. We always knew one day it would come to this, didn't you?"

I nod, feeling heat rise to my cheeks. "I've dreamed about it. More than once. I just thought it would be all of us."

He touches my chin. "It will be. It's how we'll take the Morrigan out once and for all, but for now, we need to heal, grow our power so we're ready to fight. Understand?"

I do, and I let him position me so I'm pressed against his belly and chest and I'm relieved with I feel his hard length. I exhale, feeling steady for the first time in days. There's no doubt I've been running on fumes, and this is only confirmed with the surge of power when Damien touches me.

I feel his lips on my ear and he says, "I'm going to take care of you, while you take care of Sam, okay?"

I look at Sam. My sweet, adorable Sam. His eyes are blackened, red marks ring his neck. He's even skinnier than Damien because he had less meat on him before they were locked up. I'm tentative when I reach out to him, terrified I'm going to hurt him even more.

"Touch him," Damien whispers. He's begun moving his own hands, skimming them down the curve of my hips around to my belly. I shiver and he kisses my neck, causing my nipples to tighten and point. I ghost my hand over Sam's face, his swollen neck, and smile when his eyes flicker open. There's an innate conflict—I want to sink into the pleasure of Damien's touch while also focusing on doing the same for Sam.

I've never been an amazing multi-tasker.

"Morgan?" His voice gritty and hoarse.

"Hi."

"What..." he has no voice and the thought of what caused it breaks my heart. Screaming? Begging? Fucking Casteel and his sadistic bend. I press a finger to his lips.

"Don't talk, okay? Just let me take care of you."

His eyes shift over my shoulder and Damien says to his brother, "It's time."

Sam nods and licks his dry, cracked lips.

Damien's hands wander to my breasts. I press my ass closer to his ridiculously hard cock. I've missed his body and his touch so much that I have to fight back a cry of relief from feeling him close to me again. I rest a hand by Sam's head, establishing myself in the middle of a Sam-Damien sandwich. Good thing I'm hungry, and I'm not the only one. These men have been starving for days. Not just for food and water, but for the essence of what keeps them alive: Me and the connection I bring to them.

With every ripple of pleasure Damien gives me, by tweaking my nipples or kissing my shoulders, I do the same for Sam. I take my time with him, rousing him gently, licking his skin and lathing my tongue over the red marks on his neck.

I skim my hand down his stomach, toward the soft hair below his belly button and nearly cry when I feel the hard length waiting for me. "So you've got a little left in you after all, don't you?"

His eyelashes flutter, giving me a view of his beautiful green eyes. "For you? Always."

I lift on one elbow and arch my neck to get a better look at Damien. He's watching me closely. I beckon him over and kiss him on the mouth, feeling a second set of hands reach for my body. An intense shiver rolls through my body and I know that it's time.

36

SAM

Her lips taste like salt. Her breath, like the very essence of life. It's through hooded eyes that I watch Morgan, sitting above me like a queen. Her breasts are perfect, her stomach soft, and the beckoning patch of heaven between her legs call me like an angel's song.

I've spent weeks rotting away in that filthy cell, wondering if I'd ever have the pleasure of seeing her face or touching her body once again.

I never should have questioned it. I never should have doubted.

I know immediately, instinctively, that we have moved to another level in our relationship. She's here to heal; I feel the aches slipping away with every touch, the bruises fading. I see Damien's hands. I watch my own. *I feel. I feel. I feel,* and know what will bring down the bitch sitting on her throne.

I am sure that Morgan always thought that we would be the ones that would save her—she had it wrong. She'll be the one to redeem us all.

37

MORGAN

We move fluidly. Damien follows me as I move to straddle Sam. I kiss his mouth, then his chest, lingering over his sensitive, brown nipples. I feel Damien behind me, hands firmly on my waist, as I make my way downward, grazing my teeth across Sam's sharp hip bones. He's still weak, but he watches me, hand clenched on my shoulder. When I've shimmied down every inch of his body, I rock forward on my knees, offering my backside to Damien. He doesn't hesitate, gripping my cheeks and spreading them wide.

Although it seems impossible, I focus on the hard and eager shaft between Sam's legs. With one hand on my head and another on the base he guides me toward it and I lick the tip, tasting the familiar saltiness. He shudders when I do it again and I cry against the heat in my mouth. I never knew if I'd see them again, and to have the honor of helping bring them back to full strength is almost too much.

I lick and suck and nibble and stroke, never missing a beat. Not even when I feel the pressure behind me, when Damien rubs his fingers between my legs, making sure I'm slick and ready. Not when he slips his cock between the slick folds at the entrance to my core and eases himself inside. I gasp from the sensation, never knowing—never understanding what it could be like.

Like every encounter with my Guardians we're in tune, in synch, with the pace and tone of our movements. Sometimes it's about fun. Other times it's about anger, rage, or pain. Now it's about healing—unifying. Damien and Sam fill me in two different ways and I've never felt so complete.

Damien settles for a minute, giving me time to adjust to the sensation and balance it takes to handle both of them at once. When I feel I'm ready I rock back, moving my mouth and hand at the same time. It's a slow movement and Sam props up on his elbows, fully alert and watching intently.

I like the way his eyes feel on me. I love the way Damien pushes in and out, slow and steady, hyperaware of my needs. We set a rhythm, the three of us, and soon we're a chorus of groans and pleasure. With every connection our bond rekindles and power reestablishes. I sense movement next to Sam, the shifting of the blankets, and Clinton, who'd been out like a rock, slowly wakes.

His gray eyes take in everything, lingering on my exposed breasts, on my mouth as I work Sam into a state of sheer delight. He watches Damien who grunts with every thrust.

"Damn," he mutters, fire igniting behind his eyes.

I lick my way up Sam's cock and release him, keeping the friction with my hand. Sudden nerves take hold. Two men I can handle, but three? I have no idea what to do or how to do it. But I shouldn't be nervous, because instinct takes over and I reach for Clinton, ready to bring this circle closer.

38

CLINTON

Gods above, after centuries of life, after plagues and battles and endless wars, I know for certain I've died. The Morrigan finally got me. Killed me in her filthy dungeon. I know this because an angel that looks like my soulmate is before me.

It makes sense that she'd be naked. Stripped of everything but her magnificent body. Sam's dead too, I'm sure of it; the look on his face as she runs her tongue up and down his cock is nothing short of bliss.

Damien's breathing comes hard, louder than a standard fantasy. I see the sweat on his chest, the exertion on his face, the red marks on Morgan's hips from where he grips and holds her as he pounds into her relentlessly.

Even in death I grow hard at the sight of her, at the sight of this majestic scene, but dreams slip into reality when she glances my way. Her dark eyes peer into whatever remains of my soul.

Without the slightest hesitation, she reaches for me. I blink, my ears rushing with blood. Real. This is real. *She* is real.

I shake away the pain of the dungeon, the death and destruction fostered by a ruthless dictator, and stare at the members of my family.

They're alive and rekindling the power that will end it once and for all.

Morgan beckons and I come.

39

MORGAN

Clinton wastes no time and moves toward me, kissing me hard on the mouth. The blanket falls, revealing his erection. He may have been asleep but he's ready now. Sam nudges my hand, encouraging me to go to him. Damien whispers in my ear, "Fuck him. Give him your light and love, Morgan," and pulls out, leaving me crying out with sudden loss.

The despair is short-lived. Clinton is more than up to the task, lifting me over his lap until I'm straddling his hips. I have no desire to wait, lowering myself onto his throbbing erection. Damien moves to one side and Sam, stronger now, does the same. They stand next to me and while Clinton and I quickly set a pace, I reach for both of their glistening cocks as they each fondle my breasts. I feel them everywhere. Inside, outside, down every limb. I feel the heat and power from their hard, pulsing cocks. I hear the want and connection in their labored breathing. I'm raw and ready, charged and feeling the surge of power coursing through me—through us. Sam clutches my shoulder, Damien pulls my hair, and Clinton, he stares at me with such intensity it's insane I ever thought I'd live another day without them.

We're one.

We're together.

We're powerful.

In the real world, spirits don't collide. Bodies do not work on the same time and space. But in that little cavern the three of us reach a level of pleasure, one where we stop being three different souls and forge into one ultimate power. The orgasm races up and down our bodies, tickling our senses, fraying each and every nerve. I feel it in Clinton's final thrust, hard and pulsing. I hear it in Sam's throat, his breath caught from his ecstasy, a groan so deep it makes me tremble. I sense it in the thick, white spurts of Damien's cum, warm and sticky all over my hands and arms.

And it rocks me to the core, every inch of my body, across my skin—deep in the very essence of my heart. My head spins and I grow numb, my senses on complete and utter overload.

But it doesn't matter. Three sets of hands catch me, cradle me, and love me unconditionally.

Together, we're a united force, and I dare anyone to attempt to come between us.

40

DYLAN

The castle shudders. The stone shifts underfoot, like a giant sighing in relief. Casteel groans, blood trickling from the wound on his chest. Just as I have no doubt what shook the castle like an earthquake, I have no doubt the Morrigan will be here soon, looking for the cause.

Casteel makes one last effort to raise his hand at me, but I feel the buzz, a glorious, powerful buzz, and I swing my blade, lopping off his hand at the wrist. He howls in pain and swears, "She'll castrate you for this, Sentinel. All of you."

He grips his wrist, blood flowing quickly from the wound. He crawls toward the fire—cauterizing is his only option. The Morrigan can save him or look for me. It's her choice. There's another rumbling, this time cold and bitter, a storm coming from the higher parts of the castle.

Time is running out.

I run from the room, the smell of burnt flesh followed by screaming pain chases me down the hall. I turn in the direction I came in. I know where the dungeons are. I spent weeks down in the dark pits beneath the castle. Another tremor ricochets off the walls, nearly knocking me off my feet. I right myself and continue down the stairs, following the vibrations. They're down here. I don't know where and I don't know how my girl pulled it off, but she got them together. She found her mates and opened conduits of energy and power. I feel it. I know it.

Now I just have to figure out where they are so I can get us all the hell out of here.

41

MORGAN

Wow.

That's all I can think or even feel. I coil my hand into a fist and then open it, nails elongating into sharpened points. I relish the surge of complete power flowing through my bones.

Wow. Fucking. Wow.

Three Guardians at once and I know they took it easy on me, there could be more, and like an addict wanting a hit, there is no doubt in my mind that if we survive this hellhole, it's something we'll explore again. Next time we'll do it at home, slowly, taking our time.

My skin tingles, even now that my breathing has returned to normal and my cheeks have lost the flaming heat of exertion. The men laze around me, catching their breath and going through the final stages of healing. The power that ran through me to them and back again was nothing short of epic. Together we are at full power. What will happen when Dylan joins in? Or Bunny?

If we even allow him to return.

I completely understand now why the Morrigan did what she did —why she kidnapped my men. What I don't understand, even more than before, was Bunny's betrayal. To what end? What was his point?

A knock on the door breaks me from my thoughts and I stand, wrapped in nothing but a blanket, and cross the room. I glance back and see my Guardians shift into alertness.

I open the door and Nevis stands on the other side. Bunny lurks nearby, keeping watch. He's placed a rune of protection on the door. He's trying—or at least pretending that he is.

Nevis' eyes dart from me to the men, who have relaxed, aware we're not under any threat. "Feeling better?"

"Absolutely."

"I brought you something." She reveals a folded-up outfit in her hands. I shake it out, and realize it's my suit from back home. I smile and take it from her. "I have something for them, too. Can I bring it in?"

"Thank you. And of course."

I step aside and two men enter the dwelling, carrying stacks of clothing and boots. They hand an outfit to each of my three guardians and have two extra. The material is familiar. I walk over and hold my own next to it. The fabric matches, everything from the weave to the stitching. I've seen them before—in the closet of the training room in the basement of The Nead.

"How did you get these?" I ask.

"Our people have served the Queen since the beginning—regardless of what realm they reside in." I study her hair. Her face. I think about the way she carries herself. Her strength and the lack of fear she has, despite her position.

"You got these from Davis and Sue." I look at my Guardians. They seem as surprised as I do. "I knew there was more to them than just..."

"Servants?" she says. "We're the heartbeat tying the two realms together. We've bided our time for centuries. Toiling away, working for the Morrigan, waiting for the day our savior would come and free us from oppression."

"Me?"

She nods. "Davis and Sue are impressed, which isn't easy. They've known it for some time."

The enormity of the moment slams into me, and if I hadn't just juiced up on Raven power, I'd probably crumble under the pressure. Nevis and the people down here think I'm going to save them. I look at the grim expressions on the Guardians and realize that is wrong. They think *we're* going to save them.

Which, I guess, is exactly what we had planned. There's just more at stake than I ever knew.

I steal a glance at my men, who are in the midst of dressing. In a low voice I say, "I'm going to need your help."

Nevis' eyes twinkle and she curtsies. "At your service."

◊

I IGNORE the questioning looks from my men as I take one of the extra suits and carry it outside. I'm already dressed, and I slide my sword into the sheath on my back. Bunny stands near the house, alert though obviously exhausted. I walk over to him and note that the purple shadows under his eyes are deeper than before. I expected him to get at least a contact boost from my encounter with the others, but instead he looks worse.

Good.

I toss him the suit and he catches it.

"What's this for?"

"We're getting out of here. Thought you may need it."

He stares at the fabric in his hands. "You want me to go with you?"

I take a step closer. "Not really. But I need you."

"I need you, too."

Without the slightest bit of hesitation I slap him across the face. Hard. Gods, that felt good. "You'll do everything I say. Follow every command. Each direction. Without question. Do you understand that?"

"Yes. I understand." He swallows and casts his copper eyes at mine. "Morgan, I meant it before. I'm sorry. This got out of control. It's such a mess."

He flinches when he says it, waiting for another assault. This time I rein it in.

"Stop." The feeling of power fills me in a way I never have before. I'm not even sure of how far it will reach—what I can do. "No talking. No apologizing."

He nods.

"Seriously, Bunny. Am I clear?"

"Crystal."

"Go change. We're leaving when Dylan gets here."

"Dylan? Does he even know where we are?" I hear his real question. *Do I really think he's alive?*

I nod toward the tunnel entry across the expansive grounds. Nevis has placed someone at the entrance. He moves when the door swings open and Dylan appears, blinking into the light. I smile and start toward him, but Bunny grabs my arm. "How did you know?"

"I felt him coming. Didn't you?" But I know he didn't, because just like the fact he didn't feel a boost from my connection with the others, he couldn't feel Dylan anymore. The damage Bunny has made to his bond with the five of us runs deep.

I shake away from him. Dylan sees us. Me. His heartbeat quickens at the sight of me but his eyes darken when he spots Bunny nearby. "Change," I say again, and walk toward the Raven soaked in blood and craving my attention. We're almost whole. Well, as much as we're going to get.

42

DYLAN

I follow Morgan's signal, feeling the vibrations through the stone walls in the dungeons. The path is darker than a moonless night but her soul sings to me and eventually I reach the end.

I have no idea what to expect on the other side of the passage but it certainly isn't an underground society. The gatekeepers welcome me—as though they'd been expecting me. I spot Morgan immediately, speaking with Bunny. I nearly launch myself across the caverns and kill him.

But Morgan gives me a look and I get it. Hands off. For now.

I sag against the door, catching my breath. I've suffered a loss of blood. My battle with Casteel wasn't without injury.

She's at my side in minutes. Bunny watches with a guarded expression. I don't blame him—we have unsettled business—but if Morgan has allowed him to come down here with us, I'll trust her.

"You found us," she says, touching my face. My stomach. Blood seeps through the fabric of my shirt.

"Always," I tell her, leaning against her. "I'll always find my family."

"Casteel?" she asks.

"Not dead. Severely wounded, but not dead."

She looks up at me with concerned, powerful eyes. "And the Morrigan?"

"Coming." I look across the cavern and see the members of my Guard. They're healthy and full of vigor. Morgan truly had saved them. "We need to move fast."

"I'm working on a plan." She pulls me into a kiss. I feel it in every molecule of my body. Every nerve and every muscle. "I need you strong."

"I'll be ready."

"Yes," she says, taking my hand. "You will."

43

MORGAN

I don't have time to give Dylan the full treatment, but I lead him to the clinic and assist him while he cleans up. I press my lips against every wound. I stroke his skin until the ache in his muscles ease. I do my best to ignore the hunger in his eyes and below the belt. It's impossible to turn that on and off. We don't have the luxury of immersing ourselves in one another right now.

By the time he's suited up, wearing the all black uniform and matching the other members of the Raven Guard, Nevis is knocking on the door. She asks if she can come in. I give her a welcoming nod as Dylan secures his blades in the suit. Bunny slips in behind her. He's suited up and my heart cracks a little seeing him unified with us, at least for now.

She's followed by one of the healers I'd seen in the clinic earlier. He's a small man with graying hair. "I'd hate to meet any of you in a dark corner of the castle," she says, giving us the once over. "I'd like you to meet Kuwan. He's our lead healer. His wife is the Morrigan's personal assistant."

These people are like an army of spies. No wonder their community has survived so long.

I step forward. "Thank you for helping, everyone. I know it was unexpected and probably taxed your resources. We will do whatever we can to repay you."

Kuwan nods his thanks and says, "Nevis told me about the virus that the Morrigan is spreading in your world. It sounds similar to a sickness we had here, many years ago."

"Years ago? You mean no one gets sick from it anymore?" I ask.

Dylan chimes in. "Was it cured? Eradicated?"

"No. Not exactly," Kuwan says. "When the Morrigan unleashed her fury on this realm, she destroyed all living things. After the wars were over there were still survivors, but she solved that when cold and dark days rolled over the land. Sickness wiped out the remaining clans."

"Except this one," Clinton says.

Kuwan nods. "Yes, except this one."

"How did they manage that? Just by coming underground?"

"No," Bunny says. We all look at him in surprise. "The Queen drinks from a vial like those on the counter. It keeps her young. Vital and strong—especially when faced with Morgan and her power."

"Is that true?" I ask

"Yes," Kuwan replies

"What does she take? What keeps your people alive?"

"You notice the heat—the warmth. Our ponds are filled by warm springs of clean, clear water that warms the air as well as provides sanitation for cleaning and drinking. The people on the upside were freezing to death. The water sources were contaminated. That only sped up the plague set loose by the Morrigan, and they died."

I look at Dylan and then Nevis. "You're saying the water saved your people."

"Yes," Kuwan says. "We believe it has healing properties."

"The water heals people," Damien repeats.

"Yes. Healing, longevity…"

Dylan's expression is neutral but I see the wheels turning in his head. "You're serious."

Nevis smiles and her eyes twinkle. "How old do you think I am?"

Upstairs, when she was nothing more than my servant, I thought she was a girl—a teenager. Younger than me. Her skin is smooth and her black hair is sleek and shiny. Once she saved me I saw more wisdom in her eyes but not much more age. I take a guess and high-ball it. "Twenty-five."

The others agree.

"Sixty," she announces. "This is the year I turned sixty."

"Years old?" Sam asks. Bunny watches the whole thing from the side, unable to hide his incredulousness.

"Yes."

"That's what you used on their wounds right? I noticed they'd started healing before I even came in here."

"Water," Kuwan says. "Nothing else."

There's a moment of quiet as we reflect on this. Dylan is the first to speak. "So you think this water may help cure the virus plaguing the realm we've come from?"

"The properties may shift from one realm to the other, but it's worth a shot."

The idea is exciting, liberating, but introducing a miracle cure back on Earth seems too good to be true. It's also life-changing—the kind of thing that alters the fate of mankind. The uneasy look on the Guardian's face tells me they realize the ramifications as well.

"Are you offering this to us to take back to my people?" I finally ask. The glance between Nevis and Kuwan make it clear it's not that easy. I didn't think so.

"We're willing to share—at the very least you can take it to your medics and they can assess its purposes," Nevis says.

"But..." I prompt.

"But the Morrigan must be destroyed." Kuwan stares at me. "And we can't do it alone."

I feel every male around me tense. Every single one of my guardians shifts into protective mode. A low growl rumbles behind me and I'm not sure who it comes from, but I hold up my hand. "So you want to trade our services for the cure?"

"Possible cure," Clinton bites out.

Nevis flinches from his tone, aware of the lethal power behind his words. She speaks in a calm voice. "It's not like that. We know you're already here to stop her and cure the virus. We can help with the virus, but please don't just take it and leave. We just hope that future generations can live above ground—free and not bound to the Morrigan."

I assess my men. Their expressions are hard, complicated masks. But I know they'll do what's right. Or at the very least, try. Sure enough, Dylan confirms this.

"Then we fight her," Dylan says. "We're strong. A forceful unit at maximum power. It should be easy to take her out."

"After, we'll leave," Sam says. "We go back and give the cure to the sick."

Damien nods. But his face is stoic—staring right at me. I mutter my agreements and look away, securing the blade in my boot.

It's solved. Easy as that.

Or so I want everyone to think.

44

MORGAN

The tunnel is different—leading from another part of the cavern. Nevis declares it will take us directly to the Queen's quarters. Dylan demands to go first—as is his position. The others will follow. I'll take the back—the safest place. If it goes wrong, I can run—Nevis and her people will keep alert.

She hands me six vials of water, each capped tight and wrapped in cloth.

"Just in case," I say to them. Now that we know what it can do, every soldier should carry it on their person.

I hold back emotion as I tuck a vial of water in each and every one of their breast pockets. I take a moment to check their gear. Kiss their mouths. I'm almost at full strength, only lacking the final link in the circle. Bunny's betrayal has weakened me—us—in a way I didn't know was possible. It helps me understand the pain the Morrigan felt when Cu tossed her aside at the river. Sympathetic, even.

We stand before the tunnel and the Ravens enter. Dylan, Sam, Damien...Clinton waits for Bunny to enter but I tug my betrayer by the sleeve and say, "Go first," to Clinton. He narrows his eyes and hesitates.

"He's a traitor." Clinton makes no effort to lower his voice. Damien looks over at the sound of his voice.

"He is and I'm going to deal with that. That's my job. You all have a different one."

"Deliver the cure," he replies. "It won't matter if Bunny fucks it up."

"It will matter. But that's not all I need from you. We're going to need to build an army."

"An army?" He laughs. "Where the hell are we going to get one of those?" I don't reply and finally he sighs. "We should bomb this place and never look back," he says, finally stepping into darkness.

"What was that?" Bunny asks.

"No questions. Follow orders. Remember that?"

He silently nods.

I grip his arm tighter, my nails threatening to spike. "The choices you make today will determine your future, Bunny. Don't fuck that up. Not again."

His eyes burn with pain and I release him. He's not the only one that will have regrets by the time the day is over.

∼

ONE OF NEVIS' men leads the way down the long tunnel with a torch doused in oil. Once my men have travelled deep, I allow them to get a bit ahead. When no one notices, I stop abruptly. Bunny crashes into me and whispers quietly in my ear, "What's wrong?"

"Nothing." The air shifts near me, turning cool. Bunny tenses behind me. He feels it. I reach out my hand, searching for the wall that should be there—and was moments ago. Now there's an empty gap.

"What?"

"Turn right." I glance over my shoulder. The faint light of the torches fades into the distance. My voice is barely above a whisper. "Now."

He does as I say, his toes clipping my heels. There's the faintest sound of grating stone. I reach back and the opening is gone. I count to ten and Nevis appears, holding a torch.

"They can't find us?" I ask her.

"No. And I've barricaded the entry into the caverns as well. There's only one way out and that's through The Nead."

"Good," I tell her. "Bolt that door, seal it or destroy it. Whatever it takes, and no matter what, do not let them back in."

"What have you done?" Bunny asks. His forehead is furrowed in confusion.

"That tunnel will lead them back to The Nead. Sue and Davis will intercept them."

"And what about us?" The fear in his eyes tells me he already knows. He shakes his head in disbelief. "No. This is not a good idea."

"It's the only idea," I tell him, gesturing to Nevis to lead the way. She takes us to a ladder bolted into the cavern walls that leads straight up into a dark hole. "It's the only one I've had since I gained passage into this realm. I never intended on going back."

"You didn't?"

"No. My goal was to come here and save them." I stare at Bunny in the flickering torch-light. His glasses reflect the flame. "Do I have your trust, Bunny?"

"Yes."

"Good. Then get ready to earn back mine."

45

CLINTON

I feel rather than hear the shifting of rock against stone. I spin, looking down the passage behind me. It's pitch black and I know instinctively that Morgan is no longer behind me. Neither is Bunny.

"Morgan?" I call. The only response is the echo of my voice.

I feel along the walls, searching for a hidden alcove or exit. The floor is clear. She didn't drop a thing along the way. I want to blame Bunny but I know that it's greater than him. Morgan has been calm and controlled since she saved us from the dungeons. She's changed since we've been gone.

Footsteps and heavy breathing meet me from the opposite direction. Dylan holds a torch and pushes it in my direction.

"She's gone," I confess. "Right from behind me."

"And Bunny?" Sam asks.

"Gone too."

Dylan's face clouds over and he kicks the wall, sending rocks flying. Damien begins examining the passage. When he finds nothing, he returns and says, "What did she say to you before you got in the tunnel? I saw her whisper something."

Three faces wait eagerly for my answer. I think back—it hadn't meant that much to me, I was too pissed about Bunny. Too worried about her.

"She said we needed to find—build--an army."

"Those were her last words?" Dylan asks.

"Yeah, I think so."

"Fuck," he mutters, running his hand through his hair.

"You think she's gone," Sam says. It's not a question. "She took off."

"She left me at home. Taking Anita with her—locking up Marcus in her cell. She's been different. Losing you all changed her. Her relationship with Hildi has been tense, and Hildi's partner, Andi, is sick. She feels responsible about more than just the virus. I have no doubt she think she can fix this on her own."

"If she can do it on her own, then why does she need us to gather an army?" I ask. "Why would she take Bunny and send us back home?"

Dylan's eyes shine in the torchlight, his cheeks hollow and sharp. "Because she knows she's going to lose."

46

MORGAN

"You knew all along it would come to this."

"I suspected as much," Bunny admits. "But it's never what I wanted."

"That's why you did what you did, you took everyone and locked me out. You didn't want me to come here, but the Queen wanted something and you thought you'd give her Anita."

"I needed you weak. Dylan, compromised." His eyes are on the stone floor when he says, "I won't let her destroy you."

"You tried your hardest—just in other ways."

He's silent.

"Why didn't you come to me? Tell me? Why did you think trickery was best?" I ask, watching him closely.

"Would you have listened? Taken the time away from the others?" The muscle in his jaw tics. I feel the bitterness rolling off him in waves.

"You don't understand me very well, Bunny. Don't blame me for your weakness. Your jealousy."

Knowing my Guardians are on their way back to The Nead frees me to focus on the plan ahead. Despite our tension, I give Bunny the specifics of how I want this to go down, handing him my sword and allowing him to bind my hands. We enter the castle through a grate on the floor hidden beneath a heavy woven rug. It's impossible not to ignore the wide swipe of blood covering the floors. Casteel's blood, if I had to guess.

"Go to the throne room," I say in a quiet voice. "Don't you dare hold back."

Bunny stands behind me. I feel his heart beating like a drum in his chest. He hates every part of this plan. It's risky, and the odds of us pulling it off are slim. Even if we do, it's unlikely we'll both make it out alive.

I've only seen the throne room in my dreams. The entry is huge and arched, stone pillars flanking the open double doors. The Queen is holding court even as her prisoners get away and her fierce commander bleeds out elsewhere in the castle. The voices inside sound strained, like false merriment. I'm not surprised. These people fear for their lives. Their entire existence is to humor the Queen. Soldiers spot us before we've even made it to the lush purple carpet acting as an aisle.

"Stop!" One of the men yells.

Bunny does as he's told. "I've caught a prisoner of the Morrigan's trying to escape."

He looks me up and down. Bunny holds the sharp blade so close to my throat I feel the edge against my skin. The soldier steps forward and lifts up my chin. The instant he sees my face he steps back, muttering a prayer to a god I've never heard of.

A second soldier tries to force me from Bunny's hands but my Guardian hisses disapproval. "No. I caught her. I'm turning her in. You won't take the glory for my prize."

I don't know what his expression looks like, but it must be enough because they both back off. Bunny straightens, yanking me with him, and leads me down the center of the massive throne room. We've clearly interrupted celebrations of some sort, and the people eating and drinking at the tables dispersed throughout the room come to a quick and abrupt halt, words frozen on their tongues.

Until I pass and they get a good look at my face and the whispers begin.

Who is that?

Who is that girl?

Where did she come from?

That man? I've seen him before!

All their questions come in a hurry, hushed and quiet as though they fear retribution.

The music near the throne never ends, not until the Queen herself looks up. I've waited so long for this moment, to meet her face to face. To see the woman that haunts my dreams, orchestrates my moves and dominates my life.

We lock eyes and for a moment I can do nothing but stare at the woman I share a soul with.

I'm shocked at her youth, at the lack of any lines on her face. No scars or blemishes. She's physical perfection, and although I see the resemblance, I'm nothing but a human duplicate. Sure, power runs through my veins, helped by my immortal lovers, but the Morrigan is a warrior on her own. She doesn't need anyone else to make her strong.

Or at least, that's what she wants everyone to think. She takes the elixir from underground to keep her young and virile.

There's another person on the dais that I recognize and I have to force away any reaction: Anita. She sits directly next to the Queen, in a smaller, less magnificent throne. There's no denying who should be in the empty seat on the Queen's other side, most likely set out in celebration for the ceremony Casteel mentioned. The one where we join.

I sense the presence of the weapon Bunny shoved in the back of my pants, refusing to leave me unarmed. It was foolish. I regret it now. She'll detect it immediately.

"What do we have here?" she asks, staring down at us from her massive, obsidian throne. Her eyes are deep pools of hate and anger. I force myself to hold contact. "Where is Casteel?"

"There's been a breach," Bunny says. "Casteel has been injured. Your prisoners are gone."

"Gone?" She doesn't blink.

"Yes," I say. "And I would be gone too if I hadn't taken the time to hunt down this little worm."

She watches us carefully. "You bested her?"

"Yes," Bunny replies. "She was distracted."

A wide, deranged grin splits the Morrigan's face, making her look like a jester or clown. She leans forward, laughter on the tip of her tongue, and she says, "I felt them. I felt them together. Their power and strength, it shook the castle like an earthquake. I know about Casteel. What do you think this celebration is for? It's a death watch, you see. He failed me miserably and when he finally bleeds out for good, we'll dance on his grave."

The audience cheers and everything about the moment is perverse and wrong.

She tilts her head. "Do you really want to tell me you bested her at the height of her strength?"

"I did, just like I stole her Guardians out from underneath her. Just like I opened the gates over and over again without her understanding or notice."

The Morrigan thinks this over, resting her chin on the back of her hand. "So tell me, Fallen Guardian, what am I to do? Reward you for delivering back what is mine? Punish you for allowing the others to escape? I'm not exactly sure what is happening here."

There's a pause, the entire audience is waiting for what comes next, but not even I am sure what will happen. I reach for the hidden blade and slip out of Bunny's grip. I toss him to the ground, punching him twice in his confused face, and then hold the dagger to his throat. Staring at the Morrigan, who is watching the scene like a patron at the theater, I flick my wrist, allowing the spikes to extend on one hand. She doesn't react to the move but I know she's impressed.

I press down on his chest, curving my nails like spoon to dig out his betraying heart. Without looking at the queen, I say, "You're right. I let him catch me to give the others time to get back to the other realm. They're on a ticket provided by the Shaman back home. I needed them out of here and it was easier to trick them than to kill them."

"Why?" she asks. The soldiers are inches away. "Why would you do all of this?"

"Because this is about me and you, Your Highness. It always has been, don't you think?" She doesn't look convinced. I nod at Anita. "I delivered the Third. Why would I bring her here if I didn't plan to unite with you?"

The Queen looks down at Bunny, who is frozen under the points of my blades. "What about him?"

"Kill him, hang him from the trees, use him for target practice." I spit in his face. "But you may want to thank him first."

"And why, exactly, would I do that?"

I stare down at Bunny, not having to make up an ounce of the anger and venom I feel just looking at his face. Rage rolls across every inch of my body and I make no effort to hide my emotions. "When Bunny betrayed me, I finally understood everything you went through. I felt what it was like for you that day, eons ago when your wrath took hold."

The Morrigan moves, slinking down the dais to stand before me. Her dress is tight and long, fabric trails behind her like snakes slithering across the carpet.

"Tell me what you felt."

"He was my mate. He used me. He humiliated me. He…"

"No!" Bunny shouts, his face red. "You favored the others. You never cared about me like you cared for them."

Quick as a viper I slap him across the cheek, my nails scraping the skin and leaving red, angry welts. I stand and face the Queen.

"The pain from what he did…it's too much. The anger…is consuming."

"Even with the love of the others?" she asks. "I know you fornicated with them earlier today. Your pleasure radiates off you, even now."

"To get them to leave and to build my power." I glance at Bunny, who hasn't moved even though I've released him. "And to make him jealous."

She stares at me for a long moment and then jerks her head. "Take her to my quarters. We'll see if she's telling the truth."

The soldiers move quickly, surrounding and unarming me. "What if I'm not?" I ask.

The Morrigan shrugs and waves Anita to join her. "It doesn't really matter one way or the other. You're here. You're unprotected. Your world is crumbling as we speak." She steps toward me, so close I can see the faintest cracks beneath the surface. A piece of gray hair. The thinnest of wrinkles. She smiles, linking one arm with Anita and one with my own. I fight the urge to recoil at her touch. "This way will be a lot more fun."

47

MORGAN

The room is similar to my other one, but up in the highest floors of the castle along the same corridor as the queen. Just before I enter the room, Anita slips into her own chambers, adjacent to mine. I pause, noting that a soldier remains outside her door. I have no doubt mine will be guarded as well.

This one, unlike the other, has an arched window. I walk over and take a look out. The barren landscape of the Otherside sprawls for miles. Nothing but death and decay exists where the eye can see. I lean out, smelling the sulfur and rot, and know this is what the Morrigan wants to do with my world. Trash it with hatred and bitterness. Little does she know that miles underground, life and love and happiness flourishes.

She's not as powerful as she thinks she is.

I flick my wrist, extending my nails. But that's not all. The black mists that the Morrigan controls slither from my hands and around my ankles. With the strength of my men rolling through my veins and the conviction of an entire realm at my back, all I have to do is hold her off, keep her appeased until my Raven Guard can return with an army.

Then, we will be prepared to take this world back and stop her reign of terror, once and for all.

MIDNIGHTS END

One for sorrow,
Two for mirth
Three for a funeral,
Four for birth
Five for Heaven
Six for Hell
Seven for the devil, his own self

1

DYLAN

Dawn breaks over Central Park, bringing light after another sleepless night. The Raven Guard is nearly whole, but the impact of the events in the Otherside is worse than when Bunny lost use of his wing. We're lame and incomplete, lacking a member that may never return, and painfully missing our queen.

Our mission is clear: heal the sick, build an army. Both were directives Morgan declared before she abandoned us, slipping away in the Otherside's core. None of us believe she was taken against her will. No, Morgan has a mind of her own, a plan she has chosen not to share with us, and as her loyal Guardians we have little choice but to do as we're told.

She needs us now more than ever.

"How the hell are we going to find an army?" Damien asks across the room. I listen as my brothers bicker over the same argument. Who does she expect us to recruit? How do we know who to trust? How long can she wait? What if we're too late?

"I'll make a list," Sam says. "We have allies."

Clinton replies in a low growl. "Do we? People we trust?"

I watch him closely. He's been jaded since his time in the

dungeons. Paranoid. If he hadn't had healing time with Morgan... only the gods know what mental state he'd be in now. Unfortunately, he's right. Now that the three parts of the Darkness are together, sides will be taken. Those who want the apocalypse on the Earth realm, and those who will fight with us to stop it.

"Make a list of who we need to approach," I tell Sam. "We'll find enough warriors to return with us."

"And if we don't?"

A shadow passes by the door and all of us look toward it. We aren't alone in the house. Hildi is here. Sue and Davis helped remove the corpse of her partner Andi moments before our return. We were too late with the cure, at least to spare her life. Adding another layer of grief in the house is hard to manage.

Sam's question still lingers, waiting to be answered.

I take one last look out the window at the cloudless, blue sky outside. It's the exact opposite of what Morgan will see from the Otherside. Turning to face my brothers, I declare, "Then we go back and fight alone."

2

MORGAN

The strings tighten, pulling hard against my waist.

"Ouch," I say, grunting through the discomfort and pain jabbing into my ribs. "Is this really necessary?"

"You've been invited to a formal dinner with the Morrigan and her court," Nevis says, pushing her knee into my back for leverage. I buckle, but the corset doesn't allow me to move far. "This is considered appropriate dress."

"She must plan to kill me in this. Because there's no way I can defend myself while wearing this wretched thing."

Nevis replies with final hard yank.

Truthfully, the gown is exquisite. The fabric is a dark blue silk, embroidered with tiny gold stitching. The hem grazes the floor and the skirt is fluffed out with thick crinoline. A glance down reveals that my breasts are an asset I'd never fully realized. Just seeing the whole outfit, along with my carefully arranged hair and makeup, in the mirror brings me to a halt.

I'm not here to win beauty pageants or attend royal dinners. I'm here to kill the queen, destroy the three and go home with my Raven Guard to live happily ever after.

That's the only fairy tale I want.

Nevis, on the other hand, has other plans.

"Her primary weakness is your sexuality. The way you've embraced it and your harem of lovers, her former soldiers. Your connection with them drives her mad. But most of all, it gives you strength. And you must play to your strong points over the next three days."

The Morrigan announced that the binding ceremony will take place in three days. Apparently the best time to perform such magic is during the three full moons. Once the spell and ceremony take place, Anita, the Morrigan, and I will join together into one badass queen.

Oh, and then we'll conquer the Earth realm by spreading plague, death, and destruction, just like the Morrigan did in her own world all those years ago.

At least, that's her plan. I have another. Well, sort of. It's being formulated and relies heavily on my guardians returning with an army, Nevis and her underground dwellers, and Bunny.

Yes, I'm relying on Bunny, my conflicted and confused guardian, to take down the Morrigan. What possibly could go wrong?

"So, what?" I ask Nevis, who can't stop staring at my ample cleavage. "I'm supposed to flaunt my tits and she'll back down?"

"No," the woman says, rolling her eyes. She'd been assigned to me when I first arrived, and she saved me from a violent assault from Casteel, the Morrigan's commander. I learned soon after that she was part of an entire underground community that had lived and prospered after the Morrigan ravaged their world eons ago. Nevis is clever and knows the Queen well. She has spies everywhere, and although it's uncomfortable to treat her as my slave, we both know it's for a greater good. "It will unnerve her and reinforce the fact she can never get over the Cu's rejection. That betrayal consumes her every moment and every deed."

"Won't that just make her angry?" The last thing I want is to end up in the dungeons. "And seriously, that girl needs to get over it."

"She's already angry. Your strength—your sexuality—is something she desires more than anything else. Think of how strong she would be with the true love of her own lover, much less a harem? Her jealousy will keep her focused on the ceremony and taking that strength for herself while giving us time to get ourselves in order."

I nod, hoping she's right. And I hope my Guardians return in time.

Taking one last look at myself in the mirror, I tug up the bodice of my dress, hoping to cover my chest a little better. Nevis steps forward and yanks it right back down. I sigh and hope I can get through the meal without passing out from the tight corset.

"Okay then, dinner. Anything else I should be prepared for?"

Nevis looks like a young woman but is much older. The healing springs below the castle keep her youthful but she has the wisdom of decades of life. Her eyes are steel, holding mine steady as she delivers her final directive. "One small thing."

"What's that?"

"You're going to have to forgive Bunny."

3

MORGAN

"It's not possible." The words come out in a low hiss, as we've left my quarters and are walking down the hall. Nevis is three steps behind me, partially because of her height. The rest is due to the fact she's my servant and shouldn't walk near me anyway. At least, that's what she says. I'm not well-versed in slave/prisoner etiquette.

Nevis doesn't reply and keeps her eyes trained on the ground. Two guards walk within striking distance and I know I should keep my mouth shut, but forgive Bunny?

Hell. No.

Just thinking about it makes my blood turn to a raging boil.

We arrive at the main hall and the doors open wide, revealing two long tables down the side of the room and one up on a dais, overlooking the floor. Three ornate chairs wait in the middle. There's little doubt one of those is for me.

Although the soldiers are nearby, I'm not in shackles. There are no weapons pointed at me (at least that I can see) but a wave of panic rolls over me when I spot Anita coming down the hall toward us. I reach for my blade normally tucked by my side and come up with nothing but a handful of silk.

"Oh here we go," I mutter to myself, because only the gods know what kind of mindset she's in today.

"Hello, Morgan," she says, swishing my way in a beautiful gown of her own. The fabric is in a similar cut to my own, but instead a deep emerald green that looks flattering with her blonde hair. We assess one another, physically as well as mentally. Despite her smile, I catch the tic in her left eye.

I grunt in reply.

The third piece of the Morrigan's puzzle is Anita. Her twin, Xavier, was a sacrifice to the Morrigan when our bond allowed the plague to slip from me to him. After his death, Anita took the virus from me and passed it along the citizens of New York before I caught and imprisoned her. Her connection to the Morrigan gives her immunity, but it also simply makes her a pawn.

She deserves death for what she's done but neither the Morrigan nor I can take her life. Not yet. We need her for the ceremony. My only hope is once her usefulness is over, I can slit her throat myself.

My murderous thoughts must be evident on my face, as a small cough and nudge from Nevis makes me snap my eyes to the room. All eyes are on the two of us and we line up, side by side, and walk down the black rug that leads to the main table.

Four huge stone fireplaces sit against the walls with massive fires burning in them to take the chill off the room. Tapestries hang from the ceiling, each emblazoned with images from long ago battles. The one commonality is the dark raven flying across the sky in each and every one.

"So they're letting you walk around without chains?" Anita asks, glancing around at the dozens of soldiers that flank the walls of the room. She gives the one closest to us a flirtatious smile and he stands a little straighter. "I guess most of these guys have good aim."

"Seems like you'd be a little nicer to me since I got you a free ride back to this hellhole," I reply. The men and women sitting at the tables lining the aisle watch us like celebrities on the red carpet. Many smile. A few narrow their eyes. I don't understand these people and the world the Morrigan has built for herself. Do they even know what they're missing?

"I do appreciate that," Anita whispers. "Although I do wonder how angry your little birds were when they realized you bailed on them."

I cut her a glance. We're approaching the dais, where two servants in fine clothing each extend an arm, directing us to walk away from one another and around the back of the table. Before we part, I grab Anita by the arm and she stops, studying me.

"Never speak of my Guardians again."

The smallest curve graces her lips and she nods, knowing she hit me on a sore spot. I push back my shoulders and walk up the steps, holding my hem from the ground. The instant we step behind our seats a call breaks through the crowd, echoing off the stone walls.

"All stand for the Queen of Ravens," the voice announces.

The response is instant, something I've never seen outside of a movie. People scramble to their feet, dropping their drinks to the table, scuffing the floor with their chair legs. Soon the entire room is on their knees, everyone including Anita.

A sharp jab to the back of my knees with the butt of the nearest soldier's blade forces me down as well.

She arrives in a wave of frigid air, magic in her every step. There's a darkness, an ancient power that I have tasted more than once, and the link between us begs to drink from her well of energy once again.

I swallow back the desire, seeking the peace and control my Guardians taught me to draw from. After my healing session with three of them at once and days of repeated fueling with Dylan before I arrived in the Otherside, I am strong, but just being in her presence makes me feel weaker.

The Morrigan is a stunning woman. Her hair is long and sleek, her body curvy and strong. Her eyes are the darkest obsidian, filled with eons of wisdom, rage, and death. There's evidence that she maintains her youth from the water that flows beneath the castle, and there is no doubt that everyone in the room worships her as much as they fear her.

That's when I spy the man behind her.

Bunny.

Sweet, sexy, kind, and artistic Bunny.

My betrayer.

My savior.

My...I-don't-know-what-to-do-with-him-Guardian.

As much as I hate the way the Morrigan makes me feel, dammit, Bunny makes me feel worse. Just seeing him standing there is like a punch in the gut, or really, like he's reaching across the long table and ripping my heart out with his bare hands.

"*Forgive Bunny.*" That's what Nevis said back in the room. He watches me now, his copper eyes taking me in. Despite my anger with him, the spark flares between us—he is one of my mates, after all —which is why his betrayal cuts to the bone.

There's little to no chance I'm forgiving him. Not in this realm or any other. Not for what he did to me, the risk he exposed our world to, and certainly not for what he did to the other Guardians.

The Morrigan slithers across the dais, her eyes gliding past Anita and then me. Her chair is held out and in moments she's sitting above the rest of the room, waving her hands as an indication to sit.

I stare at her, my jaw hanging because I cannot understand this world.

The Morrigan glances at me and says, "Sit, and shut your mouth. A fly will get in there."

I regain my senses. "I doubt flies live in such an icy realm."

Her black eyes penetrate me and I feel the cold, not only on my skin, but in my heart. "It's unfortunate you're only here for the three days, Nemain, we could have had such fun together."

"Nemain?" I ask, hardly aware of the servants loading the table with food. The spicy scents fill my nostrils and my stomach rumbles with hunger. "What does that mean?"

"Long ago, that was your name." She cocks a smile at me. "Mine is Anand, by the way. I'm assuming that your Sentinel never told you. God forbid he humanize me in any way." When I look confused, she laughs. "The Morrigan is my title."

"What about her?" I ask, looking over at Anita.

"Macha," the Queen replies. "Once upon a time, we were three strong." She looks out the window at the rising moon. "Soon, it will happen again."

Wine is poured and I help myself to a full glass. I watch as our plates are filled and forgo paranoia over the strange meal and dig in. The meat is tasty although of a mystery origin, and I don't dare ask what sort of animal it's from.

Bunny sits at the end of the table, just below ours. It's obvious The Morrigan—or Anand—wants him in my line of vision. She watches us, small evil smiles gracing her lips as we avoid one another. I finally turn to her and say, "Why didn't you kill him?"

She looks down at Bunny with sad apathy. "I admit he's useless as a warrior, but his skills in the magical arts are extraordinary. It would be a waste to dispose of him."

Bunny stares between the two of us. I'm unsure if he can hear our conversation. Anand tilts her head and says, "On the other hand, if you wanted to kill him, be my guest."

Bunny's wide eyes confirm that yes, he can hear our discussion.

"Me?"

"Far be it for me to judge a woman scored. I've burned a swath of revenge across this entire land. Bunny's sins are his to contend with and yours to execute." She takes a sip of wine. "But if I were you, I'd enjoy a slow and painful death."

Anita laughs, choking on her wine, finding the entire thing hilarious. Three days with these lunatics, then I can take them down once and for all.

From his spot at the lower table, Bunny makes eye contact and I hold his gaze, unwilling to look away. My rage is palpable. My heart destroyed. The Morrigan knows me better than I assumed because slow and painful is exactly how I'd fantasized his death would be.

4

BUNNY

Sitting in such proximity to Morgan is unbearable. So much so that the instant the Queen is distracted I escape the grand hall, bolting for my castle tower studio for a moment of peace.

I pass few people on the way to my studio, most still enjoying the entertainment and revelry of the banquet. The soldiers pay me little attention. They see me as nothing more than a pawn, a way to help the queen get her way, and I'm well aware she only keeps me around for my abilities.

Oh, and a reason to taunt Morgan.

Gods above, Morgan.

Seeing her in that dress, the way it accentuated all of her delicious curves, her presence, her beauty made men stop and stare at her. There was no doubt why The Morrigan needed her to bond. She was the epitome of youth and life.

I wasn't sure what would happen when she saw me, if she'd leap over the table to throttle my neck, but the feeling the magic spark between us. The fates know we are still destined, but what I've done complicates things.

Actions can carry more weight than even fate.

I step into the room and busy myself with reigniting the dwindling fire. The wood takes a minute to catch and I lean back on my heels and watch the flame lick around the edges. Once I successfully captured Morgan and turned her over, I was rewarded with a bundle of firewood and a roll of new canvas. I eagerly used the wood while I was unsure what she wanted me to do with the canvas. There's little doubt she'll tell me when she's ready.

The heat warms my small tower room but not the ice in my chest. If looks could kill...there's no doubt Morgan would have slashed my throat with her dinner knife. I knew she was angry, but I'd hoped that working together to get the other Ravens back home and initiating the plan to end the Morrigan would bring us back together and I could attempt to salvage something between us.

Maybe not what it had been before, but at least perhaps she would listen to my apology. But no, we seem past that.

I don't blame her.

And I don't blame my brothers.

The blame lands squarely on my shoulders. I allowed my insecurity, jealousy, and lack of faith in Morgan and the others to put us all at risk. I stand and walk over to the canvas and pick it up one-handed and then roll it across the floor. I stand over the beige fabric and flick the blade from my razor open, thumbing the sharp edge.

I'll have to figure out another way to get Morgan to forgive me, not only because I want her to understand but because there's no way for her to win against the Morrigan without me.

Until then, I consider, kneeling on the floor and scoring the canvas with the blade. I'll cope like I always do. Deep within my art.

5

MORGAN

When The Morrigan finally releases us from her never-ending dinner party, I'm past tipsy and on the way to drunk. The wine here is strong, the food salty, and the company unbearable. Nevis escorts me back to my room and I proceed to blabber about my thoughts on everything.

"You'd think, with so much power, the Queen would pick a nicer place to live. Somewhere with central heating and carpets on the rugs. Running water. Electricity."

We pass a window that looks out onto the desolate landscape. "And a place near the sea. That's warm. Why not Florida?"

I stumble over the hem of my dress and Nevis grips my arm to hold me upright.

"And Bunny? Did you see him? With his messy bronze hair and those adorable glasses?" I scoff. "I want to punch him in those pretty little lips."

She stops in front of my chambers and I sway back and forth before leaning against the wooden door.

"He hurt us so bad," I tell her in a whisper. "Sent my mates to the dungeons to be terrorized and beaten. Separated us, divided us to make me weaker—all for *her*. I can't forgive him."

"Are you sure of his motives?"

"I don't need to know his motives, Nevis. I saw what he did to the others. What he did to me the last time we were together. I feel my pain and I healed the wounds of my guardians. Forgiveness isn't an option." The wine swirls in my belly. "If anything, he deserves what the Morrigan suggested. Death."

Nevis opens the door to my room and nudges me in. With assistance I make it to the bed, where I push her hands away. Lying face down, the feather pillow envelops me and I grip the mattress. The spinning room finally slows.

"Go away." I tell her as she starts to help me undress. "I just need to lie here. Just sleep. Now."

"Morgan."

"Go."

I'm half asleep by the time the door clicks shut.

6

CLINTON

Cirice pushes the two bottles of ale across the bar and wipes up the wet droplets left behind with a towel. She studies them with her vivid green eyes, the gold flakes sparkling.

I swallow half the ale in one gulp and Sam drowns the whole bottle. It's been a long day.

"Didn't know if I'd see either of you back in here again," the bartender says. Sam pushes his empty bottle toward her and she slides him another. She nods at me. "What about you Clint?"

I guzzle the rest and wipe my mouth. "I'm fine."

I'm here to assess the crowd, not get trashed. Scanning the crowd, I spot a few familiar faces. The Shaman's table is empty and as much as I hate it, he's the one I'm here to see.

"Word in the alley is that you guys came back without Morgan," Cirice says.

Sam puts down his bottle. "What else did you hear?"

"That you left the prisoner of the Morrigan but came back free men—carrying a cure to the sickness plaguing the city. But you left your girl *and* one of your guard behind. What gives?"

"How the hell did you hear all that?" I growl.

"Part of the job." She shrugs and the neon lights behind the bar shine off the top of her smooth head. Her ears point slightly and her canines are a tiny bit elongated. I've heard she's from a fae realm but that's outside my concern or worry. "But you obviously came here for something. Want to tell me what it is?"

Sam and I share a look, but we both know we're short on time. Dylan estimates we have three days before the phase of three moons turns full, and that is when the Morrigan will have her ceremony.

"We need fighters. Allies. Anyone willing to go back to the Otherside and fight the Morrigan."

Her slim eyebrow arches. "You want an army?"

"As many as we can get."

She holds my eye and I feel like she's digging into my soul. I don't know what Cirice's power is, if she's gifted in any way, but from the warm charge rolling down my spine there's no doubt there's more to her than appears.

Leaning over the counter she says, "I met your girl—the human. She's strong. Went head-to-head with the Shaman and it seems like maybe she won."

I keep my face neutral. We never asked how she managed to get us all in and out of the Otherside—even using the tunnel underground. There are rules—balances between the realms. Passage doesn't come lightly.

"What's your point, Cirice?" Sam says.

"Morgan is powerful. She's smart but she's also naïve. You have to go into the Morrigan's castle fully loaded. You don't just want people in your army. You want fighters. The best." She looks between us. "People like yourselves."

An uneasy feeling emerges in my stomach. "What are you thinking?"

The gold in her eyes twinkles. "You need the Legion of Immortals."

Sam's jaw drops. "The Six?"

"No." I hold up my hands. Full stop. No.

"Without them, you'll lose the war."

"With them will cause chaos and we'll all probably die before we even get to the battle," I snap back.

She rests her hands on her hips. "You know I'm right. And you know they're exactly what you need."

"Too bad it's impossible," Sam says. "The Shaman owns their contract. I don't think he's going to hand them over easily."

"Nothing is impossible." The knowing look on her face says it all. "You just have to be willing to fight for it."

7

MORGAN

At some point during the night the walls and floors stop spinning and I fall into an uncomfortable, light sleep. My head pounds at any movement and the sun peeking in the arched, lead glass window makes my brain want to shatter into a million pieces.

"Here," a voice says. "Drink this."

I crack an eye through the sharp, spiking pain and see Nevis standing over me with a glass of water.

"Is that the good stuff?" I ask.

"Straight from the source. You'll feel better soon."

After three attempts to sit up on my own, Nevis has to help me, navigating the cup near my mouth. I take a sip of the cool water and lie back again.

"God, what happened last night? I just remember lots of wine, loud music, and the Morrigan freaking me out."

"That about sums it up, although there was the interesting part about the Morrigan trying to get you to kill Bunny."

I search my memory but mostly I come up with the image of Bunny sitting at the foot of the dais looking handsome and out of my reach. Another sip of water and my brain fog clears and I do recall the faint whispers of The Morrigan, Anand, as she called herself, taunting me with the option to take Bunny out myself. The thought, along with the gallons of wine in my belly makes me nauseous.

I look at Nevis and concede, "If you want me to forgive him and the Queen wants me to kill him, I have to trust that one of you may have a better plan in mind."

Nevis grins. "I hoped you would come around to seeing that."

Tears prick to my eyes. "Even though it may not seem like it, I do wish I could forgive Bunny. Wash it all away and make him pure again like this water." I hold up the glass. "But what he did...it was awful. Unforgiveable."

Nevis leans over and pushes my hair out of my eyes. It's a motherly move and in this moment I appreciate it. I'm away from home, without family, and sick. I'm also about to have to make a decision that could alter my life and those of my mates forever.

"I still think you should talk to him and find out why he made his decisions."

"But..." I swallow back my words and wipe the tears from my eyes.

Nevis frowns. "But what?"

Many of the emotions I've been carrying for days erupt in one emotional purge. "What if I forgive him and the others hate me for it? What if he's truly evil and it's all just a game. I'm just a pawn. They put me through tests before. What if I fail this one?" The words tumble out in between sobs. "And then there's the other side of this. What Bunny did to me was wrong and the risk he put the whole world in is unspeakable. But what he did to the other Ravens was more than I can absolve him for. I can't make that decision."

Nevis wraps her arms around me, bringing me in tight to her chest. If someone walked in on us right now I have no idea what the punishment for her or for me would be, but I don't care. I take the chance and embrace her back.

"I want you to look at something," she says in my ear. We part and I wipe my nose again on the bedding before following her to the dressing chamber. A long mirror leans against the wall and Nevis positions me so I'm standing directly in front of it. I'm in the dress from the night before. It's wrinkled as all hell. My ribs hurt from the corset as much as the crying. My face is streaked with black kohl and my hair looks like a bird's nest after a tornado.

"If you want me to look at a hot mess, I've got it. Thanks."

Her hand clasps mine and she smiles. "You may look a little worse for the wear, but there's more."

"I'm not sure I can handle any more, Nevis."

"In two days you're slated to either succumb to the Morrigan or take over. What I see in the reflection is the future Queen of both realms. The Queen of Ravens—and not the Goddess of War. If you fight through the obstacles in your way you can shine a light on this world. We need you. My people need you. Your Guardians need you." She runs a hand down my hair. "That includes Bunny. And to accomplish what you need to do to make that happen you need his help, too."

"But what about—"

"You're the Queen. You make the decisions." She touches the charm hanging between my breasts. "They are here to follow you. They trust you. And it's time for you to repair the damage between you and Bunny."

The idea leaves a sour taste in my mouth. "What if I don't want to?"

Her lips tug into a frown. "Then I'm afraid you aren't ready and it may be another millennium before we have the chance to break free from the Morrigan's reign of terror."

I'm at least a foot taller than Nevis and wearing an impressive gown. I'm young and have strength and power that I'd never expected in life, but this woman next to me seems so much stronger.

"I'm not sure if I can do it," I admit.

"You have two days to figure it out."

8

DAMIEN

"No," Dylan says. There's zero wavering in his voice. The problem for him is he's not the actual leader of the group. We all get a vote and from the set of Clinton's jaw and the tension tugging at Sam's eyes I know Dylan is not going to get his way without a fight.

I sigh and start what is sure to be a fight. "Cirice has a good point, these guys are the best. Well, other than us, but it would be better to go in with a small, solid team than with less skilled soldiers."

"They're savages," Dylan argues. "They spent centuries working directly under Camulus. His special team. They raped, pillaged, and burned their way through history."

"But these six were cast out because of their refusal to fight for Camulus in the modern era," I say. "The War God sold them into slavery as punishment and they've been under lock and key with the Shaman ever since. Maybe they've changed?"

"Or maybe they're worse than before," Clinton adds. "I, too, am worried about bringing them into the battle on the Otherside, they could easily betray us as well."

"Not if they're bound," Sam says. "We could try to win their contract."

Dylan narrows his eyes at our brother. "You want to be slave owners? I never thought I'd hear those words from you."

"I don't want to own them, but I would like to control them on the battlefield. Once the war is over we can determine their fate."

I think on it for a moment. The lives we've led and how we died and were remolded by the gods to serve the world in another way. How that time of service is now upon us. It's with that in mind that I say, "Maybe we owe them an opportunity to redeem themselves. We were given a second chance."

Dylan sighs and paces the length of the library. Being away from Morgan for this long is taking a toll on all of us. The worry. The fear. Our bond is tight. The healing between us bolstered us all in a way we'd never experienced before but even so—we are made to be a team. A unit. All of us with our mate, and leaving her behind doesn't feel right.

Finally he stops and runs his hand over his hair, leaving it in small, messy spikes. "Even if we agree to this, we have to actually procure the contract. The Shaman's fee will certainly be heavy. And costly. We already are tied to him with one debt."

The monthly fights. Adding to that debt would be a burden none of us want to bear. But even so, this is greater than the four of us.

"We're talking about the apocalypse, Dylan," Sam says. "We've spent our lives carrying the weight of the damned. One more isn't going to destroy us."

If we had to vote right now I suspect at least three of us would agree. We're desperate and most certainly running out of time. But I'm known for my impulsiveness. My willingness to take a risk. Without hesitation I say, "I'm in. Let's try to win the contract for the Legion of Immortals."

As expected, Sam and Clinton nod their approval. Dylan stares at the floor, knowing he's lost this argument. "Fine," he says. "But don't come to me to fix this when it all implodes, got it?"

We share a moment of understanding, because even though we promise we won't, we all know he's got our back—for better or worse—because that's how the Raven Guard operates.

9

MORGAN

After a bath to soothe my aching ribs, and a generous plate of eggs, bacon, and biscuits, Nevis helps me dress. My closet is filled with dresses and gowns. It feels weird wearing the Morrigan's clothing, like a lamb being dressed for slaughter, so I reach for the suit I wore from The Nead.

Nevis shakes her head. "Dress the part. Today, you're not a warrior. You're a guest of the Queen."

"A guest?" I snort. "I may not be in the dungeons, but I wouldn't call myself free."

I feel like a dick the instant I say it. Nevis is a slave and has been since birth. The Morrigan controls every aspect of her life, and the small part she doesn't is in the hidden underground community she's desperately trying to free. I reach for the nearest dress, a pale blue that has the shimmer of silver, and hold it up. "How does this look?"

"Lovely."

Nevis insists on taming my hair, using a hot iron to straighten my normally curly locks. She braids the top part so that it pulls away from my face. I'm marveling at her skills when there's a knock on the door.

Apprehension tickles my spine. I'm still reeling from the attack by Casteel. His behavior was vicious, and there's no doubt he'll be back for more once he recovers from the wound Dylan gave him.

Nevis steps forward and opens the door. Her shoulders visibly relax when she sees the courier in the hallway. He passes me an envelope stamped on the back with a wax seal. I fight the urge to laugh at the formality but it also only confirms I'm a stranger in a strange land.

I scan the card. After the courier leaves I say, "I've been summoned to the Morrigan's chambers. What do you think she wants?"

"Gods only know," she replies, bringing me a pair of soft slip-on shoes. "Just try to behave yourself, okay?"

I make a face. "I'll do my best not to get killed before my army arrives, if that's what you're saying."

Nevis smiles. "Precisely."

THE QUEEN's chambers are a level above mine and we pass through six different guards before we're allowed to enter. The first two take their time searching me for weapons. I don't blame them. Nevis had to convince me to leave the fork from breakfast on the table and not slipped into the stocking band around my thigh.

"Take your time," I hiss at one of the soldiers as his fingers linger over my waist. "Ask Casteel what happened when he took advantage."

The soldier freezes, turns pale, and abruptly steps away.

I'm not particularly surprised to find Anita on the other side of the double doors sitting on a plush, dark purple chair.

"Good morning, Morgan," she says, taking a sip of steaming tea. Her own servant stands against the wall and I recognize her from underground, although her expression is blank as stone.

"Anita." I take the seat next to her and ignore the tea.

"How did you sleep?" she asks, looking like a princess that grew up in this world. "I love these feather beds. I wish we could get something like that back home, you know?"

No. Really, I don't.

She doesn't stop, even though I say nothing to encourage her. "You drank like a champ last night. Should have told you the wine is stronger here. But their hangover tonic is to die for." She smooths out the skirt on her dress. "I really should thank you for bringing me back with you."

I fight the urge to grab her neck and snap it between my hands. Luckily, she's saved not only by my incredible self-restraint but by the Morrigan entering the room.

She's dressed to perfection in a black tunic and tight pants. The top is cut deep, revealing a large swath of pale, perfect skin. She looks better today than the night before and I wonder how much of the water tonic she took this morning to maintain her appearance. She sits, and her servant begins preparing her a cup of tea.

"Ah, Macha and Nemain. You both look lovely today." Her eyes linger over me as if she's searching for something—a crack or possibly a change of some kind. "I hope your quarters serve you well."

"Mine are fantastic, Your Majesty."

She smiles at Anita. "You always loved the creature comforts, dear sister." The Morrigan takes a sip from her cup and looks at me. "And how about you, Neman? Sleep well?"

"If you mean black-out drunk, then sure." I flash her a smile. "It was grand."

Her eyes narrow but the expression on her face doesn't change. "I called you here to explain the next few days. Last night was just the kick-off of our three day celebration leading up to the bonding ceremony. As you've seen, I've loaded your room with clothing and supplies to get you through a variety of events. All are optional but I suggest you take part in as many as you can. The members of my court and the citizens of my kingdom want a chance to see the women that will help me expand my reign from one world to the next."

"You want us on display?" I ask, trying to wrap my head around the details she's given. "Before you kill us to make yourself stronger."

The Morrigan tilts her head. "I'm not killing you, dear Nemain. We're fulfilling destiny. The fates have finally aligned. Anand, Macha, and Nemain all together on the full moons. We'll join as one and prevail over many worlds."

I open my mouth to tell her that she's deranged. Crazy. Out of her fucking mind, but a sharp look from Nevis keeps me quiet. For now.

"I'd like to proceed as though you are not prisoners here. I want you to have full access to the castle and surrounding grounds. I'll have an itinerary sent to your rooms so you can enjoy the festivities." She sets her cup on the table. Her dark eyes flick between us. "Understand you will be watched, and if you do anything to disrupt my plans, I'll shackle you in the dungeons."

"I, for one, cannot wait to join in the celebrations," Anita says.

"And you?" the Morrigan asks me.

"I won't cause any trouble," I tell her. I do not add that my guardians will do the damage for me. "In fact, I'm really eager to learn more about your kingdom. So far I'm very impressed."

The Morrigan thrusts her hand on the table and gestures for us to do the same. Anita places hers on top of the Morrigan's and I place mine on top of Anita's. The Queen lays her other hand on top, sandwiching us in. A hum of energy builds between our skin, something I've only felt with my guardians in the heat of passion. There's no denying the power charging between us. The current is strong, dark, and filled with a hunger and want like I've never experienced. It's like a shot of adrenaline. Endorphins. The most delicious drug I've ever experienced. I taste it on my tongue, feel it traveling up my arms, in my fingertips and throughout my entire body.

"Together, we can be a force beyond recognition. I hope you appreciate the opportunity I'm giving you." She lifts her hand, and like it was never there to begin with, the energy fades and immediately I miss the feeling of power coursing through my veins.

We're dismissed, and Nevis and I walk down the stone hallway back toward my rooms. Once we're out of earshot of the soldiers I grab her arm and say, "Take me to Bunny's chambers. Now."

10

DYLAN

My stomach is tight with dread as we enter the building. It's almost midnight and the earlier fights are already in process. The shouts and jeers from the crowd echo around the room and I glance back at my brothers—giving them one last chance to back out.

I'm met with three sets of determined eyes. Okay then. We're doing this.

The walkways are bottlenecked, but once we enter as a group, eyes shift our direction. We're not scheduled to fight tonight and rarely do we appear otherwise. I hear our name whispered through the crowd; the energy level rises significantly. They all suspect they're in for a surprise.

Little do they know.

"The Shaman should be down by the ring," Sam says. We break right, down the stairs and toward the ring where two female demons are in the throes of a death match.

The crowd parts, allowing us to pass. Our names are called and I hear my brothers speaking to people in the audience. I keep my eyes forward, focused. I'm not interested in friends. I'm interested in allies. It's the only reason I'm here.

When the Shaman senses our presence he glances up, making eye contact.

"You survived the trip to the Otherside," he says as we approach. His eyes flit over my brothers, searching for scars or wounds.

"With a little help, yes," I say. In the ring, one demon punches the other and a splatter of blood lands on the mat nearby. "Morgan obviously did not make it back over."

"She specifically asked for one-way passage. I wasn't sure if she got it for herself or one of you."

"You knew she was planning on staying?" Sam asks.

"She was well aware of the sacrifice she'd have to make for your safe return." He glances at the fights on the stage. "I hear you managed to bring back a cure."

"It's been delivered to the proper authorities," Clinton declares. None of us plan to reveal the source of the cure. "But hopefully the spread will end when a vaccine is made and delivered."

Admiration shines in the Shaman's eyes. "Your girl is tough. Follows through. I'm impressed."

"Well," I say, crossing my arms. "She still needs our help."

"Which is why you're here."

The buzzer for the fight sounds, thankfully, as one demon has decapitated the other and continued to bash her head on the blood-soaked mat. The fight isn't real. It's just a fantasy, but the result is still gruesome and will require a fair amount of cleanup before the next bout.

I turn back to the Shaman. "We're here to make you an offer."

The Shaman's mouth twists with interest and he leans against the stage. "I'm listening."

Clinton steps forward. "We're looking to buy the Legion of Immortals. We have cash, jewelry, or gold. Whichever you prefer."

Surprise flickers in his eyes. He waits a beat and strokes the small beard on his chin. "You know money doesn't interest me."

Damien sighs behind me. The money and gold was a wish—one we knew he wouldn't take. "But you're willing to sell their contract."

"Sell isn't the right word. I'll offer their contracts up as winnings."

I fight the urge to run. This man. Making a deal with him is like courting the devil. "What do you want? Another year of our service? Tack on another decade?"

"Let's make this interesting. If you beat the Legion of Immortals in the ring, I'll not only give you their contract but I'll tear up yours as well."

"And if we lose?" Clinton asks.

"I expand your contract for another fifty years." He pauses. "And the girl, too."

11

MORGAN

Nevis asks no questions as we hurry down the hall. The dark hole in the pit of my stomach expands as we get further away from the Morrigan.

"What was that?" I ask in a shaky voice that matches the tremor in my hands. "I mean, I know. I've felt it before but from far away. But up close..."

She leans in, clasps my hands and whispers, "The Darkness in the Queen is unmatchable. It's one of the reasons she needs to bond with you. Her body is wearing down, the power is taking a toll and unlike you, she doesn't have a harem of extraordinary beings to help balance her."

I don't tell her what I'm thinking. How my body already craves another hit of that raw power. I feel the tickle in the back of my throat and the twitch on my skin. We reach Bunny's door and she knocks, though I'm impatient and desperate enough that I would've barged right in.

There's movement behind the door and I tap my feet. Unable to wait a moment longer, I push past Nevis and fling open the door, just in time to find Bunny covering a painting attached to the wall with his one good hand.

"Morgan?" He wipes his hands on his paint-stained clothing. Looking me over, he frowns. "What's wrong?"

"Leave," I direct Nevis. The words come out harsh, like my frayed nerves. "Wait outside, please."

"Of course," she replies and walks out the door. I close it behind her and twist the lock.

"What are you doing here?" he asks, but it's clear he senses whatever is happening to me since the Morrigan shared her power.

"I need you, Bunny. If I'm going to make it through the next two days, I'm going to need your help."

"I've been waiting for your arrival," he says. "I've already told you I'm willing to do whatever it takes."

I don't want to hear his words right now. I need to feel the heat of his body next to me. I need his yin to my yang, the white to my black before whatever the Morrigan infected me with consumes me whole.

I step forward but he holds up his hands. "Wait. I don't know what this is but I definitely smell her on you." He walks to his work table and grabs a paintbrush and dips it in a jar of paint. He goes to the door and from memory, paints a large symbol on the wood in black.

"What is that?"

"A symbol that will cloak our energy. The one we create when we're together. She's highly sensitive to it and if she knows you're here..."

"Thank you," I say, feeling a wave of dark nausea roll through me. "I don't have a lot of time, Bunny."

He comes to me quickly, good hand clenched around my waist, holding me up. I feel the shift almost instantly. The balance. What brought me to these men in the first place. His beautiful face is close to mine, his soft lips, his conflicted eyes. He won't kiss me first. He's waiting for permission. An order. That's how much things have changed between us.

Another surge of darkness rocks me and I can't wait another moment. I press my lips to his, opening my mouth and drawing his tongue inside. A counter wave rolls over me. Goodness and light—I can't deny that is Bunny's core. He isn't evil. I've tasted that.

His hand does not move, although his fingers dig into my sides. I feel his hardness when he brushes against me. I feel his desire thudding in his chest. His lips move from my mouth down the column of my neck, edging across the expanse of my chest. My nipples harden and painfully point. My belly twists with a different, more carnal need.

This isn't the lost soul I've battled with. Bunny is strong. He's competent. He fulfills his duty like a soldier on a mission. My hands fall limp as he sucks at my neck, lathing my skin with his tongue.

Bit by bit, the Morrigan's darkness drains from me and when I'm seconds from crawling out of my skin with want, Bunny stops, withdrawing his mouth and blowing on the spot he'd focused on so intently.

"Don't move," he commands, leaving me and then returning with a small pot and an ultra-thin paintbrush. I recognize the gold shimmer of paint. It's the one he coated my body with at The Nead. With a steady hand, he quickly works over the heated mark. Standing back, he eyes his work with satisfaction.

"What is it?"

He holds up a mirror and although the paint is already fading, as well as the red of my skin, I spot the Raven Guard's symbol. "She thinks she can have you, Morgan, but you're already taken. That mark is just another bind to tie you to me."

A mixture of gratefulness and fear rises in me. It's the fear that speaks. "And what if I don't want to be bound to you anymore? What if I kill you like the Morrigan suggests?"

Bunny pushes his glasses up his nose, but any sign of the unsure Guardian is gone. There's no one here to back him up. He is the leader of my guard in this world. My only protector, and I realize now how much of this he planned—not to hurt me—but to end this with the Morrigan once and for all.

He gazes at my body, the one that just betrayed me so quickly and would have done anything to be closer to him. "I know I hurt you. I know the others want to skin me alive. But we're in this together and sometimes a sacrifice has to be made. Look at the Morrigan, sweetheart. Do you not see how her court will do anything for her? Xavier gave his life. Anita will give hers, and if you push me away, she'll take you, too. Everything about this world is a sacrifice. I'm just the only one willing to admit it."

"So you're saying all of this was for me. The mind-games and torture in the dungeons? Dividing everyone?" I shake my head, still unable to forgive like Nevis wants me to. "I think you just like pain, Bunny. You like taking it from me and inflicting it on yourself and everyone in your life."

His jaw tenses. "You're wrong. Open your eyes, Morgan. This is war, it isn't pretty and it sure as hell isn't without regret."

I hate the fact I taste him on my mouth. That I need him so desperately to survive the next few days. But I remember the wounds on Clinton's back. The way Sam's eyes were clouded and close to death. For them, I will work with Bunny, and for them, I will keep him at arm's length.

"Come back when you need me. I'll be here," he says as I spin on my heel and head to the door. Nevis waits on the other side; whatever she hoped would transpire in the studio falls from her face the instant she sees us.

I catch a glimpse of Bunny's face as I start down the stairs. I expect to see anger or even a little bit of hate, but I don't. I only see resolve and the smallest quirk on his lips. I throw a vulgar gesture his way and head back to my rooms.

12

CLINTON

"No," we all four say at once. Dylan shoots us a look and controls his rage. "Keep Morgan out of it."

The Shaman shrugs. Cleaners scrub down the mats so the fights can continue in a moment—if we get our way, we'll be up next. But right now the bargain is too high and the bastard knows it. "That's my deal. No offense, but without your full line-up, you're asking me for six warriors for the price of four."

"We can sign for Bunny," Sam says. "Five of the Raven Guard for six Immortals? Seems like a fair trade."

The Shaman laughs, his teeth white against his dark skin. Rings glint on his fingers. "You take me for a fool. Add in the girl and I'm game."

I grit my teeth. "Without the Legion, there may be no girl to return."

He waves his hands like it's no concern. I look to the others. There is no way we can barter with Morgan's life—her freedom. We're bound to protect her. And serve her. Not the other way around.

"I guess we come up with another plan," Sam says. Anger

mingled with defeat sparks behind his green eyes. We were so close to a solution. And so very close to running out of time.

"Or we just go on our own. We can challenge the Morrigan. We've done it before," Damien adds.

"And barely walked out alive," I growl, low under the sounds of the crowd. There's a murmur amongst the audience. Probably in anticipation of the next bout. They've no doubt been watching us and wondering why we're here. "Morgan specifically asked me to return with an army. I cannot disregard her wishes."

"You won't have to," a familiar voice says from the crowd. Looking up, I see Hildi pushing through the masses of people. Her eyes are ringed in red from grief.

"What are you doing here?"

"You need an army. I'm here to fight."

The Shaman stands and looks her up and down, a glint of excitement in his eye. "She can take the place of the girl. You five against the Legion. If you win, you take their contract and do with them as you like. If I win? I own you all for another half century."

We've made a makeshift circle and I thrust my hand in the middle, signaling my agreement to the bet. Damien follows, his tattooed hand on top of mine, Sam next, and then Dylan.

We look to Hildi and Dylan says, "It's your choice. Don't do this for us."

"I'm not doing it for me," the Valkyrie says, her voice thick with emotion. "I'm doing it for Andi."

He nods in approval and she places her hand on top. A stack of five warriors making a pact for our lives and freedom. A sacrifice risked for a better world. The Shaman's dark hand comes down on top and a flash jolts between us—tagging us as chips on the table.

"You have thirty minutes to prepare," he says, with a wicked grin. "I suggest you use it to pray."

13

MORGAN

Rejuvenated from my encounter with Bunny, I pick an option from the Morrigan's extensive list of activities surrounding the bonding celebration. Training exercises by the Morrigan's men. It seems wise to check up on the competition.

Nevis said nothing once I left Bunny's studio. It was clear I felt better physically while still warring with myself mentally. Whatever judgment she held, she kept to herself.

It felt wrong to use Bunny for his body. I mean, that was one of his betrayals. Using me for pleasure yet giving nothing in return. It had been one of the first signs something was wrong. Shouldn't I feel guilty for doing the same?

These questions linger as Nevis guides me through the castle and out the back patio where I'm met with humid, warm air. We're not outside—no, the climate is too harsh on the barren landscape surrounding the castle. This is more like a greenhouse—an enormous one with glass ceilings and walls that stretch as high and far as my eye can see.

Lush greenery climbs the walls. The scent of flowers mingles with the smell of straw, and I suspect livestock. It's an entire world here—much like the one underground--and as I look around I spot familiar faces from Nevis' home.

"What is this place?"

"It's how she stays alive. Her heart may be cold and her soul as dark as the nights, but to survive she must have nourishment and keep her soldiers and staff fed."

"Is it connected to your home?" I ask.

"Yes, the heat and water comes though pumps engineered by our people."

We walk through the maze of gardens that go for miles. Some are filled with flowers and trees. Others have vegetables and a few unidentifiable fruits. The sound of animals calls from the other end. I see a large deer-like animal with horns grazing on a patch of grass. When it looks up, I see it has three eyes and two tails, and I hold back a startled gasp.

"What?" Nevis asks.

"The animals here are not the same as back home."

She smiles. "I'm sure there are manyd differences."

We reach a terrace that looks over a valley below. The field is made of dry grass, and men in black uniforms are clumped together. Fear trembles through me when I spot a figure bellowing at soldiers.

Casteel.

"So he is alive."

"Dylan cut off his hand, but the healers were able to restore him to full capacity despite that."

"Bunny functions with only one hand—one arm, really. I doubt Casteel will slow," I say, watching him lash a whip at one of his men. From here, it looks like there are hundreds of soldiers, maybe more. I have no idea how Clinton and the others will raise an army large or skilled enough to take down the force below. I'm not even sure what to do with them when they arrive back.

Or if they will.

"Thank you for showing me around."

"Do you think it will be helpful?"

"I don't know. I'm sure the Queen added it to make me realize how powerful her army is. Just as she did this morning with the Darkness. It's all just here to keep me off balance. To question my abilities and make me heel."

"Yet you found a way around it this morning." Her comment is pointed.

"I won't give up," is all I say to her. "Not now. Not until the final moment, and I'll do what it takes to keep fighting."

14

SAM

Thirty minutes isn't much time to prepare but it's also just enough time to panic. Or maybe that's just me, I think, looking at my brothers and Hildi as we wait in the changing room.

"Any idea on how this will go down?" Clinton asks.

"I do," Hildi says. "I owed the Shaman for some gambling debts a few years ago. I paid them off by working the back. Including handling the Legion."

"What do you know about them?" Dylan asks. "I've only read about them in texts, as part of the greater mythology surrounding Camulus, the God of War. I've never seen them in person before."

"The Shaman doesn't use them for standard battles in the ring. He's more likely to send them to other realms looking for fighters to come to Earth. Where do you think he gets so many participants?"

Damien removes his rings and tapes his knuckles. "They're all in his debt, like us."

"Exactly. The Legion are different. They were tossed out of the Immortal army for refusing to continue their barbaric ways. The Shaman snapped up their contract and they've been in his service ever since."

"So they refused to stoop to Camulus' brutality. Isn't that a good thing?" I ask.

Hildi snorts. "They were part of an elite death squad. They had no civility. No moral code. They wreaked havoc and mayhem for centuries."

"Sounds like the kind of soldiers the Morrigan would love to get her hands on," Clinton says, standing and lacing his boots. "Too bad we'll get them first."

"Tell us anything you know," I say to Hildi and Dylan. We have ten minutes and I'd like to be as prepared as possible.

"The mythology states that Camulus traveled the world to find the strongest fighters for the Legion. Each were known for their heroic last stands—something that probably caught Camulus' attention. Most he collected on the battlefield, moments after their death. He granted them immortality and a spot in his special army. These soldiers cut a swath through the world with a particular kind of mayhem, but as we talked about, six men refused to continue and were released from Camulus."

"Who are they?" Clinton asks. From the set of his jaw I can tell he wants to know everything he can about his opponents.

Hildi sits on the bench next to the lockers. "They're a mixed lot. The one thing they have in common is a taste for blood. But to get it started, there's Miya. He's a Japanese swordsman who won his first duel at the age of twelve."

"So he was a prodigy," Clinton says.

"His opponent was a well-trained Samurai with a blade. Miya had a sharpened stick."

Damien winces. "Ouch."

"Then," she says, "there's Agis. He was known as the God of Death due to his refusal to die although severely injured. He kept fighting and allowed his army to get through."

"What army did he lead?" I ask.

Dylan looks at me. "The Spartans. For over a decade."

"Total badass, then," Damien says. Everyone nods.

"Next up, we have Roland."

"That's a wuss name," Clinton snorts.

Hildi rolls her eyes. "He was one of the twelve peers of Charlemagne, who we all know was a ball-busting general."

"So we have a Japanese sword-fighter, a Spartan, and an all-warrior," Clinton says in a strained voice. "Perfect. What's next?"

"Marshal, a famous knight known for sprees of murder and theft. On his deathbed, it was said that he bested over five hundred knights during his career, and took large swaths of land for his king," Hildi replies. "That just leaves Armin, a German strongman that was basically unstoppable and destroyed everything in his path, and Rupert, the child prince who ran away and joined the army at age fourteen. He was so good, people believed he had supernatural abilities."

"Did he?" I ask. I wouldn't put it past any of these men to have demon blood.

She shakes her head. "Not until he died."

"Great. How do we plan on defeating them?" I ask. "Because we have to defeat them. Not just for Morgan, but I don't want to work for that bastard out there for another fifty years."

Clinton stands just as the warning buzzer sounds from the ring. "We'll beat them like we've beaten every other opponent tossed our way. One at a time."

15

HILDI

The doors of the training room open and for a moment I'm struck still. The volume of the crowd hits me first, roaring like a freight train, so much that I almost recoil at the vibrations. But that's not what startles me. It's the arena that has replaced the old warehouse with metal bleachers soaked in beer and sweat. The stadium is wide and circular, the ground covered in sawdust and sand. The seats reach the ceiling, which is wide open, revealing a dark, starlit sky.

"Dear gods, what sort of witchery is this," one of the men behind me mutters. I look over and take in the sight of Dylan wearing traditional warrior armor, the thick coil of his whip hung at his hip. A ripple through the crowd brings me back to myself and I note the weight in my hand and lift the sword—a Valkyrie blade—and the heft of a shield on my back.

A quick glance shows me the others are outfitted similarly. Helmets, shields, chainmail linked over their broad, strong shoulders.

We're in a tunnel, the sort that leads to the center of the arena. The Shaman clearly saw fit to make a spectacle of our competition. Why not? The fight will become the stuff of legends. The sort

Morgan and Dylan will write in their history books for future generations.

All the more reason to be the victors.

The doors behind us close with a loud slam, the bolt thrown to ensure no escape. I came to this fight to do what is required to bring down the Morrigan. To force her to pay for what she took from me. The image of Andi's final breath is seared into my brain, my heart, and I felt the pain of the thousands of other deaths in the city before the cure made it into the right hands.

Morgan didn't fail me. Neither did her guardians. The Queen of Darkness must be tamed once and for all, and if that means bringing a crew of ruthless murderers into her realm, so be it.

"It's magic," I say as a reminder. Surely they know. It's not their first time in the ring nor experiencing the Shaman's mysticism. "We fight to the death."

"All six," Clinton grunts from behind a silver facemask. His gray eyes hold mine.

"I feel the eye of Odin with me," I tell them. "Thor's power flows through my fists. And Freya's lust for new souls in my blood."

There's no buzzer—not in this arena, but something louder—a gong--vibrates that the time has come. The Shaman appears in the middle of the stadium and he waves us forward, just as he waves his hand toward the opening on the other side of the field.

As though they appear from the ether, six magnificent males stride forward and the crowd falls into a hushed reverie.

Instinctively I grip my sword and I feel the others shift into a defensive position around me. I've seen the Legion before. Mentally, I understand their strength and immortality, but being on the ground with them, in their presence, even while surrounded by the strongest fighters created by the hands of gods, is humbling.

Miya's long black hair trails behind him. His goatee is trimmed and highlights the sharp lines of his jaw. His outfit is solid black. His feet are bare. Leather straps around his chest and the hilt of his sword juts over his shoulder.

Next to him strides the God of Death, Agis, carrying a metal helmet adorned with a razor sharp spike across the top. He's clad in a tight leather tunic and pants, thick-soled boots, and a silver-tipped spear gripped in his free hand.

My eyes skim over the others, trying to take in their weapons, their stature and size. I'm looking for weak spots I know I won't find. Anything to get the upper hand. Rupert walks forward in fighting leathers, brown leather gloves and boots. A quiver of arrows hangs from his back, a bow down by his side. He's next to Armin, who has on form-fitting armor from the neck down. His eyes are so blue they shine like sapphires even from a distance. His beard is thick and blond, his hair shaggy around his ears, and he's built like a gods-damned tank.

Rounding out the edges are Roland and Marshal. Roland is thin and lithe. I won't underestimate him. His reputation is that of a sadist, although it seems impossible. He looks the youngest of them all with dark, curly hair and pink cheeks. The glint in his eye and the slight tug at his lips confirm that he's eager for the bloodshed to begin.

And then Marshal. It's impossible to get an estimate of his expression with a full helmet covering his face. He moves smoothly even though he's carrying his body weight in armor, including chainmail around his neck, as well as a sword and shield in his hands.

There's an energy that rolls off of them. I've felt it with the Ravens when they've fought in the ring. But this...this is different. For the first time, I really question our decision to make this bet.

I feel separated from my body as the Shaman announces the terms of the fight. My sword is weightless as the guardians secure their armor. The only signal that the battle has started is the vibration of the gong, the Shaman disappearing, and roar of Clinton racing past me, declaring his loyalty to Morgan.

Pulling the shield off my back I follow the men into battle, prepared to meet my destiny.

16

MORGAN

After the walking the castle's grounds I fall into a deep sleep, napping before dinner. I dream I have wings, with long black feathers that guide me from this world back to my own. The sensation of Earth fills my senses. The smells. The air. The warmth of humans and society. Spreading my wings, I soar over The Nead, my stomach lurching at being so close to home, at once both excited and homesick. The kind of sensation a dream gives you—when you know it's not real. But you want it to be, so badly.

It only takes a moment to realize the house is empty. I circle, arcing over the park until I catch the faintest of scents. Then I race over the city, eyes scanning for my mates. I follow their trail to a familiar part of town. The warehouse trembles with excitement. They're at the fights—*no*, in the fights. Landing on a ventilation ledge, I peer inside.

The ring is no longer a ring, but morphed into something larger. From the inside I'm not looking through slats in a window but sitting atop a massive arena. Below, gods below...I spot six enormous fighters clashing with five familiar bodies.

The crowd screams for bloodshed, swords crash against one

another. Dylan squares against a dark-skinned man who wields his sword like a second hand. The whip unfurls in my guardian's hand and the sound of it lashing out creates a rip in the night.

I scan the others, terrified to watch any one fight; Damien, Sam, and Clinton each grunt, defending. And then in the middle, as though she's always been there...Hildi.

I have no doubt that her being here means one thing: Andi is dead. The way she goes after a man twice her size is the only proof I have. Vengeance is in her every move. I feel her pain all the way up here.

Movement catches my eye. The warriors below continue to circle one another, taking the occasional shot. I duck my head when a massive opponent brings down his weapon on Damien, a large mallet that looks as if made of stone. Damien is fast. Agile. I don't want to watch. I don't want to see this.

Why? Why are they here?

"For you," a voice says next to me. I look over and see another bird, a large falcon, perched on the thin ledge. The voice is familiar: the Shaman. I open my mouth to speak but words do not come out. I'm a bird, for Christsake.

But even though I have no voice I do hear him, and the words formulated in my head are communicated back.

"They're here for you," he tells me, nodding his beak below where the battle rages on. "They made a bet looking for soldiers for your army. If they win, they get to keep the Legion."

"If they don't?"

"They'll be in my debt."

I look down to see if I can get a sense of who is winning. It's impossible with so much metal and steel. "And Hildi?"

"She asked for a spot on the team. I always knew she was a champion."

"Do you think they'll win?"

The instant I ask this I hear the sound of a body dropping hard. One of the warriors has fallen. Blood drips from Clinton's sword. He never hesitates, jumping into the next battle. Now the numbers are even.

"I never underestimate your Ravens," he says. "Neither should you."

"Why do you think I underestimate them? I have complete faith."

"Do you?" His beady brown and yellow eyes stare at me. "All of them?"

I look down once again. Dylan yanks his whip, disarming the soldier he's fighting. In a blink he has the man bound and a knife pointed at his throat. Damien lunges nearby, sliding across the sandy floor, getting the upper hand on his opponent, while Sam has one constrained in the crook of his elbow, one hand on his head. The sound of his neck snapping is clear over the roar of the crowd.

I look back at the falcon. "You don't mean the ones on the ground, do you?"

He flexes his wings, spreading them wide. The fight below has turned into a blood bath. Five of my soldiers now against three of theirs.

"Get ready, the battle is coming for you. Make sure you're as strong and as prepared as they are." He launches from the ledge, soaring into the night. I look back down just in time to see Hildi run her sword through the gut of her victim. Turning for the falcon, I search for him. I have more questions. More thoughts. But my feathers start to fall, gloss black into the night. With the sound of the arena still in my ears I wake, arms spread across my bed, the coppery scent of blood in my nostrils.

My army is coming.

17

MORGAN

Dressed in another ridiculous gown, I await an escort to take me to dinner. Well, the word "dinner" downplays the scene in the grand hall. Really it's a formal banquet, everyone dressed in their finest, including Anita, who looks like a beacon in a blood red dress.

"Where do all these people live?" I ask Nevis as we enter the room.

"The Queen has surrounded herself with a court of loyal citizens. They stay on the castle grounds, under the protection of the Queen's magic."

"What's it like out there? Beyond the walls?" Anita asks. I'm surprised at her interest.

"Cold, dark, and dangerous. There are some small villages on the outskirts of the kingdom. Wild areas that the castle does trade and barter with. But no one has traveled further than the Queen's territory in many years. Beasts roam the hillsides, thieves and dark magic lurks in caves and the barren fields."

Anita shivers and I suppress one as well. It's hard the shake the chill of the castle. Some of it real, other parts psychological—like a dark depression. I know now though that some of this is the actual

Darkness. The power wielded by the Morrigan. The one I had a faint taste of back at the Nead, the one my guardians helped quell with their love and affection. But even after my moment with Bunny earlier today, I feel the desire for a taste of her power. It's the one thing that makes me know, she and I are one. And from the dark circles under Anita's eyes and the red scratch marks on her arms, I know she's jonesing for another hit too.

"How was your afternoon?" I ask. I'm carrying the weird dream I know the Shaman sent me deep in my chest. "Do anything interesting?"

"I spent time in the royal antiquity room. Jewels and artifacts from throughout history." She leans in. "Did you know the Hope diamond is actually a fossilized dragon's eye? The Morrigan has a matching one that she uses to control the beasts."

I wait a beat for Anita to laugh and tell me that was a joke, but no, she's serious.

"Wow. No, I didn't know that." I do notice that she sways a little and I reach to hold her steady. "You feeling okay?"

She stabilizes herself and replies in a low voice, "I've been a little rocky since that power blast earlier today. Like, I was never into drugs and stuff. Okay well, maybe a little bit of OxyContin back in college. A little boost to get through exams, and obviously Xavier dabbled, but I never knew what real cravings felt like. Not until today."

I don't reply right away but Nevis discreetly presses her heel against my toe. The pain is sharp but I bite it back. I should have the same cravings as Anita and the only reason I don't is Bunny helping me out. I can't let her or the Morrigan know I have an outlet. More than ever, she needs to think I hate him.

With the warring feelings in my heart, that won't be so hard to do.

"Yeah, I felt shitty all day. I had to take a huge nap."

She nods. "One more day and all that delicious darkness will be ours, all the time."

Instead of arguing, I lift my skirts to walk down the aisle, but Nevis holds me back.

"Tonight you'll follow the Queen down the carpet in royal formation."

"What?" I glace at Anita. She's smoothing her hair and adjusting her bodice to reveal more cleavage. Obviously she knew about this.

"It's just a formality," the servant says. "Just follow behind her. Smile and nod." Nevis narrows her eyes at me. "You can do that, can't you?"

I have no idea when I got the reputation of being uncooperative. I'm about to ask when the hallway falls silent and the Morrigan is ushered in by her protective unit.

Led by Casteel.

My instant reaction of rage and anger answers that question. These people made me uncooperative. They made me the woman I am today, one who is vengeful and determined.

The Morrigan once again wears her signature black, in a dress made of slick leather that molds to the curves of her body. It's interesting that she has me and Anita dress in such formality while she looks like a demon from the sex realm, but whatever. I guess that's her style.

"Dears," she says when she sees us, and my first reaction to her isn't hate. It's desire. Desire for her power and the dark energy that lurks in her every move. "You look outstanding. Perfect little princesses for the court to love and adore."

Anita doesn't even hide her desperation, moving quickly to touch, taste, and smell the queen. Casteel holds her back, blocking her with his arm that no longer has a hand attached. There's nothing but a wrapped stump.

"Let her pass," the Morrigan says with a stern voice. There's little doubt she dislikes Casteel's interference. Her eyes flick over me as well. "Let them both come to me. I know they need a little bump to get through the night."

I don't want to. I don't want that garbage in my system, but Nevis nudges me forward and I know I have no choice. The instant I'm in range, black tendrils of smoke swirl off her body—the kind I saw in the ring when she fought Dylan. The kind from the photos Sam took moments before he was captured. The Darkness, the Morrigan's essence, is *alive* and I watch helplessly as it wraps around my wrist like a manacle, injecting me with the cold, hard power my body is eager to taste.

It feels like a tiny prick—or dozens of them, really—sinking into my flesh. It feels good; the rush of absolute power. It hadn't been this way back home. As quickly as the smoke arrived it vanishes again, flickering back into her body.

"Just a bit, dears, to tide you over until the ceremony. I need you strong but not doped up on a level of power you can't understand."

"Thank you," Anita says, licking her lips. The rings have vanished under her eyes and she looks more alive now than before. I touch my cheeks, wondering if they have the same glow.

The Morrigan looks at me expectantly and I nod. "Thank you, Your Majesty."

She smiles and walks past us, getting into position to lead our procession. Casteel passes me and says, "You look ravishing tonight, Morgan. Not as good as you did wet and naked, but still, removing all that fabric is half the challenge."

A jolt shocks through me and I grab Casteel by his lame arm and jerk it behind his back in a quick move. He falls to the ground on his knees, whimpering when a bone cracks. The soldiers around us pull their weapons, and I feel the steel point of at least six blades at my neck and back. The strength running through me isn't my own, and when the Morrigan turns to see the commotion there's no denying the glint in her eye.

"Stand down, Casteel," she says, her lips curved in a nasty grin. "Only you would be foolish enough to push your vendetta against a woman filled with the Dark spirit. If she kills you right now, I'll do nothing but watch."

I drop him, pushing him forward. He grunts as he falls, cradling his already weak arm. I straighten and Anita smirks at me as I line up next to her. The Darkness rolls and expands inside of me, reacting to the feel of me using it.

The Morrigan turns and says, "Are you ready, girls?"

"Yes," I declare, holding my chin high.

Because yes, I think I am.

18

DYLAN

Unbelievably, in a haze of blood and sweat, the fight comes to an end. My brothers, Hildi, and I stand over the slain bodies. The roar of the crowd is both as astonished as I am and ecstatic at the results. I hardly remember it at all. Not the kills, not how we came out on top. But we did, and I'm not one to argue with the fates, so when that final buzzer rings I raise my arms like a champion and accept the win.

Now to take our prize.

"Go clean up," the Shaman says. He's not as angry as I expect. "I'll have the Legion and the paperwork prepared for transfer."

"That's it?" Clinton asks, never one to trust the Shaman. I understand. There's usually a catch, but as we walk back down the tunnel that is already shifting back to normal with a magical haze, and enter the training room, I realize that for once there isn't.

"I wish you luck," the man says, although I'm not sure he believes in such a thing. "Believe it or not, I'm on your side. The Morrigan's ways...they aren't my own. I like the balance of the realms as they are."

"Because you profit from it?" Hildi asks, the large cut on her cheek already starting to fade.

"Because it took many centuries for me to settle in. Establish my ways." He smiles. "Plus, I like the comforts of this world. Coffee. Pizza. The internet. An apocalypse isn't in my favor any more than it is in yours."

There's honesty in his words. And truth.

"And the Legion," I ask. "How will they feel about it?"

"The stories of the Legion are complex and not always as they seem. But they've waited a long time to put a god *or* goddess of war to an end. They'll be useful allies. I understand why you've chosen them."

Clinton pulls his shirt over his head, there's a nasty bruise on his side, but it too is disappearing. He jerks his chin at the Shaman. "Any suggestions on how to handle them?"

"They're soldiers. Warriors like yourself. Tell them what the mission is and they'll fight accordingly."

The Shaman spreads his right hand and waves his other across his palm. There's a ripple in the air and a roll of thick paper appears. It's old and the magic holding it together is strong enough to smell. Sulfur is the primary odor.

"Once we sign these, they're yours."

"And when the battle is over? What do we do with them then?"

The Shaman shrugs and unfurls the papers. "That's up to you."

He cuts his finger with a sharp blade and places a drop at the bottom. He passes it to me and I scan it over. I see no tricks. No manipulations. Once we sign, the Legion will belong to us. And their contract as well as our own with the Shaman are now void.

I take the blade and slice into my own skin. Blood beads at the tip of my finger and with a look at the others I seal the contract between us.

Now we're the owners of an army.

19

MORGAN

There's little time for food, and I'm definitely holding back on the drink tonight as the affair seems to be more about dancing and socializing than anything else. I still can't exactly figure out what and who the members of the Queen's court are, why they're here, but at least three handsome men line up and ask me to dance.

"Thank you," I say to the most recent one. He's blonde with brilliant green eyes. I smile sympathetically. "But, no. I really can't."

Seriously. I have no idea how to dance—at least not in the style of the Otherside.

Anita has no problem saying yes and once they walk away from me they rotate over. Her red dress flares as she spins, completely fluent in the movements of this world. Her hand lingers flirtatiously over the shoulder of the blond courtesan that I'd just rejected. He doesn't seem to mind. Why would he? Anita is at home in this world. The way she has acclimated to the kingdom brings about a million questions, and without realizing it, I scan the room for the one person that can answer them.

"It's fascinating, isn't it?" Bunny says, from behind me, like he knew I was searching for him. "How you and Anita are so different."

"Why is that?" I ask him, feeling our bond stretch with him so close. The Morrigan's Darkness tickles at the back of my throat. I'd give anything for Bunny to douse the fire with his mouth.

"She didn't have five guardians watching over her from the day she was born."

I glance over, unsure if us speaking is a good idea. There are no runes to protect us from the Morrigan's careful eye—other than the one Bunny etched on my skin. Somehow I doubt that's enough.

Yet Bunny grazes his fingers on my waist and offers me his hand. "May I have this dance?"

"I'll tell you what I haven't told the others...I can't dance."

"I'm sure we'll manage." He gives me a crooked smile and a strand of his copper hair falls in his eyes. He's wearing formal attire; black pants and a gray tunic. Add in his glasses and he looks quite distinguished.

I don't hesitate. I want his touch. I crave the way he soothes the dark power surging inside of me. My body trembles in relief when his hand takes mine and I fight to keep my knees from shaking as we walk across the marble floor. He leads me gracefully, the warmth of his hand easing into the dip of my back. There's no lack of confidence as he guides me with only one hand, but he does stand close,, using his full body to lead. Without missing a beat we fall in step with the music.

"Why are you shaking?" he asks in a low voice. People are watching, including the Queen.

"She keeps pushing her magic on me. Anita, too." I look at our connected hands. "I think she's testing me, seeing how I handle such an influx of dark power."

"So that's why you came to me before."

I nod, not feeling the slightest bit of guilt. "I can't do the job I need to if I'm drunk on dark magic, Bunny."

"You know you can come to me whenever you need to. I don't judge." He spins me around and my skirt flares like a flower. When I come back to him, he pulls me closer, dropping his hand behind my back. I don't miss the way his eyes graze over my breasts or the gentle but possessive feel of his hand. "Believe it or not, we have the same goal."

It *is* hard for me to believe that. But I think about my dream earlier in the day. My guardians are sacrificing themselves for this fight. Hildi has joined in at the risk of everything. And the Shaman, what had he said?

"I never underestimate your Ravens."

I knew at that moment he didn't just mean the ones in the fight below, but the one in front of me, too. I open my mouth to tell him everything, about the directions I gave Clinton. The dream and the warriors the guardians went up against. How I'm doing all of this to save my world, my family, and how I want to save him, too.

Our eyes meet and I feel walls crumbling between us. We're bigger than this. Bonded. Mated in all ways except one.

Before I can speak, the music changes and Bunny twirls me to the edge of the dance floor, slipping through a crowd of people until we're behind a large stone pillar near one of the roaring fireplaces.

It's against that pillar, hidden from the eyes of the court that Bunny kisses me, deliciously hard. He takes the Darkness building up inside and gives me something I'd been missing since arriving in this cold, barren kingdom.

Hope.

20

BUNNY

Gods, her mouth. Her lips and the way her breasts look in that antique gown. I love Morgan in all ways: fighting in the ring, modeling for a painting, laughing on the rooftop garden; but here, in this dress, her image burns into my mind as one of my favorites.

She's fought me for days, angry and hurt. I understand it, I do. Betrayal cuts deep, but I'd hoped she see the bigger plan. That once we were both here, free to roam and plant the seeds of a rebellion, we would have one another. Together, with the help of the Guardians, we would become whole.

She's close—nudged by the need to rid herself of the Morrigan's poison. A side effect I don't think the queen anticipated.

"She'll see," she breathes.

"She may." I peer around the pillar and find the queen involved in conversation with her courtesans. "But I've blocked her from your emotions. When we're together, she can no longer sense our bond and the strength that ties us together."

"It's still there, isn't it? The bond?"

"Only one thing will tear that apart."

Another glance tells me someone else is looking—someone dangerous. I release my hold on Morgan.

"What?" she asks. I know her worry isn't about herself. It's about the plan and time slipping away before the Raven Guard arrives. There's little time for a mistake.

"Casteel. He's watching. And waiting."

"For what?" She slips away and the coil between us ebbs.

"For an opportunity, I'm sure. To what end, I don't know. I'm sure the queen has made it clear you're off limits."

"I've made that clear, too."

I smile. "I'm sure you have."

"One day," she says, rounding the pillar to rejoin the party. "That's all we have to survive. One final day and this will be over."

I watch her vanish around the marble column and hope she realizes we will have to do more than survive for the next twenty-four hours. And if she isn't willing, then the fate of us all may succumb to the Queen and her darkness.

21

DAMIEN

The Nead, the spacious mansion that has provided the Raven Guard shelter, suddenly feels small.

I stand in the foyer and watch as Sue and Davis jump to work, figuring out places for these men—these warriors--to sleep and prepare,until we embark on our journey to the Otherside.

I don't know what to expect from the Legion. They're legends—close to a myth--that Dylan would read about in his musty books, but they're here. Standing in our foyer looking decidedly...normal.

"Does anyone need a drink?" I ask suddenly, feeling the urge. "Because I need a fucking drink."

Sam perks up, as well as Clinton, who's already headed to the library. I pat one of the warriors, Agis I believe, on the shoulder and nod for him to follow.

Clinton pours drinks and passes them around. Dylan comes in the room and shuts the door behind him. I swallow the fiery liquid in a quick gulp and wait for what comes next.

"First," Dylan says, holding his drink in his hand. "We're not looking to keep you as slaves. That has never been our interest but you how the Shaman operates. Contracts and manipulation. It was the only way."

My brother looks over the room. It's packed between the four of us, Hildi, and the six Immortals. "The Morrigan is making her move tomorrow. Her intention is to bring the Darkness from her world to this one, kicking off the apocalypse."

"The sickness," Miya says. "I've seen it before, during other times. It was made from her dark energy."

"We've managed to stop that for now," Sam says. Hildi scoffs bitterly under her breath and takes a big gulp of alcohol. Clinton refills her glass.

"That was the closest she's come to getting through in a long time. But other forces have aligned. Both of her sisters are alive right now, Macha and Nemian. Although we tried to split them using our own dark magic, it didn't work as anticipated. The Morrigan must be destroyed."

"And you need our help," says Rupert. He leans against the leather sofa as though the fight earlier didn't happen and that his freedom doesn't hang in the balance.

"Yes, we need your fighting power," I say. "We must get to our mate before the binding ceremony starts, but the Morrigan will be armed to the teeth. Her soldiers are strong and deadly."

"And after this battle is over?" Roland asks.

"You're free to go," Dylan says. He does not add that there will be conditions.

"And if we fail?" Armin asks. He's huge, even more so in human clothes where his muscles bulge against the fabric of his shirt.

Clinton places his glass on the bar. "We won't fail."

We study one another—ten men and one Valkyrie, and that much is understood. Failure is not an option.

22

MORGAN

The morning of the ceremony dawns gray like every other I've experienced on the Otherside. Nevis opens the curtains wide, blasting white light into the room, and I shield my eyes.

"Are we in a rush?"

"Preparations will last all day, starting with a dip in the royal springs and a blessing by the court priest."

"This kingdom has a priest?"

"Yes, and you're due to join the Morrigan and Anita soon. Eat your breakfast." She points to the small plate of food next to the bed.

Less than a day before the ceremony happens. I wanted to bide my time until this day, until my guardians arrived, but I feel off kilter. Like I should have done more. The harsh frown tugging at Nevis' mouth implies the same.

"What have I done wrong?" I ask her. "Where have I failed?"

"You're here, Morgan, and you're treading lightly. It's the best we can hope for."

But her disappointment is evident as she combs through my hair, working out the tangles from the night before. "Bunny and I have made up," I say. "Or at least I think we have."

"You've forgiven him?"

"As much as I can," I say, but doubt lingers. I haven't told him all of the plans. And I certainly haven't let myself truly go with him. "We're watched constantly. Even with the rune of protection he gave me, Casteel kept an eye on us both last night."

Nevis twists my hair into a tight bun and wraps my naked body in a thick robe. "Uh, no clothes?"

"I told you, bathing in the springs."

Gods, what have I gotten myself into. "And these springs? Are they the same as yours below?"

"Not exactly. They're natural but not from the same well that has the healing properties, but to keep the queen calm some water is added daily to the pools. Her vanity knows no bounds, Morgan. She feeds on her beauty and control over others. Be careful when you're with her today. You'll need all your strength as she'll be testing you, weakening you before the ceremony tonight. She can't allow anything to interfere with her plans."

"How do I fight back?" We're at the door, about to leave my room. I'm in the robe and have on felt slippers.

She turns and takes my hands. "You're powerful in your own right, Morgan. You have the tools and strength it takes to do this. Dig deep. The real challenge for you is pretending like you haven't succumbed to her will."

We're quiet in the hallway, the entire kingdom seemingly still asleep. Nevis leads me to a bathhouse. Stained glass windows line the wall and the bath itself is large and square. Steam rises from the water and just as I arrive, Anita turns the corner in a matching robe.

"Morgan," she says. "Have fun last night?"

"Sure," I reply, remembering what Nevis just said. Fake it. Pretend. Stop being such a judgy bitch and get through the day. "I've never been to anything like that before."

"Well, Mother and Daddy prepared me with cotillion and etiquette classes in high school. I loathed it at the time, but now I understand that they were grooming me for this very moment." She gives me a sympathetic grin.

Grooming. It's a strange word but obviously exactly the right one for the circumstances. "Yeah, no such luck. Somehow my parents didn't get the memo."

Nevis walks over at the same time as Anita's servant. They both reach for our robes. Anita dutifully unties her belt and I do the same, feeling incredibly awkward.

"Don't worry," Anita says, flinging her hair over her shoulder. Her body is perfection. Except for the one blemish at the base of her neck. I narrow my eyes. It looks like a hickey. "This is all just part of the ritual. The Morrigan wants to make sure we're 'pure' before the ceremony tonight."

I pretend not to care about being stark naked in front of Anita. That I'm as confident as she is. I follow her down the steps into the steaming water and quickly submerge. "What do you mean pure?"

"Pure. This water is enchanted. It will rid us of any disease or lingering energy from past lovers." She laughs and adds, "Not that your Guardians were diseased or anything, but the Morrigan doesn't want anything left of them."

I frown and glance up at Nevis. She's focused elsewhere, on purpose I assume. "Why does it matter?"

"We're binding as one, Morgan, but the Morrigan needs us to be as pure as possible to channel all of our energies together." She bobs in the water and that's when I notice the love mark on her neck fading away. Subconsciously I reach for the place Bunny marked me and gave me his rune and wonder if it's still there. I'm not sure it matters anymore. "I saw you sneak off with Bunny last night—don't tell me you didn't kiss and make up."

I shake my head. "No. We didn't."

She rolls her eyes. "Too bad. I know I spent my last night in physical gluttony." She leans forward and mock whispers. "Three men. At once. It was pretty epic."

A strange feeling blooms in my belly.

"You'd know all about that wouldn't you, though?" she says.

Feeling the urge to disappear, I submerge fully under water, pushing out the sound of Anita's voice. Even when I emerge it's like she's a mile away, blathering on about whatever she finds so important. For me it's like a bell rang, my mind clearing and reality coming into focus for the first time in days.

I guess I always assumed Bunny and I would have a chance.

I figured there would be time to fix this. To resolve our problems and repair what went wrong. But if the Morrigan succeeds tonight and one of us doesn't make it out alive, I've given up any chance of mating with him for good.

Three days ago I didn't think I would care. But now? I'm consumed with devastation and loss.

~

THE PRIEST STANDS at the end of a small garden. Roses with thorny vines climb the walls surrounding the area. The petals are a deep blood red.

Anita and I wear long white dresses, and the priest watches us carefully as we kneel before him. As usual, I'm lost and follow Anita's lead. Bowing when appropriate, nodding when necessary. I don't understand the language the priest speaks, but the sense of dread in my belly only grows when he touches my head with an oily thumb and sends me on my way.

"What's next?" I ask Nevis in a harsh tone on the way back to my rooms. "A parade?"

I'm tugging at the collar of the ridiculous gown, desperate to rip it off. Barely in the door, I yank it over my head and toss it toward the fireplace, cursing when the fabric falls short of the flames.

In nothing but the simple white bra and panties I was given after my bath, I walk to the closet and grab another outfit. That too brings about a fury of anger and I pull each and every dress from its hanger and toss them on the floor. "I'm sick of this place, the way it makes me feel. The Darkness ebbing in me even after the cleansing." I grab my arms and squeeze, trying to feel something other than the hollowness of the castle. "Everything about this world is wrong. I need my guardians. I need to get out of here."

I'm mostly ranting to myself but Nevis has closed the door quickly to make sure no one hears my tirade. The door knob jiggles and we glance at one another. I had one job. Fake it.

My heart sinks even further when the door pushes open and Casteel walks in the room.

23

DYLAN

The light flips on over my study and I stride in with Armin close behind. I'd asked who wanted to be a representative of the group—a leader for the upcoming battle. The massive warrior stepped forward.

He was silent on his way up the stairs, but now that we're in my study some of the hard expression fades as he takes in my books and maps.

"This is all yours?" he asks. I'm surprised by his grasp of the English language. I'm not sure why, he's no more American than I am. Time and magic have brought us a both a long way from who we were originally.

"This house and property has belonged to the Guardians for a long time. With the help of others that believe in our mission, we've amassed quite a collection of history and documents about the past and future."

"And your goal is to bring down the Goddess of War? The Queen of Ravens?" he asks, looking over a stack of books. "Your queen?"

"We were created by the gods to watch over her—keep her in

line. She is precariously close to crossing it." I nod to a painting leaning next to the fireplace. It's one of Bunny's that depicts the castle in explicit detail. "We are not bound to the Morrigan. Our actual queen is in that castle fighting for her life as well as the freedom of those in two realms. She left us with instructions to bring an army back."

"And we're that army," he says.

"Yes."

"And your queen. You think she's still alive?"

"Absolutely. For one, the Morrigan needs her. The other? I can feel her."

Armin frowns. "How is that?"

"She's our mate." I say it clearly so there is no misunderstanding.

"More than you?"

"All of ours." The hair on the back of my neck pricks with possessiveness.

"The Valkyrie. Who does she belong to?"

"Freya," I reply. "She's here on her own mission. A willing and capable soldier."

He says nothing else on the subject, just walks over and studies the castle. "When do we leave?"

"At dusk."

He pushes his hands in his pockets. Shoulders at ease. "And you have a plan?"

"That's why I brought you up here." I spread a map across the table. Davis gave it to me when we returned from the Otherside. "We'll make one together."

24

MORGAN

Nevis instantly sinks into the wall, trying to vanish in Casteel's presence. That move worked for her last time, but Casteel isn't the Queen's commander because he's an idiot. He shuts the door and glances over at her with dark eyes. "Don't move."

She slowly nods.

I can't take my eyes off his arm—the tied shirt covering the stump at the bottom, given to him by Dylan. There's no doubt he'll take out his anger on me. I'd narrowly escaped before, but no one is coming to save me this time.

"You have a habit of coming into my room uninvited, Commander," I say, reaching for a dress on the floor. I quickly slip it over my head. "We've just come from the blessing ceremony and my cleansing bath. You know about that, don't you?"

"Of course."

"Then you're aware of how excited the Queen is about the ceremony tonight—I'm sure you don't want to interfere with her plans." Last time, he came in looking to rape me. I ease near the fireplace, reaching for a poker. I grip the iron rod in my hand and hold it in front of me.

His good hand lingers near the sword on his belt and I'm not prepared for what he says next. "I'm not here to hurt you."

"I don't believe that."

"What if I told you I don't want the ceremony to happen tonight?"

I let his words sink in but they do nothing to allay my fears. "It would say you didn't give a rat's ass about the cleansing or blessing. It would mean my life is in danger." I swing the poker around in my hand.

"I told you, I don't want to hurt you."

Casteel is a beast of a man. Everything about him is imposing. He's the perfect foe for my Guardians and it's no surprise they've clashed more than once, and by the end of the day, I suspect they'll battle it out again. But I don't doubt his loyalty to this kingdom and the look on his face is honest—sincere.

"Then what do you want?"

"To end the binding ceremony and Anand's quest for destruction."

I glance at Nevis, who looks as confused as I must. The use of her first name, the familiarity is the most disconcerting.

"You want to stop all of that."

"Yes." He lowers his hand, no longer threatening to pull his sword. "I've been by her side since the beginning. Since she used the name Anand. Before she was the Morrigan. I fought with her after Cu's betrayal. I felt her anger and regret and I would do anything to ease her pain, even if it meant destroying the world we lived in. And together, we burned this land to the ground. She did it out of rage. I did it out of the desire to please her."

I frown. "You love her."

He nods. "Always."

"Does she know?"

"She's been unable to see anything but war since that day." He walks across the room and looks out the window. Completely vulnerable. "I want the gates closed. Forever. I want Anand to live a full life

—a real one. Not this power-hungry quest that never ends." He turns to look at me. The pain and desperation in his eyes is unmistakable. "I need her to fail tonight. And I need you to win, to close the gate and never return."

"And what about the Morrigan?"

"Leave her alive, that's all I ask and I promise we will never meet again."

I'm stunned by Casteel's revelation and as much as I believe him, I do not trust him. "How am I to do all of this? Stop the ceremony and get the gates closed. I could barely get here in the first place." I don't mention the Ravens and the warriors I know they're bringing to me now. Players are in motion—there's no going back.

"I tried to hurt you when you first came. My plan wasn't to actually harm you—but to scare you. Get you out of here for good." He raises his disfigured arm. "I paid for that—although to be fair, the Raven and I had a score to settle. There's a way to turn all of this around, but it has to be done by you. You're the only one strong enough to do it."

"I'm not sure I am. Her darkness? It's consuming—I'm no match for her."

Nevis makes a small sound and we both look over. In a soft voice she says, "There's one way to get you to the Morrigan's level."

"How is that?" I ask.

The resolution in her eyes says it all, and the way Casteel nods at me makes me know he's aware as well. There's one way for me to become stronger than the Morrigan—a way to beat the Darkness—and change the fate of all of our worlds.

They want me to close the circle with Bunny.

25

BUNNY

The star in the far right corner of the sky needs a little more shimmer. Using the end of my paintbrush, not the side with the hair, I dab a little silver and the feeling of completion settles in my bones.

I've spent the last three days, other than the time with Morgan, working on the mural. The content came to me as I worked—more muse than anything else. But now that it's laid before me, the full story of why I'm here and what I'm to be used for clicks into place.

I need to go to the underground and then...

My eyes wander over the painting. It's the entire story, from the Morrigan's creation to the death of Cu. Then the gods forming the ravens, plagues, death and war. All of that comes to the current day. Morgan as a child. The ravens in the treetops. The cat, the prince, even the loss of my arm. That, I realize now, was intentional. They'd never wanted to kill me. I was weakened physically and mentally. To get her here. To set things in motion. But another player is on the board. A shadow from the past that now pushes the pieces.

I tear off my smock and grab my things.

The clock is ticking, but the painting, it shows me that I have time.

We have time.

And the destruction can finally come to an end.

26

SAM

In the training room, seven new uniforms appear in the closet. Davis eagerly assists the Legion and Sue helps Hildi zip up her perfectly fitting suit. Each is equipped with weapons suited for our particular skills. Hildi's has a shield attached to the back and her long Valkyrie sword is nestled underneath. Her blonde hair is knotted in a dozen braids and her eye makeup is black and fearsome.

"I can understand why people would both love and fear seeing that woman come for them at the final moments," Damien says as he buckles his boot. "Not a bad way to die and go to heaven."

A few of the Immortals seem to agree. Their eyes watch her with interest. Rupert walks over to her now and engages in quiet conversation.

"This all seems a little easy, don't you think?" Damien adds. Boots secure, he checks his weapons.

"How do you mean?" The past week has been exhausting. We fought to the death. We gained contract-owned warriors. I've worried over Morgan and in my mind played out a dozen scenarios how this can go wrong.

"We have our army." He nods at Hildi. "Added a strong, loyal member, and we should get back to the castle in time for the ceremony. That all seems much too easy."

I study him for a moment. His tattoos peek above his collar. He's only wearing one ring tonight as well as just two small earrings. He's in fighting mode, as we all are, but something is bugging him. "What's your concern?"

"Bunny." He says his name quietly. "Only the gods know what he's doing."

As a group, we're conflicted about Bunny. His betrayal tears at the fabric of who we are as a unit—as a brotherhood. We've fought, lived, and now loved side-by-side since our creation. His actions hurt. Some of us more than others. Dylan and I have faith that he may have been working with us. Clinton and Damien, not so much.

"Dylan says he saved Morgan from Casteel. And she obviously still trusts him. She gave him the uniform and stayed with him on the Otherside."

"They haven't fucked," he says.

"No." We would have felt it. And frankly, I've been waiting for it. The longer it takes, the more worrisome it is. "Maybe there hasn't been an opportunity? It's not like the Morrigan will allow them to be near one another. Morgan may be in the dungeons."

"If Bunny is truly on our side, he could be dead."

I shake my head and focus on securing my belt. We would have felt that, too.

"I can't forgive him," Damien says. "Not for sending us to the dungeons. Not for hurting Morgan like that."

"I understand, but until this is over we can't do anything about it. We need him. So does she." He can't argue that. None of us can. The circle is almost complete and to beat the Darkness, Morgan needs Bunny to close the gap.

Otherwise, all of this? I look around the room. May be for nothing.

27

MORGAN

Nevis is stunned silent when Casteel reveals he is aware of her underground community.

"How long?" she asks.

"Since it began." He leads the way down to the dungeons, to the tunnel that will take us back to her people, to a safe place for the rest of the day. "There are few secrets in the castle."

"Does she know?"

"If she pressed it she would, but Anand is obsessively focused on her mission. She's just happy to have the castle run efficiently and to have the elixir from your water source to keep her healthy and strong."

The news rocks my friend and as we reach the dark end of the dungeon she stops and whispers to me, "If you stop all of this, what happens to us?"

It's an honest question—one I had not considered when agreeing to Casteel's plan. If we close the gate and contain the Darkness to this world, Nevis' people will never gain their freedom.

"I will not allow your people to suffer any longer."

"But how? How can you promise that?"

My list of challenges is growing. I pull her close and grip her hands. "Do you trust me?"

"I want to."

"I understand and if that's all you can give, I'll take it." I step into the tunnel, pulling her with me.

∽

THE CONFUSION I feel doesn't lessen as I travel beneath the castle. It does intensify when I exit the small door and stand at my full height. Bunny is already there.

"Did you..." I start to ask Nevis, but she shakes her head.

"We're short on time," she says, looking between the two of us. "Follow me."

I've learned a lot about my sexuality over the past few months. I've learned its power and the control I have over my mates. I've learned about energy and electricity. Love and compassion. Force and passion. I glance at the man walking next to me on the smooth, dirt path through the village. He's the only one that has truly hurt me. But then I wonder, as he slips his glasses up his nose with his one good hand and the other lies limp by his side, maybe he's also the one that has sacrificed the most.

Nevis takes us to the far reaches of the community, to a small but sturdy hut. The walls are made of red clay and the roof thatched from hay. She stops at the door and says, "This is our wedding house. Newlyweds come here to celebrate and consummate their relationships. You'll have the quiet and peace to figure out your next step together."

"Thank you," Bunny says, as though he's not the least bit surprised. Did he know it would come to this?

"I'll sound the gathering bell when time is close. It's important we're back in the castle and ready when the Queen sends for you."

I nod. "Yes. We'll be ready."

She gives me a tight, understanding smile. "Good luck and may the gods bless you."

She turns and walks down the path. I watch her go and then spin to face Bunny. He's already opened the door and holding it wide for me. With a knot in my belly and a grim set to my jaw, I step past him and enter the house.

The cottage is sparsely decorated. A queen-sized bed is the focal point, a white, hand-stitched quilt covering the mattress. There's a small kitchen with a table and a stove. A claw foot tub sits in the corner.

"I never thought our relationship would end like this," I say to him. "Forced. A cog in a wheel bigger than both of us." He smiles wistfully at my description. "Actually, the weird thing is I thought you'd be my first."

"In a different life I probably would have been."

We stand before one another, neither dressed in our finest as we were just the night before. At the banquet there had been at least a sense of danger. Of desire. Definitely desperation as the Darkness surged in me and needed quenching. If we'd been pushed together at one of those times I easily would have succumbed, but now I'm cleansed. Clean from that dark energy—primed for the Morrigan's binding.

Now I just feel helpless. Hopeless, despite what Casteel told me in my room upstairs. There are too many balls in the air; my guardians, the warriors they bring with them, Nevis and her people and the whole gods-damned world back home that doesn't even realize they're on the edge of a knife. There are too many people counting on me, relying on me, and I'm nothing but a girl.

"I don't know what to do," I say to him in a whisper.

He lifts his hand and tucks my hair behind my ear. Instinctively my body reacts to his touch; butterflies flutter in my stomach, my knees tremble, and my nipples tighten in anticipation. His pupils dilate, the dark center spreading over his copper iris. I feel his fingers clench in my hair and I lean into his palm.

"Do you trust me?" he asks.

"No." I shake my head. "I don't."

He tilts his head and his hair falls into his eyes. His tongue darts out and my traitorous lips quiver, thinking about kissing him. "You don't have to. It's okay if you don't. But we've got to do this, okay?"

I nod. "Okay."

He grazes my neck with his hand, the pads of his fingertips rough from use. A chill runs down my spine—the good kind—and he brushes his warm lips against mine. There's no hesitation, there's no time for that. I'm thankful because it's time to turn off my gods-forsaken brain for just. One. Fucking. Minute.

My body responds to his like a flower to sunlight. I lean into him, tasting his mouth, sucking his tongue. The layers of conflict fall between us, like the shedding of our clothes. I unbutton his shirt, slipping the wide metal buttons through the slits one after the other. The solid curves and planes of his bare chest peek out at me along with the taut ladder of his abs. His body is unfamiliar to me, I haven't had the pleasure of spending time exploring him and today would be no different.

He bunches my dress in his hand, lifting it up my body, his knuckles grazing my stomach. My belly clenches and there's no denying the warmth between my legs. Our mouths part but our breath mingles as we remove the final barriers between us.

Bunny nudges me toward the bed and I fall back, knees dangling over the edge. He stands before me, hard. Ready. Big.

His eyes drink me in. I brace myself for him, half eager, half feeling a pit of hollowness deep inside. It shouldn't be like this—out of our control. My fingers clench the bedding and I close my eyes.

I feel nothing but a flutter by my legs, knees brushing knees. I blink and find him over me. His mouth is inches from mine and he whispers, "I can never take back the pain of what I did, but I can redeem myself in the eyes of the gods and my brothers and you."

His length is between us; pressing and solid. My legs part and his hand ghosts down my inner thigh. I shift, welcoming him, my core slick.

The energy between us ebbs, the Darkness beaten back inch by inch, and something different rises, something I've only grasped in my fingers like the wind. I cling to the feeling, the power, and lasso it around us like a bond. I touch his chest, feel the pebble of his nipples beneath my fingers. With my mind—my body—I pull, bringing him closer. To my mouth, to my body, and with one hand I guide him toward me. The goddess flares the instant we meet. I roar against his lips and he pushes in, slowly, achingly.

Finally.

He enters me and it's like a link in the chain. A piece of the puzzle clicks into place. A rush washes over me. *Everything* makes sense. Feels right.

And it's not enough.

It's like a trigger, those pieces clicking together, link by link and the swirling energy kicks me to life.

"Oh," I say to him, to the world. "Oh, Bunny. I..."

I push Bunny off and on his back, his expression shock and regret. I feel the loss of our connection but that is short-lived. The entity inside me understands. She knows the path we're on and is no longer allowing the weaker side of me—the human part of both of us--to fuck this up.

His head presses into the pillows and I straddle his hips. His cock is slick with my heat and I don't hesitate before sinking down, guiding him to the depths of my core.

"Uhhhh," I cry, followed by prayers to the gods. The flip switches in Bunny's eye and once he understands how this is truly greater than the two of us, he reacts with force.

His hips buck against me and I ride him hard, feeling every inch of him, from tip to the base of his cock when he slams into me. Sweat pools between us, I feel it on his fingertips when he pinches my nipples and on his face when I suck his jaw. The walls fade, the bed disappears and we're just two, bonding, binding, and mating.

We close the circle, the one that started with Clinton and forged with Sam and Damien. Strengthened by Dylan but left incomplete. On purpose. I see that now. He was waiting. I was forced back. Now is the right moment for us to complete the bond of the five. Our eyes meet and for the first time I know the path ahead.

28

BUNNY

A goddess, with hair of ebony and eyes as dark as obsidian hovers above me. Her body is perfection, her skin smooth as silk. I grip her hip and pull her to me, harder and harder she rides, tumbling us both toward ecstasy. Her hair spills over her shoulders, bouncing with her breasts. Morgan's lips part and the moan that comes from her sounds like an angel singing.

Tension builds in me but I know this is a moment about both of us, a unique point that ties us all. My brothers surely feel the mounting energy, the power surging in his glorious woman. She's in control. She *owns* us all. Her skin burns as if on fire. Her lip trembles and everything from her sharp breaths to her shaking shoulders sets me on edge. Coiling and twisting in frenzied harmony.

"Do you feel it?" she grinds out.

Fuck yes, I feel it. Her. Everything. I can't speak. I can't formulate words. But my eyes meet hers and I nod, grunting with every thrust. Her hands move to the slab of headboard and she grips it as she cries out. It's not just pleasure. Certainly not pain. The essence of Darkness releases from her body, every dark tendril lingering from the Morrigan's touch. The infection festering deep in her soul.

Bright light engulfs us. Warm and full of charged energy. Tilting her head back she spirals, biting down on her lip. I let go, the room fading around us. It's just us and warmth. Love and righteous power. Once we ascend to this, everything I've held back for so long frees—I groan.

"Gods above," I grind out, my teeth clenched. My eyes squint, trying to look at her with the glow of power behind her. I spill everything I have into Morgan just as she tilts her head back. She tightens around me and mercy, it feels like nothing I've ever dreamed of. Nothing a mortal man could know. We writhe against one another, riding out the moment, the event, because nothing in our world will ever be the same.

We're one.

We're bonded.

We've mated.

And as Morgan's body slows and the bright light fades to a hazy glow, she smiles down at me. Her is mouth lazy and her eyes are glazed and there's no doubt in my mind we've changed the fate of humanity.

29

CLINTON

Deep in the bowls of earth, the ground shudders beneath my feet. I touch the wall for purchase. That's when I realize that it's not the floor or even the walls. It's coming from inside my body. My chest.

"Morgan," Sam says. He's right behind me. "Do you feel that?"

"Yes," Damien replies. In the torchlight, Dylan nods. The Immortals and Hildi look at us with confusion.

"She closed the circle."

Which means one thing. She and Bunny have consummated their relationship. What we don't know is Bunny's frame of mind. Did he do this for us or the Morrigan? Which side is he on? Whatever the case, we now have a united bond. It also means that her power is fully balanced. She doesn't need us to keep her even. She'll have full control over an enormous amount of ability that she can use for good *or* evil.

"Do you think she's ready?" I ask.

"I think Morgan is strong and steadfast," Dylan replies.

A second wave rolls over me—us, and I cling to the wall. It's not a bad feeling. Just overwhelming. I can't help but ask, "And Bunny?"

Damien pushes past me to walk down the hall, his torch taking the light with him. "We'll find out soon."

30

MORGAN

I can't see the power, but I feel it. It's in every inch of my body—trembling beneath my skin, in my muscles. Everything changed the instant Bunny entered me. No, everything changed with that first kiss from Clinton months ago. That simple touch cumulated in this event. My body hums in awakening. Not just physically but mentally as well.

Bunny lies next to me, his cheeks red. His copper eyes are clear and I lay a hand on his chest, feeling the heartbeat inside.

I understand now. His motives. His fears. His loyalty.

"I forgive you," I say to him.

"I'll earn that forgiveness for the rest of our lifetimes." His fingers graze the underside of my breast and a pool of heat gathers below my belly. There is no ache left in me, not after the explosive orgasm we just shared, but my body crackles and sparks with renewed desire.

I lean over to kiss him. It's a kiss of forgiveness. A promise.

"They're coming," he says. Our noses are inches apart. "They're in the tunnels."

"I feel them."

"They felt us," he replies.

I open my mouth to tell him about my command; that they bring me an army, but a wave of chimes sounds from outside the cottage. There's no mistaking. It's time.

He kisses me where he marked me days ago and the rune ignites.

"Will that help?"

He shakes his head and slips his glasses on. "You don't need my protection anymore. You're strong and ready." He touches the spot. "That's for me. For you to remember who you belong to."

I look down and see the outline isn't the symbol from before but a darker brand.

Five flying ravens.

～

THE WHITE GOWN clings to the curves of my body like a second skin. I've seen the design before, it's identical to the style the Morrigan prefers. It's no surprise when I enter the enclosed field behind the castle that Anita is wearing the same one.

It's dark, but the stone walkway leads to a paved area in the middle of green grass surrounded by flaming torches. Moonlight filters through the rooftop. The ceremony begins at midnight and we wait in a hidden area away from the crowd. Soldiers are positioned three feet apart. They're *everywhere*. I strain my ears and search my heart for any signal of my guardians. I find nothing but the steady beat of my own pulse.

"I spent the afternoon reading books from the Queen's library," Anita says. Her face looks fresh, but I also see a bit of tiredness in her eyes. Her human vessel is feeling the strain of the Morrigan's presence. I've had my guardians to help carry the weight of the Darkness. "I couldn't sleep. Too excited, you know?"

"This is really what you want?" I ask her. She had a life. A family.

"More than anything." She gives me a curious look. "I know

you've been brainwashed by those roommates of yours to fight against this, but you have no idea what awaits on the other side."

Heavy footsteps echo off the ground. I look toward the castle and see Casteel walking down the center path. He's escorting the Morrigan personally. She glides across the stones toward the small platform in the middle of the field. The audience, I'm assuming the most loyal of her court, watches in silence as she takes her place. Her dress is black, made of a shiny, tight fabric that looks like wet paint. Her hair is back and she wears a headdress made of glossy feathers. A crown of glittering black jewels sits on top.

There's no sense of betrayal on Casteel's face. Nothing but stone-cold loyalty. The priest from earlier in the day steps on the platform and nods at the Morrigan.

It's time.

My Guardians are not here.

The priest says something in a language I do not understand, but a wide smile appears on Anita's lips. There's a nudge at my back. The blonde woman next to me links her arm with mine and we leave our spot in the shadows and enter the ring of fire. At the edge of the platform Anita leans in and whispers, "I forgive you for what you did to me back home. Today we start new. As one. I'm thankful you're my sister."

The priest doesn't smile when he sees us. Neither does the Morrigan. Her eyes are closed as if in prayer. With the help of assistants, we take our positions, each on the side of the Queen. I feel the Darkness ebbing off of her but it's different. It's like the energy bounces off. I have a shield of protection.

"We shall now begin the ceremony," the priest says, now in English. Or maybe, I think, watching his lips, I can just understand what he's saying? The shape of his mouth doesn't match the words and they echo in my head.

"At the beginning of time, a child of the gods was born, blessed with three souls. Macha, Nemain, and Anand. These three culti-vated and protected land and agriculture, fertility, and the art of war.

Together they were equals. United, they held magnificent power. Betrayal and deceit split them apart and only one remained to protect and fortify these lands." Every eye watches the priest as he spins his tale.

"Anand, the goddess of war, has ruled the Otherside since that time. But her true glory is to leave this realm and conquer others. And to do that she must unite again with her sisters."

At the back of the circle is a flat stone table, or altar, and the priest turns toward it. "We start with a sacrifice of one of the gods' chosen. His blood will act as a conduit to bring these three together."

A sacrifice? Seriously, where is Dylan? Clinton? Right about now would be a good time to come in and shut this nightmare down. But there is no cavalry. No heroic entrance, just the sound of a man being dragged from the back of the gardens toward the altar.

It's Anita's gasp followed by a gleeful laugh that forces me to look up at the man gagged at the mouth and bound at the ankles. I stare into those deep copper eyes and choke back on my emotions.

The Queen plans to sacrifice Bunny.

31

DYLAN

Light greets us at the end of the tunnel, along with the sharpened tips of blades. Nevis is at the front, and they wear mismatched clothes but clearly want to be seen as a united force.

"Why the blades?" I ask, stepping into the humid cavern. I have my hand on the handle of the coiled whip at my side.

Nevis looks over my shoulder, sees the men pushing out of the tunnel. Whatever she's thinking, I hope it's not some sort of attack. Her people look strong but not Legion of Immortals strong.

"We've decided to join your fight, but Morgan has changed the terms of our agreement. She no longer wants to kill the Morrigan."

"What? Why?" Damien asks, moving next to me.

"The Commander made a deal with her. He bought her time. Allowed her to be with the last of her mates. She's at full strength."

"We're aware," Clinton says. "What are the terms of her agreement with Casteel?"

"Morgan spares the Queen and leaves, closing the gate forever." Her eyes grow tight. "This leaves us with a problem. There's no assurance we will not continue to be the Kingdom's slaves."

"Morgan won't betray you," I say, but I don't know that. I don't know how having so much power will change her. I don't even understand why she'd give Casteel a chance.

Nevis nods. "I hope not, but we're willing to reveal our numbers to the Kingdom. Risk our peaceful society for a chance at the future." She grips the handle of her sword. "We'll lead you to the battle and fight by your side, and if Morgan fails we will kill the Queen ourselves."

It's a bold move. Most likely suicide, but I understand. Being under the control of a sadist makes it worth taking the chance to end it when you have it. And this may be the only one they get.

"Casteel...he wants to save Morgan and see the gate closed?"

"Yes."

We're walking across the cavern to one of the pipes that leads to the castle above. I wave my soldiers through and they are followed by the people of the underground, some who will surely never see this place or their loved ones again.

"Why is he doing this?" I ask, trying to wrap my mind around the change.

Nevis stops and looks up at me. She's so small but also incredibly strong. In the heart and mind, if not physically. "He loves her."

"Morgan?"

"No, Anand, his true love from the days before. She's his mate."

Those are words I understand. Feelings I can comprehend. I nod and move toward the pipe to follow the others to the battle above. We've all done foolish things for love, I'm doing my own now.

32

MORGAN

"I told you to kill him."

The Morrigan's words cut into my mind like a razor. I don't need to look away from Bunny lying flat on the altar to know she has a smile on her face.

"You think I didn't know you were going to him? That you'd forgiven him? Your weakness brought us to this moment, Nemain."

I finally look at her. I'm not the only one; Anita, the audience, Casteel, and even the priest is clinging to her every word.

"What are you talking about?"

"You think I don't want you at your peak strength before we bond? That I don't want your raw power? You're both alive because I need it that way." She glances at Bunny and sneers. "Or did."

The power she speaks of crackles in my fingers; if the Morrigan feels it, she doesn't care. She nods at the priest. "Kill him and begin the ceremony."

He walks to the altar and pulls out a sharpened blade on a small shelf beneath. Three goblets sit beneath Bunny's head, a slanted piece of wood falling toward each one. The goblets are to be filled with blood. Bunny's blood.

Although I feel my guardians in this world, they are not here. My eyes connect with Bunny's. There isn't an ounce of fear in his eyes. He's always known it would come to this. Sacrifice is his role. His destiny.

Not if I can fucking help it.

The Morrigan, too caught up in her dramatics, turns her back to watch the priest work. I do what I came here to do. Channeling my lessons and training, I go for the weakest point, lunging for Anita and gripping her by her stupid, perfect hair.

"Ahh! Morgan!" she shrikes. I close a hand around her throat and the sound becomes more guttural. The Morrigan spins, anger twisting her lips. She doesn't even have time to speak before I whisper in Anita's ear and wrench her neck to the side, severing her spine in one snap.

Her body drops to the ground with a thud.

My strength surprises me. Clinton and Dylan taught me that move, but I'd never had the power to pull it off. But just then I knew I possessed it. I used it, and just as quickly I tear the slinky white dress at the collar down to my feet and step out of the shell of insanity in my fighting suit.

"I don't need her," the Morrigan says. She flicks out her hand and whatever light—whatever energy Anita possessed--lifts from her body in a swirl and slams into the Queen. She licks her lips in pleasure. "She was rendered weak during the original split. She was nothing but a pawn and her duty is fulfilled. But you...you're magnificent, Nemain. So much rage. So much anger. Don't pretend you don't feel the dark power surging in you. I can taste it from here."

"But I don't. That's what you don't understand, Your Highness," I take a step forward. Casteel and his men haven't made the slightest move. On her call or his, I do not know. "The Darkness is gone. Banished by the love of that man right there." I point to Bunny. His eyebrow lifts at the word love. "You can kill him but you can't take away what he's given me. What we have together."

A commotion rises at the edge of the field. I smile.

"What we all have together," I amend. I pull my sword from my back, the one that works well in my world but is a force in this one. The jewels sparkle on the hilt. "Say goodbye to tyranny!" I shout to all of the Otherside.

And we begin to fight.

33

BUNNY

Chaos explodes when Morgan raises her sword. Casteel's men scatter to the edges of the field. The priest drops his knife and runs. Two queens face one another mere feet away.

I wriggle my feet and wrist against the tight rope.

Morgan, never taking her eyes off the queen, lifts her hand toward me. Warm air blasts in my direction and I squint against the draft. The ropes twist and slither apart, alive with whatever power she blasted my way. The instant they are free I jump from the altar and pick up the priest's discarded weapon. It's ceremonial, I see, flipping it in my hand, but it will do.

I don't know what Morgan's plan is or how she wants to end this, but I know the Queen is hers to take. I hop off the platform and search the field for my brothers. It's not hard to find them. A sea of scuffles move along the edge.

I move to join my brothers when a massive hand grips me on the shoulder. I look back and see Casteel. I tighten my hold on the blade.

"Weapon down," he says, jaw tight. "Your true Queen has a handle on this. Your fellow Guardians will fall in line. You're needed for something else."

I frown, confused by his words. "What is that?"

"You painted the mural. You've seen the prophecy. Only you can close the gate for good."

"You want the Morrigan locked in?"

He nods. "I'll clear you a path."

I don't understand what's happening here but if he's willing to betray the Morrigan, I'm willing to follow his lead. I step into his shadow and we push through the sea of kingdom soldiers fighting for their lives. I spot Damien breaking a man in two. I see Sam clashing with a man twice his size. There are others, faces I don't recognize, but they're wearing our uniform and as Casteel leads me away from battle I pray to the gods I will see them all once more.

34

CLINTON

Morgan is too far away for me to see but I feel her—sense her. She's claimed her power. It's possible she didn't need us after all.

The kingdom's soldiers swarm, hundreds of men charging toward us with a taste of blood on their tongues. We've been asked by the people underground not to kill the queen—that Morgan has a bigger plan. I have to trust this is true but we were not asked to take it lightly on her army, and I plan to slash and slay my way to the platform.

It's eleven against hundreds, but we still have the edge. I slam my foot into the chest of the nearest soldier. I plunge my blade into his throat. I do it again. Jabbing elbows, kicking in kneecaps. I break necks. Shatter spines. Blood coats my hands. My face. The air fills with blood and screams. Glancing to my right I spot Agis rip the arm off a foe. I'm pleased to see he doesn't smile. That the act takes him to a deeper place. I've been there. I *am* there.

War is fucking hell.

Miya cleans up my mess, taking down swaths of charging men with his double-edged sword, and slowly we creep toward the middle, stepping over the slain on our way to the beckoning light.

We need our mate and then we need to get the fuck out of this gods-forsaken hellhole for good.

35

HILDI

Inch by inch we creep toward the center of the batshit crazy atrium. Nothing about this place makes sense, especially the crazy-as-hell woman up on the platform. We've cleared enough distance that I can finally see her—my friend—Morgan and my enemy—the Goddess of gods-damned War.

A body slams into me and I stumble. I'd let myself get distracted and now I'm on my back with a blade plunging toward my face. A pair of hands grips my shoulders and pulls me to my feet. Another figure moves like a wall of thunder, pummeling the soldier into dust.

"Thanks," I say to Armin. His blue eyes make me unnerved. I nod at Dylan, who pulled me away. He stares at me with judgment.

"Stay focused," he says.

"I am." I prove this by knifing a soldier running at us.

"This is not about revenge. We promised Nevis."

"You promised her," I reply, already stepping into the fray. "I joined this army on my own terms, Dylan."

"This is bigger than you," he argues, but there are too many soldiers to fight and too little time to get to his precious queen on the platform. I don't care about some lame request by a bastard commander. I care about what that bitch took from me. I promised to make her pay.

I unsheathe another sword, this one ancient and filled with the wrath of Freya. I always keep my promises.

36

DYLAN

Keeping one eye on Hildi and the other on the blood-thirsty soldiers, I let my heart guide me to Morgan. It seemed impossible when we first entered the field—the platform too far away—but now a sea of black uniforms covers the ground and my Queen is in reach.

I'm not a fan of this plan, allowing the Morrigan to live. Casteel isn't to be trusted and I doubt the gate can truly be closed. Nevis obviously agrees, which is why she waited for us at the tunnel entrance.

But what none of us understood then and what I'm barely grasping now is the immense power Morgan yields now that she is complete. She's an entity of glorious energy, equal to if not dwarfing the Morrigan next to her. I'm not sure she's even aware. When she moves, the earth trembles under my feet. My heart clenches with love. And my body aches to be possessed by her.

She is the true goddess...almost. There is one final move.

"Kill her," I say under my breath. "Take her life. Claim the throne."

Her ebony eyes connect with mine.

The blades of the soldiers still fighting drop to the ground. They fall to their knees and the Morrigan's face freezes, her expression caught in that moment.

The ten other members of my army stand ready. Even the Immortals feel her power. We wait to see where she leads us.

"Your army has fallen," Morgan says, walking across the platform and facing the Darkness. "Your court has abandoned. You have nothing now."

"Nothing?" The platform shudders. The grass shrivels under my feet. "I will eat you alive."

"No," Morgan says. "You will submit."

"Never."

"Submit and I'll spare your life." The sword hangs in her fingertips.

The Morrigan smiles—no, laughs. "Little girl, you're nothing in this world. A speck. Once the heady glow of your mates wears off, you'll understand. Once they leave and betray you as I've been betrayed."

Morgan points her blade at the Queen's heaving chest. Black smoke swirls at the Queen's feet. Morgan raises her other hand and white light shoots to the glass rooftop.

The Guardians and Immortals are now surrounding the stage. Rupert stands next to me, watching the scene unfold. Hildi is between me and Armin. Rage vibrates off her body. I don't know about the others, but I feel the immense, conflicting power churning in the two goddesses above.

"Do you see this light? This power?" Morgan says, drawing it back to her and cradling it in her hand like a pliable ball. "It didn't come from the Darkness, it came from a well of hope. Of love." She glances down at us, making eye contact with each of her guardians.

"Love is for fools."

"Turning your back on it is even more foolish," Morgan replies. "I know what you did. You tell the story of your betrayal, but what about your own? How you scorched me and Macha into the ground.

How you rallied an army to destroy everything before you." She moves inches away from the queen and I take a step forward protectively. Morgan holds her hand up, telling me to stand down. "You had love, Anand. You had it all around you and you gave it up for a bastard demi-god who wanted nothing more than to use you."

"Cu was my everything."

Morgan shakes her head. "Gods that is sad. Pathetic. As much as I hate Casteel, you really don't deserve him."

The queen frowns. "Casteel?"

"Are you truly unaware of his dedication to you? His loyalty?"

"Of course I am." She's barely holding on to her rage but Morgan has kept her interest. The words of truth will do that.

"He loves you, you know, but if you do this—continue this desperate crusade and cross realms, you'll lose him forever."

Footsteps sound on the stairs to the platform and Casteel emerges from the field of bodies. I tighten my grip on my sword. One false move and I'll end them both.

"Tell her," Morgan says. She certainly isn't afraid of the Commander, not anymore. The soldier stands before the queen.

"I love you, Anand. I have since the days before, when this land and the people on it flourished."

Her expression is one of confusion. "You love my power."

"No." He laughs bitterly. "If I could I would banish The Darkness to other realms. Back to the underworld where it came from."

There's an identical look of surprise on Morgan and the Queen's face when the commander steps to Anand and touches her cheek. Something flickers in her eyes and for once it's not anger.

Slowly, I move to the platform and my brothers do the same.

It's time to take Morgan home.

37

MORGAN

We're close. So close, but I know my job isn't done. Casteel may have asked me to spare her life but I owe a debt to Nevis and her people. Not only did she save and support me, but the underground dwellers came up and fought with my men. They built an army. And it's time they shared a spot in this kingdom.

There is only one way to do this. And I look down at Anita's dead body thinking of how this started. One vessel to another. Sharing. Spreading. Sacrificing.

I sense Dylan behind me. Damien is close. Sam and Clinton right behind. I don't just feel them—they boost me—fill me. I want nothing more than to get home and spend time with each one of them. Alone. Together. A whole life filled with peace and love. A family. Babies.

But that will never happen if I leave things as they are. And the choice I must make is a long shot. The Shaman knew it when he gave me passage. The odds of me coming home alone are slim.

I snatch a moment and turn to face my mates. There's no time for words but I connect with each, staring into their eyes. Blue, green, gray, and purple. As usual I'm missing one but I have no doubt he's working to get us out of here.

"Whatever you're thinking—don't," Dylan says. I smile and walk away. There's a skirmish behind me and it only takes a glance to see my guardians restrained by the men they brought with them. The Ravens fight back, but these men...they're strong and they were sent here for a purpose. Emotion isn't part of their job.

"Love you, girl," Hildi says, pushing through the commotion. There's no doubt she gave the order to this group of soldiers. She may be just the kind of woman they need to tell them what to do.

"You, too."

I walk across the platform to Casteel and the Morrigan. They're lost in their own world. I extract my sword and press it into Casteel's spine. He looks down in confusion.

"You asked me to fix this so I am."

I expect him to fight but to my surprise, he doesn't. Everyone knows, including the Queen. I stand face-to-face and say, "Thank you for revealing my true powers. I couldn't have done it without coming here, having my feet on this land and being in your presence."

"You're not stronger than me."

I glance at my Guardians, my friends and the people filling the ground, some of their faces feeling the moonlight for the first time in ages.

"Oh but I am. I am so. Much. Stronger."

I push up on my toes, because my sister is taller than me. I don't know what she expects but it's not this—not a kiss, and when our mouths touch it's like a bomb goes off. Good versus evil. Light against dark. Two queens battling for control.

The difference is, she's alone. Her soldiers are dead. Her commander had dropped his weapon. And the light comes shining through. I feel the relenting on her lips. In the taste of her tongue. The Darkness is foul and it fills me, angry and bitter. We're nothing but vessels and this one is up for sacrifice. Pain fills my limbs, my fingertips and toes. Poison attacks my organs, stabbing away at the muscle of my heart.

There's one final moment, right after the Darkness consumes me, when I'm filled with centuries of hate and pain and destruction, that I see the true face of Anand. Her eyes are bright—and green. Her cheeks are rosy. Her hand slips into Casteel's and she kisses me on the forehead.

"Thank you, Morgan," she says, realizing what I have done.

I've freed her and the people of the Otherside. I fall forward but I'm caught by many hands. As they lay me on the ground I look to the sky and see one last thing.

The sun.

38

BUNNY

I hear the pounding of footsteps as I blow on the painting. The magic is weaker when wet, but there's no choice. Casteel wants the gate closed but we've got to be on the other side before that can happen.

A wave of Darkness hits me in the gut moments before the sounds in the hall. Morgan. She's hurt. Or injured—or worse. I clench the rolled-up mural in my hands. The final scene of a rising sun. A goddess in white on the ground.

There's no mistaking the imagery.

"Bunny!" My name is a desperate shout. I run to the door and down the hall. I meet the frantic faces of my brothers. I look for kingdom soldiers chasing them. No one follows but their allies.

Who I don't see is Morgan, and I scan the group. My eyes finally settle on Clinton, who's carrying her in his arms. Her face is pale. Black stains her chin. The hollow in my stomach grows.

"Tell me you're ready," Dylan says. "Because we've got to get the hell out of here and lock the door behind us."

"I'm ready," I tell them and jog up the stairs to my studio. I lead them to the window looking out over the kingdom. The sky has parted blue and the land as far as the eye can see comes to life. I glance back at Morgan and realize that it is because she's carrying the Darkness and it's killing her.

I've already drawn the symbols around the window, the ones that will allow us to pass and then seal the gate behind us. Casteel made that clear. Do not return and do not give her a chance to get out.

"Once I activate the gate we'll only have a few moments. Go first," I tell Clinton. "Get her back."

What we'll do with her is beyond me. I pray the gods will have an answer.

Clinton doesn't hesitate. He carries Morgan like she's light as a feather. He steps to the edge and the outside world vanishes—instead, he's looking into the dining room of The Nead. He steps through and they both vanish.

Dylan hurries the others through. Hildi and the six warriors I do not know. Sam and Damien, each giving me a look that contains less hate than I imagined. Once Damien crosses over, the edges of the window turn fuzzy and the kingdom comes back into view.

"Go," I say to Dylan.

He steps to the edge and puts his feet in first. I watch as the gate closes on itself, bricking up like the window never existed.

"Bunny." He stares at me, his eyes imploring. I shrug. If this is my penance, I'll take it.

There's a beat, a moment, and the bricks build one by one closing one realm to the other. Dylan reaches out his hand and grabs me by the collar—yanking me through.

39

MORGAN

I'm drowning in a lake made of black oil. The surface is on fire. Liquid clogs my throat. I gasp for air, for the edge, but there's nothing there but Darkness. Dank, foul, darkness.

I fall...slipping into nothing until my feet touch solid ground. I blink, thinking my eyes are closed but no, just black. So much black. I open my mouth and scream. This time it works. I hear my voice. The sound of my fear. What happened to my Guardians? The castle and the Morrigan?

I still taste her and the filth I consumed in my mouth.

Taking a step I move across the void, my feet echoing in the nothingness. I knew it was a risk—a sacrifice I was willing to make. But this? This is what her soul looks like?

I scream again. "Hello!"

My voice mocks me in return. I hold my hands to my ears and scream. Scream for the loss of my mates. The loss of my realm. Scream for wanting it back—the feeling—the love.

Hands grip my arms and pull them away from my ears. White teeth shine in the dark. Long braided hair hangs over a broad shoulder. "Why are you screaming, child?" the Shaman asks.

"Did you bring me here? Drag me to this place?"

"You consumed the poison. That was not my doing."

"How do I get out of here?"

"I don't know." He clasps his hands together. I count three rings on each hand.

"I took the darkness and gave her my light."

He frowns. "That doesn't sound right."

Wings flap overhead. I look up and spot five ravens, all flying in a row. One carries a charm in his beak. My mind breaks and I grip it with my hands.

"Dig deep," the Shaman says. "You can't give away what isn't yours."

I feel in my belly. I reach in my heart. I feel a pebble—round and perfect. I pull it out and see it is a shiny pearl—white and bold. I hold it to the sky. A raven, the biggest of them all, swoops down and takes it in his beak and flies away. The pearl leaves a trail, glossy like a satin ribbon, and I glance at the Shaman. "Follow it, child. That's your way home."

I pick up my feet, sticky from the black goo, and chase after the raven.

~

"Morgan."

"How much longer?"

"How the fuck should I know?"

"Shut up. She's moving."

"I can't handle this."

"I can't handle your mouth."

"Seriously, is this what you want her to wake up to? The five of you acting like assholes?"

The final voice cuts through my mind like a knife.

"Hildi?" I rasp. My voice feels like sandpaper mixed with tar.

"Babe." It's her voice but I feel five other sets of hands. Strong, capable hands. Familiar hands. I blink and spot my guardians. Hildi elbows Dylan out of the way and brings a glass of water to my lips. The liquid is cool and I gulp it down faster than I should. She wipes my chin and says. "Nevis sent it to help you heal."

The wicked feeling in my throat vanishes, soothed by the water. It settles in my belly and I feel the magic working. I look at Hildi and the first thing I think of to say is, "I'm so sorry about Andi."

"You tried." She brushes back my hair. "You should have killed her."

"Death would have been too good for her. This way, she has to live with the consequences and redeem herself to the people in her kingdom." I search for a pair of copper eyes. I find them near my feet. "Redemption is good."

I wiggle to a sitting position, feeling almost back to normal. I'm on the bed in my room. I look around at my things, my books and journals. The trinkets I've collected during my time in New York. It truly feels like home.

Again I focus on Bunny. "Did you close the gate?"

"Yes."

"And the Darkness? I know I carried it with me."

Dylan takes my hand. "The Shaman was waiting for us when we came through. He cured you."

"What was the cost?"

"He took the Darkness with him," Damien says. "Locked up tight. I made the box myself."

That news doesn't sit well with me and from a glance around the bed, not with anyone else either. Clinton stands, arms crossed, to my left.

"We didn't have a choice," Sam says. He leans over and I brush his hair out of his eyes. Gods, I've missed him. All of them.

"Okay, it's time to give Morgan a little rest, everyone out." The directive comes from Sue and I smile thankfully at her. I love my men. I adore my mates, but choking down an unhealthy dose of evil wore me out.

Everyone leaves, but I grab Dylan's hand before he leaves the room.

"Hey," I say quietly. "Do me a favor."

He touches my hair and runs his fingers down my cheek. "Anything."

I nod at Bunny, who is leaving the room. "Be nice to him. Things got complicated."

He smirks. "He's one of us. Don't worry."

"That's exactly why I am worried. It's not like you guys are easy on one another."

He leans down and kisses me on the forehead. "You got it, Your Highness."

"Don't call me that."

He nods and heads for the door, but the glint in his eyes says this is just the beginning.

Of so many amazing things.

40

MORGAN

Recovery comes slow. Not just for my body but for my mind. For the harem and the new people that have entered our group. There's a different feel to the house, with it being so crowded, but it's also nice having people around that understand what you've been through—people who willingly fought by your side.

Hildi still occupies the guest room—not wanting to go back to the apartment she shared with Andi. I like having her here, having another woman in the house. My ravens are amazing, but a friend who is just a friend with zero complications? It's a gift.

The men—the fighters that joined our army—they've camped out in the basement, near the training room. Davis and Sue created bedrooms down there. They keep to themselves for the most part but I've seen them come and go from Dylan's room. Negotiations are in progress. They aren't slaves, Dylan told me. But they are caught in a bit of transition. Where do they go from here? And how does he make sure they've adjusted to modern ways?

I've taken to writing again. About the Otherside and the Morrigan. I've shown some of my work to Professor Christensen, who thinks it should be documented. Maybe. I just like feeling the normalcy of pen on paper again.

There's a knock on my door, firm and quick. I lay my journal on the window seat and cross the room. I open the door and find Damien on the other side, leaning one arm against the frame. He's wearing low-slung black jeans and a long-sleeved gray shirt. A thin strip of his lower belly peeks out. My eyes linger on the scattering of hair that travels below.

When I look at his face, my heart pitter-patters. His eyebrow is raised.

"Hey," I say, happy to see him. His smile in return confirms he's been looking forward to our meetup as well.

I spot a fresh tattoo on his arm depicting the fight with the Morrigan. I reach for his arm and run my fingers down the ink. The heat and electricity between us crackles.

Yeah, there's that.

In the dark place, when I was consumed by the Morrigan's waste, the Shaman tried to tell me something. The pearl. That is the light inside of me. It wasn't gone—just overwhelmed by the Darkness. I didn't lose that. I carry it with me—the tiny piece of the goddess that lives inside. That piece. It burns with hope. With love.

I hold Damien's violet eye.

And a little bit of lust.

I still need these men to balance me. They're my mates.

He holds up his hand and shows me a sleek black helmet. "Want to go for a ride?"

"I'd love to."

I grab my boots and slide them over my jeans. Damien comes up behind me and wraps his arms around my waist. His lips find my throat and he showers me with warm kisses.

He spins me around and pushes my hair out of my eyes. "I'm glad you're feeling better."

"Thank you," I say, kissing him on the mouth. "I'm glad you came back for me."

He smirks. "There was never a chance of that not happening, babe."

"Need me too much?" I ask.

He pulls my hips to his and I feel his hard length. "You have no fucking idea."

It's my turn to give a wicked smile. I fist his shirt and say, "Take me on a ride and bring me back and show me."

"Deal."

My knees buckle just having him near me, but I gain composure and lead the way to the garage. There's one thing I've learned about Damien. If I hold off a little bit longer, cruise through the city with my arms tight around his body and bide my time, I'll be rewarded with the ride of a lifetime.

～

"I TOLD them to be nice to you."

I dip my fingers into the salve and gently touch the bruise on Bunny's cheekbone. He flinches but steadies himself and allows me to rub on the cream.

"You didn't need to do that," he says, wincing in pain. He's on the bed, head pressed into pillows. "It's sort of...um, a ritual."

The Ravens beat the shit out of Bunny.

Betrayal comes with a price, even if it's for a reason.

"It's not the first time one of us has had to run the gauntlet." He holds his ribs when he says it. "Dylan had to run it once. Clinton twice."

I stare at him for a minute, not really wanting to know more than I already do about the archaic punishment system that involves sticks. A little of my concern fades when his lips twitch into a slight smile. He and his brothers are right again and that's all that matters.

"No more secrets, okay?" I tell him. Everything we went through on the Otherside together brought us closer. We had to learn to trust one another.

"Yeah. I learned my lesson on that one." He reaches out and grazes my cheek. "Never underestimate what you can handle."

I take his hand and kiss his knuckles. "Same."

I continue checking his wounds. The bruises on his ribs are dark purple. The one on his back looks painful and red. I sigh and drop his shirt. "You know, I haven't tested my healing powers on anyone since we returned home."

His quirked eyebrow peeks out over the frame of his glasses. "Interesting."

"I mean, obviously I would have to be gentle."

He nods. "I can do gentle. I mean, you know, if you're up to it."

I don't tell him that I've been looking for a chance to be close to him again. On our own terms, without danger and obligation over our heads. I knew the opportunity would come for us—there's been no rush.

"Let's see if my mojo still works," I say, genuinely curious.

I take my time peeling off his shirt. His body is still magnificent, regardless of the beating. I strip him completely, removing his pants and boxers. He's not too injured that his body isn't reacting and I'm pleased to see his reaction to me, despite the pain.

I crawl up the bed, kissing every bruise. I breathe hot air against his skin and his cock grows harder with every touch. His hand pushes against the hem of my shirt, nudging it higher and slipping his hand underneath. His fingers find my breast, grazing then tugging at my nipple.

"Gods, Bunny," I mumble, feeling the sensation ripple down my body. I lay my hands on his abdomen, on the ladder of taught muscles, and miraculously the bruises fade. Just in time because I'm dying to straddle him, feel him between my legs.

Even so, we take our time, hands wandering, bodies connecting. His wounds heal, slowly fading with every touch. I shimmy out of my skirt and his fingers grip the side of my panties, tearing them off in a snap. I smile at his eagerness, the way it excites me, and I climb in his lap, wrapping my legs around his back. I kiss the wound on his cheek, the bridge of his nose and his lips. I taste his blood, suck on his tongue and cry into his mouth, begging for him to enter me.

"Fuck me," I whisper.

Better now, he stands and drags me to the edge of the bed, tapping my knee with his hand. I open for him and he looms over me, a god in his own right. He's gorgeous, hair flopping into his eyes, jaw tight with want. His torso tapers into a muscular V, pointing at the hard length bobbing between his legs. He dips his fingers against my core, feeling, to makes sure I'm wet and ready.

I moan and writhe against this fingers, letting him know I am.

I really, really am.

I issue a prayer that he doesn't make me wait, and thank the gods when he enters me quickly with a relieved groan. "Feeling better?" I ask as he takes a moment to stare at me, our bodies adjusting to one another.

"You have no idea how much."

My fingers weave into the blanket covering the bed. "Don't make me beg," I say, pushing against him.

"Queens don't beg," he replies, pulling back just an inch before slamming into me.

But I do beg, not because he isn't fulfilling my need, but because I can't get enough. I start a chant as he plows into me, more forceful than I knew Bunny could muster. He sets up a rhythm, a mixture of hard and deliriously slow. I bend my knees and inch down the bed, feeling each hit all the way to my teeth.

His thumb grazes my clit, sending sparks across my body. All thought of healing Bunny are gone—all thoughts entirely are gone. My mind is filled with nothing but the feeling of him inside of me. The way he looks at me. How his jaw tenses with every thrust. How his knees shake as he gets closer.

Our eyes connect and a lazy smile falls across his lips. It's mimicking my own. I feel it. I feel him. After all our struggles, the pain and distrust, I'm not just healing Bunny.

We're healing each other.

NOTHING GETS a Southern girl more excited than snow.

And New York's first snowfall is a doozy.

"Come outside with me?" I ask each and every one of my Ravens. They all shake their heads and mumble about other obligations. I'm starting to think they're afraid of snow. "Really? No one?"

Hildi dashes downstairs and I'm not even brave enough to approach the Legion. Damn, those guys are terrifying.

"I'll go," Sam says after a long pause. "Let me get my camera."

I wait in the foyer, dressed for a blizzard. I'm tugging my fuzzy black hat over my ears when he walks in wearing a normal jacket.

He looks me up and down. "Warm enough?"

"I don't know," I reply. "I was thinking I may need some of those foot and hand heaters."

"I'll keep you warm," he says with a smile. He's not even wearing gloves.

We step out of The Nead and into a world of white. It's like the sky dumped a cloud on the city. I shiver. "Seriously, aren't you cold?"

"We're like, half bird, Morgan. We don't get cold."

"You're not a bird."

He shrugs. "I promise we do not get cold."

This could explain some of the reason they weren't affected by the Morrigan's freezing castle. I tug my scarf up over my neck and we cross the snow-covered road into the park.

Everything in sight is covered in a thick layer or ice and snow. The tree limbs, the railings. I run my hand over a pristine, snow-covered bench and gather a clump before crunching it into a hard ball.

"We don't have this back home." I smell the snowball. "Maybe occasionally, but it's more of a mess than anything else."

I look up and see that Sam has his camera out; he takes a series of photographs and I strike a variety of silly poses.

"Want to take a look?" he asks, holding out the camera.

I'm not sure I do. Not after the last images he captured. But those days are over. The Darkness is gone, the Morrigan is contained and things are even and balanced between the realms.

I take the camera and look into the screen. There's nothing but blue sky, white snow and me looking like a dork.

"It's really over, isn't it?" I ask him.

His eyes are the brightest of greens and he wraps an arm around my waist. "You stopped the apocalypse, Morgan. You saved us all."

My cheeks heat with embarrassment. I wrinkle my nose. "I didn't do it alone."

He presses his lips to mine. They're cold. So are mine. Our tongues are hot.

"We all made sacrifices along the way, but you were the one chosen to stop her. And you did it. I'm proud of you."

Before I can speak I hear laughter, the sound of a group of girls walking down the path. Their voices turn to a whisper and I look up to see them glancing over at us—well, really, at Sam.

When they see us looking they pick up the pace and race through the snow, across the park.

"They think you're cute."

He smiles. Adorably. "Jealous?"

"Should I be?"

"Only one girl has my heart." He grabs the front of my coat and pulls me to him.

"Is it weird, that five of you have mine?"

"Not for a minute." He lifts his palms to my cheeks and they're oddly warm against my cool skin. "This is who we are, Morgan. Why we were made and who we will be for an eternity. The gods blessed us with the sole job of loving and protecting you."

Snowflakes fall and one lands in his eyelash. I wipe it away. "You're really good at that, you know."

"At what?"

"Charming me."

He smiles. "Well, you know the other part of it..."

"What's that?"

"That you're way too much for one man to handle. The gods knew this and had to send reinforcements." His lips quirk teasingly.

I wrap my arms around his waist and hold on to him. I snuggle in the crook of his neck and say, "Thank you."

"For what?"

I kiss the tender flesh of his throat. "For being you."

Because he's relaxed, he's also unaware. I take the snowball still in my hand and crash it over his head. Ice explodes and he shouts in surprise.

"You didn't."

I shrug, but the glint in his eye changes to something mischievous and I turn on my heel, running for cover just as a barrage of snowballs comes my way.

I run, but I don't really hide.

I've never wanted to be found so much.

～

It's after midnight when I make my way into the kitchen. Sue has long gone to bed but there's half a chocolate cake on the counter left over from dinner. I hold the knife over the cake and start to cut a wedge. What the hell? I move it over half an inch. What the hell. I take the whole thing.

I really like chocolate cake.

Setting the plate on the table I move to the refrigerator, looking for milk. Swinging the door open, I spot the carton.

Fuck.

It's Dylan's milk.

It says so in black Sharpie. I scan the rest of the shelves. Nope. Nope. Nope. No other milk.

Fuck.

Dylan is...particular. About his things. His wants. He marks his food. His books. Hell, he's even marked me.

MIDNIGHTS END

I glance at the cake. So moist. So delicious. It would be a waste not to eat it and a shame not to wash it down with a cold glass of milk. Without another thought I grab the carton and fill the glass. Shit. Too much, that's like, the whole carton. I pour a little back in and maybe he'll just think he drank it all. Sue will get him more.

I'll leave her a note.

I sit at the table and like a bloodhound on a trail, I've barely got the first forkful in my mouth when Dylan walks in. Shirtless. Pajama pants low on his hips.

"Hey," I say around a mouthful of cake. Did it just get hot in here? I turn around and take a gulp of the milk. Then another, and hide the glass under the table. Then I wipe my mouth and ask, "What are you doing down here?"

"Couldn't sleep. Thought I'd come down for a snack."

"You never sleep."

He shrugs and walks to the cabinet, pulling out a glass identical to mine. I shove a hunk of cake in my mouth and start to stand. I've got to get out of here.

The next minute passes in a blur of cake, refrigerators, and milk cartons. Dylan lifts the carton and shakes it, the little bit left swishing inside. He looks at me. I look at the door.

I bolt for the hallway but his gods-forsaken excessively long arm shoots out and blocks me in. "Did you drink my milk?"

"Hmm?"

"You know the rules, Morgan." He points to the carton. "My name is right here."

"It wasn't me."

Stares.

"Seriously."

Harder.

"I didn't drink your milk, Dylan."

He doesn't move. His eyes are narrow and I've never truly been afraid of Dylan. Well, at least not in a long time. We've been through a lot together. So much. We've fought and killed for one another. But now? He has murder in his eyes, directed squarely at me.

"So look..."

His eyebrow quirks. His chest and torso are very close. His arm, lean and taut with corded muscle takes up much of the space. It's hard for me to take my eyes off of that part of his body.

"What if I did drink your milk?"

"So you drank it."

"No." I hold up my hands. "What if I did drink it? I'm asking...hypothetically."

He moves his arm but still takes up the entire doorway with his wide shoulders and long body. He crosses his arms and tilts his head. "I don't know, Morgan. Theft is a pretty big deal."

"What if I worked off the debt?"

He looks me up and down, blue eyes skimming over my tank and shorts. "I'm listening."

I don't need to tell him what I'm thinking. I simply touch the fuzzy hair trailing down his lower belly. His stomach twitches but his jaw remains set.

His hand grips mine and stops me from moving any further. I look up at him curiously, but he moves with cat-like reflexes, lifting me off the ground with one arm, clearing the table with another, and dropping me on the edge.

"Lay back," he commands.

I nod and do as he asks.

His hands find the top of my shorts and he tugs, pausing for me to lift my hips. He leans over me, mouth inches from mine and whispers, "I told you I came down for a snack."

I wait for him to kiss me but he pulls back and vanishes. That's when I feel his hands on my inner thighs and his mouth...

"Oh," I gasp, feeling the warmth of his breath, the tickle of his tongue. I reach for the edge of the table. My legs hang over the side but he pushes my knees back, spreading me wider. He works his tongue, his lips, his breath. My hips raise off the ground pushing, pushing for more friction.

I close my eyes and sink into the feelings, the care and determination Dylan uses with every flick. Each stroke. But he also leaves me hanging, pulling away just as I'm tumbling over the edge. Drawing me further and further into a spiral I can't quite catch. I hear a strange sound and it comes from deep in my throat.

I hear a sound, a sharp intake of breath across the room and open my eyes. Clinton stands in the doorway watching. Waiting. Our eyes connect and I lick my lips, knowing what it feels like to have more than one set of hands on me at once. What two mouths can do. He doesn't move. He simply observes and it sends a shudder of pleasure down my body knowing that he's there.

I have little doubt Dylan knows he's there and when he gives my clit one final suck and lifts his head and nods at his fellow Raven, butterflies race through my belly. Clinton stands before me, runs his fingers down my thighs and says, "Is this okay?"

I nod. "Yes. Please."

I hear the sound of his zipper over my heartbeat. I feel the hard tip of his cock as it teases the slippery wet of my core. I turn my head in search of Dylan and find him leaning against the counter top. There's no mistaking the tent in his cotton pants.

Clinton lays his hands on my breasts, fondling my nipples, and my toes curl. I'm thankful that he doesn't make me wait long, running a hand down my belly and grazing his thumb across my clit. I bite down on my bottom lip when he enters me. I glance to the side just in time to see Dylan reach his hands into his pants.

It's a trio of sounds: deep grunts from my chest as Clinton claims me, the rocking of the table with every punch, and the short panting from my left as Dylan's hand moves in time, pumping up and down.

Clinton's dark hair spills into his face, his jaw is tight. His eyes focused. Dylan got me ready and I'm already teetering on the edge. The man inside of me grows frantic, lifting me off the table and pulling me to his chest. He kisses me, fucks me, consumes every inch of me. We share it all. Energy. Life. Love, and just when I think my body may break, that it may all be too much...I shatter.

And he comes, slamming into me so hard I cry for mercy.

I fall back against the table, breath ragged, Clinton still twitching inside of me, and glance over at the third member of this late night club. Dylan hasn't come but he's moved closer and I splay my hand on my belly. He leans down and kisses me, hard and possessive. Dark like his soul. Consuming like his passion. And he comes in an explosion of cum across my stomach. His head tilts back and his hand grips my head and fuck, fuck, fuck.

"Fuck," he mutters.

Yeah, I'm at a loss for fucking coherent words, too.

Clinton's gray eyes scan the table behind me and narrow.

"What?" I ask, exhausted and unable to lift myself to see what he's looking at.

"Did you seriously eat all the cake?"

41

MORGAN

"So is this dinner thing mandatory?" Hildi asks. She's standing in front of my closet, flipping through my clothes. Nothing but a dress will fit her and even then it will probably only come to her mid-thigh.

"I'm surprised it took Sue this long to work out a configuration in the dining room to fit all of us."

She holds up a black dress. I shake my head. On me it looks okay. On her, I think it may veer into street walker territory.

"Hold on," I say, digging through the outfits. I pull out a dress that hits me below the knee. It's a green and white wrap dress. A little cool for the weather but it will have to do. "Try this."

She takes it and nods in approval.

It doesn't take long for us to get ready and together we walk down the three flights of stairs. "I'm really glad you've been staying here," I tell her. "Being the only woman around can get a little crazy."

She laughs. "I never understood your whole...thing with the guys. I mean, I get it, they're hot and they're all completely devoted to you, but..."

"It's a lot of work. We've established some rules. And now that the end of the world isn't crashing down on us we have time to feel things out a little better."

"Like fucking on the kitchen table?" She shakes her head.

I pause, fingers gripping the bannister. "You know about that?"

"Everyone knows about that."

My cheeks heat up. "Even the guys downstairs?"

"Yes." She sighs. "Really, we're going to have to look into some different living arrangements. It's fun being here but the, uh...sexual tension? It's a little much for outsiders and those boys...it's a whole lot of testosterone in one place."

"We'll tone it down," I say. "Promise."

"No, you've sacrificed enough. Live. Love. Be happy," she says. There's a touch of pain in her voice but not as much as a week ago. We're down in the foyer and I spot the Legion walking into the dining room. I expect Dylan is handing out drinks and everyone is waiting for us to arrive.

I grab her arm before we reach the door. "I am happy," I tell her, wanting to add that I wish her happiness as well. She'll get it. I feel it. "Take your time. We've all been through a lot."

We cross the threshold and I don't know what Sue and Davis did, perform a magic spell or hire a carpenter, but the dining room feels wider and longer. The table is big enough for all of us and is set with The Nead's finest china.

I make eye contact with Clinton first and he pushes his hair behind his ear, no doubt to see me better. Damien stands next to him; ink peeking out from his shirtsleeves. He looks adorable in a short-sleeved button-down complete with a bow-tie. I can't help but smile when I look at him. Sam has out his camera and blinds the two of us before we can even get in the room. His smile is more blinding than the flash.

Bunny sidles up to me, latching his hand to mine. I'm so thankful he's here. That we worked through all our differences. Trust is important—we've learned that the hard way.

"Come on," he says, "Sue set you up at the end of the table."

Because, in this world or the next, I am still the Queen.

I take my place and watch as my guardians stand behind their seats, Dylan across from me, eyes ever alert. His face is different, more relaxed, and I think for once he feels secure. We all do.

The six members of the Legion of Immortals take the remaining chairs. They look adorable—okay, super hot—cleaned up and dressed in formal wear. With a little assistance I have no doubt they'll find a place in our society.

Davis fills each goblet with deep red wine, finishing with the glass in front of my plate. I lift it up and hold it out.

"Thank you for being here," I begin. "For being part of a remarkable point in history. We stopped a plague. Saved the world. Foiled an apocalypse. Does anyone know? Nope. Not really. Does it matter? Nah. We've don't need glory or recognition." I stare at every face. My mates. My best friend and the new friends that helped us accomplish our mission.

"Thank you," Dylan says, cutting in before I can finish. It's clear he speaks for everyone at the table. "You brought us together. Made us whole."

I raise my glass and they all do the same; we're a table of magic, power, and mystery. I can't wait to find out where destiny will take us next.

EPILOGUE

"Do you think it will work?" Sam is the only one that dares ask the question out loud. His green eyes are a mixture of excitement and fear. Damien can't even look at my face—his gaze planted firmly on the ground.

And Dylan? He's across the rooftop, unable to even be near us.

"I did the spell. Accurately, I think." Bunny nods his approval. He helped me, along with Tran at the magic shop.

"The Shaman had nothing to do with this, right?" Clinton asks. His jaw is set and shoulders tense. This means so much to them. If it fails...if I fail...

"Do you think I'm crazy? No freaking way I involved that bastard in something so important."

"So what do we do?" Sam asks.

"Well, it should be like riding a bicycle, don't you think? Instinctive."

Damien finally looks up. "It's been a long time since we've shifted."

I take his hand in mine. "Today is the day you reclaim your

wings. Don't be afraid. Embrace it the way we do everything. Fear doesn't guide my Raven Guardians, even when it comes to this."

I tug him by the shirt and his violet eyes flash at me. His lips are sweet when I kiss him for good luck. The best part about my harem is they do not fight and squabble over the attention I give to the others. They're patient.

Good things come to those that wait.

The kiss seems to have calmed him down, and he walks across the garden to stand with Dylan. I take time with the others. I feel the tension ease off Clinton as our mouths connect. I taste the excitement from Sam in the way his fingers dig into my sides. Bunny wraps me in a nervous hug, using both arms. Yes, both. The extent of my power is great, and with the books in the library downstairs, I can do many things. Healing Bunny was the first. Giving them back their form is the second.

After years of not being able to use both arms, Bunny has made up for lost time, linking his around me at every opportunity. Battling the others with newfound speed. He kisses my neck, biting my chin and finally crashes his mouth into mine.

"I have no doubt you pulled this off. I know what you can do. What you've already done." He holds up his reclaimed arm. "The power you hold, thank you for using it to give this back to us."

I touch his cheek, so thankful we're all back together again. I want it like this always. Forever.

The others wait, ready to begin the process. Dylan still stands by the edge of the roof, looking out over the bare trees of the park. The sky is a gorgeous blue. Cloudless and crisp. I roll my eyes at the others and they fight back a laugh. Someone always needs a little extra coaxing. I cross the garden and slip my hand into his.

"They're waiting."

He looks down at me. His eyes reflect the blue of the sky. "They should go without me."

"They won't. You know that. They need your eyes and your leadership. You're the Sentinel."

"Someone should stay back to protect you."

I snort. "You really think I need protecting? From who? Sue's cheesecake? That thing needs protecting from me."

He shifts on his feet, biding time to make up another threat. "The Legion is still here. Gods know how many enemies they have."

"Hildi has them under control." More like under her spell. I've never seen a group of men so fascinated by a woman. Well, other than my own. "Stop procrastinating, babe. This is my thank you for everything you've done. For your love and devotion. For your protection and grace." I squeeze his hand. "Not to mention the sexual awakening I've had. Can you believe I was a virgin when I got here?"

At that he smiles, because he remembers the meek, curious girl with a head full of stories and imagination that arrived here months and months ago. That girl had no idea what was in store for her future.

"I guess it would be rude not to accept your gift."

"Terribly rude," I agree, feeling the ice melt. He's always the last one to commit, but when he does, he's all in.

He finally relents and goes to meet his brothers. I go with him, making a circle of six. The incantation isn't difficult—it's the final part of the spell. When the last word parts my lips, the air shimmers, the ground trembles, and my men slowly vanish into glossy black. Their feet do not hit the ground. Their wings take over naturally, instinctively, and without another look in my direction they lift off the rooftop and soar.

∼

I RETREAT to the cushioned bench that overlooks the city. I've watched many things from this perch. Fireworks. Sunsets. Snowfall and rain. But feeling the passing shadow from overhead and the widespread wings of my ravens soaring through the sky is the best.

They go for hours, sailing out over the park and reaching the high peaks of New York's skyscrapers. One always remains in sight. I'm trying to learn who is who in this form. It's harder from a distance. Up close I can see their eyes and then, without a doubt, I know.

The sun begins to fade and a chill rolls over the rooftop. One by one, my ravens meet in the sky, flying in formation. The first, Dylan, drops to an ornamental tree in the garden, plucking something out of the branches with his beak. He joins the others in a circle overhead. I shade my eyes and see whatever it is in his mouth fall from the sky. I hold out my hands and it fumbles twice before I catch it.

It's a box.

Butterflies form in my belly and the shadows that cross over me are no longer winged and in flight, but human and standing before me. That is, until they kneel.

Their hair is wild. Their eyes bright. A smile tickles their lips.

"What is this?" I ask. The box is square, light, and tied with a bow.

"Open it," Damien says.

I do and find the most amazing diamond and platinum ring inside. I hold it up and it sparkles in the fading daylight. It's a circle of five crows, linked one after the other, encrusted in jewels.

"What is this?" I ask again, unable to say anything else. That's when I notice the piece of paper tucked inside. With a shaking hand, I lift it out.

Sam clears his voice. "Read it. Please."

My voice cracks when I speak, "We waited a thousand lifetimes for you. Those days were dark. Listless. But we knew something was on the other end. Something good, we hoped. Something we could fight for. The gods never told us it would be you. So strong. So beautiful. So sexy and perfect and full of life." I pause, blushing hard, and with tears filling my eyes. Bunny nods for me to continue. "Share our life with us. Fill our beds. Make us a family and lead us to the future. Seal our destiny, Morgan, Queen of the Ravens, by declaring yourself ours and us yours officially."

The paper trembles in her hand and Clinton takes it from her. They're all still kneeling, but Dylan steps forward.

"Marry us," is all he says.

I spot the tears welling in the corners of his eyes. I look at the faces of the others. I love them all so much. I don't need the ring to prove that. Or a ceremony, but they want it, and I want them. An image of the five of them dressed in tuxedos flashes in my mind. And then the honeymoon. I bite my lip and blurt out, "Yes. I will take you all as my husbands. It will be an honor to be your wife."

I hold out my left hand and with the others' permission he slips the ring on my finger, sealing our promise to one another for the rest of our lives.

ACKNOWLEDGMENTS

Thank you for reading The Raven Queen's Harem. This is the final book although keep your eyes out for a few follow up novellas and additional stories. It may be a little too hard to let Morgan and the Raven Guards go.

Special thanks to Vanessa, AG (for my covers), Jennifer for the awesome beta work, Soobee for being an awesome cheerleader, My Riverdale Girls with Pep!
The Raven Queen's Harem FB group which is so fun and gives me a chance to engage with new readers and I LOVE THIS. The whole community and of course Lisa who pushed me in this new direction that set our careers and friendship in a whole new direction we never saw coming.
I hope you all follow my work toward the new adventures, but if not, we've always got these sexy, hot ravens!

angel

ALSO BY ANGEL LAWSON

Angel Lawson Books

∽

(Reverse Harem)

The Wayward Sons (Contemporary YA)

Starlee's Heart

Starlee's Turn

Starlee's Home

∽

The Allendale Four (Contemporary YA-Series Complete)

A Piece of Heaven: The Allendale Four

Holding on to Heaven: The Allendale Four Book 2

The Road to Heaven: The Allendale Four Book 3

Seventh Heaven: The Allendale Four Book 4 (November 2018)

∽

Boys of Ocean Beach (Contemporary YA- Series Complete)

Summer's Kiss (The Boys of Ocean Beach)

Summer's Fun (The Boys of Ocean Beach 2)

~

Raven Queen's Harem (Series Complete)
Raven's Mark (Part 1)
Ebony Rising (Part 2)
Black Magic (Part 3)
Obsidian Fire (Part 4)
Onyx Eclipse (Part 5)
Midnight's End (Part 6)
*Raven's Gift (Holiday Novella)

~

Huntress: Trial of Gods

~

(Reverse Harem Alien Romance)

Taking Mercy: Planet Athion Book 1
Finding Mercy: Planet Athion Book 2
Saving Mercy: Planet Athion Book 3

~

(Reverse Harem Superheroes)

The Elites: Supers of Project 12
Sentinels: Supers of Project 12 (Book 2)

Rogues: Supers of Project 12 (Book 3)

Heroes: Supers of Project 12 (Book 4)

The Death Fields: A Post Apocalyptic Thriller

The Girl Who Shot First

The Girl Who Punched Back

The Girl Who Kicked Ass

The Girl Who Kissed the Sun

The Girl Who Broke Free

The Girl Who Saved the World

Creature of Habit Series (Paranormal Romance)

Creature of Habit (Book 1)

Creature of Habit (Book 2)

Creature of Habit (Book 3)

A Vampire's Seduction (Ryan's Story Book 4)

A Vampire's Fate (Sebastian's Story Book 5)

The Wraith Series (YA Paranormal Romance)

Wraith

Shadow Bound

Grave Possession

Printed in Great Britain
by Amazon